A TRIBUTE OF FIRE

A TRIBUTE OF FIRE

SARIAH WILSON

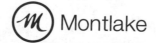 Montlake

Published by Montlake, Seattle

www.apub.com

Amazon, the Amazon logo, and Montlake are trademarks of Amazon.com, Inc., or its affiliates.

ISBN-13: 9781662525933 (hardcover)
ISBN-13: 9781662525148 (paperback)
ISBN-13: 9781662525131 (digital)

Cover design by Elizabeth Turner Stokes
Cover image: © Separisa, © Peratek, © Studio77 FX vector, © Vasilius / Shutterstock

Printed in the United States of America

First edition

For all my Reylo friends
and for everyone who adores enemies to lovers

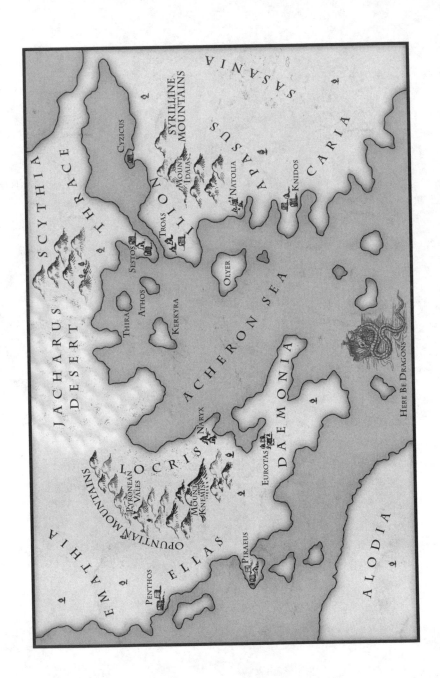

But I shall cause grief to many women in the future
bereft of their maiden daughters. They will long bewail the
commander,
the breaker of sexual law, the thief of the . . . goddess;
they shall send their girls to a hostile place,
deprived of wedlock.
. . . Locrians . . . and the valleys of Pyronae
All of you, because of his impious sexual intercourse with me,
will pay requital to . . . the goddess
for a thousand-year period, nurturing until old age
the unmarried maidens, chosen by [lottery].
Foreigners in a foreign land, their sad grave . . .
shall be washed away by the sandy breakers,
. . . burn their limbs with logs
from barren trees, and shall sprinkle into the sea
the ashes of her who perished . . .
Others, like women about to die, shall arrive by night
at the fields of . . . Sithon,
peering round for secret out-of-the way paths,
until they are able to run into the house of [the goddess]
and kneel in prayer as suppliants . . .
They shall sweep and decorate the goddess's sacred ground
with pure water, escaping the hateful anger
of the citizens. For every man of Ilion
will be watching out for the maidens, holding a stone in his hands,

or a black sword, or a hefty
bull-killing axe, or a . . . club,
keen to satisfy his hand which thirsts for blood.
The people shall, by an inscribed law, honor the slayer . . .
and grant him immunity.

Lycophron, *Alexandra*, lines 1141–73

CHAPTER ONE

I took the corner too sharply and nearly tripped over my own feet, slamming hard into the stone wall. Pain bloomed in my shoulder. I grit my teeth together and kept running, breathing hard, sweat pouring down my back and making my tunic cling to me.

"That way!" I heard a soldier call out behind me, and it gave me a burst of energy, propelling me forward even faster.

An arrow whizzed by my head, so close that it nearly nicked my ear. I gasped and fought the urge to freeze in place.

Stupid girl, remember that a moving target is nearly impossible to hit! My mentor's words echoed inside my head, reminding me that I needed to keep low to the ground and run as fast as I could.

There was an unfamiliar whirling sound one moment, and then in the next, my legs were suddenly swept out from under me. I tumbled to the ground, my armor clanking. I hit the earth so hard that my breath was knocked from me.

I was dazed for only a moment and then I looked down. They had thrown a bola around my ankles. I pushed the heavy helmet from my head and reached down to tug the rope loose from my legs.

The men's voices were getting closer.

With a silent groan I got to my feet and ran. I went left through the maze, then right. I had lost track of the course and didn't know where I was. Fear flooded my system, making it even harder to think, harder to focus on a way of getting out of this alive.

A spear whooshed past me, piercing the hem of my tunic before it slammed into the ground, wobbling in place. I ran by it and turned left again.

A few more turns and I would reach the temple. Sanctuary.

My breathing turned even more ragged as I dug deep, willing myself to fly the rest of the way. My limbs burned, my lungs protested, but I had to keep going.

Another arrow. This one went wide but I still felt the rush of hot air as it cut through the open space beside me.

"We almost have her!" a man's voice called out in triumph, and the panicky adrenaline coursing through me said he was right. Too close. They were too close.

I heard the sounds of swords being drawn from scabbards as the soldiers behind me closed the distance between us.

I came to a crossroads. Right or left? I couldn't remember.

With no time to think it through, I chose right.

And after two more turns, I realized that I had made a fatal mistake. That path came to a dead end. There was only a stone wall ahead of me. I banged my fists against it in frustration.

I was trapped.

A dozen soldiers crowded together behind me, their weapons pointed my way. I pulled out my dagger but knew that I wouldn't be able to fight my way clear. Maybe if there had been only a few I might have had a chance.

"You are caught," the man in front announced with delight.

"Not yet," I hissed back.

He stepped forward with his own dagger drawn and I grabbed his wrist, turning it so that he dropped the weapon. I elbowed him hard in the face and pushed him into the man behind him.

Someone lunged at me on my right, and I sidestepped the swing of his staff and used his momentum to shove him off-balance.

Arms went around me, grabbing me hard about my waist and lifting me. To the soldier's surprise, I went completely limp and fell to the ground. It was the worst possible defensive position to be in, but I'd had no choice. I grabbed the back of the attacker's knee to propel him forward so that he tripped over me, and I kicked out at the two closest men, clearing a spot to leap to my feet.

I got back into a defensive crouch, holding my weapon out. My pursuers spread out in a line and my stomach sank. I knew it was over.

My only hope had been to fight them one at a time.

As I feared, they attacked all together and I had a dozen sets of hands on me, pulling me down. I struggled against them, pushing and kicking, but it was no use.

Demaratus was already yelling as he shoved his way through the crowd. "Stupid girl! What did I tell you? Never, ever allow yourself to be cornered. And you never let yourself get flanked that way!"

The regiment released me and I huffed out, "I know." When my mentor was in this mood, which was essentially all the time, I was better served by being meek and agreeable. Arguing only made him worse.

Someone from my regiment offered me their hand to help me up and I accepted, brushing dust from my tunic.

Demaratus's face finally came into sight and I breathed deeply to fortify myself. I was very tall for a woman, but he was a head taller than me. He was nearly as old as my father but moved like a much younger man. He radiated anger and frustration. Even the patch over his missing right eye seemed angry with me.

"You are not as strong as them," he yelled. "Hide! Evade! Run! You don't try to fight your way clear." He gestured toward his soldiers, who had all been sworn to secrecy. "They have more training and they are stronger than you. You will not win in hand-to-hand combat. You must stay out of arm's reach! Once they get their hands on you, it's over."

"I know," I said again as my breathing returned to normal. I looked at my shoulder, which had already started to turn a darker color.

The bruises were getting harder and harder to explain.

Then Demaratus was directly in front of me, grabbing me by my breastplate the way he would any of his other soldiers and pulling me up to his face. His breath reeked of alcohol, as it normally did.

"No quarter will be given! You will not be taken alive. If they catch you, corner you, you will die!" He roared the words so loudly I wondered if everyone in the palace could hear him.

The former Daemonian general spent his time either not speaking at all or yelling at the top of his lungs. During our training, there had been no middle ground.

I didn't even know if he knew my name. He only ever called me "stupid girl."

"What happens if you get within reach of those Ilionian men?" he demanded.

"They will kill me." I understood this better than everyone else here, as I was the one it would soon happen to.

I had been training with Demaratus for the last year in preparation for the selection that would take place in two days' time. The Seven Sisters constellation had appeared in the sky a week ago, letting us know that the time had arrived.

And the main thing that I had learned in practicing hand-to-hand combat was that no matter how many techniques I learned, no matter how agile or nimble I might be, if more than one soldier could get their hands on me, I was finished. Demaratus was right—they were stronger than I was.

My only hope was to keep my distance. I wouldn't be able to fight my way out. Getting cornered would mean certain death.

And you got cornered in a place that you're familiar with, that worried voice inside me pointed out.

When this happened for real, I would be in a city I'd never stepped foot in before.

I stumbled a bit as he finally released me. Seeing that Demaratus had finished lecturing me, the other soldiers dispersed. I'd wondered more than once what the general had threatened them with to get them not only to help me train, but to keep silent about our activities. Because they were the biggest bunch of gossips I'd ever met. If I wanted to know what was happening in the palace, I only had to ask one of them.

"At least when I go to Ilion, I won't have this much armor weighing me down," I said as I undid the buckles at my shoulders, letting the breastplate drop.

Demaratus watched as it hit the ground. Before he could yell I reached over and picked it up. I could already hear him in my head. *Stupid girl! A warrior's armor deserves respect!*

But to my surprise he spoke in a rational tone, one I normally only heard when I visited him in the evenings after he'd become completely drunk. "There used to be a racing event called the hoplitodromos. It was a footrace run with full armor on."

"Was the point to torture the athletes?"

He ignored my jest while I undid the bracers on my wrists. "Centuries ago, there was a battle between the Sasanians and Daemonians. The Sasanian archers expected to pick the Daemonians off easily, given the superiority of their arrows. What they did not expect was a phalanx line of soldiers rushing them in full armor, plowing into their front defense. Training with armor made the Daemonians able to run long distances in it, unlike our enemies."

"I'm not going to battle with the Sasanians," I said, bending to remove my leg plates.

He grimaced, as if annoyed. "You race with armor now so that when it matters, you will be accustomed to a heavier load and you will be faster when you run without it. And it strengthens you to train with it on. A warrior who sweats more in training bleeds less in war."

I had certainly sweat enough to ensure that I wouldn't bleed at all when the time came. I gathered my armor, holding it against my chest. "One of those arrows almost hit me."

"You have to learn to be unafraid of being shot at, and there's only one way to do that."

"By shooting at me."

He grunted, and if he were the sort of man who ever smiled, I was sure he would have.

"At least no one threw an axe at me this time," I said.

"I didn't want to risk injuring you. Not so close to the end."

And despite the fact that I knew it was coming, that I was aware of the fact that the Ilionians would be landing on our shores in two days to collect their tribute, a bolt of fear struck my heart, shuddering in place the same way the spear had earlier.

I immediately suppressed the sensation. Demaratus had drilled into me the need to control my fear. Panicked warriors made mistakes.

I could not afford to make any mistakes.

He reached for the wineskin at his side, deftly undoing the ties with his right hand. Although I had never asked him about how he'd lost his left hand, I'd always been in awe of how easily he fought without it. There wasn't a soldier in the entire Locrian army who could defeat him now.

He must have been terrifyingly lethal when he'd had both.

Demaratus surprised me by offering me the skin.

"What's this?" I asked.

"Wine," he said.

I took a deep swig and then had to fight the urge to spit it out. This was what he drank all day, every day? "That is not wine," I said with a grimace, passing the skin back to him. "It tastes like vinegar."

His expression didn't change, but I heard the slight defensiveness in his voice. "It's Daemonian wine."

Daemonians were renowned for their skill in battle—but their wine left much to be desired.

"No wonder the Daemonians aren't afraid to die." I could have sworn that a ghost of a smile hovered over his lips. "Why are you being so nice to me? Is it because you're worried I'm about to die?"

My mentor was the only one I could joke with about my situation. To be more accurate, I joked while he glared.

Much as he was doing now.

"I would tell you to do better tomorrow, but this is our last training session. I will have to hope that you've retained some small part of all that I've taught you. If not, at least you will have an honorable death, which is all anyone can ask for."

This entire conversation felt surreal. He never spoke this much unless he was about to black out.

It made me think he really was worried that I would die.

Which I understood because that fear had kept me up many a night.

"Put your gear away," he said, interrupting my thoughts. There was so much I wanted to say to him in that moment, to thank him for all his guidance, his teaching, the skills he had drilled into me.

For giving me a fighting chance.

But he walked away before I could speak.

I trudged back to the armory, glad that I would never have to wear this blasted armor again. It was ill-fitting and often made me chafe. When I entered the room, my regiment were stowing their equipment, teasing one another.

"There's the thigh-flasher!" I heard Linus say, and they all started laughing. I glanced down at my tunic. In Locris it was considered improperly short, showing my upper legs, but Demaratus had told me that it was what the Daemonian women wore when they exercised and trained. It was much easier to run without lengths of cloth wrapping around my ankles.

I wouldn't make it very far with a regular tunic.

And my daringly short hemline was the reason I kept a cloak in the armory. If I went into the palace dressed like this, there would be questions I wouldn't want to answer.

"Why are you looking at my thighs?" I retorted, which set off another round of laughter as the regiment mocked Linus for his remark.

I stood there and watched them, still holding my armor. I was hit with a wave of sadness as I realized that I would never train with them again. They had been my constant companions for this past year. I had spent hours with them every day.

And I never would again.

I put my armor up on my designated shelf, patting it one final time.

"Maybe that's the reason Telamon grazed Lia with that arrow," Linus said. "Because he was so distracted by her legs!"

"Or his aim is just as poor as yours," I responded, which set off another round of laughter, squeezing my heart so tightly it felt like it might break.

"I wouldn't have almost hit you if you could manage to run faster than a wounded animal," Telamon told me.

"Wounded is the only way Telamon catches any woman!" Polymedes said with a loud laugh.

This group of men had always treated me as one of their own. From the first day, when Demaratus told them that I would be joining their ranks, not a single soldier had muttered a complaint or protested against having to train with a woman.

I knew there were many who would have.

My throat felt tight, like there was a large lump that I couldn't swallow. "Thank you."

At my words, the men fell silent, all their faces turned toward me.

"Thank you," I repeated. "For all your help and for including me. And for not telling anyone."

Andronicus, their captain, got to his feet. He was twenty years old—a couple of years older than I was—and coming to the end of his mandatory service in the army.

"You have earned our gratitude and loyalty," he said. He balled his hand into a fist and laid it across his chest, the gesture one soldier made to another. "Every one of us would take your place if we could, and we respect the sacrifice that you are going to make for Locris. One for many."

Then every other member of the regiment stood and did the same. Tears filled my eyes, but I would not cry in front of them. They would never respect me again if I did.

I put my fist over my own chest, returning the honor they'd given me. "One for many," I repeated.

We all stayed there for a bit as I drank in their faces, committing them to memory.

Then they began to move, the moment over, making plans for their evening.

Telamon approached me, shyly. "Do you want to join us at the tavern?"

More than anything, but that wasn't the sort of place I could go without being discovered.

Not to mention that I understood what he was asking without saying the actual words. I'd never had romantic feelings for Telamon. He had indicated possible interest in the past, but I hadn't seen the point.

"I appreciate the offer, but I have a family dinner tonight."

He smiled and ducked his head, taking the merciless ribbing his compatriots now offered him.

Linus crowed, "She turned him down! I told you she would. You owe me three drachmas."

"You ruined your last chance," someone added, but they were all out of the building now and I wasn't sure which one of them had said it or how long Telamon had been planning to ask me to spend time with him before I left.

The armory was now completely silent, and I took one last look around the room. While I knew I should have returned to the palace, my feet took me in the opposite direction. I walked through the dilapidated maze. No one knew why it had been built. Polymedes had conjectured that it had been meant as a defensive measure to keep the temple safe. I knew he was correct but had kept that information to myself.

The doorway of the temple had broken during an earthquake a thousand years ago, crushing the wooden doors, but there was still enough of an opening for me to sneak inside. Water dripped slowly down one wall and the entire place smelled dirty and musty. I headed through the main room toward the staircase, making my way down to where the statue of the goddess lay in pieces.

Just before I reached the last step, I crouched down to raise the top of the stair and pulled out the ancient box within. I opened the box and took out the book it held, walking over to the statue.

I sat on the overturned column near the goddess's head and brushed some dust off her face.

Her large, empty eye sockets seemed to stare back at me, mocking my pathetically sparse plan.

This might be the last time I visited this temple. My grandmother had brought me here two years ago, just a few months before she died. She was the one who had shown me the false step with the box. The book was so old I had been afraid to touch it.

"What is this?" I had asked her.

"It is a record of Locris, our home. Of stories that have been banned and forgotten. Words about the goddess, who we used to praise with songs and prayers. Until she cursed us and our land, destroying her own temple."

I took the book reverently and began to read. I remembered that rush as I turned the pages, learning so many new things. I had known about the temple, passed by it many times, but I'd never gone inside. I hadn't realized that it was significant in any real way.

I was familiar with the yearly tribute we paid to Ilion, and the reasons why, but was shocked at the discovery that Locrians had abandoned their entire belief system when we were cursed.

Stories of the greatness and power of the earth goddess, how she had blessed our lands for millennia, before everything was destroyed by the actions of one man.

My ancestor.

"Not even your father knows about this book," my grandmother had said.

"Why did you give it to me?" I asked, not understanding why she would take such a risk. My father would be forced to destroy the book and punish his own mother if he ever found out.

A chill ran down my back as I recalled the way her gaze had bored into mine—so clearly, so certainly. "You will be the one to carry this legacy forward. You will keep the word. Someone in Locris must remember the old ways, how we worshipped the goddess, and find a way to regain her favor to restore our lands. Your older sister will marry and leave. Your brother will be beholden to the law and his people. But you? You will have a choice about your life's path. And you should choose to remember what was and what might be."

What if I don't want it? I wanted to ask but knew that I wouldn't. I understood that this was too important to reject. This legacy was now mine, regardless of how I felt about it.

"You must always remember that all the answers you need are in the written word," she continued. "In scrolls, in poems, in songs, in books. Find the right words and you will have your answer."

She had turned out to be right. A single line in the book had caught my attention and changed the entire course of my life.

Only the eye of the goddess can restore Locris.

The sound of rocks falling down the stairs had me on my feet, my blade drawn, heart pounding in my chest.

Because I knew I would be executed if anyone found me with this book.

CHAPTER TWO

"Lia?"

I immediately relaxed and sighed. It was just my sister, Quynh.

"You scared me," I told her when she peered down at me from the top of the stairs. She was always too frightened to come all the way down. I sheathed my dagger and then returned the book to its box, replacing the stone lid. "You'll remember to take this to Kallisto if I don't return?"

Someone in my family would have to carry on the legacy if I wasn't here to do it.

"Yes, I'll remember." She sounded so annoyed that it reminded me of Demaratus. "But you're coming back."

We both knew it was more likely that I wouldn't. No other maiden ever had.

But she and I never spoke about that.

"Mother is looking for you. You need to get cleaned up and ready for dinner," she said. Outside of Demaratus and my regiment, Quynh was the only other person who knew what I'd been doing the last year, and so she could always find me easily.

I nodded and took one final glance around the temple before I went upstairs to join her.

"Hurry!" she said, pushing against my back when I reached the top floor.

"Why are you in such a rush?" I asked.

"After dinner I have plans to meet with Andronicus," she said with a secret smile.

I smiled back. "Will he finally ask for your hand?"

"He knows not to. Not until I know . . ." Quynh's voice trailed off.

"Not until you know my fate," I finished for her. "I don't want you to put your plans aside for me. You should marry if that's what you want to do."

She shrugged and we walked back to the palace. Somehow I attracted even more dirt, while she managed to remain pristine, like she was floating over the dusty, arid earth.

My stomach growled. "I'm starving."

The only good thing about the Ilionians coming was that they would bring an extravagant feast with them to celebrate the selection. There would be all kinds of rich and delicious meats and vegetables, fruits and grains that no one in Locris had the opportunity to eat any other time of the year, savory, flaky fish, and such a variety of sweet desserts that last year I'd nearly wept when I saw them all.

We subsisted on so little here in our desert kingdom that it was difficult to remember that others routinely had access to so much more than we did.

And that the Ilionians were to blame for cutting off our trade access.

"Here," Quynh said, reaching into her tunic pocket and pulling out a cloth that she had wrapped around—

"Pasteli!" I exclaimed as soon as I saw it. It was a thin bar made of honey and sesame. My mouth watered and I eagerly took the piece she offered to me. "Where did you get this?"

Had the Ilionians arrived early?

"Andronicus bought some this morning at the docks and gave it to me."

Feeling guilty, I tried to hand it back to her. "You should keep it. He intended for you to have it."

Half the men in the palace were in love with Quynh. Not only because she was beautiful physically, with her silky, black hair hanging to her waist, her unusual long and thin eyes, her high cheekbones that always seemed to be flushed pink, but because she was so beautiful inside, too. Kind and generous and selfless in a way that I could only aspire to.

I always felt gangly and awkward around Quynh, and wished I could be more like her. Not so short-tempered and judgmental or impatient. She had definitely been a good influence on me, something our mother noted often.

Quynh had joined the palace when we were six years old. Her ship had been destroyed and she had washed up on our beaches. Shipwrecks weren't unusual—the strange and high reef formation along our shores to the south had ruined many vessels. Thanks to the Ilionian blockade, we had become a nation of traders and scavengers, taking whatever the ocean offered since the earth had been denied to us.

My older brother and I had been searching for seashells when we found her. I stayed with her while he ran back to get help. Everyone was surprised that she had survived. She spoke a fair amount of the common tongue—she had been able to tell us her name and that her family were merchants who had traveled from a land called Goguryeo, far in the east. They had been blown off course by a storm that had torn their ship apart.

I had felt an instant kinship to her, as if we had been meant to know one another. My soul recognized hers. Orphans were usually taken by a couple unable to have their own children, but I had begged my parents to let her come home with us.

They had permitted it and she had stayed.

Quynh was family. My sister.

And my best friend.

"Andronicus won't mind if I share the pasteli with you," she said, gently pushing my hand away.

"He meant it as a token of his affection," I tried to insist, but somehow the pasteli made its way to my mouth. I tried not to moan when I took my first bite and the sweetness of the honey exploded across my tongue. It really had been a romantic gift—the honey was symbolic of love and passion, the sesame of fertility.

It was a treat often served at Locrian weddings. It spoke very clearly of Andronicus's intentions once his military service ended.

We went into my room and she shut the door behind us. "He has shown me his affection in countless ways already. I'm sure he plans to show me his affection again later tonight."

It was as if Quynh lived in a secret world that I'd never even glimpsed, let alone entered.

I went behind my dressing curtain and washed my body quickly with a sea sponge and cold water, changing into the tunic she had left waiting for me.

"Sit down," she said when I emerged. My clothes always felt voluminous after training and it took me a bit to readapt to them. I sat in the chair at my dressing table, positioned in front of my polished obsidian mirror. I looked at our reflections and again felt inadequate. I knew I was not beautiful. Not like Quynh or our sister, Kallisto. Kallisto resembled our mother with her dark hair, short stature, and generous curves. I looked more like our father and brother—too tall for a woman, with lighter brown hair and eyes that couldn't decide whether they wanted to be green or brown.

"You know that I can style my own hair," I told her. I wouldn't do it as well, but I was capable.

She ignored my offer. While Quynh was usually the type of person who would go along with what others wanted, when it came to things that were important to her, she was obstinate and immovable. She would perform this task for me whether I liked it or not.

"I'm going to have to put some scented powder in your hair," she grumbled, more to herself. "You'll have to wash it before the selection."

I would. I couldn't sail off to my death with dirty hair.

Especially since it was my one vanity. The color was plain, but it was thick and curled slightly at the ends. Like all Locrian women's hair, it hung down past my waist.

Quynh had just started to comb through my hair when she came to a sudden stop and I felt a snag. "What is it?" I asked.

"My bracelet. My bracelet is caught." I heard the strong emotion in her voice.

"Cut my hair," I said. It was the most serious offer I could make her. No woman of Locris ever cut her hair. But that bracelet was the one thing she had left from her parents, and I would never let it be ruined. Better my head be shaved than for Quynh to lose her bracelet.

"I think I can work it free," she said. It took a couple of minutes, but she finally managed it. "There!"

She held her wrist out in triumph and I examined the bracelet carefully. It was constructed from green and white silk, with a large green gukwa knot in the center that resembled a flower. Smaller knots kept beads of jade and pearl in place.

I let out a sigh of relief. It was her most treasured possession. It was important to me that she still have it once . . .

Once I'm gone.

"So what exactly do you have planned with Andronicus tonight?" I asked, wanting to redirect my thoughts.

Her cheeks reddened slightly and she ducked her head. "This and that."

"Kissing?" I asked, and she flushed even harder.

"I'm surprised that nothing has happened with you and any of the men you train with. How did you miss how handsome Andronicus is?"

Because I'd never thought of him that way. Andronicus was my captain and the person who had given me a black eye on my second day of training. I'd had to blame it on running into a door to shake off my mother's suspicion.

I'd never considered any of the regiment as prospective romantic partners. They were my friends, my fellow trainees. I had been solely focused on my mission, and there hadn't been time for boys or kisses. And Demaratus would have killed any soldier who tried to kiss me.

Not to mention that I was betrothed to the Ilionian prince and probably shouldn't have been kissing other men.

But now I regretted my choices. Quynh had described how exciting kissing was, the way it made you feel warm and shivery all at once, how you lost track of time and your mind shut down—I wished more than anything that I had experienced it myself.

Maybe I should have gone off with Telamon so that I could have tried it.

I sighed. I didn't want to die without ever kissing someone.

Quynh finished brushing my hair, creating two braids in the front that she pulled back and tied together. "There. At least you actually resemble the princess that you are."

There was no real way to tell now. My grandmother had described to me once what their lives had been like when she was young. How their tunics had been created from a linen so fine it was nearly see-through, soft and luxurious. The jewels they had worn on their ears, their necks, their wrists, the crowns on their heads.

But in order to survive the Ilionian tariffs, my family had sold off almost everything we'd once owned.

The tunic I wore, although one of my finest, was indistinguishable from the ones worn by the servants in the palace.

Quynh and I left for the dining room, walking together down the stone hallways lit by torches.

Our relative poverty was one of the reasons why my betrothal to the Ilionian prince was so important to my parents. I was supposed to convince him to decrease the tariffs imposed by his blockade. It was rumored that the king of Ilion had fallen ill and the crown prince had increased the taxes, from his own people and the blockade, to waste on whoring and drinking.

When the goddess had cursed our lands, Locris had been a lush place full of flocks and grain, cheese and honey. But she had turned our once-rich soil to arid dust and now nothing would grow. Water wasn't a problem—we still had plenty of it, but the ground was barren no matter how much water was poured on it.

For a thousand years we had been able to import everything we needed, exporting salt and blocks of marble from our quarries.

But with the increased tariffs taken by the blockade, fewer merchants dared to travel here, and the ones who did had much higher prices, passing the cost along to us.

I'd overheard my father in meetings with his advisers where he was told that the quarries were nearly empty.

The young people of Locris had forsaken their ancestral lands and homes and set out for other places to start over. They saw what I did.

My nation was dying. If things continued as they were, it wouldn't be long before there was no one left.

Which was probably the point. Ilion had always been our mortal enemy, and they had found a way to destroy us without shedding blood.

Well, besides the blood of the maidens they demanded as tribute.

We entered the dining room and everyone was waiting for us.

"Quynh and Lia! There you are! We were about to send out the guard to search for you," our father, King Ephesus, called out from the head of the table. Our mother, Queen Hypatia, sat on the opposite end and beamed at us. Our elder sister, Kallisto, also smiled, pleased that we'd arrived.

My heart twisted in my chest. This would be the last dinner I ever had alone with my family.

And they didn't even know it.

CHAPTER THREE

I sat down across from Kallisto, who reached over to take my hand and squeezed it. I returned the gesture with all the love I had for her. She was the most incredible sister. She was a lot like Quynh, very sweet, generous, and compassionate. She loved our family dinners. She had never enjoyed bigger social gatherings, preferring the solitude of her chambers over having to converse with strangers.

It must have weighed heavily on her shoulders that she was soon to be queen of Locris. Her betrothed, an Ilionian nobleman named Lykaon, had written to say that he planned to join the selection envoy so that they could finally meet in person.

His imminent arrival unnerved her, but she tried not to show it to anyone and I admired the strength it took to put on a happy face.

My almost sister-in-law, Doria, sat next to Kallisto. Unlike my sister, Doria never tried to conceal her pain or heartache. She was in a perpetual state of mourning for my brother.

My father lifted his cup. "To Haemon."

We raised ours in response. "To Haemon."

Every dinner started with a toast to my only brother. Two years ago he had set out to find a new trade route that would allow us to rebuild our kingdom, and he'd never returned.

Doria insisted that he was still alive—that she would know if he were truly dead. But Haemon, like Kallisto and I, was one of the

Aianteioi. Descendants of Ajax the Lesser, who had committed an unspeakable crime.

Laws had been passed a millennium ago regarding how the Aianteioi were to be treated, protections that we would be afforded. One of them was that we would have to be ransomed if we fell into enemy hands. The goddess would punish those who ignored this rule.

So I knew Haemon wasn't alive. We would have received word long ago. After seeing what had been done to Locris, no one would dare to risk the goddess's wrath. He must have drowned at sea.

Haemon and Doria had been betrothed as children, as she was the daughter of one of the Hundred Houses, the nobles of Locris. They had fallen in love the first time they met. I still remembered the way they were with each other—the laughter, the secret touches, the longing in their eyes, the stolen kisses. They had shared an emotional and physical connection despite their marriage being arranged. He had promised to wed her as soon as he returned from his voyage.

They had openly declared their love for one another from the beginning. Saying "I love you" to a romantic partner was an unbreakable bond and commitment. Doria had once told me that saying the words had stitched her soul to Haemon's in a mystical way she couldn't properly describe. The goddess punished those who said it lightly, or those who said it but then did not honor their vows and their relationship. Doria and Haemon had meant the words and I knew they would have lived a very happy life together.

It was something else the Ilionians had stolen from me—their blockade and rising tariffs had taken my brother's life and I would never forgive them for that.

Neither would Doria, who had never moved past her grief. I'd heard a story once that Sasanians burned their dead in a giant pyre and that sometimes wives would join their husbands in the fire rather than live a life without them. I knew that would have been Doria's choice if it had been offered to her.

She dressed like a widow and had become a shadow of her former self. She had not even been granted the position of wife, which would have afforded her some protections and inheritances. Her family had rejected her, angry that she hadn't elevated their status by becoming a princess and then queen, furious that she had spoken of her love for Haemon, rendering her unable to marry a different man. So my parents had taken her in, welcoming Doria as another daughter.

We all shared in her sorrow. Haemon had been the light and promise of our family. I could still hear his laughter, as clearly as if he sat at the table now. In the chair next to Doria's that was always left open for him.

His death had drastically changed all of our lives. Kallisto had been betrothed to the Ilionian prince, but it had been broken because she had to stay in Locris and eventually become queen. The new match with the wealthy Ilionian nobleman had been arranged instead. He would become her prince consort, and their oldest child would be the next ruler of Locris. Her betrothed's wealth would bring much-needed relief to the kingdom.

And where before there had been possibilities for my life as the youngest sibling, all those options had been taken from me. Someone had to marry the crown prince to create an alliance with our worst enemy, and that lot fell to me.

But I had decided on a new path.

Dinner began, and as always, it was barley flatbread and salted anchovies with a bowl of watery broth. Before I had started training, Demaratus had often joined us for dinner. He had thoroughly enjoyed the very basic food we ate but he would wax nostalgic for the dish he had shared with his fellow soldiers while he'd trained—black broth— which was meat cooked in blood, salt, and vinegar.

It sounded as foul to me as that swill he called wine.

Which he somehow managed to import and used to black out on a daily basis after we'd all eaten together. In fact, it had been at a family dinner much like this one that he had inadvertently set me on my mission. I had learned all I could about the eye of the goddess in Ilion, but I wasn't sure how I could make it to the Ilionian temple. Being chosen in the selection would give me a chance to reach the temple but I knew I would be slaughtered. While I worried over that reality, Demaratus had drunkenly boasted that he could turn anyone into a Daemonian warrior—even a woman.

I had approached him the next day and asked if he would train me. He had too much pride to back down from his claim and he'd taken me on. I assumed that was why he had stayed away from family dinners ever since—he didn't want to risk lying to my parents.

And I wasn't sure if my parents were just completely unaware of what I'd been doing every day or if they knew and had decided to keep it to themselves. Now that I was an adult and my betrothal was arranged, my days were my own. My mother would have preferred that I spend my time learning how to run a royal household, weaving in her sitting room with Kallisto, Quynh, and Doria, but I had other plans.

Before Haemon's death, my mother would have lectured me and insisted I join them. But the last words she had exchanged with Haemon had been angry ones and she'd never forgiven herself. It made her afraid to discipline me or my sisters.

"Is everything ready for the Ilionians' arrival?" my father asked and I nearly dropped my spoon.

Their arrival meant my departure.

"Yes," my mother said. "Everything is as it should be."

There wasn't much for her to do to prepare. The Ilionians would bring everything they needed with them. They knew how poor we were, and that we did not have the resources to properly host them.

It was another way they shamed and humiliated us.

"You should destroy their ship before it even docks," Doria muttered to absolutely no one's surprise. She also blamed the Ilionians for Haemon's death and it had made her bloodthirsty.

I liked her more for it.

"We don't need to destroy the Ilionians," I said carefully. I had wondered for a long time how much my parents knew or remembered about the old myths and legends, the way that the Locrians used to worship the goddess. Maybe if they could believe in her, believe that there was a

22

way to save our nation, it would be easier for them when I left. "If we could restore the goddess's favor, find a way for her to remove the curse from our lands . . ."

Everyone was staring at me as if I'd sprouted a second head. It should have made me stop talking, as it was forbidden, but I continued. "If we can find the eye of the goddess, we can save Locris."

"'Eye of the goddess.' Why would you speak such heresy at my table? Who believes in those kinds of ridiculous superstitions?" my father scoffed angrily.

How would he respond if I said I did? I wanted to argue with him, to show him that there was another way than to just give in and watch as our people died, but I didn't want my defiance to be his possible last memory of me.

My mother changed the subject, speaking of the materials Lykaon's letter had promised so that she and my sisters could make Kallisto's wedding dress.

"You could join us, Thalia," she said to me. It was the closest she came to being annoyed these days—using the name I was known by to the rest of the nation.

My actual name, Euthalia, was never used. I had hated it since I was a small child and had insisted on my nicknames. Princess Thalia for more formal occasions, Lia for my friends and family.

"All I'll do is tangle your careful threads," I said. While I'd always enjoyed weaving, I wasn't as good at it as my siblings were.

I also could not make promises that I wouldn't be able to keep.

Then Doria asked Kallisto what type of embroidery she planned on doing along the edges of her dress and the rest of the dinner was spent discussing my sister's bridal wardrobe.

But all I could think about was my father calling the eye of the goddess superstition.

It wasn't. It couldn't be.

The curse was real. I knew for a fact that the eye was real, that Locris had had its own eye a long time ago.

I wondered how many generations it had taken for people to forget, to turn their backs on the goddess the way she had turned her back on them.

When dinner was over I went out onto the balcony that overlooked the ocean and sat down on a stone bench. Usually it brought me peace to sit out here, but my father's words were causing me to doubt myself and the plans I had put in motion.

My mother joined me on the bench and asked, "Are you nervous about your own marriage?"

Suppressing a laugh, I said, "No." It was entirely truthful. I wasn't the least bit worried about having to marry the foolish, wasteful, selfish prince of Ilion, because no wedding would take place. In a week I would be dead or an acolyte in the temple of the goddess. "I was thinking about what Father said. That he thinks that the eye is superstition. Magic is real. We've seen it."

I shouldn't have been pressing the issue, as it might arouse her suspicion, but she didn't look for a deeper context for my statement. "It's easier for women to believe in magic because we have the ability to make life and carry it inside us. We're already magic. And it is a magic no man will ever understand."

In a sense she was right, but that wasn't what I was talking about. I did consider what she was saying, though. That I carried a spark of magic in me that I might never get to experience.

Initially, after Haemon's death, I had assumed that I would do what was required of me—I would marry the prince and bear his heirs. Even before my brother had left, I had imagined that I would someday marry and have children.

Become a mother.

One more dream I was most likely going to have to give up.

A horn bellowed, loud and deep. I got to my feet as my racing heart leapt up into my throat.

A giant ship came into view.

The Ilionians had arrived early.

CHAPTER FOUR

I slammed open Demaratus's door. He was lying on his bed in the corner of the room. "The Ilionians are here," I said as I shut the door behind me. His room was devoid of any personal touches: no tapestries, no rugs, no decoration—nothing that would speak of comfort. No mattress, no pillows. He wouldn't even use a blanket when the weather turned cold.

"The Ilionians must have had good winds," he said, slightly slurring his words.

Definitely drunk. It would make conversation possible. I sat in his one chair and balled my fists up on my lap. "I want to go down to the docks and meet them with a blade and stab every last one of them."

"Where is the best place to stab someone?" he asked, still in his role of teacher.

"Anywhere is a good place to stab an Ilionian," I muttered. At his annoyed expression I said, "For an armored soldier? The eye, throat, and armpit." The parts not protected that would also cause the most damage.

My correct answer seemed to satisfy him.

"Not that I would be able to accomplish much," I said as I tried to sink into his uncomfortable chair. Why wouldn't he use cushions like a civilized person? "There's too many of them."

"The size of the enemy force does not matter," Demaratus corrected me. "A Daemonian never backs down, never gives up the fight. What else does the code require?"

Was this meant to be an examination? Why wouldn't he let me just complain in peace? "To always behave with honor—"

He nodded and interrupted me. "Self-control is vitally important."

"Your words might carry more weight if you were not drunk right now," I told him.

He ignored my observation and kept speaking. "You must always be the master of yourself and your emotions. A Daemonian king infuriated with his servant told the man, 'I would kill you if I were not so angry.' That's the sort of self-control you must have."

"And not just control of myself and my emotions, but most importantly a mastery of fear. Obedience to the law. To fight to the death. One for many." There was one more, but I couldn't remember it.

"And never flee a battle," he prompted.

"Yes. Never flee a battle. Although you've been doing nothing but teaching me how to flee this battle."

"Because there is a larger battle at play. Recovering the eye and restoring your nation." He said this with a slight note of sarcasm because he didn't believe in the goddess or magic. He had told me on more than one occasion that the only thing he believed in was steel.

"Did you flee a battle?" I asked, holding my breath. I might be dead soon and I would prefer to die with all of my curiosity satiated.

There was an uncomfortably long pause before he finally responded. "Yes."

"Why?" The question was out before I could stop it. He was the bravest man I'd ever met. I couldn't imagine him ever leaving a battlefield.

"I lost my shield."

"How?"

He looked at the stump at the end of his left arm. "In a moment of danger, I raised my shield to cover my best friend and saved his life. But the enemy's blade cut off my hand, which had been holding my shield. There is nothing worse to the Daemonians than a dropped shield. I lost my honor."

Despite all his teachings, I was confused. "But you saved your friend. That should be all that matters."

Demaratus ran his right hand over the stubble on his scalp. He had always kept his hair shorn since I'd known him. "If I had dropped a weapon or a piece of armor, I would have been fined or punished. A sword or a helmet is meant to protect me. But a shield protects every warrior in the phalanx. A Daemonian who loses his shield is forever dishonored. The group comes before the individual. One for many."

He hadn't lost his shield, though—it had been literally cut away from him. "But why come to Locris? Why didn't you return home?"

"Here if a man is a coward, it will not change his life or his family's lives. He may still go to the market, still meet and visit with friends, still meet a foe on the battlefield. You even make him commander of your army. But in Daemonia? I would not be welcome. I would be beaten and rejected from everywhere I tried to go and my dishonor would become my family's. My wife and children are better off without me. My actions shamed them, and if I had returned to them, it would have ruined their lives. I would never do that to them."

I put my hands over my heart. That was so unspeakably sad I wasn't sure what to say.

He made an uncomfortable sound, as if he'd shared too much. "We were flogged repeatedly as boys, to see who could endure it best without complaining or crying out. I should have flogged you to toughen you up."

Respecting his desire to shift the flow of our conversation, I said, "Whip scars on my back would have been difficult to explain to my parents."

"You're a creative liar. You would have come up with something."

His assessment was correct. Necessity had forced me to become a very creative liar. "Your childhood sounds terrifying."

"It was all in service of becoming the best warriors we could be," he countered. "It helped."

I'd personally experienced one particular form of his childhood training that I had not enjoyed—Demaratus often had members of my regiment randomly sneak into my room to attack me. I was to never let my guard down—I had to always be ready, always prepared, never in a sleep so deep that I could be taken by surprise.

Demaratus had also attempted to teach me lock picking. He meant to encourage me to steal if necessary in order to survive, as the Daemonians would, but I was hopeless at it. He had given up after calling me "stupid girl" more times than I could count.

He had listed off all the things he'd stolen when he was younger, and I'd tried to look impressed. When I'd wondered aloud if it had been dishonorable to steal, he had rushed to assure me that the honor was in not getting caught. It seemed like strange logic to me, but it worked well for my current situation, in which I very much planned on stealing something priceless.

"Here everyone is soft and weak," Demaratus complained, his words slurring even further as sleep started to claim him. "Do you know that there are no defensive walls in Daemonia? Only cowards have walled-in cities."

Whatever he'd been about to say next was swallowed up by a snore.

I walked over to the model of Troas, the capital city of Ilion, that I had constructed based on the information that I'd gleaned over the last year.

The palace lay in the middle of a massive maze of walls. It had been designed to keep invaders out. Demaratus had noted that it would have been very easy for archers to walk along the top of the high walls, out of the infantry's reach, and pick off the enemy one by one.

The other parts of the city were only accessible through the maze, and I had spent hours poring over this model, memorizing every turn and dead end, where each sector of the city was located, so that I could reach the temple quickly.

Looking at it again wasn't going to do me any good. I already had the entire layout in my head. I glanced at Demaratus, knowing he wouldn't come to any of the celebrations and that this might be my final chance to say goodbye.

I went over and kissed him on the forehead and said, "Thank you."

He grumbled and turned over. I wished he'd been awake to hear my gratitude.

I walked from the barracks back to my room, sneaking through shadows and staying out of sight. It was good practice.

Quynh was waiting for me. "I was worried about you," she said when I entered.

"I'm fine. I'm in no danger in my own home," I said as I went over to sit next to her on my bed.

A few heartbeats passed before she said, "The Ilionians have arrived."

"I know. Mother said the selection will still take place in two days even though they are early. They sent a messenger saying that they will have a feast tomorrow evening to celebrate Lykaon and the betrothal." Much as I wished for a painful death for all Ilionians, I didn't mind the extra opportunity to eat their food.

Even if they did mean it as an insult.

"Wouldn't it be easier to just marry the prince?" she asked. "If you were the princess of Ilion, then you could look for the eye as much as you wanted."

The princess of Ilion. That thought made me feel physically ill. "Only the priestesses and the acolytes are allowed in the temple."

When I wasn't training, I had gotten two or three members of the regiment to go down with me to the docks to badger the incoming traders for information. It was how I had been able to construct the model of the capital city of Ilion. The traders had also warned me that there was one way to gain entry to the temple.

The selection was my only chance.

"Are you concerned that there will be repercussions from you not marrying the prince?" she asked.

I shook my head. "I am not a woman men would go to war for. I am no Menelaia."

"Who?" she asked.

"She was the most beautiful woman in the world, who ran away with her lover and started the Great War," I said. I wasn't surprised that Quynh didn't remember the name. It was usually not spoken in Locris, as her selfish actions had caused us so much pain and loss. "Regardless, I still have the right to choose whether or not I'll wed. And how can the prince be angry? I'll be in his kingdom, serving in his goddess's temple. He can be upset at the goddess if he would like. That won't turn out well for him, though."

"You know how some men are. He might be vain and proud. He might wage war on our family for damaging his pride."

That wasn't something I had considered before, and it made my stomach feel queasy. "That would be a foolish choice. There's nothing to be won here. They're already choking us to death."

"Lia, you might be a steadying influence on him. Help him to see reason."

I was probably the last person who could do that. "If he's as reckless and irresponsible as they say, my marrying him won't change anything. There is only one way to save Locris and it isn't by becoming a bride."

"Maybe you can marry him when you return."

I didn't know how long it would take me to find the eye and return to Locris. I intended for the prince to not ever find out what I was doing. I hoped my parents would delay the betrothal for as long as they could to give me enough time to search and make my way home.

When I returned, it would be with the eye of the goddess in my hands. Which might lead to a new set of problems with Ilion and the prince beyond a delayed wedding.

But I would face that when the time came.

I only needed to concentrate on the here and now.

"Perhaps," I agreed. "Or you could marry him. You would make an excellent queen. And there isn't anyone else alive who could touch the heart of that horrible man the same way that you could."

"I have no desire to be queen," she said. "I have seen what it entails and would prefer a quiet life with a man I love."

"Like Andronicus?" I teased and she shrugged.

As much as she seemed to enjoy being with him, I realized that she hadn't once said that she loved him.

It spoke volumes.

"You should tell our parents about what you're doing," she said. "They should be given the chance to prepare."

"If I tell them, they will find a way to undo what I've done," I said. "Everything is in place."

"It will destroy them to lose another child."

Her words thrust into me like a sword, just under my ribs and then dragged up to my heart. I had considered what my death would do to my family, but not too closely. It was too painful. "I'm not going to die. You know how stubborn I am."

Quynh laughed, which had been my intent. "Lia, you are the sister of my heart."

"And you are of mine," I said as I hugged her. "I will come back. I will restore Locris and save the people. One for many."

"I just wish you didn't have to be the one," she said against my shoulder.

With a sigh I said, "It had to be someone. It might as well be me."

CHAPTER FIVE

The palace was a hive of activity as everyone tried to prepare for the Ilionians' arrival. My mother refused to be embarrassed that her home might not be up to their standards, so we were all roped into cleaning. I had hoped to spend this day talking to my family, saying all the things I needed to say, but instead I was sweeping stone floors.

Quynh proved why she was my favorite person when she found me and said that she had sweet-talked Hippolyta into drawing a bath for me. The water was warm and soothing and I sighed as I lowered myself into it. I thanked Hippolyta for fetching the water. She was one of the few maidservants that we had left, and she was always so helpful and sweet.

I dunked my hair under the water, and Quynh insisted that she help me to wash it. Usually we would work sand into it to clean it and then brush it out, but given that it was a special occasion, we dipped into our ever-diminishing store of soap. It was created from tallow and ashes, and it was a complete luxury to have such clean hair.

"Do you think we'll have to do this for the male guests?" I asked. In some countries it was normal for the virgin daughters of a household to bathe male visitors. It wasn't something that any of us had done before, but I had heard rumor that the Ilionians might expect it. I'd never seen an unclothed man before. I was a tiny bit curious.

"I hope not," she said. "If you're allowed around naked, unarmed Ilionians, my fear is that they will wind up murdered and then we will certainly have to go to war."

"True," I mused. "The temptation might be too great for me to withstand."

The Ilionians weren't the only visitors we were expecting. People would arrive from all over Locris to attend the selection.

To bear witness.

Quynh helped me to get ready for the festivities. I looked down at my plain tunic, knowing that I was about to be judged on my appearance by hundreds of people.

I raised my chin. I was a princess of Locris. I wouldn't allow others to make me feel small.

"Mother wanted you to wear Grandmother's pearls," she said.

There was a pang of regret that I had to brush aside. I had sold them to ensure my plan was successful. I just nodded.

"I'm going to go check on Kallisto and see if she needs anything," Quynh said. After she left I studied my reflection for a moment longer before going out into the hallway.

I walked toward the throne room, where all festivities and celebrations were held.

There was a muffled cry, and then I heard a short scream and the sound of someone being slapped. I darted left and went down a hall toward the sound.

Hippolyta was on the ground, covering her head with her hands, wailing, and a strange man was hitting her. I ran over and threw myself between them.

"What do you think you're doing?" I demanded.

Without answering me, he caught the side of my face with the back of his fist, flinging me backward, knocking me off my feet. Pain exploded where he made contact, stars blooming to life in front of my darkened eyes.

My first thought was that my regiment had been pulling their blows during our hand-to-hand training. I realized that none of them had ever hit me with their full strength, as this man just had.

This was why Demaratus had told me to keep clear.

"Learn your place and obey your betters," the man said, spitting on the ground next to us. I took in as many details about his appearance as I could. I wanted to be sure that I could find him again later. His hair was a strange color, almost yellow, and he had dark, cruel eyes. He stared back with a sneer, and then he left. I had no weapon and my mentor would have been furious with me. *Stupid girl, no Daemonian warrior should ever be more than an arm's length away from their sword!*

Ignoring my inner voice, I crawled over to Hippolyta.

"Are you all right?" I asked, looking her over.

"I'm fine," she said in between sobs.

There weren't any visible bruises now. That didn't mean there wouldn't be any later. "What happened?"

"I don't know," she said as she attempted to stop crying. "He told me to bring him something to drink and I suppose I wasn't going fast enough."

"So he hit you?" I asked, completely shocked. I had heard of this sort of thing happening in some other nations, but I had no experience with it at all. The men of Locris were gentle and kind.

I held her tightly, rocking her until her cries came to an end. When her breathing returned to normal, I released her and said, "I'm going to tell my father."

"Please don't," she protested. "I don't want to make any trouble for your family. They've been so good to me."

I had no problem lying to her. "Of course." It was the first thing I would do when I found the king.

He needed to know that one of his guests hit defenseless women.

"I should go back to the kitchens," she said, her voice wobbly.

"Only if you're certain," I said. "And maybe you should find someone else to serve the guests."

"There is no one else," she said in a way that broke my heart.

I knew what that felt like.

"Call on me if you need my assistance," I said. Hippolyta nodded and headed toward the kitchens.

Adrenaline built up inside me. I wanted to hit something.

Or stab someone.

I got up, intending to head back to my room to get my dagger. I wouldn't be caught off guard without it again. I went around a corner and nearly smacked straight into Andronicus. He put his hands on my shoulders to steady me. "Lia! I was looking for you. I have a surprise."

He reached behind his back and pulled out my dagger, handing it to me. As if he knew exactly what I needed in that moment.

"You're giving me my own weapon? I'm only going to tell you this because you're courting Quynh, but women don't like getting presents that already belong to them." I had to tease him just to soothe my own nerves, which were unsettled by the coincidence of him bringing me what I had intended to retrieve.

Andronicus smiled. "No, I had it sharpened for you. Quynh handed it off to me this morning. I thought you might need it."

The dagger was in its scabbard, but the straps I used to tie it to my leg were most likely still in my room. "I wish I'd had it two minutes ago."

"Why?"

"One of our 'guests' was hitting Hippolyta and I got backhanded in the face for interfering."

He pressed his lips into an angry line, his eyebrows narrowing. "Where?"

At first I didn't know what he meant. Where had it happened? Or where on my face had I been hit? I figured it was the second and pointed at the area where the man had struck me. My jaw still burned with pain, but I had learned a long time ago to push past that sensation.

"I don't see anything," he said.

That was good, but as I'd noted earlier, just because there wasn't a bruise now didn't mean there wouldn't be later.

"Can you assign someone to watch over Hippolyta?" I asked. "I don't want it to happen again."

He gave me a curt nod. "I think Telamon's off duty tonight. I'll get him to do it."

"Good. And thank you for this." I held the dagger up.

"You're welcome. And if you find the man, point him out to me. I might like to have a word with him," Andronicus said and then left.

I wondered how bad it would be for my parents if I went to hunt down the man who had hit me. I hadn't asked my captain for a guard and he hadn't offered me one.

We both knew I didn't need it.

With a weapon in my hand, I could hold my own against any man, just so long as I didn't let him touch me.

I was usually very good at darting and ducking away from being hit, at getting in blows and cuts while avoiding the swing of my opponent's weapon or fists. This stranger attacking Hippolyta and me—in our home, where we should be safe—had just been so unexpected that I'd been unprepared for it.

I wouldn't let that happen again.

Demaratus would never let me hear the end of it if he ever found out.

I decided to go back to my room to get my leather straps for the scabbard. I'd only gone a few steps when I heard my father's voice. I looked at the dagger in my hand. I had no place to hide it and no way to explain it. I searched around me, desperate, and my gaze landed on a serving tray that someone had left behind. I grabbed it and hid my dagger underneath it.

My father saw me and smiled. "Are you joining us?"

"Yes, of course. I'm just going to put this away. I'll be right there."

He frowned slightly. I knew it bothered him that he wasn't able to give us a life of ease and luxury, that we had to help with the running of our home. But he nodded and continued on his way.

There was a large group of people following him and I inclined my head as they passed by me.

Several feet behind the last person, I saw two more men walking toward the dining hall. My heart slammed into my ribs as I realized that one of them was the man who had hit me.

Red flashed at the edges of my vision as my blood boiled. My fingers tightened around the handle of my newly sharpened dagger. I wanted nothing more in the world than to run over and slit his throat.

Stupid girl, a warrior must obey the law.

It would be against the laws of Locris for me to harm this guest in my father's home. He had been offered hospitality and protection by my father—they had shared salt between them and that was a sacred bond that could not be broken.

Even though I very much wanted to kill this man where he stood.

And I would certainly have the element of surprise on my side. I briefly let myself imagine the way his eyes would go wide in shock as my blade whispered across his throat, just before he collapsed to the ground.

Self-control in all things, I reminded myself.

I had to get away from him before I did something foolish and reckless. Desperate to regain control of my impulses, I turned and walked outside to a courtyard I almost never entered.

A very large, ancient olive tree stood in the center. During the daytime it would shade the entire area. At night, it blocked out the stars.

I closed my eyes and leaned against the cool stone wall, willing my anger to dissipate.

There was a noise, like a leather sandal moving against the ground. My eyes flew open and I gripped the dagger under the tray I still held.

"Is someone there?" I said, wondering if that man had come to meet his fate. If he attacked me again, the law would clear me if I spilled his blood. It would be self-defense.

But the sound had come from the opposite end of the courtyard, deep in the shadows. A figure stepped around one of the columns and came closer.

A different man.

And as soon as I saw his face, my heart whispered, *Oh, there you are. I've been waiting for you.*

CHAPTER SIX

It was exactly the same feeling I'd had when I'd first met Quynh. A recognition, a remembrance, rather than encountering someone for the first time.

As if we had been destined to meet.

My soul calling to his.

There was a difference, though—I knew Quynh was meant to be my sister.

And there was nothing familial about the feelings I was experiencing for this man.

"Good evening," he said, bowing slightly. His voice was rich and deep, like the honey in the pasteli I'd eaten yesterday.

My mouth gaped open and I couldn't answer. Protocol had been drilled into my head from when I'd first started to talk, and now I couldn't have spoken if my very life had depended on it.

Did he feel the same?

Even if he did—what did it matter? Nothing could come of it.

It crushed me that this had finally happened just as I was about to risk my life.

He was tall. Taller than even Demaratus. Broader, too. His indigo-blue tunic was simple, belted at the waist. He wore a darker blue cloak, fastened with a pin over his right shoulder. Which left his right arm exposed, and I could see muscles that spoke of the hard work he must have regularly performed.

He was young. Not a boy, but a man. He was probably only a few years older than me.

His golden-brown skin was darker than that of most men I'd met. As if he spent all of his time under the sun. His hair was midnight black, gleaming in the torchlight, and the ends curled slightly, reminding me of my own hair.

I couldn't see the color of his eyes, but his lips were full. Kissable.

And he had a healed scar on the right side of his face, beginning above his dark eyebrow, traveling across his high cheekbone, and ending at his strong jawline.

I wondered who had cut his face and if it would be all right if I stabbed them for it.

Perhaps the scar should have marked him as dangerous, the sort of man who got into knife fights, but it only made his face even more interesting.

He had to be from one of the Pyronean valleys, where the Locrian quarries were situated, as he had on the distinctive amber bead necklace all the people from that region wore.

But I had never seen him at court before. I knew I would have remembered him.

My body's reaction to him was the same as if I were about to fight. My heart raced, my skin tingled in anticipation, my blood pumped hard through my body, my breathing became difficult to manage.

It was hard to keep a clear head.

This must have been the attraction that Quynh had spoken of—this spark, this longing, the desire to be closer to him.

What would it be like to be kissed by a man like him?

He did not seem to be affected in the same way. He wasn't even looking at me, while I drank in every detail about him. His gaze was pointed at the tree's branches and he skirted along the trunk, running his fingers over the bark.

"I had heard of this tree and wanted to see it for myself. The last tree in Locris, left as a reminder of all that was lost." He paused and then shifted his gaze back to me, causing my heart to beat even more rapidly. "It doesn't bear fruit?"

"No," I said, relieved that I had regained my voice.

"Another admonishment from the goddess."

It was unusual to hear someone speak about her so casually. As if there were no question that she was real and not something to be brushed under a rug and ignored.

He said, "And it is why the women of Locris all have long hair. Because it is the only thing that grows here."

Was he asking me or telling me? I couldn't be certain. All my senses were clouded, confused.

"Is this your first time at court?" I asked, pleased that I was able to form an entire sentence and that my voice didn't shake.

He leaned against the tree trunk, as if he expected me to come closer to him. He crossed his arms against his chest. "It is. I had supposed it would be grander. More impressive. It's a bit sad, honestly."

While I probably shouldn't have felt personally insulted by his slight, I was. I said with a twinge of disgust, "You're an elitist."

He grinned at me, as if my reaction delighted him. "I generally think I'm better than most people, yes."

His words were ruining him for me. I should leave before he made things even worse. "As entertaining and enlightening as our chat has been, I have other duties to see to."

"What happened to your face?" he asked, gesturing with his hand.

A bruise must have appeared. I swallowed back a groan. How was I going to explain that to my mother? I wanted to press my hand against my cheek but I was still holding my dagger and the tray. "I stopped a man from harming a maid."

"Why would you do that?" he asked, incredulous.

"Why would I stop a man from physically hurting someone smaller and weaker?" I asked, just as incredulous.

"Yes, you could have been seriously hurt. It seems foolish."

My spine tightened and I stood taller. "Should I have waited for someone else to arrive to save her?"

"Yes," he said, as if that were obvious.

"I put a stop to it." With my face, but that seemed like an unnecessary detail at the moment. "I saved her and I'm more than capable of saving myself."

"Are you?"

What was he getting at? "Yes."

"And what do you plan on saving yourself from?"

"At the moment? This conversation."

"Don't go."

I would have had a difficult time explaining why his entreaty softened me. It wasn't spoken as a command or order. I'd certainly had plenty of those over the last year.

Instead he said it like he didn't want to be parted from me.

I knew what he was doing. He was wielding his charm and handsomeness like a sword against me, and despite my earlier declaration, I felt helpless against the onslaught.

Maybe I did need someone else to save me.

"Why shouldn't I go?" I asked.

"Because you want me to kiss you and I would be happy to oblige."

"What?" My limbs were shaking, my heart pounding so loudly I was sure he could hear it.

I couldn't just kiss some stranger in the courtyard of my parents' palace. And it was humiliating that he'd correctly read my desire for him. I never would have acted upon it. I couldn't. My mother would be shocked, my father furious. This was not how people like me were supposed to behave.

The smart thing to do would be to leave. To walk away and pretend that this had never happened.

I didn't do that.

He sauntered over to me slowly, as if he had all the time in the world. My heart somehow managed to beat even faster, drowning out everything else. He came to a stop in front of me and his warmth washed over me. He reached for my tray and took it, intending to set it down.

My dagger clattered to the ground and his eyes followed the sound. He gave me a half smile while he placed the tray next to my knife. "A dagger? Do you have need of a weapon?"

"I suppose that would depend on what you plan to do."

Another smile. "I only plan to do things that you will enjoy. But if you were thinking about stabbing me, just know that you would not be the first woman to do so."

Was that meant to be a warning? I should have taken heed, but I was watching him instead, completely enthralled, unable to flee.

"You have been looking at my lips since you first saw me." He murmured the words so softly that I had to lean in slightly to hear them.

"I have not," I protested just as quietly, but it was because I didn't think I was capable of raising my voice at the moment. I felt as if I had no control at all over my body.

"You want me to kiss you." He said this as a statement of fact and I wanted to protest that I did not because something at the back of my mind that sounded suspiciously like Demaratus's voice was telling me, *Stupid girl, this is not how a betrothed princess should behave!*

I knew that. But in a week's time I might be dead.

Time to push propriety aside.

"If you want me to leave, I will," he said.

"I don't even know your name." My voice was breathless, unsteady.

"Jason."

"I'm Lia."

"Your heart is beating very quickly, Lia. I can see your pulse in your throat."

"Oh," was all I could manage to reply.

He touched the spot with his warm fingertip and I felt that same pulse jump in response.

Jason moved his mouth closer to mine but kept it tantalizingly out of reach and my core tightened in anticipation. "You're trembling. Have you ever been kissed before?"

My heart reverberated inside my chest like a massive drum. "No."

"Are you betrothed?"

I supposed it was good that one of us was worried about it. "I am but won't be for much longer." I probably should have lied, but I found that I didn't want to.

Not to him.

"Does your betrothed know that?"

I shook my head. "Not yet."

His lips somehow came closer without touching me. "I would hate to kiss you and ruin you for any other man's kisses."

The absolute arrogance in his statement should have cooled my ardor.

It did not.

If anything, I wanted to find out if he was as adept as he claimed to be.

And I would have happily let Jason ruin me for kissing with any future partners if it meant he would finally press his mouth against mine.

"I don't normally kiss women like you. Untouched. Innocent. You never know what their fathers might insist on."

A desperate need for him to continue, to satisfy my curiosity and kiss me, took residence in my stomach, urging me to destroy all his excuses. "I won't tell him."

"Neither will I." There was a gleam in his eyes, and I wished I knew what color they were in daylight because currently they were inky pools of blackness, drawing me in. "You have to say the words, though. That you want me to kiss you."

The Lia from ten minutes ago would have punched him. But the person I was now? What he had reduced me to without even touching me? I briefly wondered where my pride had gone before I said, "I want you to kiss me. But I don't know what I'm doing."

"It's easy. Do what I do. Follow my lead."

The entire world ceased to exist and everything was focused in on this moment—where his mouth finally descended. My eyes fluttered shut and I made a sound when he gently kissed me, his lips seeming to melt into mine. It was strange but not unwelcome. Our mouths were the only place where we touched. I briefly wondered what it would feel like to have those large arms of his wrapped around me.

At first I was overly aware of what I was doing. I paid close attention, trying to be a good student. To do what he was doing, mimicking his movements as his lips shifted and pressed against mine.

But then something changed. Instead of focusing on what he was doing and trying to figure out how I was supposed to respond to it, I began to let go and soon everything felt natural. The kiss was something I was a part of and was enjoying, instead of being tense and anxious about it.

It felt a little like slipping into my bath earlier. I was warm and comfortable and my limbs felt pliant and loose, like I was drifting along in a cozy haze. His kisses were gentle and soft, as if he intended to keep things sweet between us.

While this was nice, it wasn't at all what I'd been anticipating. It was not what Quynh had described to me.

Like a piece was missing.

He pulled back, as if he sensed my inner turmoil.

I was the one who spoke first. "Do that again. But this time, do it right. I know that there's more than that."

His jaw clenched, his brow furrowed, his eyes darkened. "You want me to show you more?" His voice was raspy and tight, which was inexplicably thrilling.

"Yes."

He raised his hands to my face, cupping it. His eyes stared into mine for several heartbeats and the intensity there was hypnotic. I wasn't sure that I could have resisted, even if I wanted to.

And I did not want to resist.

Then . . . he devoured me. There was no other word for the frenzied passion of his kisses, the desperate way that he moved his mouth against mine. He showed me exactly what I had been missing out on.

I understood that he had been holding back in his first attempt, the same way my regiment had pulled their punches for an entire year. This was not at all like climbing into a warm bath.

It was like being tossed into an active volcano, where molten heat coursed its way through me, licking along my veins, turning me into a mindless body filled with an aching need that I somehow knew only Jason could fulfill.

He pulled back suddenly and his thumb tugged at my bottom lip. "Part your lips for me," he said.

I did as he instructed and his tongue invaded my mouth. A bolt of shock slammed into me until he stroked his tongue along mine and my knees buckled. His hands tightened around my waist and he lifted me up, holding me against him. He picked me up as if I weighed no more than a feather.

His size and strength should have scared me, but I found them intoxicating.

He began to tease me with his tongue. He ran it softly across my lips, then back into my mouth, stoking the inferno he had set to life inside me. Everywhere he touched me with his mouth and his tongue sizzled, as if he'd marked me his. Branded me permanently.

No wonder Quynh liked this so much!

"You should not let strange men kiss you this way." His words were broken against my lips. He seemed surprised by my reaction. As if he had been prepared for a slap or a protest, and not my enthusiastic participation.

I slid down his body, able to stand on my own feet again. "And you should not let strange women—"

He swallowed my retort with his mouth. His hands were everywhere—in my hair, holding my neck, at my waist to pull me closer. I could only briefly register his constantly moving touch, too caught up in what we were doing with our kiss.

I finally understood what was happening between us. It was swordplay with an entirely different type of weapon. A type of combat that would end not in pain, but in a pleasure I hadn't even imagined possible. Press forward, retreat, keeping my footing, engaging my hands, plunging into battle.

And I knew how to fight.

I gave as good as I got, matching him stroke for stroke, taste for taste, touch for touch, kiss for kiss.

"You taste like honey," I murmured against his mouth.

Jason smiled. "You taste sweeter than honey."

I put my hands on his broad shoulders and maneuvered him to the tree. When his back made contact, he smiled again. "I'm meant to be leading you, not the other way around."

"I've always been a quick study," I said, leaning up to fuse our mouths together again.

He groaned low in his throat at my action, his body a hot, strong line against mine as I pressed into him, and I realized that at some point he had changed from an arrogant, smug braggart to something else.

Something I'd turned him into.

He was no longer in control or instructing me, no longer amused by me or the things I was saying. No, he unraveled against me, bit by bit. His breathing was ragged; his heart thundered in his chest. He shuddered against me.

Jason was not unaffected.

I had only a moment to glory in the victorious feeling this gave me, as if I'd somehow won this battle, when his mouth went wild against mine. Now I was the one moaning against his lips and his onslaught.

Exquisite sensations racked my body, like an icy fire that raced up and down my veins. I was burning and freezing at the same time, which both confused and exhilarated me.

I had often wondered what it would be like to wield magic, and I couldn't imagine that it was much different from this—the magic two people could create just by kissing. It was almost otherworldly.

And whenever I thought there couldn't possibly be more passion, more intensity, more desire, that the kiss could not be any deeper, wilder, or hotter, he repeatedly proved me wrong. He transported me to a dizzying height that made my mind go hazy, unable to think about anything other than his kiss and touch.

I'd never fainted before, but it started to feel like a real possibility.

I had an overwhelming need to be closer to him. My hand was in his silken hair and I traced it down his face to rest on his neck. His skin was so warm, so alive, so soft but strong at the same time. I wanted access to more of him. To rip apart every barrier between us.

He pulled back and smiled at my whining nonverbal protest. "There is no need to rush," he said and I wanted to heartily disagree.

But then he distracted me by pressing soft kisses along my jaw, down the side of my exposed throat. This was new and interesting and delightful. I leaned my head back to give him better access and sighed. I could feel his smile against my skin.

His voice was rough and deep. "I would have come here a long time ago if I had known that all Locrian women were so welcoming to Ilionian men."

CHAPTER SEVEN

It took a moment for my mind to clear, and for me to properly understand what he had just said.

The second that the full impact of it slammed into me, I threw myself back, rolling to the ground for my dagger. In one swift movement I had it unsheathed and was back on my feet, holding it at the ready.

He didn't seem concerned, though. If anything he seemed amused. "Was the kiss not to your liking?"

"Who are you?" I demanded, crouching into a fighting position.

His smile grew bigger. "We've already had this discussion. My name is Jason."

"An Ilionian." I spat the word out.

"Yes. I also just made that clear."

I used my dagger to point at the amber beads around his neck. "You're wearing Pyronean beads. I thought you were a Pyronean nobleman."

"I'm not a nobleman." If he was at all concerned about me pointing a weapon at him, he didn't show it. He was the picture of ease and amusement. "I'm a sailor. First mate to Trierarch Nereus. He is the captain who oversees the transport of the maidens every year."

That was so much worse than simply being from Ilion. Jason was actively involved in the sacrifice of maidens. I raised my dagger higher.

He uncrossed his arms and took a step toward me. I held my ground while he kept speaking. "I found a very accommodating Pyronean woman earlier today and she gave me these beads as a token of her affection."

Bile rose up in my throat. What was wrong with me? How could I have imagined that my soul had recognized his? I wondered what it said about me that I'd thought I was fated to be with an Ilionian sailor who actively participated in killing innocent maidens and apparently had spent his entire first day in Locris kissing every woman he came across.

I scowled. He had just cheapened everything that had passed between us. It had meant nothing to him—I was just another willing woman who had been fool enough to fall for his charm. To not recognize the danger he presented.

I really was the stupid girl that Demaratus constantly accused me of being.

There were two things I wanted in that moment—the first was to return to my room and scrub everywhere he had kissed or touched me.

The second was to give him even a fraction of the pain he had just caused me. He was only a sailor. My father wouldn't be too angry with me for disemboweling a sailor, would he?

Especially one who took maidens to Ilion?

As if he could hear my thoughts, Jason said, "You should put your dagger away. I wouldn't want you to hurt yourself."

"I'm not the one who is going to get hurt. I am going to cut out your lying tongue."

"That would be a shame, seeing how much you just enjoyed it." He purred the words, his voice silky and slightly menacing. My body traitorously shivered, enjoying his tone and what he'd said. I shook my head. I would not be tempted by him ever again. He took another step toward me.

"You should have told me from the beginning that you were from Ilion!"

"What would be fun about that? To be fair, I didn't tell you anything. You made an assumption."

Jason was not going to turn this around on me. I tightened my hold on my weapon. "I will slit your—"

His movements were so quick that I didn't have time to react, to come up with a countermeasure. He swept my feet out from underneath me while simultaneously knocking my dagger out of my hand.

Before I could slam into the ground, he was there, catching and lowering me down the last bit. Then he pinned me into place, his hands holding down my wrists as he sat atop my hips, straddling me.

I struggled, attempting to move, but it was like being held by a stone wall. I was stuck.

We were both breathing hard as he stared down at me. My body tingled at his nearness and I tried to stop it. But it was as if it were working independently from my mind and I couldn't control its response.

His gaze dropped down to my lips and I was torn between wanting him to kiss me and finding a way to get my hands free so that I could squeeze the life from his neck.

For several long, aching, desperate heartbeats, I didn't know what he was going to do.

Or how I would respond to it.

Then his voice was low, full of deadly intensity. "If you intend to slit your opponent's throat, you should not talk about it first. Do not hesitate. Act immediately. Your enemy will do the same."

I was going to headbutt him, but he moved out of the way so that I couldn't reach him while still managing to hold me down. I tried thrashing my torso up and had to strangle back a scream of frustration.

"I will kill you," I told him.

"You wouldn't be the first to try. I owe gambling debts in every port in the Acheron Sea." He flashed a charming smile and we lay there on the stone floor for a few moments more.

Until I remembered myself and my training. I stopped struggling and did the maneuver Demaratus had taught me. I bucked my hips up while yanking my elbows down. It caused him to lurch forward, releasing my wrists, and I grabbed his waist, pulling my head up against his stomach.

"What?" he said, but I was already moving. I locked my left arm around his right elbow, yanking it down, and used his surprise to roll us to the left. The second he was on his back, I pulled myself free and moved away from him.

My breath turned metallic as I put my hands up defensively and waited to see what he would do next.

He gave me another amused grin and stood up. He bowed slightly and then left the courtyard. Leaving me stunned and not sure what had just happened.

I couldn't believe that I'd let him beat me and get me to the ground. I hadn't been that humiliated in a long time—not since I'd first begun my training and had been a complete novice. It was the second time today that I had been caught off-guard and bested by a strange man.

Something I would not allow to happen again.

I located my dagger and picked up the tray. I had wanted to satiate my curiosity, to kiss a man before I was consigned to die, and this was the goddess having a laugh at my expense. She had sent me a man to kiss, only he was Ilionian.

It was frightening how easily Jason had disarmed and incapacitated me. I had completely forgotten myself because I'd been so seduced by his kiss.

No wonder Demaratus had counseled me so many times to have self-control. To not let my emotions or feelings dictate my actions. Because I had done just that and wound up kissing my enemy.

I carried the tray and the dagger back to my bedroom. I kept checking behind me, like I expected to be followed.

But there was no one there.

I closed my door and locked it for good measure. Just in case. I set everything down and went over to my basin, pouring in cold water.

I used a salt scrub on my face, determined to wash away all traces of Jason.

It wasn't working. If I closed my eyes, I could still feel his arms around me, crushing me to him, his mouth feverishly working mine, and my stomach tightened and swirled with that molten heat.

"Bah." I made a sound of disgust. I should go tell Demaratus exactly what I'd just done and then he could yell at me for a few hours and that might make me feel a bit better.

If nothing else it would at least distract me.

Instead I located the bands for my scabbard and tied the dagger to my thigh. That gave me some measure of relief.

But it did nothing to ease the wanting I felt, the heat prickling along the back of my neck from the idea of seeing Jason again. I had to get that under control somehow.

I briefly considered hiding in my room but knew that someone would come looking for me.

The dining hall was packed full of people eating and drinking, laughing.

With our enemies.

Although there wasn't much I could say on that matter, considering what I had just been doing with the enemy.

While Locrian festivities were more formal affairs, sitting at tables while being served our meal, the Ilionians had a more relaxed way of celebrating. The food was set out and the guests were free to partake of any of the dishes they wished. There probably had been a line earlier, but no one stood by the food tables now.

I hurried over and my eyes watered, my mouth salivating, at what lay in front of me. A roasted boar with an apple in its mouth. Lamb shanks crusted with onion, garlic, mint, and fennel. Hare stew, featuring carrots, turnips, leeks, and cabbage. Venison cooked with dill, cucumber, and garlic. Whole chickens roasted in butter, parsley, and thyme. Cyprus snails basted in wine, vinegar, and olive oil.

And that was just one table. There were so many others laden with all sorts of delights. There were vegetables—lettuce, radishes, asparagus, celery, artichokes—all prepared in a variety of ways. Some were mashed, some raw, some sautéed in sauces, others cooked with seasoning. There was also a massive spread of fruit—grapes, olives, apples, figs, pears, plums. Like the vegetables, they were offered in various forms—alone, in their own juices, drizzled with honey, cooked, dried.

I counted twelve different types of bread, with everything from unleavened flatbread to the coarse brown bread made from wheat to the soft, pillowy white bread made from the finest ground flour.

The desserts! My heart fluttered at the sight. There were cheesecakes drizzled in honey or grape molasses, honey cakes, dried figs, raisins and pomegranates, sweet rye buns, thin pastry embedded with walnuts, almonds and honey, fried dough laced with syrup, puddings, pastries cooked from flour and sweet flavorings.

Of course there were salt bowls everywhere. And in another nation, it might have seemed extravagant or excessive to offer so much, but it was going to quickly become the only good we had left to export.

There was a loud note blown from a horn and I turned to see what was happening. A life mage was on the dais. He wore a dark green tunic and had wrapped a thin cloak around himself so that only one arm could move.

An Ilionian servant approached with a plant in a terra-cotta flowerpot. He set the pot down on the table next to the life mage. The mage reached into his tunic and pulled out his amulet. The green gem sliver sparkled even in the torchlight.

The man closed his eyes and muttered some words to himself, his right hand waving over the plant. For several beats nothing happened, and then a large bulb started to grow at the top of the plant. It got bigger and bigger until it burst open, revealing a dark pink flower. The flower slowly opened until it became a full bloom.

The audience broke into respectful but bored applause as the life mage collapsed into a chair behind him, completely drained from that small bit of magic he'd just displayed. He would remain that way, oblivious to the world, for several more hours. Doing magic seemed to severely drain the user.

No one was excited because we had seen this trick performed every year before the selection. I still remembered the first time I'd witnessed it—it had shifted everything I had thought to be true. When my grandmother told me the ancient stories, how could I not believe? I had seen magic performed in front of me.

At last year's selection, after the mage had been roused, I had proceeded to get him very, very drunk. He had been a timid and quiet man who became the opposite when he drank.

He had shared a great wealth of information with me.

Most importantly, he had told me what had happened to the Locrian eye, which used to be housed in our temple.

After the curse, our eye had been taken by Ilionian mages. They had cut up the green gem into tiny pieces and each man took one for himself, embedding it into an amulet. They wore the destruction of our nation around their necks. Their amulets were passed from father to son and allowed them to do small, meaningless pieces of magic—like forcing things to grow or wither away. He had spoken of the power he felt while wearing it—a tiny, constant hum that buzzed against his chest.

After he'd passed out, I'd stolen his amulet. It did nothing for me, though. I hadn't felt the hum he'd spoken of and I didn't know how to wield magic.

I had decided that there were two reasons it hadn't worked. First, the piece of the gem wasn't big enough. I would need the entire eye to restore Locris. The second, and most important, was that only men could wield the magic of the goddess.

Which meant I was going to have to kidnap an Ilionian life mage and bring him back with me after I stole their eye.

With the show over, I turned to get something to eat. I wanted to try everything and was having a difficult time deciding what to take first.

"Good evening, beautiful Lia."

Jason was standing next to me, on my left. He'd disarmed me, held me down, humiliated me in the worst way possible, and now he was mocking my appearance? I was not going to make a scene in my parents' palace. "Go away."

"Is that any way to treat the man who gave you your first kiss?"

Would he be able to stop me before I went for my dagger?

He leaned his head in so that his mouth was next to my ear. "Look at how you flush. Very alluring."

I had to swallow hard and stop my eyeballs from rolling back into my head due to the sensation caused by the faintest brush of his lips against the shell of my ear. I reached for a chicken leg and put it on my plate, determined to ignore him.

Jason wasn't interested in being ignored. "I thought I would come over here and inform you that if you'd like to sneak off to a shadowed corner, I'm available."

"I'm sure you are," I said through gritted teeth.

My body still flamed in response to his offer, though. *He is my enemy*, I tried to remind myself. *I want to run him through, not kiss him.*

But my trembling hands hadn't received the message.

"I would have to request that you leave all pointed objects behind, though," he said. "I prefer to keep all of my body parts where they are currently situated."

"No deal," I shot back.

He laughed, but thankfully we were interrupted.

"May I have your attention?" My father's voice boomed across the hall. "Thank you all for coming to celebrate the betrothal of my daughter Princess Kallisto to Lykaon, son of Pelias, of Ilion."

No mention of the selection that would take place tomorrow.

My sister smiled sweetly and waved to the crowd, who cheered for her.

And then her betrothed turned to face the room and I dropped my plate to the floor, where it broke.

The man standing next to my sister was the same man who had hit me.

CHAPTER EIGHT

Several people turned in my direction and I immediately bent down to pick up the broken clay plate.

My gentle sister, who just two days ago had wept over a dirty seagull that had crashed into the outer wall of the palace and died, was to be married to that monster?

I had to stop this from happening. But how?

It was nearly impossible to undo royal marriage contracts once all parties had agreed to them. The only reason my parents had been able to break the original one with Prince Alexandros and Kallisto was because they could offer me as a substitute.

And I had seen the marriage contract from Lykaon's family in my father's study. It had been written to be favorable to his family, not ours. There had been some legal blustering over the fact that we had previously broken another contract and they wanted to make certain that they wouldn't be put aside so easily.

At the time I had wondered why my parents had agreed to such a heavily slanted document, but now I understood that things in Locris must have been more desperate than I realized.

The terms of that contract could ruin us. Lykaon's family could instill serious financial fines if my parents reneged. And I knew they would end it once I told them what Lykaon had done to me. They would do it to protect Kallisto.

There had to be another way. If Locris could be restored, we would have the resources to fight back or to pay off Lykaon's family.

Either that or I would have to find my dead brother and figure out a way to resurrect him. As the eldest the throne would have belonged to him. If he had lived, Kallisto would have been safe. I wondered how far a life mage's powers could extend with a full eye.

"What's wrong?" Jason asked as he stooped down next to me, trying to help.

I hit his hands away. "I'm just clumsy."

Then I made the mistake of glancing over at him. His gaze latched on to mine, not allowing me to look away. "You are not clumsy. You are very practiced, sure, and confident in your movements. Even with ones you've never done before."

He didn't have to clarify his meaning—I could feel my own cheeks burning under his words and implication.

I gathered all my mess just as Hippolyta walked by with a tray. I called her over and put everything on the tray for her to discard.

Jason stayed close, even though I had clearly indicated that I was done with him. He nodded at the dais. "I feel sorry for her."

"For the princess?" I asked. When he nodded, I added, "Why?"

"Lykaon and his father are well known in Troas for their cruelty. I would be willing to bet that as soon as the princess gives birth, Lykaon will have her killed so that he can take her throne."

My mouth dropped, my hand going over my roiling stomach. This was so much worse than I'd initially thought. My mind frantically tried to think of a quick solution.

"Perhaps there is another man from Ilion she could marry. A wealthier man." One who could protect her from the financial penalties Lykaon's family would impose.

"His father, Pelias, would never allow it. There is no one wealthier than him in all of Ilion and they have influence everywhere. No one would dare cross him."

"Not even the prince?" I asked. Maybe I would have to reevaluate my plans if Prince Alexandros would be a viable path to help save Kallisto.

"Especially not him," Jason said with a laugh. "The prince is a powerless, pathetic man."

My hopes were dashed. "Do you know him?"

"I've never had the pleasure. In my experience royalty doesn't spend much time with people like me."

That wasn't currently true, but I wasn't going to share that information with him. Instead I found myself asking, "Have you seen the prince in a royal processional? Or . . ." What else did they do in Ilion where the royals might make an appearance? "A religious parade?"

"I don't spend much time gawking on parade routes. I have a job to do."

My blasted curiosity forced me to keep asking him questions. I'd never spoken to an Ilionian before and Prince Alexandros was supposed to have been my husband. I wanted to know more. "I heard he's malformed."

"In what way?" he queried.

"Some traders say he's half-man, half-beast."

Jason shrugged. "Since I haven't seen him, I can't confirm if this is true or not. I lean toward believing it to be a fabrication."

That wasn't a no. The prince might very well be some kind of mythical monster from one of my grandmother's stories. If Alexandros had looked at all like Jason, I might have considered changing my mind about my scheme.

And I hated that I thought it. I should not feel that way about an Ilionian.

"I've also heard that the king has a terrible temper and beats his children." I said this in a low voice, not wanting to risk being overheard. A merchant had told me this one night after being deep in his cups, as if it were a giant secret. In Locris we valued our children. I couldn't imagine how a parent would ever harm a child, especially their own.

"I've heard that rumor as well."

It didn't surprise me. If we'd heard it all the way here in Locris, it made sense that he would have heard it in Ilion.

"Where's the other one?" he asked.

I wasn't sure what he meant. "The other what?"

"The other princess. The captain mentioned something earlier about her being betrothed to Prince Alexandros and that we would be bringing him here in a couple of months. Then you and I can both get a good look at him and see if he's part bull."

I was not going to be here and I didn't like Jason making it sound as if we'd be seeing each other again. There obviously wouldn't be any future where someone like him and someone like me could be together. Not only because of our differences in station, but because I would not marry an Ilionian even if my life depended upon it. I glanced around the room, as if searching for someone.

"I don't see her."

He smiled. "I can't imagine that she would be as beautiful as the woman the prince would like to marry."

Why did part of me feel indignant that Prince Alexandros wanted to marry someone other than me? I didn't want him either, but that seemed beside the point. "What is she like?"

"Chryseis? She is said to be the very image of the goddess—sweet, kind, and demure. They say that all the men of Ilion wish to make her theirs."

"Do you wish it?"

"I'm a man of Ilion, aren't I?" he asked with a wolfish grin that made my stomach flutter. I angrily told it to stop being attracted to a philandering man who stole kisses without consideration and was talking about how he wanted another woman.

"She's Lykaon's sister," he added, and it made me dislike the prince even more. If this Chryseis was even a tiny bit like her awful brother, she didn't deserve anyone's undying devotion.

Although once the prince discovered that I had escaped our betrothal, maybe he wouldn't take his anger out on my family—he would be free to wed his goddess-like harpy. It might be a good thing that there was someone else to distract him from my actions.

Not wanting to continue this conversation any further, I turned my back on Jason and returned to the food tables, intending to pile my plate high.

Realizing that he'd been dismissed, he decided to take one last swipe at me. "When you're done with your chores this evening, let me know if you've changed your mind about sneaking off somewhere together. I'll be at my ship."

He walked away and I couldn't help but stare after him. Chores? He assumed that I was a maid. To be fair, there was nothing in my dress or appearance that might make him think otherwise. And most princesses probably didn't pull out weapons and threaten to kill people.

I wasn't mad about that part, but I was infuriated by the notion that he thought I was so desperate for his kisses that I would go looking for him. How could he think I would ever voluntarily spend time with him again? I was more likely to burn his ship to the ground than I was to sneak onto it, trying to locate him.

Although I could picture myself doing just that.

With a groan, I forced myself to pay attention to the food. Demaratus would want me to eat as much meat as I could before I left. He believed that it strengthened a warrior going into battle.

And I was about to leap into the fray.

While I ate, I kept an eye on Lykaon and Kallisto. He was all easy smiles punctuated with laughter. I saw my sister's shyness lift bit by bit as his charm worked on her. What special power did these Ilionian men possess? How did they know exactly what to say and do to make Locrian women let their defenses down?

I was as guilty of falling for it as anyone else.

My sister was too kind, too soft, for this sort of political game. Despite his outward veneer, her betrothed had a sly and calculating face.

Kallisto would never survive with him as her husband.

Quynh's queries from last night had been haunting me the entire day. What would I do if my plan failed? Shouldn't I tell my parents what I was going to do? Try to find another solution to save Locris and my family?

But as I watched that monster woo my precious sister, the answer was very clear. There was one option. It might not have been a great plan, but it was the only one I had and I was going to find a way to make it work.

I tried to focus on eating and it didn't take long to fill me up. My stomach had turned after everything I had experienced today, my fears and worries ruining the taste of what I'd chosen. Perhaps it would be better for me to return to my bedroom and give myself time to calm down. Maybe practice stabbing the wooden target Demaratus had given me. After I'd worked out some of the aggression I was feeling, I could sneak into the kitchens to finish up whatever desserts were left over.

When I left the throne room, I came across Telamon in the hallway, trailing after Hippolyta.

"Thank you for watching over her," I said.

"You're welcome." He paused and then cleared his throat. I immediately felt the shift in the air between us. Something was about to change. "But I'm not doing it for her. I'm doing it for you."

"Oh, Telamon . . ." I felt incredibly bad that this was happening now. I had hoped last night would be the end of it.

"I know how things are. I understand my place and what you're going to do." He seemed so nervous and uncertain and it made my heart twinge. He was my friend. I didn't want to hurt him. "Maybe I could send you away with a goodbye kiss."

Before I'd met Jason, I might have done it. Just to find out what it was like. But now I knew that it wouldn't have been fair to me or to Telamon.

It wouldn't be right to let him believe that I had feelings for him that went beyond friendship. I leaned over and kissed his cheek quickly.

"Thank you for everything. I hope you find a woman worthy of your affection."

Then I turned away, not wanting to see his expression. I wanted my memories of him to be when we had laughed and fought together, not when I had disappointed him. I walked quickly back to my room and wasn't at all surprised to find Quynh there.

She always seemed to know when I needed her.

I filled her in on what had happened with Lykaon and how afraid I was of what he would do to our sister and to Locris. Her eyes grew wide and I briefly wondered what she would think if I told her about the kiss I'd shared with Jason.

It was too humiliating to tell anyone about, though. I would keep that to myself.

"If I don't see Demaratus before I go, I need for you to tell him about Lykaon so that he can keep an eye on Kallisto."

She nodded. "I will. And I will be certain to stay by her side whenever that Ilionian monster is near."

While I appreciated the sentiment, I didn't know that Quynh's presence would be enough to deter him, and the thought that he might hurt both of my sisters made me murderous all over again.

We sat in silence, both of us staring at the far wall.

"Are you sure this is the only way?" she asked.

I supposed she had to make at least one final attempt. I patted her hand. "Now more than ever."

CHAPTER NINE

The day of the selection was as busy as the one before had been. There was much to clean and prepare and it felt good to lose myself in mindless physical labor. It helped to distract me from what was to come.

There was another dinner celebration, but I begged off, claiming my head hurt. I wouldn't get to spend time with my family anyway and I was too queasy to keep anything down. Quynh stayed with me in my room, holding my hand while we both waited until it was time.

I dressed carefully with Quynh's help. I wanted to look my best when I was chosen. She silently cried. I felt her tears landing on my shoulder. I clenched my teeth together to keep myself under control. I couldn't afford to let myself cry.

Because I feared that if I started, I might never be able to stop.

The Ilionians were ordered to stay either in the palace or within the confines of their ship, with the exception of one man.

The Ilionian witness.

It had been the same man at every selection I'd ever attended. He had been chosen because he was unable to read, and his tongue had been cut out so that he could not speak.

There had been a period of time when the Ilionian envoy had told their people which families the maidens had come from, and the maidens had been captured by the Ilionians and held for ransom. The families had paid it, but the maidens had still died as the Ilionians weren't willing to put themselves at risk by breaking the rules. As a precautionary measure, the current witness could not communicate the names of the maidens or their families.

He would verify the maidens' identities by nodding as they boarded the ship. There had been many a wealthy family who had tried to substitute their daughter for someone else. The witness had to ensure that the maidens who sailed to Ilion were the same as the ones who had been initially chosen—the law could not be subverted.

There was only one way to make certain that a daughter was not picked. Those who still had the resources bribed the selector to keep their child's name from the lottery.

And it was the reason I no longer had my grandmother's pearls. I had pawned them and given the coins to the selector to make certain I was chosen.

There was never any guarantee, of course—a man who could be bribed was a man without honor. He could ignore my request and choose another.

My name might not be called.

It was a risk I'd had to take.

We all gathered in the main square of the agora. The marketplace had been emptied out, all of the stalls and booths shut down. Only Locrians were allowed at the ceremony. No outsiders today.

The air was uneasy, the tension obvious. Dust swirled around thousands of feet. People did not make eye contact with one another. Parents hugged their daughters, afraid of their names being called.

All the girls between the ages of fifteen and nineteen gathered together toward the dais that had been constructed in the center of the agora. There was no separation by status or rank. We were all, supposedly, equally at risk of being chosen.

I was extremely grateful that Kallisto was too old to be called.

One of my father's advisers, a historian, stepped forward to tell us the tale that we had heard so many times before. He was an elderly man with a long, white beard. His gray robes were faded and tattered. They must have been beautiful once, but time had not been kind. He held up both of his hands, indicating that we were to be quiet and listen.

"All who have assembled, we bow our heads and take our solemn vow now not to repeat the story that I am about to share, and to never speak the names of the maidens selected. Say that you swear it, or your life is forfeit."

This event was the closest we came to having any kind of religion. Taking the oath was sacred, and Locrians protected our own. Especially the maidens. Everyone bowed their heads and said, "I swear it."

Satisfied, the historian began his tale, his voice booming through the open marketplace.

"The prince of Ilion offended the goddess by kidnapping the most beautiful woman in the world and hiding her behind the walls of Troas. That woman's husband assembled together the greatest warriors the world had ever known, including Prince Ajax of Locris. These heroes called themselves the Achaeans, and they were those who honored the law of hospitality and the sacredness of marriage. They fought the Great War for years and years until finally, the Achaeans emerged triumphant, defeating the Ilionians."

I pressed my lips together tightly, my stomach clenching. I hated the next part.

"As was custom, the Achaeans began to divide up their well-earned spoils of war. An Ilionian princess and priestess named Kysandra fled the palace instead of submitting herself to the victors, as required. Ignoring their instruction, she ran to the temple of the goddess and claimed sanctuary, throwing her arms around the feet of the goddess's statue. Ajax of Locris found her there and punished her for what she had done."

It wasn't until I was fifteen years old that I had been told what that vile punishment had entailed. Ajax the Lesser had sexually assaulted Kysandra. Violated her in the worst way possible, despite the fact that she had been a virgin and had claimed sanctuary.

Ajax had violated the laws of man and the laws of the goddess.

My father had tried to explain that things were different then—that women had once been considered part of the spoils to be taken—but it still disgusted me. I was ashamed to be descended from such a man.

"The goddess was angry with Ajax of Locris for what he had done and swore in her wrath that Locris would pay for his crime. She cursed us with barren ground so that nothing would grow. Prince Ajax denied that a crime had taken place—he said that he had only pulled Kysandra from the temple by her hair. The Achaeans believed his account. Kysandra fled, hoping to use the labyrinth to evade the Achaeans and escape the city. Ajax ordered his men to give chase. They pursued her, caught her, and . . ." His voice trailed off.

They killed her, I finished mentally. Those men had hunted her like an animal and murdered her in the streets.

The historian cleared his throat. "The goddess expected that the Achaeans would punish Ajax of Locris, but they did not. Furious, the goddess commanded the earth to open, and it swallowed Ajax whole in front of his fellow soldiers, burying him while still alive. The goddess then sent foul winds and thunderstorms to ensure that the Achaeans would take years to travel home as retribution for turning their faces away from what had happened in her temple."

It was one of the reasons why no other nation had come to aid Locris after the goddess's punishment. No one was willing to risk her wrath. Some people hoped to curry her favor by taking things a step further. Many mercenaries began to hunt the descendants of Ajax, the Aianteioi, and a council of nations passed laws to protect us, as they reasoned that we had done nothing wrong and did not deserve a death sentence for our ancestor's crime.

"The goddess then demanded that Locris replace her lost priestess—that we were to pay tribute every year of two maidens, drawn by lot, to serve in her temple. We honor Periboea and Cleopatra, the first two maidens sent to appease the goddess."

Our laws always dictated that retribution be made twofold. If one priestess had been taken, then two must be sent to repay the debt.

We all bowed our heads, honoring the first maidens with a few moments of silence. The only time that the goddess was ever spoken of in Locris was at the selection. The rest of the year everyone acted as if she didn't exist, and to even mention her was blasphemy. It had always seemed strange to me that in this one instance she was talked about in this manner—as if she still had control over our lives.

Which I supposed she did.

Despite wanting to claim that they were past religion and no longer believed, even the Locrians did not dare to offend the goddess further by removing her part in the retelling.

"But the goddess had devised further punishment for all Locrians. The journey for the Locrian maidens would not be easy. They would be allowed to serve as priestesses, but only if they made it to the temple alive. They were to race through the city of Troas, and if they reached the temple, they would be received as acolytes. But the goddess instructed the men of Ilion to gather their weapons—their stones, their swords, their axes, their clubs—and attempt to slaughter the maidens before they could reach the temple. She promised that she would absolve them from shedding innocent blood for doing her will. The goddess wants a blood sacrifice but gives our daughters the opportunity to survive, a courtesy not extended to Kysandra."

That was the part I had trained for. Every man in the city would be waiting for me, wanting to kill me. A reward was given to the man who slaughtered a maiden, and he was honored by his people.

No Locrian maiden had ever reached the temple alive, and so every year Locris had to send two more maidens to replace the ones who had been butchered in the streets of Troas.

There was a reason "brief as a Locrian rose" was a common saying.

At first Locris had simply refused to send any maidens to Ilion. A terrible plague broke out that killed nearly half of the Locrian population. The oracle in Phocis had been consulted, and she said that it was a punishment by the goddess for not sending the maidens—that our entire nation would be utterly destroyed if we did not obey.

Then the Locrians looked for ways around the decree. They sent two infant daughters with their nursemaids, thinking it would stay the Ilionians' hands.

It did not.

Some maidens wore armor for protection under their tunics, but all it did was slow them down and allow them to be caught faster.

Locris tried to argue to the council of nations that we should only be required to send one maiden, but the ruler of the council, King Antigonus, disagreed. The law was the law. Two maidens would be sent, drawn by lot, with certain compensations made to their families. Nothing would change.

So every year, without fail, the Ilionians arrived to take their human tributes, and the Locrians did not resist.

The historian said, "We sacrifice to the goddess two of our treasured, precious daughters so that we may keep the rest. We know that those who are called upon to serve have the strength to endure this ordeal."

This was another aspect that had always bothered me. This belief that women were special enough to be pleasing to the goddess, but that we were ultimately easy to discard and unimportant. Strong enough to be slaughtered but not important enough to fight for.

And so it had fallen to me to step forward. I would fight.

I would change the curse and the fate of every woman destined to follow by myself.

"The maidens will enter Ilion by night and race to the temple of the goddess. If they are caught they will be killed, and their bodies burned on a pyre of barren branches and their ashes thrown into the sea."

It was how criminals were executed. With the branches of trees that produced no fruit, and not allowed the privilege and honor of a proper burial in the earth. It was said that the spirits of those who had not been buried lingered, unable to find peace in the next life.

I had wondered more than once whether Haemon was a spirit, never able to find his way home.

"The parents of the chosen maidens will receive fifteen minae and they will be exempt from taxes as gratitude for the ultimate sacrifice that they have been called upon to make."

A restless murmur shifted through the crowd. It was nearly time.

The historian had finished his recitation and nodded to the selector. The selector was dressed in a black tunic and the dust of Locris clung to him. His clothing marked him as an outcast. He was the most hated man in our nation—not only because he drew the two names every year, but because he profited off the misery of so many.

He held up the leather bag that had the name of every eligible girl from the capital city of Naryx, as it was our turn this year for the lottery. He opened the top and reached his hand inside.

This was it. I held my breath, clenching my fists so tightly that my nails dug into my palms.

"The first maiden selected is . . ."

Despite how many people stood in the agora waiting, there was absolute silence.

"Thalia, daughter of Ephesus and Hypatia."

The first thing I felt was a strange kind of relief that everything had worked the way I had planned. The events were now in motion.

The second was sheer agony at the inhuman sound that ripped from my mother's throat. I turned to watch her collapse, my father kneeling down beside her, holding her close as she screamed. The noise pierced my very soul and it took all of my strength to step forward so that the witness could see my face.

I knew my mother didn't want to lose another child.

But I didn't intend to be lost.

Maybe I could even find a way to end the tribute. To protect all the Locrian maidens.

I knew this would be hard for my parents, but if I succeeded?

I would save all of Locris.

Although I should have been facing forward, I couldn't help but turn my gaze toward my loved ones. I wanted so badly to run to them, to comfort them. To let them know that things were going to be all right.

"The second maiden selected is . . ." The selector reached into his bag, pulling out another inscribed stone. He peered at it before announcing, "Quynh, adopted daughter of Ephesus and Hypatia."

CHAPTER TEN

I dropped to my knees, my hands pressed hard against the dusty earth. A high-pitched shrieking noise blocked out all other sound, and it took me a while to realize that it was coming from me.

No.

No, no, no.

Terror clawed at my throat as my breaths rasped hard in my chest. There was no air. I couldn't breathe.

Not Quynh. Anyone but Quynh.

This was a mistake. It had to be a mistake.

Quynh stepped out next to me and I wanted to push her back into the crowd. This couldn't be happening.

I had known that another maiden would be selected.

But I'd never even considered the possibility that it would be someone I loved.

Demaratus had warned me about the second tribute on our third day of training.

"She will be the first casualty of your war," he said.

"What do you mean?"

"I cannot train you to protect yourself and another. You will only be able to save yourself."

That had bothered me. I didn't want to have to sacrifice anyone to attain my goals. Perhaps I could convince another woman to train with me. Two would be better than one, wouldn't it? It would certainly increase our odds that one of us would make it into the temple alive. "Maybe I can bribe the selector with a second name. I can find someone who would want to work with us."

"You do not have the resources, nor do I believe that you would be able to find another maiden willing to do what you're doing. You can only attempt to control your own fate."

I'd accepted on that day that I would have to abandon whoever was chosen along with me.

I shouldn't have listened to Demaratus. I should have forced Quynh to train with me. She would have hated every moment of it, but at least then she would have had a fighting chance.

Or I should have murdered every Ilionian as soon as they got off their ship, the way I'd wanted to.

She crouched down next to me and there was a heated knot in my larynx. "I'm so sorry, Quynh. So sorry."

But instead of responding, she just wrapped her arms around me and I finally let myself cry with her.

I would have to be strong going forward, get my emotions back under control, but I would allow myself this moment to grieve our intertwined fates.

A dark future I never could have imagined.

I became aware of hands reaching for us. Our father had lifted Quynh to her feet and was helping her walk back to the palace. I saw that our mother was lying completely still and had been placed on a litter to be carried back by several of the guards.

Andronicus got me up, wrapping his arm around my waist to support me. If I had been myself, I would have been embarrassed to have my captain seeing me in this state.

I might not have been screaming on the outside, but it was still happening inside my mind.

Not Quynh.

"You have to protect her," he said.

"I know." It was the one thing I was absolutely sure of in that moment—that I would give my life to save Quynh's. There was no other option. "I will."

"How?" Andronicus asked.

That part I did not know. I had no idea how to help an untrained woman survive an entire city trying to kill us. She wouldn't be able to run as fast as I could. Couldn't fight. Wouldn't know the way to the temple.

What was I going to do?

"Where's Demaratus?" I asked.

"Passed out."

"Already?" It was early.

"Because of you," he said.

I nodded. Demaratus and I knew what we had signed up for. We were aware of the risks and all the possibilities.

But Quynh wasn't.

This was so unfair.

Father tried to take Quynh into her room, but she immediately protested and he brought her to mine instead.

"You should rest for now. I will find a way to save you both," he said as he helped us climb into my bed. His voice was so desperate, so scared. Despite his words, I saw how bleak his gaze was. He knew the truth as well as I did.

There was no escape from this.

At that moment I decided not to tell him what I had done. It would be better for him and my mother not to know, to think that this had all just been random, meaningless. If they knew I had caused my selection deliberately, it would destroy them.

"Don't tell Prince Alexandros," I said.

Father briefly knit his eyebrows together. "Why?"

"Because Quynh and I will find the eye and return to Locris." Priestesses didn't leave the temple. It was supposed to be a lifelong commitment, but I didn't care. I would come home again with the eye and my sister. "I don't want anyone in Ilion to know that I'm there. Pretend that I'm still at the palace. Delay him and the betrothal however you can."

My father's expression indicated that he didn't believe in the eye of the goddess but he didn't contradict me. He only asked, "What if the prince sends ambassadors here to meet you?"

"Then I'm ill and can't receive anyone. Send letters on my behalf if you need to. Don't break the betrothal and risk Locris. We will be back."

I'd never seen my father look so sad, not even when we realized that Haemon was gone.

"We will do our best to keep the home fires burning until you both return," Father said, leaning forward to kiss me on the forehead. Then he kissed Quynh's forehead as well. His voice broke when he said, "My little flowers, you have always been so brave."

"We will keep being brave," I said. "And we will return."

Although he didn't say it, I saw from his face that he didn't believe me.

He kissed us again and told us to send for him if we needed him.

After he closed the door, I lay back and Quynh curled up next to me. I didn't know what to say to her. I wanted to make this better but realized I couldn't.

"Maybe it's symbolic," she said. "Maybe the chase is a ritual and there are dozens of Locrian maidens serving in the temple."

"It's not symbolic." The traders at the docks had shared too many horror stories about what happened to the maidens. "I wish that it was."

She didn't respond for so long that I thought she had fallen asleep, overcome by the day's events. But then she asked, "Can I sleep in here?"

"Of course." When Quynh had first joined our family, she had been terrified of the dark. We had shared a bed for years after she'd arrived.

And now we were about to head into the worst darkness imaginable.

"If something happens to me," she said, "and I am caught, you need to continue on without me."

That wasn't even a possibility. "If you are caught, I will stay and help you. I will protect you."

"Lia, not even you can fight an entire army by yourself."

Maybe not, but I was going to try.

It didn't take long for her to fall asleep, her breathing evening out. I envied her the chance to escape for a few hours.

I would have to strategize alone. But no matter how much I tried to figure out a way for us to live, I kept going back to Demaratus's words from a year ago.

That I wouldn't be able to save us both.

A few hours later our older sister sneaked into my room. "Lia?"

"I'm awake," I said. She made her way over to my bed while I sat up. She hugged me fiercely, burying her face in my neck.

"I can't believe this is happening," she said.

"Neither can I."

She released me, leaning back to peer into my face. "How are you?"

"I'm fine." And it was partially true. Because it was imperative that I regain control of myself and my emotions.

Quynh's life depended on my ability to do so. To plan, to find a way out of this situation.

"You're doing better than our parents," she said. "I've been sitting with Mother, who can't stop crying. Every time she gets up to come see you, she collapses again. The physician just arrived to tend to her. Father has shut himself up in his library with his advisers and lawyers so they can find some way out of this."

"They won't. If the tribute could be circumvented, someone would have figured it out in the last thousand years."

"Well, I'm not going to give up hope. We still have until morning."

I hadn't given up hope. I was being realistic. "I need to ask you for two favors."

She squeezed my hands. "Anything."

"The first is that Grandmother left me a book about worshipping the goddess and other banned religious stories from our history. It is in the bottom step of the temple. The stair is fake and there is a box inside of it. Grandmother wanted me to pass the book along to the next generation, to learn the stories for myself, and if the worst does happen, I have to give that legacy to you."

"You won't—"

"The second thing," I said, interrupting her, "is about your betrothed. Lykaon. He is a dangerous man." I told her what he had done to me and Hippolyta.

Her mouth hung open. It was a testament to our closeness that she immediately believed me.

"You must never be alone with him," I said. "Ever. For any reason. I don't care what he says or promises or threatens. Always have Father or one of the guards with you. Someone who can physically stop him if necessary."

"You're scaring me," she said, and her trembling voice proved her words.

But it was a good thing for her to be scared. She was too naive, too trusting. "Maybe he won't hit you. I'm not willing to take that chance, though." I wasn't going to tell her about Jason's prediction that Lykaon would kill her after she gave him an heir. There was only so much Kallisto would be able to handle and I was already pushing up against that line.

Her hands had gone clammy in mine, affirming that I was right to keep the worst part to myself.

"Kalli," I said.

She glanced up at me in surprise. I hadn't used her nickname since we were small. But I needed her to know how important this next part was.

"You have to delay the wedding. Give me six months. I will come back with the eye of the goddess and restore Locris."

"Lia, you can't possibly believe in that—"

"I do believe! Someone has to or else we're all doomed." I gripped her hands tightly. "Six months. Tell him that you have to finish your

77

dress before you wed him. And then every night undo whatever you've woven that day. Anything to delay."

I'd already lost Haemon, might potentially lose Quynh. I wasn't going to let Kallisto be destroyed by an evil man.

"Swear it to me," I said.

"I swear it. Six months."

A sigh of relief escaped me. One less thing to worry about. It wasn't in her nature to scheme or lie, but she had sworn it to me, and Kallisto always kept her word.

"I should go check on Mother," she said.

I nodded and we hugged before she quietly left my room.

When the door shut and the darkness enveloped me again, I knew that I should try to sleep. I needed it.

But it eluded me. I lay there with my eyes wide open, staring at the ceiling. There were only a few hours before the sun would rise and it would be time to leave.

I had to hope that the arrival of the dawn would bring me a solution to keep both Quynh and me safe.

CHAPTER ELEVEN

But all the dawn brought was a knock on my door, telling me that we had to dress and prepare to leave.

In the past the maidens had been given a week or more with their families after the selection, but too many either tried to run away or had chosen to take their own lives to avoid the tribute, so the process moved more quickly now.

Quynh and I got ready in silence. I strapped my dagger to my thigh. I highly doubted that the Ilionians would bother to check whether I had a weapon. I took my potful of Locrian soil and covered it with a tight cloth, putting it into my satchel.

Along with two tiny daggers that I planned on sliding into my belt later.

I also packed up food for once the race began, along with a full waterskin. I had several bags of salt that were worth their weight in gold in Ilion. Demaratus had always taught me to overprepare.

My family waited for us in the hallway outside my room. My mother immediately burst into tears, throwing her arms around my neck. I kept trying to soothe her, but she was bordering on hysterical.

Then she turned her attention to Quynh, continuing to sob. Quynh cried with her.

I held to my promise to myself. I would not shed another tear. I would master my emotions. They would not control me.

I would stay calm and clearheaded. No matter what.

Mother was saying something, but her words were unintelligible. I went over to hug both her and Quynh, and then our father and sister did the same. We stood there as a group, Mother's heart still loudly breaking, until Andronicus approached.

"It's time," he said, his face lined with grief and pain.

I was the one who pulled away first. "I love all of you. So much." I was doing this for them, and it was destroying me that I couldn't tell them.

And each one of them said they loved me in return. I let those words sink deep into my heart. I would use them as fuel for my fire so that I would keep going no matter what. Quynh shared her own words of love and gratitude that were returned.

"We will walk with you," my father said.

"No." I wasn't sure I would be able to maintain my composure if I had to see them standing on the docks as we sailed away. "Let this be our goodbye. And we will do everything in our power to return to you."

Father nodded and I saw the unshed tears in his eyes.

"We are so proud of both of you," he said. "I'm so grateful that I got to be your father."

I shook my head. I wouldn't let him do that. He would continue to be our father for the rest of our lives.

Which I intended to be long.

I reached for Quynh's hand and took one last look at our family. Father and Kallisto had their arms around our mother.

"Let's go," I said. We began to walk away and our mother screamed and it took all of my willpower not to go back to her.

There was nothing I could do for her now.

I would have to wait until I could return with Quynh to ease her soul.

We headed down toward the docks and the scent of sea salt and brine rose up to meet us. There was no trade happening today, no fish being brought in. Out of respect, the Locrians stayed away from the docks and the sea. Life stopped for this moment to honor us.

But Demaratus was no Locrian. He stood at the pathway that led down to the docks, waiting.

"Go on," Andronicus said to me. "I would like to speak with Quynh alone."

Nodding, I walked over to where my mentor stood. It never ceased to amaze me how he could black out from drinking and be completely fresh and focused the next day.

I wondered if there was a lesson in that.

"What happened to your jaw?" he demanded, turning my head to see the bruise more clearly. My jaw ached from where I'd been hit, but I'd been shutting the pain out.

"Lykaon of Ilion. My sister's betrothed. He was beating a maid and I tried to stop him. He is still at the palace. I don't know how long he's staying, or if he'll return to visit while I'm gone, but I need you to keep an eye on him. To warn the guards to do the same. I don't want him to ever be alone with Kallisto."

"Do you want me to remove his head from his neck?"

More than anything, and I knew that if it was my final request Demaratus would see it done, even if it cost him his own life. "I don't want any wars started while I'm gone, so no. When we return to Locris, I will do it myself."

He nodded, his gaze turning toward Andronicus and Quynh. Andronicus was soothing her while she cried. "I heard your sister was selected."

"Yes. How do I keep her alive?"

Demaratus gave me that piercing, withering look of his. The one that said I already knew the answer. "You don't. There is no way for you to succeed and keep her from dying. Sometimes sacrifices must be made. Even of our loved ones."

"You lost your hand to protect your best friend!" Surely he would understand.

But he did not. "It is too late for you to make that same choice. You can no longer protect her. You might still be able to protect the rest of your family and your nation, but your sister is already lost to you."

"I don't accept that."

"Whether or not you accept it, it is still a fact. I'm sorry for your loss, but there is nothing that can be done. She will weigh you down."

I wanted to tear my hair out by the roots in frustration. This was not the answer that I wanted. I needed Demaratus to fix this. To have some special Daemonian method or trick that would help me. He was supposed to be the expert, the master strategist.

"Weren't you the one who told me the greatest pleasure in life is doing something everyone says is impossible?" I asked. "I want to live by my choice, not by chance."

He didn't address my question or my statement and only replied, "You'll have to leave her behind."

"I won't," I said with a shake of my head.

"Then you'll both die and all of this will have been for nothing."

His words hung in the air between us. I knew he meant them and some tiny part of me suspected that he was right. "This wasn't quite the inspirational speech I thought you would share."

He considered this information and then said, "I can give you the same one my last commander gave me when we were faced with an undefeatable foe. 'Breakfast here, dinner in the underworld.'"

For the first time since the selection, I actually had the desire to smile. "That is terrible."

He nodded, as if agreeing with me. "I have something for you."

A gift? That wasn't at all like him.

Demaratus reached to his side and pulled out his xiphos. He laid the sword across his left forearm and offered it to me.

I hesitated, sure that I was misunderstanding.

"It's all right. I want you to have it."

Swords of this type were very expensive and were usually passed on from father to son. I reached for the handle and held it up. It was double-edged with a leaf-shaped blade, forged with Chalcidian steel. Wider at the tip, cinched in the middle, tapering in at the bottom just above the cross guard.

The weight at the top made it perfect for hacking, slashing, and thrusting.

It was an elegant weapon and fit perfectly into my hand.

The xiphos was the most meaningful and thoughtful gift he ever could have given me.

"I thought you sold this years ago for drinking money," I said, trying to swallow down the lump in my throat.

"I did. But then I persuaded the man who had bought it to return it to me."

"By the goddess, Demaratus! Is he still alive?"

"Yes," he said defensively. As if the buyer's death weren't a very real possibility. "It's much better than the toy you've been carrying around with you."

The sword was only twelve inches long—not much longer than my dagger. "My dagger isn't a toy. It stabs people just fine."

"This will stab people better."

I tested the weight, slashing through the air in front of me. "Why is the Daemonian xiphos so much shorter than other swords?"

He shrugged one shoulder. "Battles were becoming too easy. We had to do something to keep the fighting interesting."

I let the sword drop to my side in my surprise. "Was that a jest?" I asked, shocked.

He raised both of his eyebrows but didn't respond.

I'd finally gotten Demaratus to joke with me and all it had taken was me facing death.

He cleared his throat and said, "Hundreds of years ago, when the Sasanians invaded our lands, they sent envoys that demanded a tribute of earth and water. They were symbolic tokens of complete submission. Do you know how the Daemonians answered their request? They threw the envoy down a deep well."

"They did?"

"Yes. The envoy was told that he was free to gather as much water and earth as he wanted at the bottom." Demaratus crossed his arms. "The Ilionians want the same from you. You and your sister are the tribute of earth and water. They want your total surrender, to give up everything and everyone you hold dear. Do not give it to them! Instead, shove a tribute of fire and steel down their throats!"

I had to look away from him, down at the ground. My throat was thick, my eyes burning. "I will." It took me several seconds before I got my emotions back under control and could face him again. "I promise."

He nodded in satisfaction and we stood there in silence for a few beats before I said, "You've been very verbose today."

Demaratus reached for his wineskin. "I needed to start drinking early."

And while he didn't say that I was the reason, I knew that I was.

"Remember to not panic," he reminded me. "Panic always leads to death."

"I know. I won't." Then I confessed the thing that I had been carrying around inside me, because he was the only one who would truly understand. "I'm afraid."

"The code says that there is no honor in a man who rushes to war because he doesn't care if he dies. There is valor in battle for those who desire to live. Courage can only exist in the same space that fear does."

I'd heard this before. "Why do you still hold to the code of a nation who rejected you?"

He considered my question before answering, "I suppose you can remove the man from Daemonia, but not Daemonia from the man."

A sailor standing near a rowboat at the farthest dock whistled. It was an indication that our time was up.

"Thank you," I said to Demaratus. "For everything. If I live, it will only be because of you and all that you've taught me."

"If you live, it will be because of you." He cleared his throat again, and I wondered if he was wrestling with the same kind of emotions that I was. "Hold to the code and you will be fine."

"I'm not Daemonian," I reminded him.

"In all but birth, you are."

It was the most complimentary thing he'd ever said.

"Well." He gave me a slight, uncomfortable nod and then began to walk away. I watched him for a moment. Then I turned, intending to retrieve Quynh and be on our way.

"Stupid girl."

Demaratus had never said those words to me in that tone before. He was usually angry and shouted them at me. Now they were soft, sweet. There was so much emotion in his voice—regret, concern, and something that felt like love.

But when I turned to face him, his expression had gone blank, his voice closer to his regular monotone.

"Try not to die."

CHAPTER TWELVE

I swapped out my dagger for Demaratus's xiphos and placed the dagger into my pack. Andronicus saw me approaching and gave Quynh one last hug, then one last lingering kiss.

She was crying as we made our way to the rowboat. The witness stood there and verified with a nod that we were the right maidens. A sailor offered me his hand to help me into the boat, but I ignored him and climbed in alone. I very nearly capsized us both but found my footing and stabilized myself.

Despite living near the ocean, I hadn't ever spent much time on boats. The Ilionians had made it a crime for us to build any ship bigger than a fishing vessel, to ensure that we could never go to war against them again. My brother had sneaked past the blockade on a foreign trader's ship.

I helped Quynh into the rowboat and we sat down together on a bench near the front. The witness and the sailor who had whistled us over climbed in after me, and the men began to row.

My face was turned toward the shore. I stared at the palace, the only home I had ever known, pushing down the emotions that were fighting to surface.

Then I turned my eyes toward Mount Knemis, the highest point in the Opuntian range. Those mountains were the western border of Locris, impassable, hemming us in.

Mount Knemis would be the first thing that I saw when I returned to my country and I wanted that image burned into my mind.

It didn't take long for us to reach the Ilionian ship. I turned and saw that it was no ordinary vessel. It was a trireme—a warship.

I shook my head in disbelief. They had sent a warship to retrieve us.

Was that to intimidate all of Locris, or had it been meant just to scare Quynh and me?

The trireme was approximately a hundred feet long, twenty feet across at the widest part. The ends of the ship came to sharp points, where they were covered in bronze shielding, and there were massive eyes painted on each end. Giant masts shot up straight to the sky, but no sails were up.

There were three banks for rowers. The top bank was on the deck, the other two on the levels beneath. The three levels were where the ship got its name. Oars stuck out of holes in the side, their tips covered in leather.

Haemon had been fascinated by ships, especially triremes. He had told me on more than one occasion that they were deceptively light and strong, capable of easily navigating very deep or extremely shallow waters. That they could take a lot of damage and holes but stay afloat.

I wondered if a ship like this one had been responsible for his death.

And I hated that I would never know.

I saw the ship's name painted on the southern end.

Nikos.

It meant "victory." I decided to take it as an omen, a message meant just for me.

I was going to win and save everyone.

The rowboat pulled up alongside the trireme and there was a rope ladder for us to climb. I went up first, wanting to make sure the way was clear for Quynh and that I would be in a position to help her if she struggled to make it over the top.

It wasn't hard for me to ascend over the railing—this was the kind of thing Demaratus had made us all do repeatedly in training.

"Why?" Polymedes had asked. "There's no chance that we'll ever be in a sea battle."

"Quiet!" Demaratus had roared back. "You don't know what you will or won't face!"

Maybe he'd done it for my benefit so that I wouldn't have to be hoisted on board by my enemy.

My decision to go first had been the right one, as Quynh couldn't figure out how to position herself as she neared the top.

"Give me your hand," I told her. She grabbed on and I pulled her up. It wasn't easy and I was grateful that she was so small.

"Let me help," I heard a voice say and I ignored him, lifting her by myself.

Jason.

When Quynh's feet were safely on the deck, I turned to glare at him.

His expression was remorseful and I couldn't tell if it was sincere. Then I noticed the shade of his eyes. A beautiful golden brown.

Of course his eyes were the color of honey. The goddess seemed intent on torturing me.

A pulse of want throbbed inside my gut.

Why was I attracted to this man?

He spoke, interrupting my internal struggle. "Lia. I'm sorry you were chosen."

"I'm sorry you're Ilionian," I spat back, and walked away from him, bringing my sister with me.

Quynh's eyes flew to mine in confusion. I probably should have told her about him. Part of me had hoped that he would be staying behind in Naryx with Lykaon, even though he had told me that he was first mate to the captain of the tribute vessel. I should have expected that I would see him again.

"Hoist the anchor! Rowers to positions!" an older man called out behind us, presumably the captain, and the deck was a hive of activity as men raced around, following orders.

Pegs were hammered into place, oars striking against their rowlocks as they prepared to be lowered into the sea, grunts coming from the men pulling up the anchor.

"Forward!" the captain called, and the ship suddenly lurched as the oars hit the water. I felt uneasy and I wasn't sure if that was due to Jason's nearness or if it was the way the wooden boards seemed to roll and move under my feet. It was unnatural. I didn't like it.

A drummer and flautist were playing, keeping a steady beat that the rowers followed.

No one gave us any instructions and I assumed we were to look after ourselves. There was a wooden crate next to the ship railing, and Quynh curled up next to it. She pulled her knees up to her face, wrapping her arms around her legs. Her eyes fluttered shut. She didn't seem to mind the rocking ship at all. She did this during stressful events—she would take quick naps to restore her spirits and to briefly escape whatever was upsetting her. I envied her ability to sleep anywhere, anytime.

I wouldn't sleep, though. I had to see where we were headed.

Only a few minutes passed before we reached the blockade. A line of ships extended in both directions, as far as the eye could see. I gripped the railing tightly.

I wished I could take command of this ship and ram into every vessel here, destroying them so that I could lift the overwhelming economic burden my country had been put under.

And very few smuggler ships dared to run past them, as the Ilionians were merciless against those who disobeyed their rules. Because Troas's location was central to several major trade routes, no other nation wanted to be shut out of those by crossing Ilion's line.

Control of the trade routes was one of the reasons why Ilion had been able to rebuild so quickly after the Great War, and how they were able to raise enough money to create the blockade, so that they could punish us not only for Ajax's sin, but for the destruction that had been visited on their capital city.

"Admiring the view?" Jason asked as he came to stand next to me.

"I was wondering how long it would take those ships to burn."

"You shouldn't joke about such things. Sailors are a superstitious bunch, and fire is one of our worst fears. 'Fire, women, and sea, evils three.'"

That made absolutely no sense as sailors spent all their time at sea, but I wasn't interested in engaging with him. I wanted him to leave me alone.

So that I wouldn't remember what it had felt like to have his muscled arms crushing me to him.

His hot mouth ravaging mine.

"Go away, Ilionian."

"My name is Jason," he reminded me.

"Ilionian suits you better."

"Except most of the men on this boat are Ilionian, which might get confusing."

Not all the men were Ilionian? That was interesting information. Had they hired mercenaries to help with the rowing? Men who worked for money could be bought. Their allegiances switched.

As I looked over the rowers on the top deck, I realized that there was no way to tell where each person had come from. Locris and Ilion had descended from the same group of ancestors.

Jason's gaze was on me, and my skin seemed to burn in response. "You never did tell me who hit you."

He reached out his hand, as if he intended to touch the bruise on my jaw. I stepped away from him and his arm dropped.

"Because you aren't owed an explanation." We rowed past the blockade, to the open ocean.

He stayed quiet for a few beats before saying, "I had heard that Locrian men were barbarians."

And while I knew he was goading me into answering, I still took the bait. I whirled to face him, reminding myself not to reach for my sword. "We aren't the ones who butcher women."

"A crime was committed—and it must be repaid."

"It has been repaid two thousandfold with innocent blood," I fired back. "That should be enough to satisfy your bloodthirsty, vengeful nation."

"Ilion is not the one who requires it. The goddess does."

It was infuriating how calm he was, how rational. I wanted to strike him. "And who speaks for the goddess?"

His eyebrows lifted slightly. "That is bordering on blasphemy."

"Better to be blasphemous than to stand by while innocents die."

"By decree of the goddess, Ilionian citizens are not allowed to assist any Locrian maiden."

I hadn't heard that before, but Jason had no reason to lie to me. "It wasn't a Locrian who hit me. It was one of your countrymen. Lykaon."

Anger flashed in his eyes—he clamped his teeth together, his cheeks flexing in response.

And I wasn't sure what he was mad about, nor did I care. "There. Now your curiosity has been satisfied. Don't you have work to do?"

"Not everyone agrees with what's happening to you. If I were captain of this ship, I would return you to Locris."

Again, I believed him and I hated that I did. And I hated even more that his words had the effect of softening the edges of my anger toward him.

I glanced over my shoulder at the trierarch, who was still giving orders to a small group of men assembled around him. "I could kill the captain and then you'd succeed him."

Jason grinned at me, like this amused him. "We have three hundred men on board who wouldn't allow that to happen. He is beloved and I am not ambitious. But none of us can disobey the goddess. This is what she demands."

"It's been a thousand years. You'd think her bloodlust would have been sated by now."

"If you make it to the temple, maybe you can tell her as much."

While I had pictured myself throwing open the temple doors and crossing the threshold, not once had I imagined what would happen after Quynh and I arrived. What did priestesses and their acolytes do? I had no idea.

Would I actually be able to communicate with the goddess? Was there someone in the temple who spoke for her?

The captain and another man approached us and Jason snapped to attention. I nudged Quynh with my foot, aware that something was about to happen.

"Greetings. I am Trierarch Nereus. Welcome aboard the *Nikos*."

"Thank you," I said, even though I died a little inside at having to be polite to a man who made a living in part by transporting Locrian maidens to their deaths. Quynh stood up and hid herself behind me.

"This is Acmon." Acmon was an older man, his face lined with wrinkles, and he had dark brown sunspots on his face. "He will escort you downstairs to your cell."

"Cell?" I repeated. "I thought we were supposed to be your guests."

"With this crew it will be the safest place for you. It is my responsibility to keep you secure and whole until we arrive," the captain said dismissively. "Jason, may I have a word with you?"

Acmon held his arm out, pointing us toward the stairs. As we descended I heard the bleating of goats but didn't see them. At the lowest level we walked toward the back of the ship, where they kept amphorae and crates filled with goods.

A large metal cage waited for us, the door open. There were buckets inside, blankets and pillows, and hay spread along the floor. Quynh went in first and everything inside me protested at entering. I knew there was no other option here, and I would rather choose to walk into the cell than to be dragged in by someone like Jason.

I stepped inside and Acmon closed the door behind me, turning the key in the lock. "I will bring you your midday meal soon. Let me know if you need anything."

As if he were our servant instead of our captor.

He hung the key on a post too far for me to reach. Then he shuffled away and I watched him retreat.

I really should have paid better attention when Demaratus was trying to teach me how to pick locks.

"At least we'll be protected from the crew," Quynh said, and I could only nod as I leaned my face against the bars.

I highly doubted this was for our benefit. We were captives and were being treated as such, kept "secure and whole" until the citizens of Troas had the chance to tear us limb from limb.

CHAPTER THIRTEEN

Within a couple of hours of being in the cell, I became extremely ill. Quynh told me I had seasickness, and if the sea had been a person, I would have stabbed it. I'd never been so ill. I was clammy, sweating, dizzy, my head throbbed, and I kept vomiting. I was curled up in a ball in the corner of the cage and had started to consider asking her if she would put me out of my misery.

"This will pass quickly," she said.

"Why aren't you sick?" I asked while shivering.

She put another blanket on top of me. "I've been on ships before, remember? You will adjust. Hopefully sooner than later."

I slipped in and out of consciousness. I heard Demaratus yelling at me several times.

Stupid girl! Get control of yourself. You can fight off this sickness!

At some point I became aware of Jason coming close to the cell and Quynh talking to him.

I pried my eyes open and saw that he was giving her a cup and a bag with food. "She needs to eat something. And I've mixed some powdered ginger with water. It will help with the nausea. Have her drink it."

"Are you sure it won't hurt her?" she asked.

"I've used it many times," he said. "I promise it will help."

Quynh pushed my sweaty hair from my forehead and pulled me up by my neck so that I could drink.

"I don't want it," I protested weakly. "I don't want his food or medicines."

"You're being irrational."

"You would be too if your insides were trying to escape through your mouth."

She ignored me and made me drink and eat. The water had a peppery but slightly sweet taste to it. And to my chagrin, it did help. I threw up a fair amount of it, but she was relentless and kept shoving food into me, pouring medicine down my throat. By the next morning I felt more like myself again.

Jason came to check on us while Quynh was still sleeping. I think it had exhausted her, watching over me.

"Feeling better?" he asked. "And you're welcome."

I glared at him.

"Ah, there's that look of hatred I know so well," he said as he came over to the cage, sticking his arms inside and leaning against the bars. He passed a bundle through, dropping it onto the ground.

"Breakfast," he said.

I briefly considered pulling my sword and slicing him open but didn't want anyone on board to know that I carried weapons. It wouldn't be worth it, even though it would have given me a great deal of satisfaction.

"Don't you have anything better to do?" I asked him.

"At the moment? Not particularly."

Then he stood there, staring at me. The desire to make him bleed increased with each passing moment.

"Aren't you hungry?" He inclined his head toward the bundle.

I was starving, as I'd spent the last twenty-four hours repeatedly emptying myself out.

"No."

Then my stomach betrayed me by rumbling loudly.

He laughed. "Your body begs to differ."

Yes, my body and I had been having some very different opinions lately. Especially when it came to Jason. I wanted to either ignore him or introduce him to the pointed end of my xiphos; my body wanted to lure him into the cell and have its way with him.

Quynh stirred beside me and grumbled something, but I kept my gaze trained on him.

I reached for the bundle and undid the knot. I couldn't help myself—I gasped when I saw the contents.

"Pasteli?" I took a bite, closed my eyes, and let out a happy sigh.

When I opened my eyes again, he was wearing an incredulous expression. "Why are you so excited about pasteli? It's what soldiers carry in their packs to eat before they go to battle. What sailors bring with them on long voyages. Because it's inexpensive and it keeps well."

I understood what he was saying. That this was a common food and I was behaving as if it were one of the finest dishes ever created. His disdain would not hinder my enjoyment. "Thank you for making sure to fatten us up before you lead us to our slaughter."

The smile fell off his face and he nodded, chastened. "I'll let you eat."

Why was a tiny part of me disappointed that he was leaving?

When he got a few feet away, he stopped and turned back to face me. "Lia, it may not be my place to say anything, but there is something different about you. As a gambling man, I would lay odds that you'll make it."

I snarled, ready to tell him what he could do with his wager, but he turned a corner and was out of sight. A moment later I heard him clomping up the stairs.

Even if he was right and I could reach the temple, I still hadn't come up with a way to make sure that Quynh made it as well. It should only take four or five days to cross the Acheron Sea, and I'd wasted one of them being ill.

What could I teach her in a few days? There was no way to train her or to share any of my skills with her. She couldn't fight. Hadn't practiced running several miles every day. Had never faced a man in combat. No one had shot arrows at her so she could keep moving even when she was petrified. What if she shut down completely?

My sister was strong, but she wasn't invincible. I didn't know what to do.

Other than not leave her behind.

"What was that about?" Quynh asked, her dark eyes blinking at me.

At first I wasn't sure what she meant, given where my thoughts had gone, but then I realized she was talking about Jason. She sat up next to me and stretched.

"With Jason?" I clarified. "He was just bringing us breakfast. Pasteli. You should have some."

I didn't manage to distract her, though.

"How do you know him?"

"I met him. The day of the celebration for Kallisto's betrothal."

She wasn't put off by my casual evasiveness. She studied me before announcing, "Something happened between you two."

Were my cheeks red? Had I somehow tipped her off? "What would make you say that?"

Quynh arched one eyebrow at me. "How well I know you."

I should have taken that into account before I'd started trying to avoid her question. "I met him in the tree courtyard and we might have . . . we kissed."

"You kissed an Ilionian?" She practically shrieked the words.

"Not on purpose!"

"I just . . . can't believe your first kiss was with an Ilionian."

"Neither can I. The thought of it makes me sick."

That wasn't true. The memory of that event excited me, and I wanted to seek him out and do it again. To see if it would be different this time now that I knew who he was.

To find out if I would enjoy it as much.

I suspected that it would be just as intense, just as satisfying, which was concerning because I didn't know what it said about me.

But I could never share any of that with another person. It was far too humiliating to say out loud.

"You shouldn't have been alone with a man you didn't know," she said, and I could almost hear my mother's voice, as she had told us the same thing many times over. "He could have seriously hurt you."

"I . . ." My voice trailed off because I realized that once he'd stepped out of the shadows, there had never been a moment where I had feared that Jason would harm me.

Maybe that had been due to my naivete or just the power of his kisses, but I hadn't been scared of him. Even when he'd held me down and I couldn't move.

Unlike Lykaon, whom I had immediately found terrifying.

"You're right," I finally said, since I had sat there in silence for too long. "I should have left the moment I saw him. Then I never would have kissed a horrible Ilionian."

"They can't all be bad," she said.

"They can," I disagreed. "Especially Jason. He's transporting us to be hunted."

I wouldn't say that he was taking us to be killed. When I spoke to Quynh about what was coming, I would stay positive for her benefit. Maybe if she believed that she would make it through, then she would.

"We're all subject to the same rules," she said. "He's no more at fault for this than we are."

That seemed like a weak excuse to me. "Someone should stand up against this archaic event."

"Someone is. You."

While I hoped my actions might lead to abolishing the tribute, we had no guarantees that they would. I was more focused on restoring Locris. Once that had been accomplished, I could turn my attention to dealing with Ilion and their unreasonable demands.

She said, "The next time he comes in here, maybe you should talk to him. He's sought you out more than once now, even though he has responsibilities. I think that says something. That it might be more than just a kiss to him."

I would not let her sentiment move me. And I would ignore the excited shiver that had accompanied it.

Because there was no point. If I made it to the temple, I would become the goddess's servant. When I found the eye and Quynh and I returned home, I would have duties and responsibilities to my nation. I would never be able to marry a simple sailor.

I hated that I felt regret. That part of me wished that I could be an ordinary girl so that I could have entertained a courtship from someone like him.

All it had taken was one moment to put me in this position. If I had made a different choice, if I had left the courtyard instead of staying, I would have removed a layer of difficulty for myself. There wouldn't have been any connection between Jason and me, and I wouldn't have been internally wrestling with the attraction I continued to feel for him.

He had become a distraction, and I couldn't afford any of those right now.

"Why do you always look for the good in others?" I asked Quynh.

"It's a personal failing," she said with a small smile.

I returned it. "I suppose it is. You should stop doing that." After a beat I added, "You know I don't mean that."

Her generosity of spirit and positivity were two of the best things about her.

"I know you don't."

Thinking of how one moment with Jason had altered my life made me think of all the choices, all the twists of fate, that had brought us here to this very moment.

How Quynh's parents' choices had inadvertently led to this.

"Have you ever wished that you could go back to your parents' country?" I asked her.

"I wouldn't have been able to go there, even if I'd wanted to."

"We could have hired a merchant to take you."

She shook her head. "Our family doesn't have the money to do so. And even if we did, what would I have done when I got there? I would have been surrounded by strangers."

"It used to be your home. You might have family there."

Quynh held up her wrist. "I might not. My only hope would be that someone would recognize my bracelet and direct me toward my parents' families. Because they wouldn't be my family. You, our parents, Kallisto—you are my family. The only one I remember. My home is with you."

CHAPTER FOURTEEN

"Lia."

Jason was whispering my name against my throat as he alternated between licking my skin, leaving hot kisses, and nipping me. He said my name like a prayer, as if I were the goddess he wanted to pay homage to.

I ran my fingers through his dark, silken hair, marveling at how many textural differences he had. Soft hair, a rough, stubbled jaw, warm, velvety skin over hard muscles. Each one begged to be touched, explored.

And I planned to do just that. But first, I needed him closer.

He moaned against my collarbone as I wrapped my legs around his waist, holding him to me. We were lying in his bed, in a room I'd never seen. An inn? His home? I wasn't sure.

I could feel how much he wanted me, and molten heat pounded its way through me, leaving me an aching mess. One who could no longer speak, only feel. I desired him more than I'd ever desired anything.

His lips returned to mine, heated and possessive.

You are mine.

He didn't speak the words, but I felt them in his kiss.

But I couldn't be his.

This had to stop.

He had braced his arms on either side of my head so that he could kiss me deeply, but I needed his hands on me. I wanted to tug him down so that his weight would deliciously press into me, leaving his fingers free to wander.

He moved his mouth away and pressed fervent kisses along my cheekbones, my jaw, marking me so that I would never forget that I belonged with him. I burned for him, so brightly and intensely that I worried I might set the bed beneath me on fire.

"Yield to me." He murmured the words against my skin and I both heard and felt them. "Give in."

Why was I resisting? I didn't want to. But I found myself saying, "I can't. You know that I can't."

"You can," he encouraged me, his hips pressing into mine, and I bit back a groan at the exquisite ache that caused. "Surrender. I want to make you mine."

He stopped kissing, stopped moving. He held his face above mine, and we stared into one another's eyes. His gaze never left mine, but I felt his fingers reaching up to push the sleeve of my tunic from my shoulder, leaving scorching trails everywhere they touched my bare skin.

"Lia. Please."

I was on the verge of saying yes when he disappeared, the bed and the room along with him.

Suddenly I was in the training fields in Locris. Demaratus yelled at me while Andronicus swung his club at my head. I ducked out of the way and reached up to punch him as hard as I could in the kidneys.

He bent over slightly, letting out an "oof" as he dropped his club. Then he grabbed the back of my breastplate with both of his hands, heaving me into the air, directly at the rest of the regiment.

The others were laughing as I fell into a heap on the ground.

Demaratus stood over me, the veins in his neck bulging.

Stupid girl! Stay out of reach!

Everything around me shifted and changed and a field of wildflowers spread out in front of me. I marveled at their beauty. I'd never seen so many in one place, growing out of the ground like this. I reached out and felt the soft petals of a bright yellow flower with a black center as high as my shoulder.

I saw a tall woman, taller even than Jason. She had long golden hair that hung to her ankles. It gleamed like sunlight, rippling as she walked. Her eyes were bright green, her tunic a brilliant white. There was a strong scent that seemed to come from her robes, sweet but earthy at the same time. The flowers in the field turned their faces toward her, as entranced by her otherworldly beauty as I was.

The sun was rising in the east and she turned her face toward it, bathing in its light, her skin aglow.

She spoke, and the sound of it overwhelmed me.

Euthalia.

I wanted to follow her. To do whatever she asked of me. To promise my allegiance.

The ground beneath me opened up and I fell, slamming into the dust of Locris with Demaratus leaning over me, screaming.

Stupid girl, wake up!

I let out a gasp as I sat straight up in my cell. I had fallen into a deep enough sleep to dream. It had been a long time since that had happened.

Men were shouting. I looked to the porthole to the left of our cell, and even though it was dark, I saw another ship. It was far too close. Swords clanged against each other, and there were thumps from the decks above us.

My heart pounded in my chest and a metallic taste filled my mouth. Were we in danger? What was happening?

I pulled out my sword and crouched into position. Should I wake Quynh up?

While I was debating that, torchlight appeared from the stairs. Someone was coming.

My lungs tightened while my breath solidified inside me.

A man came into view, his face illuminated by the torch. I didn't recognize him, but there were so many men on board that wasn't surprising. Ever since we'd been put in our cell, we had only seen Acmon and Jason as they brought us food and water.

The man slid the torch into a bracket and took the key from where it hung on the post. He reached into a pouch at his side and threw something on the floor. I heard a kind of hissing sound as it hit the planks, but I was unsure of what he'd just done. He walked over to me and came to a stop about an arm's length from the cell.

"Who are you?" I demanded. Could he see that I was armed? I kept my sword at my side, and hoped it was hidden in the shadows.

"Your savior."

He had the same dark hair and brown skin of an Ilionian or Locrian, but his accent was unlike any I'd ever heard.

I stayed quiet, assessing my situation. He had a sword at his side that he hadn't drawn yet. But he had the key and could open the door to our cell.

Could put his hands on me or Quynh.

"We've come to free you," he said.

For one quick moment I thought I could send Quynh with them. I would continue on to Ilion, but she could escape with these men and be safe. It seemed like a perfect solution.

"You can trust us. We mean you no harm," he added, and it felt like a step too far.

Things that seem too good to be true usually are.

Now it was my father's voice I heard in my head. Warning me.

Something was off.

"Would you like to come with us?" he offered.

The sounds of battle raged above us, swords meeting swords, bodies hitting the deck as men were struck down. Which side was winning? Would I have to face this one man alone or would there be more?

"No thank you," I said. "I think I'll stay here."

He made a tsking sound and shook his head. "That was the wrong answer."

There were more footsteps on the stairs and the man was joined by two others. The newcomers already had their weapons drawn.

An eerie calm settled into my nerves as I prepared for what was coming. The man would have to unlock the cell to get at me, and then I would have the chance to strike. I could do a lot of damage to him before the others could reach me.

"Maybe your little friend would like to join us. We'll wake her up gently and then we'll ask her. And we'll make sure she enjoys our particular kind of questioning," the man said, and his companions laughed.

I raised my sword then, fury gripping my gut. "I will kill you if you touch her."

"With your tiny little knife?" he asked, amused.

"Many a man has lost his life to this blade. I would be happy to add you to the list." I hoped he wouldn't see through my bravado. There was no way I would be able to defend us against three armed warriors.

The men above deck were all fighting for their lives. No one had time to worry about me and Quynh.

We were on our own.

"Lia?" She chose that moment to wake up, and my stomach dropped down to my feet. It would have been better if she'd stayed asleep. I didn't want her to see what was going to happen next.

"It will be all right," I told her in a soft voice. "Stay low and out of the way as best you can."

She immediately scooted herself into the far corner of the cell.

The man held up the key, letting me know that he intended to open the door. "I was hoping you'd make this easy, but it will be much more fun if you're going to put up a fight first. We know how Locrian women like to be treated."

I didn't know what that was even supposed to mean, but I wasn't going to ask him for a further explanation because it didn't matter. It was obvious that they intended to hurt us.

At least the Ilionians were only planning on killing us and had no intention of violating us first.

The man darted forward, fitting the key into the lock and turning. At the same time I reached through the bars and stabbed his thigh. It was the first time that I'd ever deliberately drawn blood. He roared and threw the door open, immediately retreating. He swore viciously at me, then shifted into a language I didn't know.

He drew his sword as he said something to his companions. The other men spread out and I saw that they were going to attack from all three sides of the cell. Quynh understood this and, without my telling her to, moved directly behind me, up against the wooden wall of the ship.

As far out of range as she could get.

There was no way they would attack simultaneously. I would deal with the one who got to me first and do my best to avoid the blows of the other two.

I almost wanted to laugh. I'd been so concerned about Quynh and me being struck down in the streets of Troas that it had never occurred to me that we might not survive the ship ride there.

"You should have taken our offer," the first man said as he raised his weapon. Then his eyes bulged as a sword plunged through his chest, the tip gleaming in the torchlight before it was quickly withdrawn.

When the man crumpled to the floor, I saw Jason behind him.

Then Jason tore through the other two men as if they were made of papyrus. His sword arced and sliced as he danced around the two invaders, moving faster than I'd ever seen a man move in battle before.

Before the second man could even raise his weapon to defend himself, Jason had already struck him down and moved on to the last. He dispatched the third man so quickly that Jason had already sheathed his sword before the man had finished falling to the ground to join his companions.

Like some kind of battle magic. As if he were goddess-blessed.

I still held my sword aloft, expecting that Jason would attempt to disarm me.

"Are you all right?" he asked, and I couldn't respond.

He stood there for a moment longer, his eyes raking over me, and then he ran back upstairs to rejoin the fight.

With the danger over, the adrenaline quickly left my system and I dragged air back into my lungs. I dropped my sword to the ground and then fell to my knees as I thought of what Jason had just done.

He had saved us, but all I could think about was that if a sailor could fight like that, what hope would Quynh and I have against the trained citizenry of Troas?

We would die before we even got six feet away from the ship.

CHAPTER FIFTEEN

After that wave of terror passed, I got up to pull the cell door shut and locked it, keeping the key. The battle was still raging and I didn't know if we would get more unwelcome visitors. I held my sword in my right hand and waited.

"Those men were going to kill us." Quynh whispered the words. I wished more than anything that I could protect her from all of this.

"Yes. They must be pirates." For years traders had complained about how prevalent pirate attacks were becoming. I had often wondered if that was how my brother had died.

But if these men were just pirates, how had they known Quynh and I were Locrian? And what ship we'd be on? They'd made it seem as if they had come here specifically to find us.

This attack wasn't random.

I heard someone yell, "Retreat!" and there was more shouting and the sounds of feet racing across the deck. I watched as the oars from the pirate ship sank down and cut into the water, propelling their ship forward. The crew of the *Nikos* roared their victory, congratulating each other, finishing off the men who hadn't made it to their ship in time.

I sat down next to Quynh and wrapped my arms around her. She was trembling and I hoped she couldn't tell that I was shaking, too.

Every time before this encounter had been practice for me. Pretend. When I'd lunged at Polymedes or Telamon, I'd never made contact. I'd never truly stabbed someone before. I'd never watched someone die.

It was more unsettling than I'd thought it would be.

There was a splash, then another, and another. I realized that they were throwing dead bodies into the ocean. I wondered how many losses had been suffered on each side.

There were multiple sets of feet on the stairs, heading down. Jason came into the room with three other men. Without saying a word, the three men each grabbed one of the pirate bodies and began hefting them back upstairs.

"I'll be on watch tonight," Jason said to me after the other men had left, and I wasn't sure why.

But he went up the stairs before I could ask.

"He wants to talk to you," Quynh offered. "Alone."

"Why would he want that?" I asked.

"Maybe you should go and find out. He might have answers."

I hated not knowing things. Even when I'd been a little girl, I had constantly pestered my tutors and parents to fill in the gaps in my learning. I wanted to know everything, to understand exactly how things worked and why, and hated when people couldn't explain it to me.

It was one of the reasons why my brother's death haunted me. No one could give me any details so that I could arrange the pieces together to my satisfaction.

Quynh could be right and Jason might have answers about what had happened tonight. I couldn't miss out on the opportunity to get them, especially since he was probably the only one on the ship who would share what he knew with me.

"If I go, I'll lock the door and leave you both of my throwing knives," I said.

"All I want to do is sleep." Her voice sounded anxious and stressed, and again I wished that I could take this burden from her. That I could run through the city alone.

Today had been just a small taste of what we'd be facing. The worst was still to come.

The splashing had stopped and I heard the men settling into their hammocks in the decks above us. Jason had mentioned that during the day the rowers worked in shifts so that each man was given a chance to recuperate and rest. The rowers sang the same song over and over again in a foreign language. Since I'd been forced to listen to it all day, the melody had been seared into my brain. Eventually I was able to phonetically sing along, even though I didn't understand what the words meant.

I knew from my interactions with the traders that nearly everyone on board slept at night, except for the men who kept watch.

And tonight Jason would be one of those men.

Within minutes Quynh was fast asleep. I eased her onto the floor and put the knives far enough away from her that she wouldn't accidentally roll over on them while sleeping but could still easily reach them.

I got up and let myself out of the cell, ensuring that the door latched before I locked it. I had put my xiphos back into my thigh sheath and kept the key in my hand. I didn't want anyone to be able to get into the cell without me there.

I went up the stairs quietly until I reached the top deck, half-expecting a guard to jump out or to question me.

When I stepped foot on the planks, there was a granular feel there. As if someone had spread sand all over the deck. It was odd.

There was a lighthouse off to my right. I'd never seen one in person before, only drawings. I knew they used mirrors to reflect the sun during the day, and fires to light them at night. It looked as if we had anchored not far from the shoreline.

"Over here."

I couldn't see Jason, but I followed his voice. He was sitting in between the two steering paddles at the back of the boat, hidden in shadows. I approached him carefully, keeping an eye out. I didn't see anyone else. I crept over until I stood directly in front of him.

"You should try to sleep," he said.

It was an odd thing to say, given that he had essentially invited me to join him. Unless Quynh and I had misunderstood. "I'm too worked up to sleep."

He nodded. "So am I. It's why I volunteered to take this watch. If I'd been on watch earlier, maybe I could have prevented all this. Kept everyone safe."

Some part of me liked the idea of Jason watching over me, protecting me. I was also thrilled by the knowledge that he could have torn those three men apart with his bare hands if he'd chosen to.

"I've never seen anyone move the way that you do." The words were out before I could recall them. I didn't want him to know that I admired something about him.

"You've seen me move that way before. When I had you in my arms."

His silky, seductive words made the back of my neck prickle and sweat break out along my hairline.

"I've always been handy in a fight," he added, dismissing his skill as if it had been nothing.

Demaratus had trained with the greatest military the world had ever known, and even he did not move as quickly or as lethally as Jason had.

Although I told myself I was only here to find out what had happened, the truth was that I was drawn to him. He was my enemy, had been paid to bring Quynh and me to our deaths, and still I wanted him. The sheer deadliness I'd seen from him earlier should have terrified me, but it had only served to make him even more attractive.

My heart quickened as I studied his face. I swallowed hard and all my questions flew out of my head. He was so beautiful, so masculine and strong, and I knew that he kissed as if he'd been created solely for that purpose. The air between us became thick, making it hard for me to breathe.

My lips tingled in anticipation, urging me to take what I desperately wanted.

"What did you come above deck for?" he asked, his voice deep, an invitation. A pang of lust pierced me, making my stomach tighten with need, and it took all of my willpower not to climb into his lap and kiss him with everything I felt for him.

"I came here . . ."

But then my ability to speak left when he reached out and took my hand in his. He enveloped me with his warmth and strength. "After a battle it's not uncommon for a soldier to fall onto the first willing woman he comes across, to remind himself that he's still alive."

That instantly cooled my ardor. I yanked my hand free, disgusted. Was that what this was to him? He saw me as nothing more than a body to be used, to remind him that he had lived?

Or was he implying that it had been my motivation? That I had come up here solely for that reason?

Either one was terrible.

My inclination was to leave and lock myself back up in my cell. But I still didn't have my answers about earlier and my curiosity would not let me exit with my dignity still intact. "I came up here to ask you what happened."

He grinned. "Well, when a man and a woman desire one another, they often begin by kissing and then—"

I immediately interrupted him, ignoring the way his words heated my insides. "I don't . . ." I found myself incapable of saying I didn't desire him. I did.

Meanwhile he desired every woman that he'd ever met.

Clearing my throat I said, "I meant what happened with the attack."

He shrugged one shoulder, as if the battle had been routine. "Pirates. They're fairly common. It's why we sail during the day and anchor close to the coast at night. It's not usually worth the risk for pirates to come this close to the shore. Not to mention that we aren't carrying any cargo worth stealing. I don't know what they were after."

Me. And Quynh. They were trying to steal us—not silks or spices or salt. I didn't tell him that, though.

I couldn't let myself trust him. To break down another barrier I'd erected to keep him out.

Someone approached, and in the moonlight I saw that it was the captain. My fingers twitched, ready to go for my weapon.

"Jason." He nodded to his first mate.

"Captain."

"Why have you released the prisoners?" Was he about to order Jason to escort me back to my cell?

"If they were going to flee, they would have done it when they had the chance," Jason said.

Nereus nodded, taking in this information. "Make sure to wake the next man when your shift has ended."

"I will."

The trierarch lingered for a moment, as if he wished to say something more, but instead he just turned on his heel and headed below deck. I wondered if he had a hammock with the other men or if he had his own private quarters.

Then I wondered why Jason hadn't shared all that he had seen and done during the fight near the cell. He hadn't reported to the captain that he'd unilaterally decided to let Quynh and me keep the key. What else was he hiding?

"Are you going to tell him that I'm armed?" I asked.

"No." Jason's answer was quick, no hesitation.

"Why didn't you try to take my weapon from me?" I had wondered it ever since he'd left after dispatching those pirates. Given how fast and strong he was, it would have been easy for him to do so.

"I recognize a Daemonian xiphos when I see one. Which means you killed one and took it from him, or it was given to you from a Daemonian as a gift, and either way it means you are not someone to trifle with."

This pleased me, although it shouldn't have.

"I don't envy the men of Troas," he added.

The way he spoke made it sound like he didn't plan on participating. "You're not going to hunt me?"

He went absolutely still, his intense gaze boring into mine. "I would never hurt you."

And again, I believed him. Although why I took the word of and felt safe with a womanizing man who never stayed in one place for very long because he was saddled with substantial gambling debts, I wasn't sure.

"At least you'll get a day or two of reprieve," he said as he turned his head to the left, toward the lighthouse. "The pirates left a lot of holes in the hull that will need to be repaired before we set sail."

"In a way, that's almost worse. I don't like delaying the inevitable."

"Neither do I." And that honeyed tone was back, the one that promised all sorts of delights and pleasures if I would just agree.

I remembered my dream, of him kissing me, lying on top of me, while begging me to yield, to surrender.

"There is no one here but us," he added. "No one to see if you'd like to reacquaint yourself with my other set of special skills."

A spike of desire struck me hard, making my legs feel weak. Maybe his suggestion, as repellent as I'd found it, that those who survived a battle sought others out in order to remind themselves that they had lived merited some consideration.

Because I'd never felt quite as alive as I had when he'd kissed me.

It would be so easy to accept. To kiss him again in the shadows, to lose myself in his touch, to let him make me forget all that was coming.

A good memory to carry with me once we landed in Ilion.

Just as in my dream, I didn't want to say no.

CHAPTER SIXTEEN

But even though I didn't want to refuse him, I had to. I had to stay in control of myself and my emotions.

No matter how difficult that might be.

Needing to put some distance between us, I walked over to the railing on the coastal-facing side of the ship. I knew that he would follow me, and he did.

Maybe he felt the draw as strongly as I did.

There was a strange light coming from the water. It glimmered in a vibrant shade of light blue and white, almost as if it were alive, pulsating and moving with the waves as they traveled to the shore.

"What is that?" I asked, fascinated.

Jason stood next to my left shoulder, peering over to look. My breath caught from his nearness, from that warmth he gave off, like he was the sun and I wanted to bask in his rays. "No one is certain. Magic? Spirits? The gods?"

"Gods?" I repeated, turning my gaze to him. "As in, more than one?"

"There are many people who worship many different gods and goddesses."

"I hadn't realized." My worldview had been so limited. The book my grandmother had given me only contained stories of the goddess. I'd never even imagined that there could be a god or goddess besides her.

"Are you afraid to die?" he asked, and I was surprised by the question. I probably shouldn't have been, given how many times I had thrown my possible demise in his face.

"I'm not afraid. I don't want to die. I want to succeed." But if saving Quynh cost my life, I would gladly pay that price.

"What of your family?"

I couldn't help but let out a short, bitter laugh. My family was in complete shambles. I didn't know if my mother would ever be whole again unless Quynh and I returned. "My elder brother died a couple of years ago. They got past that; they will get over our deaths."

"'Our'?"

"Quynh is my sister. Adopted, although that makes no difference to me. I love her as I do my other siblings." As if my mother were at my elbow, reminding me to treat others with courtesy and respect, I felt compelled to ask, "Do you have siblings?"

"A sister and three brothers," he said, but there was a tightness to his face that made me think I shouldn't ask any further questions about his family. Was he not close to them? Did they disagree with his decision to make his living this way? Had something happened to them?

My curiosity would be the death of me one day.

If a sword didn't take me out first.

I had to stop thinking about Jason altogether. I needed to remember why I was here and how I could prevent Quynh's death.

"Is there anyone on the ship who can be bribed?" I asked.

He leaned against the railing, folding his arms over his broad chest. I had seen the members of my regiment without the top of their tunics many, many times, but I was overcome with a desire to see what Jason would look like underneath his clothes.

To run my fingers over the ridges and planes I'd felt against my chest when he'd held me close.

His slightly sarcastic response snapped me out of my reverie. "I haven't had an occasion to test whether or not my crew places money above honor."

"What about the captain?"

"He's sworn an oath, like all trierarchs do. Who do you plan on bribing?"

"Anyone who would take Quynh and drop her off somewhere. It doesn't matter to me where she'd go, just anywhere that's not Troas. When we arrive in Ilion, we can tell whoever's in charge that she died on the voyage over. Maybe when our ship was attacked by pirates." This was brilliant—why hadn't I thought of it before? We were already so close to land. We could dispatch the rowboat now and be back before anyone even missed us.

Jason seemed to consider my request seriously before answering. "I am sorry, but we've already had this discussion. Our hands are tied. The goddess wants her priestess replaced."

"She would have had that two thousand times over if she'd allowed the maidens to live."

"We do her will."

"Even if her will is terrible?" I countered.

"Even then, unfortunately."

I'd never been able to ask anyone about the tribute who might have witnessed it. "What if Quynh stays on the ship? Refuses to get off or participate at all?"

"Then someone will come and drag her out and they'll kill her on the docks. Neither one of you will have a choice but to run."

He was knocking down every plan that I had come up with so far and I felt my vexation and anger mounting. There had to be something I was missing, an angle I hadn't considered.

"You may have more of a chance than you realize," he said. "There are many in Ilion that disagree with the tribute. Just past the docks and before you enter the city's walls, there is an open area called the Fields of Sithon. The men who will participate in the hunt will line up there. Those who do not want to take part will stay in their homes, living their lives as usual. Many have said the tribute should be done away with completely. But it takes time for these things to change."

"I am out of time," I told him. "And I'm terrified that Quynh will not survive the race!" I hit my fists against the railing out of frustration.

"She matters that much to you?"

Hadn't I just told him that she was my sister? "She matters more to me than almost anyone in the world. I will not see her die. Please help me find a way to keep her safe."

He was silent for a long time. "I wish that I could. But I'm only one person."

"It only takes one person to change the world, one person to save a life," I snapped back. I was furious with him and myself. I should have known better than to ask for his help. He had shown me that he was a man who cared only for himself and his desires.

I pivoted and strode away from him. He called my name, but I didn't look back. There would be no more clandestine meetings on the deck at midnight.

I would not allow him to distract me further.

The next morning, two members of the crew came in to mop away the blood that had already stained the planks of the lower deck.

They were also cleaning up the red dirt I had found around my cell. I'd gathered a handful of it and studied it. This was what the first pirate had retrieved from his pouch and thrown on the floor. It also must have been what I had felt under my feet when I'd gone up to the top deck last night.

Why would someone throw dirt down before they began a fight? I knew so little of the world that it might be some battle ritual that I was simply unaware of. I had no memory of Demaratus mentioning it.

Although he had said something about ancient Sasanians demanding a tribute of earth and water.

Was this tied to that? But how? If anything, the pirate had given me the tribute. He hadn't demanded it in return.

It didn't make sense, and I was annoyed that I didn't understand and that I couldn't ask anyone about it.

Jason might have had the answers I wanted, but I'd promised myself that I wasn't going to interact with him at all.

Over the next few days, I kept my word. Jason and Acmon took turns bringing us food and fresh water, and I ignored Jason whenever he came in. Quynh exchanged pleasantries with him, and I could feel his gaze upon me every time he approached the cell, but I only showed him my back.

I spent those days sharing as much knowledge as I could with Quynh, the things Demaratus had drilled into my head over and over again. To stay out of reach, to never let an attacker get his hands on me, to make myself small. That a moving target was nearly impossible to hit.

That she would have to keep running no matter how tired she got.

I also wanted her to remember that she had to go on if something happened to me. "If you make it to the temple and I don't, you have to get the eye and go back to Locris. Kidnap or bribe a life mage to help you." I didn't need to tell her the plan, she already knew it. I'd certainly run it past her enough times.

"You should take my bracelet. Just in case." She started to untie it, but I put my hand over hers.

"No. You're going to be wearing it when you walk through the temple doors."

The sadness in her eyes told me she didn't agree with my prediction. "Lia—"

"Don't." I heard from her tone exactly what she was about to say. "Do not ask that of me. You can't. I won't leave you, no matter what. Promise me that you won't give up, that you'll stay with me."

The corners of her mouth turned down, and after several long heartbeats, she finally said, "I promise."

It felt like I could breathe again. She had brought up me leaving her behind so many times that I was afraid she would find a way to force my hand. But Quynh never broke a promise.

"Good."

The rowers on the deck above us began to sing that infernal song of theirs and I wanted to pound my head against the wall until I passed out so that I wouldn't have to hear it again.

Quynh seemed to share in my frustration and asked for a distraction. "Can you sing me one of your Daemonian songs?"

Demaratus had told me that before battle the Daemonians would sing songs to soothe themselves, but the only ones I knew from him were drinking songs. And while they did little to ease my worry, they did make her laugh.

I had reached the first chorus when the entire world went black. Someone screamed, and there was the sound of confusion as the crew called to one another, of oars being dropped, a bench being knocked over.

"What's happening?" she asked.

"Let's go find out," I said. I opened our cell and took her by the hand, climbing the stairs to the top deck.

I shaded my eyes and looked up. It was an eclipse.

Acmon was at the back of the ship, curled up in a ball, screaming.

"We should throw him overboard," I heard a man say. "He'll bring a harbinger upon us."

Jason seemed to materialize out of nowhere, so quickly that I nearly jumped out of my skin. "Sailors are superstitious," he said, and I didn't know if his words were meant for me or himself. "They already don't like having women on board, and Acmon behaving that way, as if he's taken leave of his senses . . . they won't tolerate it. It'll spread like a disease."

He headed over to Acmon's side. What was he going to do?

Another man behind me said something about Acmon cursing the ship with his hysterics, and with a sigh, I realized that I couldn't let anything happen to Acmon. He had been very kind to both Quynh and me since we'd come on board. My conscience wouldn't allow me to stand aside.

Jason was talking to him, but Acmon continued to shriek loudly, and his words were hard to make out. I heard "sun," "blotted out," "death," "omen," "all die." There was an easy way to handle this.

I grabbed a cloak from one of the nearby sailors, ripping it from his shoulders. He protested, but the cloak fell easily into my hands.

When I'd been very young, we'd had horses. I remembered a large chestnut stallion who had been spooked by something the rest of us couldn't see. He had bucked off his rider, throwing his body around the pen, slamming into the fencing, braying continually.

The trainer had thrown a blanket over the stallion's eyes and he had immediately calmed down.

So I did the same. I threw the cloak over Acmon's head, and just like the stallion, he stilled.

"Take deep breaths," I told him. "In and out."

The crowd who had been watching him dispersed. Thankfully, now that Acmon was calm, there was no more talk of throwing him into the ocean.

From underneath the cloak he moaned, "The sun has abandoned the earth. We have displeased the goddess. Something terrible is about to happen."

I pulled the cloak from him and held it aloft. He blinked at me several times as his eyes adjusted to the light.

"See this?" I asked, shaking the cloak. "An eclipse is like a large cloak being thrown over the sun, only bigger and farther away. Nothing more. It's not a bad omen."

"You've studied Aristarchus and his heliocentric model of the universe?" Jason asked. I'd honestly forgotten he was there.

I heard the shock in his voice and it was understandable. While Locrian women could read, most did not have tutors or attend specialized schools. And from our interaction at the palace, he thought I was a servant. Quynh nudged me with her elbow—she had come to the same conclusion. I had to tread carefully here.

"My father is interested in astronomy," I said. That was certainly true and I hoped it was enough of an explanation to deter him from investigating further. "I have this in hand. You can go."

He didn't move and I resisted the urge to shove him, knowing that it would be like pushing against a stone wall, an exercise in futility and frustration.

I turned my attention back to Acmon. "Will you be all right now?"

He nodded, but I had my suspicions. I felt like I should stay above deck until the eclipse had ended. I walked away, leaving both Jason and Acmon behind.

"That was close," Quynh said worriedly, and I nodded. The last thing I needed was the crew of this vessel to discover my real identity.

I hadn't managed to shake Jason and his questions, though. "Why did you help Acmon?" he asked.

I could hear in his tone how important this question was to him, even though I didn't understand why. I answered honestly. "Because he needed it and he has been kind to me."

The look in his eyes made me think that he wanted to protest that he too had been kind to me, had even saved my life, but he didn't. "As you like to keep reminding me, he is one of the men that is taking you and your sister to Ilion."

Maybe Quynh and Jason were right and I shouldn't blame any of the men on the *Nikos*. They weren't personally responsible for this system. Just as I was not responsible for the actions of one man a thousand years ago. But here I was, still paying that price.

"There is no reason to give in to ridiculous superstition," I said. "That eclipse is based on a physical phenomenon. It doesn't mean that there's magic involved or that something terrible is about to happen to us."

A loud, watery roar emanated from the depths beneath us, making the entire ship vibrate and pitch.

"What was that?" Quynh asked, looking every bit as terrified as I felt.

"A dragon," Jason responded as he pulled out his sword.

CHAPTER SEVENTEEN

"How many elements are there?" my grandmother had asked as we looked through the book together.

"Five. Earth, air, water, fire, and aether."

"Correct. And what creature represents those elements?"

"Dragons." There were dozens of illustrations—the earth dragons whose scales resembled rocks, the blue-green air dragons with their massive wings that allowed them to fly, the red-scaled fire dragons who could burn an entire forest with a single breath. There weren't any drawings of aether dragons. No one had ever seen one—their very existence was questioned.

But the water dragon had been the one that had scared me the most. It looked more like a serpent than a dragon, its scales shimmering in iridescent blues, its eyes just above the water as it hunted prey. They lived in the deep ocean and had destroyed entire fleets of ships. They could swallow massive whales whole.

Unpredictable, deadly, destructive.

"They never come this far north!" someone shouted, and I realized that there was complete pandemonium among the entire crew. I'd been caught up in my memory and had shut everything else out.

A dragon.

There was a water dragon beneath us.

My heart slammed against my chest and there was a high-pitched ringing in my ears. I shook my head. I needed to pay attention to what was going on.

"The goats! Get the goats!" the captain yelled.

"I told him not to throw those bodies into the ocean," Jason growled. "We chummed the water. We were begging it to come find us."

Quynh's hand tightened around mine, looking for reassurance, but I had none to offer. My throat felt like it was going to close in on itself. There was no way to escape the water dragon—if we jumped into the ocean, we'd be eaten. And there was no place to hide on the ship. If it chose to, the dragon could snap the hull in half to better pick us off, one by one.

Maybe we should have moved closer to the center of the trireme, but I couldn't bring myself to do it. I had to see what was happening, what the dragon's next move would be.

Three crew members ran onto the deck, each carrying a large goat in their arms.

"What are they doing with the—" Quynh started to ask, but then the men heaved all three goats overboard.

"No!" she gasped and ran to the railing.

I pulled her back from the edge. "Don't look."

She buried her face against my shoulder, but I couldn't take my own advice. I watched as a massive blue reptilian snout emerged from the sea, sunlight and water glistening off its scales. He opened his jaw wide, which caused the water to stream from his teeth, off his snout.

The dragon swallowed all three goats so quickly that it was shocking. Would that be enough food? Or was he still hungry?

I thought he might dive back down. It would be the smartest maneuver—he could disguise his movements under the cover of the ocean, and we wouldn't be able to predict what he would do next.

The dragon didn't do that, though. Instead it began to raise itself slowly out of the sea. Silence fell over the deck, all the sailors motionless. Rivers of water poured down the dragon's lanky sides as he grew taller and taller. His long, sinuous body seemed to sway slightly back and forth. His massive claws looked like swords, shining and sharp. There was a staggering and terrifying amount of power and potential destruction on display.

His terrible golden eyes stared directly into mine. Was I supposed to look away? Would staring at him be seen as a challenge? I couldn't help but continue to stare—something about his gaze was unearthly, powerful, and I felt hypnotized.

A low humming sound seemed to reverberate inside me. As if he were singing to me. Calling.

No, not he. She. She was beckoning me.

My arms dropped from Quynh and I took a step forward. Did the dragon intend to snap me up from the ship, the same way she had the goats in the water? Quickly swallowing me whole?

I should have been afraid, but I wasn't.

"Lia." Jason's voice pierced through the haze. His voice was deceptively calm as he wrapped his hand around my wrist and gently tugged me down from the railing.

I didn't remember climbing it.

He pulled me against his chest with one arm; the other held his sword. Which he kept down at his side, most likely so that the dragon wouldn't see him as a threat.

"Are you trying to get eaten?" he demanded quietly, his words hot and angry against my ear.

"That would be one way to avoid the tribute," I said with a tiny laugh, still caught up in some kind of connection with this magnificent creature that I couldn't have explained.

He did not seem to share in my amusement.

The dragon watched us for a few moments more and then lowered herself into the water so carefully and quietly that it was like she had never even been there at all.

I glanced down at Jason's strong forearm, still clamped against my shoulders, pushing my back into his front.

Why was I drawn to such dangerous and deadly things?

A giddy excitement filled me, and I wondered what he would do if I turned around and pressed myself to him, my softness against his strength. What would his reaction be if I kissed him? Here, in front of everyone?

I ran my fingertips along his forearm, his skin warmed by the sun. I traced the outline of the veins along his hands. Without thinking I lowered my head slightly and pressed my lips gently to the top of his wrist. His arm tightened against me as he softly swore.

"What just happened?" he demanded, and for a moment I wasn't sure what he was referring to. Me touching him? The accidental kiss? Or the dragon?

He quickly cleared up my confusion by asking, "Do you speak to dragons?"

Were there people who could talk to dragons? Could life mages do so? What a marvelous power that must be. I shook my head. I didn't know what had occurred. I hadn't spoken and neither had she. But the compulsion to join her had been there all the same. As had this residual, elated feeling that made me want to kiss Jason.

"Are you all right?" Quynh demanded, and only then did Jason release me. I took a few steps away from him, regretting each one. I was overcome by this strange desire to kiss him and stay close to him.

Her question almost seemed silly. I felt exuberant, as if I could conquer the world. I hadn't been harmed. If anything, I'd been reenergized. "I'm fine."

"No one said anything about dragons," Quynh said accusatorially to Jason, as if she held him personally responsible for it.

"We don't generally see them," he said as he sheathed his sword.

"What if he had tried to attack us?" she demanded.

"She," I corrected. "The dragon was female."

They both stared at me for a long while before Jason spoke. "Dragons are sacred to the goddess. We have been taught to respect them and we try to do our best to leave them alone. That doesn't mean people haven't occasionally slayed one from time to time, but usually as long as you feed them, they're fine. It's why we bring goats on every voyage. Just in case." Then his heated gaze turned toward me. "And as a general rule you shouldn't offer yourself up to one as a midday snack."

"Air dragons pull the goddess's chariot," I offered to no one in particular, and it had the effect of causing both Quynh and Jason to stare at me as if I'd gone mad.

Some detached part of my mind wondered if I had.

"Isn't that why you paint eyes onto your ship?" Quynh asked. "To scare off monsters?"

"If it is, I don't think it works," I added.

"It does not," he agreed in a tone that sounded almost cheerful. The rowers had returned to their stations and the boatswain was playing a fast tune, to quickly get us as far away as possible.

But as we glided along, I found myself wanting to throw myself overboard to find the dragon. It seemed clear to me now that she had wanted me to join her. Not to be eaten, but for some other purpose.

It was only Quynh's grip on my hand that kept me tethered in place.

The next two days passed by far too quickly. I showed Quynh basic fighting techniques, how to block a strike, how to look for an opening, constantly encouraging her to remember that she would have to keep her wits about her and fight off any fear she was feeling.

Jason and Acmon continued delivering our meals and water. And although I didn't ignore Jason, I no longer spoke to him. I was embarrassed by what had happened between us when the dragon appeared. I had no explanation for my behavior, and that knowing smirk he sported whenever he saw me didn't help things.

The end was quickly approaching and the only person I could care about right now was Quynh.

The night before we were to reach the docks, Acmon brought us a great feast. I was surprised by the number and variety of dishes. I realized that they were marking us as important, honoring us. Treating us like royalty. They had no idea that two princesses had been selected and they had no need to pretend.

I wasn't one to turn away food. My stomach was upset but I forced myself to eat. I needed the strength it would provide. They also gave us pure, sweet, unfiltered wine and I allowed myself only a small sip. I had to keep all of my wits about me.

Quynh was surprisingly calm and it helped to steady my own nerves.

After the feast had been cleared, Jason came down carrying bundles of cloth. He passed them through the bars of the cage. "They want you to wear this."

They were gleaming white tunics.

"Yes," I said as I held mine aloft. "We want to make sure that we stand out so that it will be easier to locate us. We wouldn't want to blend in. And probably more importantly, we want to make sure that our blood is clearly visible for the man who claims our lives."

Jason looked ashamed, as if my words pained him, and I was glad. He should feel bad.

But after he left, I was the one who felt terrible. I had been trying so hard not to speak about our deaths as a given in front of Quynh.

"Let me do your braids," she said. This was not only because our hair had become so dirty, but we had planned to put it up as a safety precaution.

I sat down on the floor in front of her while she rummaged through her pack. While I had made sure to bring weapons, bribes, and food, Quynh had brought a comb and hairpins.

Now I was glad for it—our long hair would put us at a disadvantage as we ran. It would be too easy to grab and yank. We'd decided yesterday to create braids that we would pin against our scalps so that we wouldn't be offering any kind of loop for anyone to hold on to.

"We will stay in the shadows," I told her. "If we get a chance to steal some cloaks or change our clothing, we will do it."

I hadn't accounted for having to wear something that would make us easier targets.

But instead of agreeing or saying anything in response, Quynh began humming a tune I hadn't heard in years. It was one my mother had sung to us when we were little, about how we had no reason to fear the dark, that we were safe, that she would watch over us.

We were no longer safe.

My mother wasn't here to watch over us.

And we had every reason to fear the dark.

CHAPTER EIGHTEEN

The captain had personally come down to escort us from our cell, asking us to join him above. Given the two armed guards behind him, I understood that it was not a request. Quynh and I held hands as we walked up the stairs until we reached the top deck.

We were taken to a spot at the front of the ship. The *Nikos* had just entered the Troas Harbor. There were so many ships—hundreds. All carrying precious cargo to trade.

Quynh and I were being shown off as the rarest of cargo.

And we captured the attention of every ship and boat we passed on our way in.

The city of Troas came into view and I realized two things simultaneously.

First, we were headed for the docks. I had assumed that the trierarch would let down the anchor and we would wait for nightfall, arriving at the docks then.

The second and even more alarming one was that my map was wrong. I had so carefully constructed it, but it had either been full of lies or mistakes. I thought of all the bribes I'd paid to sailors and traders, and how I had been led completely astray.

The temple of the goddess was supposed to be in the center of the maze, but there was no center.

My confidence evaporated and was replaced by a crushing terror that made it so I couldn't breathe.

I knew that I couldn't let myself give in to the absolute panic I was feeling. Nothing that I'd planned for or had anticipated was happening.

We would be running and I would have no idea which way to go.

There was at least one thing I might be able to control. I whirled to face the captain. "We are supposed to arrive at nighttime."

He sounded sympathetic. "The people won't wait. They will row out to the harbor and claim you here if we try. We should have arrived last night but were delayed because of the pirate attack."

We needed the darkness and shadows as cover.

Quynh had been vomiting all morning and now I was the one fighting off the desire to throw up last night's feast over the side of the ship.

We were going to die.

It seemed totally inevitable.

The city was massive, bigger than any I'd ever seen. It spread out in front of us, as if to mock me and my plans. The palace was at the farthest point and there was nothing beyond it. It stood on a hill, above the rest of the city, encircled by labyrinth walls, with cliffs on the far side.

But that was the only identifiable building. The labyrinth walls were sand-colored, narrow, and intertwined. And there were large openings crammed full of buildings. Hundreds of pockets interspersed throughout the maze. The temple of the goddess could have been in any one of them.

I saw only tiled and flat roofs everywhere I searched. How would I ever locate it?

The dream I'd had, where I'd seen the beautiful woman in a field of wildflowers, suddenly filled my mind. I remembered that she had been watching the sun rise in the east, her face turned that direction.

What if that had been some kind of clue? My mind seized on the possibility. If it was, then it would make sense that her temple would lie in the west so that her statue would soak up as much light as she could.

Or it might have been located in the east so that she would be closer to the sun when it rose.

Desperation scrambled my ability to think clearly, to decide.

Because if I chose wrong, if we ran in the wrong direction, it would mean certain death.

Hope was all I'd had left, and it was quickly abandoning me.

"None of my men will participate in the event," the captain said behind me, and I didn't know what he expected us to do. Thank him? Was it an attempt to comfort us?

But he walked away before I could formulate a retort, letting him know exactly what I thought about his declaration.

Quynh's hand shook in mine. "It's so big."

She was giving voice to my fears, and I was determined to chase them away. "We will find it. Don't worry."

The water in the harbor was deep enough, and free of dangerous reefs, so that we could go directly to the docks and weren't forced to travel by rowboat as we had when we'd left Locris.

As the men threw ropes to those who waited on the wooden docks to catch them, I felt even more eyes on us. Everyone openly stared. Another wave of nausea rose up in my throat, but I swallowed it back.

Jason coughed and then announced, "The captain is waiting for you by the gangplank."

I nodded and turned to look at him. There was something in his eyes, something I couldn't have described with words. Instead I felt it, deep in my stomach.

He didn't want me to go but was just as powerless as I was to stop it.

"May I ask a favor from you?"

His expression showed me that he understood how difficult it was for me to ask. "Anything, if it is within my power to do so."

"If one or both of us makes it to the temple alive, I left a small pot in my cell. Will you bring it there?" I had my pack with my dagger, the bags of salt, food, and water. My throwing knives were in my belt, my xiphos attached to my thigh.

I had brought the pot with Locrian dirt to test once I found the eye and a life mage. I would put the eye in my soil and make sure it grew plants. I had to know that the eye would restore my kingdom before I returned home.

But there was no point in carrying something so heavy on my back when I wasn't sure whether I'd make it.

"Yes," he said. "I swear it."

I was used to him being more insufferable, more arrogant, and wasn't sure what to make of this serious man swearing himself to my request.

We reached the gangplank and the captain dismissed him.

Jason leaned in close to me so that no one else could hear and said, "If I could save you, I would."

And I believed that he physically could have. That he would have fought off every crew member and then cut his way through the crowd gathered at the dock. The others wouldn't even be able to reach for their swords before he would slice them open. He was capable of it, and for a brief moment, I allowed myself to fantasize that he would do just that—save Quynh and me by facing an entire army alone and succeeding.

"But you can't. And you won't. Your words don't matter very much right now," I said.

He lingered for a moment longer, as if he wished to say something else. But he didn't and instead went and picked up a broom leaning against the main mast. To my astonishment, he started sweeping the deck.

I didn't know what I'd expected, but it hadn't been for him to start doing chores.

He began to sing, his voice strong and clear.

To the blue, to the blue
Head to the blue, the blue
Where the sea meets the sky
On the water we'll fly
Off to sail, off to roam
Salty waves are our home
To the blue, to the blue,
Head to the blue, the blue

It was the song the rowers had been singing nonstop since we'd boarded. It seemed entirely unsuitable for him to be singing some sea shanty, given my situation. While a tiny part of me was glad that I finally knew the words in the common tongue, the rest of me was in total disbelief.

At least his actions gave me some clarity. I had thought I'd mattered to him, even a little bit. But he had been very honest with me about the kind of man he was, and I was the fool who had wanted to pretend otherwise.

I had been a willing pair of lips, a port in the storm, nothing more, nothing less.

The captain walked us down the gangplank, surrounded by several members of his crew, who had their weapons drawn. I wondered if it was to scare us, or to keep the gathered crowd in check.

Perhaps a little of both.

I headed down first with Quynh right behind me. I wondered how many other maidens had only gotten this far. How many had declined to come out of their cell? Off the ship? Had refused to go beyond the docks, futilely hoping for safety?

How long had it taken for them to discover that they would have been better off running, making an attempt to reach the temple?

I glanced at Quynh and could see the fear written all over her face. Had the other maidens helped each other the way I was going to help her?

Or had it been every woman for herself?

As we exited the docks, we walked past sagging buildings. I saw signs indicating that they were warehouses, trading offices, shipbuilders, recruiting offices. The ground here was not dusty, but a rich, dark, deep brown soil, nearly black.

And there were trees. So many trees. Everywhere I looked I saw green leaves.

I'd never imagined that there could be so much green in the entire world, let alone on a single street leading from the docks.

As we drew closer to the city walls, I became acutely aware of everything around me. The sound of metal being struck, the delicious smell of bread combined with newly cut wood and the saltiness of the ocean. Seagulls flew lazily overhead, calling to one another, while the sun beat down on us. My lips were dried out, but I didn't reach for my waterskin.

There would be time for that later.

We got past the shipping district and reached the place Jason had told me about, the Fields of Sithon. They were large open areas, covered in grass. I had the urge to reach down and touch it, but I refrained.

Jason had told me that not all the men of Troas participated in the tribute, and so I had imagined that there would be a few dozen, maybe less.

But there were hundreds of armed men lined up. Maybe even thousands.

My heart sank to my feet as I realized the impossibility of what I was going to try to do. I'd been so arrogant in my assumptions that we could survive this.

Many of the men had on armor but not full sets. Mostly breastplates with some bracers. I supposed that they probably weren't wearing additional pieces because they had surmised it wasn't necessary.

It hadn't been necessary against every other maiden until now.

But I was going to fight back.

I recalled how fast Jason had been, how hard Lykaon had hit me, and resolved to do my best to follow all of Demaratus's training and not let anyone here catch us.

A line had been drawn at the opened city gate, marked by a purple flag that bore the crest of the royal family.

I'd certainly seen it on enough wax seals on correspondence in my father's library to recognize it.

The gateway soared above us. The outer walls were thirty feet high. At least the traders had been correct about that. The walls looked as if they'd been built to keep monsters out.

Two men were situated near the line. One held a brass horn in his hand, while the other had a small water clock on a makeshift table.

Nereus greeted the two men and then turned to speak to us.

"This never gets easier, no matter how many times I do it," he grumbled to himself. Then he cleared his throat and loudly announced, "Locrian maidens, there is only one rule: survive. And there is only one way to win: enter the temple of the goddess."

I nodded, swallowing back the boulder that had taken up residence in my throat. I'd had so long to prepare for this moment that I should have been calm. Instead my heart was crashing into my ribs like a battering ram.

"A horn will sound to indicate that it is time for you to race. You will be given a one-minute head start. The horn will sound again to signal that the chase can begin. Do you understand this?"

"Yes." It was difficult to speak.

He nodded, accepting my answer. "May the goddess bless you."

I understood that he'd meant it kindly, but it felt like he had just pulled out his sword and stabbed me in the gut.

Then the captain left with his guards, back to the ship.

Where Jason was probably still singing his infernal song.

I didn't know how much time I had before the trumpeter blew his horn. I pulled out my sword, undoing the sheath and stowing it in my pack. I used the xiphos to cut off the bottom of my tunic, getting rid of the ridiculous length.

Then I did the same to Quynh's tunic. The excess fell to the ground in a pool around her feet that she kicked away.

If anyone was upset or concerned that I had a weapon, they didn't say anything, and no one tried to take it from me.

I felt hollowed out inside, as if I'd become detached from my body. Fear bubbled into my lungs as my heartbeat slowed to a loud, heavy thud. I grabbed the flagpole and cut off the flag, letting it flutter away. I handed the wooden pole to Quynh.

"Hit anyone who comes too close," I said. I'd offered her my dagger earlier, but she'd said she was afraid she'd do more damage to herself than to someone else. I wanted her to have some kind of weapon.

She nodded and her eyes were bright with unshed tears. She was holding it together remarkably well and I felt a swell of pride in her.

"Ready?" I asked. "We can't stop. We can't hesitate. We can't rest. We will have to keep pushing forward until we reach the temple, no matter what."

"I understand." Her hands tightened around the pole. "If this is the end, then I'm glad that I'm with you."

"It's not the end," I said. I took her by the hand and crouched into position, waiting.

I watched as the man lifted the horn to his lips and blew with all his might, a long, solid note.

"Go!" I yelled and we began to run.

CHAPTER NINETEEN

There was a familiarity in my actions, as if my body remembered exactly what to do because I'd practiced so many times.

Just beyond the main gate, the labyrinth split into eight different sections. I saw that the four on the west had dirt paths, while the four on the right were all cobblestones.

If I took a western path, they would be able to more easily track us. But I had decided that the temple would be in that direction.

"This way," I said as I tugged Quynh's hand, forcing her to keep up. Demaratus had made me train with armor so that it would weigh me down because of how much faster I'd be able to run without it.

Neither one of us had anticipated that I'd be carrying an even heavier burden now.

The maze walls were not as high as the outer one, maybe twenty feet tall. I glanced up, making certain that no archers were waiting for us.

They were clear.

I ran along the path, choosing left or right based solely on my gut.

The pathway emptied out into what appeared to be a residential area. There were cramped and poorly constructed apartment buildings all on top of one another. Some small children were playing in the dirt outside their homes, shaded by trees. We ran through a mostly deserted street and I felt the eyes of people watching us from their windows.

I wondered if they would help the men following us, telling them which way we'd gone.

Quynh was already panting behind me and it caused a knot to form in my abdomen. Her breathing hard wasn't good. The chase hadn't even begun yet.

I considered slowing down, not pushing so much, but I had to put as much distance between us and our pursuers as I could. I turned up an alleyway, looking around at the buildings as we ran. This was not the kind of place that the temple would be built in. It would be in a more expensive area.

We cut through several more alleys, some open squares, and down a street to find another opening into the labyrinth. I plunged back in, never letting my grip on Quynh go, even though my hand and her wrist had become sweaty.

The second horn blew, although it seemed a long distance off. Had we come that far that quickly, or were the walls distorting sound?

There was a thunderous roar as the men yelled, beginning their pursuit.

How long would it take them to catch up? Quynh had a short stride, and many of those men had been very tall and would eat up the ground quicker than we could.

Stupid girl. You should leave her.

Demaratus's voice filled my head, but much as I had before, I refused to listen.

I wanted to ask Quynh if she was well, but I was afraid that if we spoke, it would make it easier to find us. I would only speak to her if it was absolutely necessary.

We made a left turn and I saw that there was a dead end approximately fifteen feet away. I slid to a stop and then turned, dragging Quynh along as I went right instead.

She was wheezing but still managing to keep up with me. And although I wouldn't have admitted it, I had slowed down a bit for her benefit.

Demaratus's voice was still in my head, telling me what a bad idea that was, but I had no choice.

The maze opened into another pocket, a marketplace. Would they have put their temple in a square like this one? Or would they not want commerce to be mingled with their worship?

"There they are!"

I looked over my shoulder and saw a group of men, maybe a dozen, with their swords raised. They'd entered the agora from a different tunnel and I pivoted, banking hard to my right, and headed into the marketplace.

While I hated to harm the livelihoods of the people who weren't participating, Quynh's survival was worth more than a few coins.

Stupid girl, don't forget that chaos and confusion are your allies in battle!

I cut the leg of a table piled high with melons as we passed so that all the melons poured onto the ground. I heard several of the men tripping and falling—they'd been running too fast to come to a stop.

Quynh and I turned a corner and I saw a pen full of goats. I undid the latch, opening the gate. I yelled, waving my hands, and the goats barreled out, straight into the oncoming group of men. There was more swearing and confusion as we left them behind and I turned right down a narrow alley.

I considered the possibility that someone might be waiting for us at the other end, and I had my sword ready.

But when we entered the street, all I saw were carts full of hay. "Stay here," I told Quynh.

There was a fire in a pit nearby, and I grabbed one of the logs and brought it back to the carts, setting fire to as many as I could before I heard the shouts of our pursuers.

They were headed down the same alley. I pushed one of the carts in front of the exit. People emerged from their homes and shops to help put out the fires, not realizing that I had deliberately set them.

One man did. He pulled his sword out and came toward me.

Before he could act I ducked down and sliced across his abdomen. Not deeply enough to kill him, but enough to stop his pursuit. His hand went to his gut, shock all over his face as he started to bleed onto the sidewalk.

Fire and steel.

I ran back over to Quynh and grabbed her by the wrist. I pulled so hard that I nearly yanked her shoulder from its socket.

"Sorry," I said. I felt invincible, as if I could cut down any foe and bend the world to my will.

Was this what Demaratus had meant when he'd spoken of the thrill of the fight?

Despite my distractions, we were still being pursued. I spotted an open-air tavern and altered our course to head straight for it. When I crossed the threshold, I began to upend tables, sending drinks flying.

Drunken men yelled in protest but turned all their anger to each other and to the men following us as we darted away. I heard the sound of fists meeting flesh as I located an exit point.

We went back into the maze of walls, which somehow seemed slimmer than before. I had to let go of Quynh's wrist as she could no longer run at my side but had to be directly behind me.

Would this get worse? Would there eventually be a point where the walls closed in completely and were impassable?

My fear was immediately eased as we entered another path and the walls widened again.

I had no idea how this labyrinth connected across those multiple paths I'd initially seen. While men had successfully tracked us down, I had to assume that there would now be hunters in front of us as well as behind us.

Those men knew this city and I did not.

Which might have also been helping me. There was no way to predict my travel route since I had no idea where I was going.

We turned a corner and I heard Quynh scream. I spun and saw a man who had latched his left hand on to her tunic, pulling her toward him.

"Lia!"

In my panic I did something entirely foolish. I ran at the man, slamming into him, but he batted me away as if I were a fly.

"I have one!" he yelled, and I wondered how many people were going to join him. Quynh still strained forward as he pulled. I considered grabbing her hands, trying to wrench her free, but quickly realized that wouldn't do me any good.

He was too strong.

I whirled around, raising my sword, and then brought it down on his wrist, as hard as I could.

He screamed as his left hand fell to the ground.

The scent of blood filled the air and Quynh crashed into the far wall, the momentum propelling her forward now that he was no longer holding on to her.

I was sickened by what I had done, but there had been no other option.

"Let's go!" I yelled to Quynh as the man grabbed his left arm, falling to his knees and still screaming. I ignored the metallic taste that filled my mouth and went deeper into the maze.

I went right and there was an extremely long passageway. I headed down, spotting some buildings just beyond the walls. There had to be another opening.

But when we reached the end, I realized that it had been an illusion. There had appeared to be an exit, but it was sealed off just out of sight.

A dead end.

I didn't even need Demaratus to yell at me for this one. I knew better. "Back the way we came," I said, but it worried me. That was where I'd cut off the man's hand, and he had called out to someone.

It might be a trap.

I heard someone huffing and realized that we were about to crash into another hunter at the end of the passage. I turned to Quynh. "Get on the ground. Pretend to be hurt. Cry."

"I don't have to pretend that," she said as she collapsed into a heap and began to wail. I crouched down next to her, placing my sword on the other side of her body, where it couldn't be seen.

A man carrying an axe ran around the corner, spotting me.

"Please," I said as he approached, holding his weapon up. "She's hurt. We need help."

He slowed down to a walk, his eyes darting as if he expected someone else to jump out. He was cautious, but hopefully not cautious enough.

"Come on, come on, come on," I muttered under my breath. I needed him to hurry up.

When he was finally within reach, I grabbed my sword and plunged it into his thigh. His eyes went wide. He didn't make a sound and just fell backward. He must not have been a soldier—if he had been, he would have taken my head off with that axe before he'd collapsed.

"On your feet!" I told Quynh.

We made it back to the entrance of the dead-end passage and went right. The buildings I'd spotted had looked as if they'd been constructed from expensive materials. Maybe the temple was there.

Then I was being yanked off my feet as an armored man grabbed me by the shoulders, slammed me into a wall, and knocked the breath from my lungs. I pulled up both of my feet and kicked as hard as I could against his chest, getting him to release me.

A wooden pole hit me across my back and I turned to see Quynh, her mouth wide open. "I'm so sorry! I was trying to hit him!"

Taking advantage of the distraction, the man picked me up under my armpits, as if he intended to toss me into the stone wall headfirst.

Instead of resisting or fighting back, I remembered what I had done during my last training session in Locris and went completely limp. It surprised him, as I'd thought it might.

He let go, and when I hit the ground, I rolled myself behind him. I cut the backs of his calves, the closest and most exposed part of him.

Sariah Wilson

The man swore and tried to reach for me, but Quynh finally connected and swung her pole into his head, hard.

He twirled in a complete circle before collapsing, and she and I stood there for a moment staring at each other. Quynh began to laugh.

I joined in, until a man bigger than a horse wrenched my sword from my hand and punched me in the face.

CHAPTER TWENTY

Demaratus was swearing at me in my head for not paying closer attention, for not checking to see if the first man had been alone before I'd prematurely celebrated my victory. My head throbbed and I turned over onto my back, intending to crawl for my sword.

I saw Quynh attempting to hit the man, but he took the pole from her while shoving her away. Her head hit the wall and she went completely still.

"Quynh!" I screamed, now trying to get to her side.

The man snapped her pole in half over his knee, like it was a child's toy, and then tossed it aside. I took out my throwing knives and heaved one at him, but it went wide. He ran over and kicked the other one out of my hand.

He yanked me up and slammed me into the stone wall. I leaned forward so that my head wouldn't hit. I couldn't lose consciousness.

"That is my brother!" the man hollered at me as his hands closed around my throat, inclining his head toward the armored man currently on the ground, bleeding out.

My attacker was so strong. His fingers pressed in and I clawed at his hands as he began to crush my windpipe. I tried to lash out with my feet, but he was tall enough that he could keep clear.

"I'm not going to use my knife on you," he growled at me, baring his teeth. "I want to squeeze the life out of you with my bare hands. Every Locrian deserves a painful death."

His grip tightened and panic tore up my deprived lungs as I hit the man's hands, trying to make him let go. Nothing was working. Stars exploded behind my eyes, and the edges of my vision had started to turn black.

This was it.

It was over.

As the world began to go dark, I saw Quynh, standing off to my right, holding my sword, offering it to me.

I reached out and took it, bringing it up swiftly to stab the man in the neck. Blood spurted out, covering my weapon as his hands fell away from my throat. I collapsed to my knees, gasping and drawing in deep breaths, feeling as if I'd never have enough air again.

"Lia! Are you all right?" Quynh got on the ground next to me, her fingers gently pressing on my neck, checking.

"I'm about as good as can be expected," I finally said, my voice sounding rough. "You didn't have to give me the sword. You could have stabbed him."

"I was afraid I'd hit you again."

Forcing myself to get up, I shook off a wave of dizziness. There had been little possibility of her missing and accidentally stabbing me, given how massive her target would have been. "I appreciate your consideration."

She gave me a small smile and we gathered all our things before heading back into the maze.

My body felt shaky, my throat ached.

But my senses were not entirely dulled, and I heard the sound of a spear cutting through the air. I dived at Quynh, knocking her down to the ground as the spear flew past.

I immediately helped her back up and we continued running.

"That spear almost—" she said.

"I know," I interrupted her. "Don't talk. Save your breath. Keep moving."

We continued west, heading for those rooftops I had seen. We were fortunate that, other than our first encounter, no one had attacked us in a group. That we'd only been dealing with one man at a time. I was concerned that was going to change.

That while there were some hunters who wanted to get the glory solely for themselves, the rest would figure out that they'd be better served to hunt us in packs, like wild animals.

"Lia!" Quynh called, and I turned, my xiphos up, ready to defend her.

"I have to rest," she said. "I'm sorry. I know we can't stop, but I have to drink something."

The sun was past its apex in the sky and had started its slow descent down. It would be hours until nighttime. We would have had a better chance to stop and recuperate under the cover of darkness. I wanted to keep going, but she deserved a break for how well she'd been keeping up with me.

If anyone came down this passage, they would instantly spot us. There was no good place to hide. And someone had already thrown a spear at us; there was no question we were still being pursued.

I handed Quynh my pack, and she found the waterskin. She took a long, deep drink. "Not too much," I warned her. "Your stomach will cramp up."

She nodded and handed it to me. I had just gotten a mouthful when I sensed someone behind me and immediately ducked down and pivoted, moving my body away. The tip of his blade kissed my cheek. I lashed out, bringing my sword up, deflecting his motion while knocking his weapon loose.

How many times would someone be able to sneak up on me? My concern for Quynh was distracting me. My attacker reached for my tunic and got a fistful of cloth at the shoulder. He raised his right hand, intending to punch me. I turned my face at the last second so that his fist met my hairline above my forehead, and although the shock of the impact rang through me, he had it worse.

He yelped, a high-pitched noise, as I heard the bones in his hand break from hitting the toughest part of my head instead of my cheek. It was another maneuver I'd only ever actually practiced—I hadn't realized that it would work so well.

"Go!" I shouted to Quynh. She began to run while I turned to finish with this man. He picked up his fallen sword in what was obviously his nondominant hand, and I was easily able to parry his thrust while running my own blade up the inside of his arm, spilling his blood into the dirt.

Considering him sufficiently dealt with, I grabbed all my things and raced after my sister. She had come to a crossroads.

"Left!" I shouted to her. I caught up and went to take the lead.

Which turned out to be a good thing as a tall man stood in our way. He held a broadsword and a massive shield and filled the entire path, making it impossible for us to pass.

Grabbing one of my knives from my belt and holding my xiphos aloft, I barreled straight toward him. He lifted his shield up, expecting me to slam into him, widening his stance as he braced for impact.

Which was exactly what I'd wanted him to do.

At the last moment I slid along the ground between his legs and sliced at the backs of his tendons as I went past.

He roared with pain and went down.

I got up and looked for Quynh, but she was already racing past me. When I caught up to her, she said, "Your leg!"

I glanced down. My outer thigh was shredded, streaks of red showing underneath the dirt. "I don't even feel it!"

It was true. Just as Demaratus had taught me, I was beyond pain.

We continued to run hard until we came to a crossroads where there were three different paths. "Wait," I told her.

I knew we were being followed, but we couldn't keep running and hoping we'd accidentally trip across the temple. I tried to get my bearings. The sun was going to the west, which meant the palace was directly north of us. I looked up at the walls and realized for the first time that there was faded paint along the edges.

One was purple, one blue, one yellow, and the other green.

There had to be a reason behind it. What was it?

It felt like the answer was right there, at the edge of my consciousness, but I was too beat up and too exhausted to figure it out.

"What are you staring at?" she asked.

"The edges of the walls. They've been painted." Had they been that way the whole time and I just hadn't noticed? Too focused on being pursued and not paying enough attention to my surroundings?

"Why?"

It was a good question. Why would someone paint the walls? The colors were faint. Someone not from Troas, like me, would easily overlook them.

Which meant they'd been created for the people of the city.

Then the answer hit me like a bolt of lightning.

Directions.

They were coded directions.

Jason's voice filled my head: *Head to the blue, the blue.* The blue must mean the way to the docks, next to the blue ocean.

And purple would lead me to the palace, the color of royalty.

I didn't know what the yellow meant—the marketplace, full of bread made from wheat, maybe?

But green . . . green was the color for the earth goddess. The color of her trees, bushes, and grass.

While Jason couldn't assist me, he had given me a clue without my even realizing it.

Excitement bubbled up inside me. "The green paint will lead us to the temple!"

"How do you know that?" she asked.

I briefly explained my thought process as we followed the green path. While this would make it easier to reach our destination, I understood that it was also going to put more hunters in our way.

"I'm not sure if I'm right," I said when I finished, "but it's better than us wandering around."

"Agreed," she said.

The green path led to an opening, and the buildings here were nicer than the first residential area we'd gone through. I saw a mixture of homes and businesses, and we had just stepped onto the street when I heard a sound I recognized.

I wasn't fast enough this time. I called out a warning, but a bola wrapped around Quynh's ankles before I could get her out of the way. She went down, face-first. I dropped my sword and raced to help her.

When I rolled her over, I saw that her face was bloody. My heart leapt into my throat, pulsating with terror. I quickly realized that she had only scraped it up and had hit her nose, which was where most of the blood was coming from.

"Behind you!" she called out.

A man had started to thrust down at me with his sword, and I realized I wasn't going to be able to stop him. I crossed my arms at the wrist, knowing that they would absorb the blow but that I was about to lose one or more limbs and bleed to death. Now I wished I had worn armor.

I braced myself, waiting for the moment his steel sank into my unprotected flesh.

It never came.

A loud whistle was the only warning of the arrow that struck the man full in the chest, knocking him back. I watched in disbelief as the bright yellow feathers at the end of the shaft quivered.

I got to my feet, looking for the shooter while I went for my sword. I had no defense against an arrow attack, other than to keep moving. I turned my gaze in the direction the arrow had come from but didn't see anyone.

The only sensible explanation was that someone had been aiming for me and had missed. But if that was true, then there would have been a follow-up arrow, as an archer would do if he'd failed to hit his target the first time.

There were no more arrows.

Quynh groaned and I went over to help her get the rope off her ankles. When she got to her feet, she immediately collapsed, and I had to put my arm around her waist to keep her upright.

"My ankle!" she exclaimed through clenched teeth.

"Try to put your weight on it," I said.

She did as I instructed and yelled out, falling against me.

"I think it's sprained," she said.

There was no way we could keep running. She would have to rest for a little while because, much as I might have wanted to, I couldn't carry her to the temple. Even if I had known exactly where it was.

Stupid girl, use your surroundings! Focus!

Again, Demaratus was right. I glanced around until I saw words pressed into the dirt that said "Follow me."

I tightened my grip around Quynh. "I know where we can go to get help."

CHAPTER
TWENTY-ONE

We moved as quickly as we could. It was obvious how much pain Quynh was in, but she didn't complain.

I felt incredibly guilty, as if I had caused this. Earlier I'd told her to pretend she'd been injured and had somehow willed it into being. This evil existed because I had spoken the words.

"You should leave me," she said. "I was worried about slowing you down before, but now? There's no way we can make it. We'll both get caught."

The footprints with the words went left and I continued to follow them. "I will tie you to me if I have to. I'm not leaving you."

"Lia, you must see reason. I can't go on."

"Yes, you can. We might be close. We'll get to the temple and then you'll have plenty of time to heal."

The footprints led to a wooden door that had been painted red. I knocked on it, and when it opened slightly, I jammed my foot inside and entered the front room. The woman at the door gasped as I pushed past her. Several other women were gathered inside, all wearing fine-twined linen in various bright colors.

Quynh realized where we were. "Hetaerae."

Hetaerae were expensive courtesans, the very best of what their profession had to offer. And my regiment had shared with me that the hetaerae would often custom order sandals with the words "follow me" embedded into the soles with metal spikes so that potential customers would be able to find their business easily.

I was so glad that the same thing was true in Ilion.

An older woman came downstairs. Her rich black hair was piled up on her head, her dark, piercing eyes taking us in. "What's all this? Who are you?"

"We are the Locrian maidens. My sister has been injured, and I've come to ask you for a place to rest, to heal." My heart thundered inside me. I knew this was a big risk, but we had to get off the street.

The woman shook her head at me. "We cannot help you."

"No citizen of Ilion may assist us. Are you a citizen?"

At this she hesitated. "No. I am Sasanian." She showed me her right wrist, and there was a tattoo there. A small dot surrounded by four oblong petals, representative of their nation.

"Then you can help us." All the hetaerae in Locris had been from other places, and I had gambled on the fact that the same would be true in Ilion.

"Your presence here endangers my girls."

She would be taking a risk by sheltering us—I understood that. "The men of the city are hunting us, and we're both injured. I'm asking you, woman to woman, to please help us. We'll die without it."

If anyone understood the situation we were in, what it was like to be at the mercy of men, I hoped it would be her. The woman considered my request.

I took the chance to press things further. "We weren't supposed to enter the city in the middle of the day. We were supposed to be afforded the protection of night, and we haven't even been given that. Please let us have a fighting chance."

I held my breath and waited.

She was obviously someone well practiced in disguising her emotions, as I couldn't guess at what she was thinking.

"All right. Until nightfall. Our clients will begin to arrive at that time, and it should be easy enough to sneak you out in the confusion." She turned to the girl I'd pushed past. "Close the door."

Relief flooded my body. "Thank you. Thank you so much."

"Come upstairs. There is a room you can use. I'm Mahtab."

We followed along behind her with Quynh still making a small sound of pain with each step.

"I'm Lia, and this is my sister Quynh."

Mahtab raised her eyebrows slightly, as if surprised at my declaration because we obviously weren't blood-related, but she didn't comment on it.

"Could we get some fresh water? And bandages? And brown or beige tunics? Something most women would wear so that we won't be noticed," I said. We obviously couldn't go out in the bright yellows, pinks, and oranges the hetaerae downstairs were wearing. "We can pay you."

Once we were upstairs, we walked down a long hallway to a small room they used for storage. It was too tiny for a bed or any other furniture. "I will bring you what I can," she said. "Stay here and I'll return."

"Thank you," I said again. She nodded before leaving, closing the door behind her.

Sunlight streamed into the room and I lifted Quynh's ankle so that I could better examine it. She hissed as I gently touched it. It looked a little swollen, but it wasn't bright red. I didn't see any broken bones.

I also didn't know how long it took a sprain to heal, but I suspected that it wouldn't be quick enough for us to keep running.

Mahtab returned along with one of the women from downstairs and they carried all sorts of supplies, including a washing basin. I reached into my pack and gave them one of the bags of salt I'd brought. It was worth far more than they had given us, and I saw the other woman's eyes widen when she realized what it was.

I again angrily thought of the wealth Locris might have if not for the tariffs imposed by the Ilionian blockade.

"We cannot tell you where the temple is," Mahtab said, handing the bag of salt to her companion. "If we tell you, we would be put to death."

"I think I know where it is," I said. "We won't ask. You're doing so much for us and I wouldn't be that ungrateful."

"You will have to leave at nightfall," she repeated. "They will organize a search and go house by house until they find you. I won't let anyone who lives within these walls be put in danger. They're all under my protection."

"I understand."

She nodded and left us alone again.

I helped Quynh to wash her face and change out of her tunic. She grimaced and grunted the entire time, and I could plainly see how much her ankle was hurting her.

You won't be able to save her.

I pushed Demaratus's words away, but they took up residence in my mind, repeating over and over again. After I changed into my own tunic, cutting it short, I washed up the best that I could, flinching when I ran the washcloth over my thigh. It throbbed with pain but it would be fine. At this point nearly every part of me ached with some kind of bruise or cut. I wrapped a bandage around my leg and another around Quynh's ankle, as tightly as I dared.

We both went completely still when we heard a man's voice outside yell, "Has anyone seen the Locrian maidens? You will be rewarded for information!"

No one answered him, but it took me several minutes to relax as I waited for the door to burst open or for one of the women to volunteer our location.

It didn't happen.

Quynh leaned her head against the wall, clearly in a great deal of pain. I passed her the water, making sure she drank.

She barely took any.

"You're going to need water," I said.

She gave me a tight smile. "I know."

"Are you hungry?" They had brought us some nuts and fruit. I divided them up in half and gave Quynh her portion.

But she didn't touch it.

Instead she began to undo her bracelet. "I want you to put this on."

An alarm sounded inside me and I was filled with dread. "Why?"

"My mother told me that it would bring me good luck. And it did. It brought me to you and our family." She struggled with the knot and I didn't try to help her.

"You still need the luck," I reminded her.

"I have you, and that's luck enough," she said. She finally managed to get it loose, and I realized that I'd never seen her without it. Not once in my entire life. She even wore it while she bathed.

Part of me was terrified that this meant she was giving up, but she had promised me that she wouldn't.

"I can't accept it," I said when she offered it to me.

She let out a sound of frustration. "I don't typically ask anything from you, but I am asking you for this."

"I feel like if I take it, I'm admitting that we'll die." Or that she would die and I would have to carry on and keep her bracelet safe.

"Lia, please." Seeing that her entreaty wasn't working, she changed tactics. "I will not take another step unless you promise to take my bracelet and keep it safe."

Seeing no other recourse, I took the bracelet. She helped me tie it onto my wrist. It felt wrong on my arm, like it didn't belong there. "I will guard it with my life."

"I've already said this to you, but if something does happen to me—" She held up both of her hands as I began to protest, stopping me. "If something does happen, please don't let it be in vain. Promise me that you'll go on."

The unshed tears that collected in my throat were hot, burning me. "Don't make me promise that."

"Do it, Lia."

She wouldn't give in on this, I could tell. So I nodded. "I promise."

"Good." Her entire body relaxed, and within a few minutes, she had gone to sleep. I was glad—her body needed the chance to recuperate.

I leaned against the far wall and considered our options. I thought about offering Mahtab another bag of salt and asking her to watch over Quynh here, but I understood that she would refuse. That it would bring death on her house, and while she was kind enough to offer us temporary shelter, she would not be willing to put the lives of those she looked out for on the line for us.

It wasn't like I could go out and look for another person to take Quynh in. There might be men searching this area already, and I would be caught and killed. Even if I did find someone, they might lie and turn us in.

The only thing I could do was press forward. The temple might be two streets over or two miles away. I had no way of knowing. It didn't matter, though, because we would find it.

Both of us. Together.

Hobbling the entire way if we had to.

As I nibbled on the nuts they'd brought us, I thought about how, while we were resting, our hunters could be doing the same. There would be some who were still searching and tiring themselves out, but not everyone would do that.

They would be fresh and ready to meet us, while Quynh and I had been severely hurt.

We weren't going to stand much of a chance.

The sun continued to sink, bringing us closer and closer to the time that we would have to leave. I didn't want to risk going to the window for fear that someone might recognize me. The odds were small but I wasn't willing to tempt fate.

Darkness came, rolling in like a wave from the sea. I heard the front door open and then men's voices downstairs, sounding happy. I found my sheath in my pack and tied it back onto my leg.

The door to the storage room opened and one of the hetaerae stuck her head in. "Mahtab sent me. You have to go."

I had already gathered my things together and leaned over to gently shake Quynh, wanting her to have as much time to rest as possible before we had to run. I said her name and she immediately woke.

"Is it time?" she asked, and I nodded.

"There is a ladder here that will take you up to the roof," the woman said. I had been worried about how we would get past their clientele downstairs, and this was a perfect solution. It would also keep us off the streets, where the men had been searching for us.

Quynh again collapsed against me when she stood, burying her face into my shoulder. I had desperately hoped that her condition would improve, but that hadn't happened.

We would just have to do the best we could.

I had her climb the ladder first. The woman Mahtab had sent put her hand on my shoulder. "My mother was Locrian. And the temple is half a mile north from here. Above the temple doors there is a stone carving of trees and barley. It is easy to recognize."

"Thank you," I said, nearly overwhelmed with relief and gratitude. "You've saved us."

She nodded and then quickly left. I finally had hope again. We were close.

Quynh had reached the top rung when I heard a man behind me say, "The Locrian maidens! The Locrian maidens are here!"

He was half-undressed and started running toward me. I got my sword out and began to climb but watched as Mahtab appeared behind him, grabbing the edge of the rug and pulling it out from under the man, sending him flying forward.

She ran over to check on him, cooing and asking if he was all right, while giving me a quick nod. I climbed up quickly and slammed the door down. There was a large clay vase nearby, and I rolled it on top of the door to slow our pursuers. The roof of the hetaera house and the surrounding buildings were all flat. We could run up here and stay off the street.

But that man calling out had sent up an alarm and I heard men below us, mobilizing. It wouldn't take them very long to figure out where we had gone.

I helped Quynh the best that I could, but we were far too slow. At least now we had darker clothes and the night to help protect us. We crossed onto another roof, and then another.

A shattering sound cut through the night air. The pot I'd put on top of the door.

"We have to hurry," I said unnecessarily. I knew she was doing her best. But I didn't know how many men were behind us or how hard it would be for me to fight our way through.

There was a gap between the roof we were on and the next one. I didn't see a way down. We would have to jump.

"I'll go first, and then I'll help catch you," I said. "You'll have to run. It will hurt, but you can do this."

She nodded. It wasn't a difficult jump, but my ankle wasn't sprained. I made the leap easily and then pivoted around, getting close to the edge. "Your turn!"

Hobbling back a few steps, she did her best to run, but my stomach bottomed out when I saw her make the mistake of leaping from her injured foot. It caused her to miscalculate the jump.

Fear squeezed my heart with its icy claws.

Quynh wasn't going to make it.

CHAPTER TWENTY-TWO

Her jump was short, but she still managed to grab the ledge. She quickly started to slip but I dived onto my chest, latching on to both of her wrists.

"I've got you!" I said. I began to shift my position so that I could pull her back up. I had no leverage currently.

"The maidens are here!" a man said from below us. I couldn't see his face, but I heard the sound of leather sandals running along the roads and sidewalks. People began to converge beneath Quynh's feet.

"Help me," I told her. "Grab on to me."

But Quynh looked up at me with an expression that made my fear a thousand times worse.

"No!" I shouted.

My hands were sweating and her left hand came loose. I reached for it but missed.

"Lia." She'd never sounded so calm, so collected. "It's time. Let me go."

"Get a ladder!" someone beneath us said.

"We don't have time for this. Give me your other hand, right now! Quynh, please! Don't do this!" Hysteria and terror pushed out every pain, every other emotion. "I cannot lose you!"

"I was lost the moment my name was chosen. We have only been delaying fate."

Grabbing her right wrist with both of my hands, I tried to pull her up, but she wasn't helping me and had gone slack. "We're so close. We can make it. Give me your other hand!"

My arm burned, and my shoulder felt like it was about to be ripped out.

"I love you," she said, and there was a finality to it that exacerbated my frenzied dread.

Sweat broke out on my back and it took everything I had to hang on to her. My strength was waning.

"You promised me," I said with a sob. "You promised me you wouldn't give up."

"I'm not giving up. I'm giving you a chance. Let me go."

"I won't!" I yelled the words back, my chest and throat aching.

There was a sharp tug. The crowd had torches and I blinked, realizing that I could see them clearly. They had found a ladder and a man had climbed it to pull at her feet. His skin was as pale as a ghost, his hair redder than flame. As if he were an apparition from the underworld, come to claim my sister.

"Quynh!" I pleaded. "Please!"

She had been holding on to my wrist, but she let go, unwrapping her fingers. "One for many," she said.

I screamed as she was ripped away from me, her wrist sliding through my hands.

I rolled over, lying flat on my back while I listened to her scream. I couldn't watch. I should have. I should have given her that honor, borne witness to her death, but I couldn't.

That image would have immobilized me and this would have been over.

I put my hands over my ears, wanting to block out the sound, squeezing my eyes shut. The desire to give in, to let them take me so that I could join her, was overwhelming.

Stupid girl! Don't let her sacrifice be for nothing!

We had both come too far for me to give up now. I had promised her I would go on.

I got up on shaky legs and began to run along the flat rooftops, looking for a way down. While being up here was currently better so that I could evade pursuers, it would also make me easier to find, up high, not able to run down alleys or dart through buildings to hide. I was too exposed.

Quynh's name pounded in my heart. Every beat was for her.

I went north, the direction that the Locrian hetaera had told me to run. Not only was I being hunted on the streets, but there were men following me, a rooftop or two behind.

In the moonlight, I saw the temple with the stone carving. It wasn't far.

We could have made it, my heart wept bitterly, but I knew it wasn't true. There were too many hunters now. My only hope was to run as quickly as I could and outpace them.

I saw a tall white canvas just ahead. A sail merchant had one of his wares out on display. I took out my throwing knife and jumped toward the sail, reaching out to pierce the canvas so that I could safely travel down its entire length.

I landed a bit more abruptly than I'd anticipated and rolled into it, jumping up and continuing on. There were arrows, spears, rocks.

But I knew how to deal with those kinds of missiles. *Just keep moving.*

An arrow did manage to nick my shoulder, but what was one more scar?

A man crashed into me, shoving me back against a wall. I wasn't stunned or surprised and tried to absorb the blow as best I could. He made the mistake of raising his arm to swing his axe at me, and I took the opening to stab him in the armpit.

Demaratus would have been so proud of me.

A detached part of my mind wondered if my attacker would die. I had killed men today. That probably should have felt more significant to me, but those men had been trying to hurt me and Quynh.

Or maybe it was because Demaratus had spoken of slaying enemies in battle so often that I had become hardened to it.

And the loss of Quynh . . . that was payment enough. I had no more tears to shed, no guilt to feel over men who wanted us both dead.

It felt completely unreal that she was gone. After everything we'd been through, everything she had survived, to have it end up like this?

I couldn't think about it now. I had to keep running.

A hunter waited for me in the middle of the road, his spear held out in front of him. Like I would be enough of a fool to impale myself on it. I hit it out of the way with my sword and swiped at his back, feeling my blade cut into him.

Part of me wanted to turn around and face my would-be attackers. To take out as many of them as I could before I joined Quynh in death.

But Kallisto was the only sibling I had left. I couldn't let her marry Lykaon, couldn't let her be queen of a dead land.

There were still many people I needed to save.

The full moon hung low in the sky, as if it were guiding me. I turned a corner and there it was.

The temple of the goddess. Beckoning to me.

I assumed that there had to be a trap waiting for me. If I were hunting someone and knew the exact place they were headed, I would plan an ambush with a line of armored men with shields and weapons.

There were men there, but they were lying in the street and on the sidewalk. Asleep? Dead? I didn't know and I didn't care.

The way to the temple was clear. I didn't feel relief or gratitude. I was numb. There was a fence with an open archway and I ran through it. A fountain quietly burbled in the middle of a stone courtyard. I raced past it, running up the steps and through the giant columns that held up the stone carving and the roof.

The doors were massive and made of bronze. An arrow hit the wall next to me, and I turned to see several men at the archway. They did not enter the courtyard, did not come up to the long porch where I currently stood.

As if there were an invisible line holding them back.

It didn't stop them from shooting their arrows at me, though, from taunting me, trying to call me back to them.

I ignored them and placed my hand on the door and pushed.

Nothing.

It didn't give at all.

I fought off a wave of panic and tried again as another arrow came close to hitting me.

Then I pushed the other door, thinking the first one had been stuck.

Neither one worked. Both doors were locked.

I took a step back, keeping a stone column between me and the group of hunters outside the courtyard.

There weren't any windows, no way to get in. I banged against the door, thinking someone might come and open it for me.

No response.

At some point those men were either going to come in here after me or they would ring around the temple grounds and fire off a shot that would hit me.

I slumped down to the ground. I'd come so far. I'd made it only to find the doors locked, and it was just a matter of time before one of these men killed me.

Now what should I do?

Stupid girl! The doors aren't the only way in. Go up! Climb!

I hurriedly got to my feet and ran around to the side of the temple. It was at least twenty feet high, but unlike the smooth facade on the front, the rocks here were unfinished and provided foot- and handholds. I slid my xiphos back into its sheath. I was going to need both hands.

With a grunt I began my ascent. There was still yelling and commotion outside the archway and beyond the fence, but none of the men tried to physically follow me. They continued to shoot poorly.

My legs and hands were burning. This was more difficult than I'd thought it would be, requiring a great deal of balance and strength.

I was nearly to the roof but realized that there wasn't anything else to grab on to. I looked around, desperate to find something to use as a handhold, but found nothing.

Stuck. I was going to be stuck.

Then, like an answer to a prayer, a spear embedded itself into the wall next to me. The thrower must have been exceptionally strong to get the spear into place, or the stone was softer than I thought. Either way it was exactly where I needed it to be. I tested it and found that it could support my weight. I used it to keep climbing and got myself to the edge of the roof.

The edge jutted out from the wall, and the only way up would be to leap out and hope that I caught the eave before falling. I took out my sword and used it to reach up and hit the clay tiles at the edge, knowing that if I grabbed them they would slip away, as they weren't attached to anything. They began to fall, one after another in a cascade, until there was a spot clear for me. I put my xiphos back in the sheath.

I counted to three, held my breath, and then I jumped.

My fingers curled around the edge and I gripped tightly as I began to swing. I would need enough momentum to get myself up. I kicked out with my legs, rocking back and forth, harder with each pass.

It took me a couple of attempts, my arms weakening from the strain. I reminded myself that I hadn't come this far to fail now. With one final burst I finally managed it, hooking one of my elbows over the edge, then the other, and using them to leverage myself up.

The edge of the roof scratched me as I climbed, but I didn't care. I turned over when I'd pulled myself up completely, lying against the cool tiles under my back. But then another spear clattered uselessly a few feet away from me as a reminder that I had to keep moving.

The roof was slanted and the tiles farther up were bolted into place. I climbed carefully, not wanting to slip or fall. At the top I took my xiphos out and used the hilt to break the tiles apart, making a large enough hole for me to fit through. I saw the wooden support beams underneath. I lowered myself down, my feet touching a thick beam. I leaned forward and unfurled my legs behind me. Gripping the beam tightly, I hung there, seeing how far I had to drop to the stone floor.

This was going to hurt.

I grit my teeth and let go.

CHAPTER
TWENTY-THREE

The ground rushed up to meet me as I slammed into it. The pain was instant and crushing. I lay on the stone floor, unable to catch my breath. I was fairly certain I'd broken a rib. I moved my legs and they seemed intact, no bones protruding through my skin. That was good.

Each breath I pushed in and out burned. Not only because of whatever injuries I'd sustained, but from the loss of Quynh.

I had made it to the temple, but it had cost me her life.

It wasn't a bargain I would have ever agreed to.

"Your kind are not welcome here."

I rolled slightly to locate the voice speaking to me and realized that I must have hit my face at some point because my left eye was swollen shut. Three women stood in the middle of the room. They were dressed in green tunics, all different shades.

The one in the center wore a veil that covered her entire face. The woman to her left looked to be only a few years older than me, while the one on her right was elderly, her silver hair in a long braid over her right shoulder.

The veiled priestess repeated her words. "Your kind are not welcome in the sacred place. You need to leave."

Did she mean Locrians? "My kind were ordered to survive and to serve the goddess if we made it to the temple alive," I said, trying to sit up as the blinding pain made me groan aloud. I forced myself up. I wanted to stand but didn't think I would be able to support my own weight right now.

"We are under no obligation to keep you," the priestess said. "Throw her out onto the street."

This woman would never understand what this had cost me. I wouldn't let her toss me aside. I would stay in this temple until I got what I came for. Then, and only then, would I leave.

She was not going to send me away, especially not now, when those hunters were most likely waiting for me. "You *are* under an obligation to keep me."

I wished that I could see her face. Her entire body tensed up, though, as if preparing for a fight. Where had my sword gone? Although . . . what good would it do me? I couldn't battle anyone right now.

"I am not," she said.

"Yes, you are. I am Aianteioi. As a religious institution, by law you must offer me hospitality and sanctuary if I seek it or risk offending the goddess." I was extremely grateful my father had required me to memorize all the laws that protected the Aianteioi.

Because those laws were about to save my life.

There was a very long silence as I got to my knees. Everything hurt and I didn't think I would ever feel whole again without Quynh, but I was prepared to do whatever I needed to stay right where I was.

"I wouldn't think that a priestess of the earth goddess would willingly break her laws," I said. "I would assume that there would be great consequences for doing so." Although I could not see her face, the other two women's expressions were answer enough. They were shocked and even looked a bit . . . frightened?

Another long silence, and then finally the priestess spat, "Fine. Stay. But you will be treated like the Locrian that you are. Find her more suitable clothing and shave her head."

The younger woman left the room, presumably to carry out the instructions.

For a moment I thought I had misunderstood. Had she just told someone to shave my head? She couldn't be serious. Did they not know what my hair meant to me? But two more women entered the room carrying black cloth, scissors, and a razor.

"No," I protested, but my arms were held in place and I was hauled to my feet. I nearly passed out from the pain, but noticed that these women seemed ridiculously strong, lifting me as if I were a child when I was a head taller than most of them.

Or maybe I was incredibly weak after all I'd endured.

My tunic was roughly removed, and a black one put on. The same kind that criminals and outcasts wore.

I was pushed back down onto my knees, and a strong hand on my right shoulder held me in place.

They were going to cut my hair. Shave my head. Again, as if I were a criminal.

"You cannot cut a Locrian woman's hair! It is sacred to us!" I protested, but no one responded.

With a sense of resigned dread, I understood that this was going to happen. I couldn't stop it. There was nothing else they could have done that would have dishonored me more.

Demaratus would have rather I strike down everyone in this room than let them take my hair and my honor.

But I wasn't a Daemonian. I was a Locrian who still had a mission to carry out.

It was only hair. It would grow back.

I clenched my teeth together and held completely still as they pulled and tugged at my hair, unpinning the careful braids Quynh had made. They cut them off with scissors and I watched as the braids fell like thick ropes onto the floor around me.

With my gaze pointed down, Quynh's bracelet caught my eye. I reached over to touch it, to feel the flower knot under my fingertips.

She had known at the hetaera house what she was going to do. She had been planning her sacrifice even then. Maybe longer.

I couldn't think of her alone somewhere, in the dark. She would be so scared. No, not scared. She would never be afraid again. She was gone. And they were going to burn her with wood that bore no fruit, her ashes tossed into the sea. I wouldn't even have the chance to give her a proper burial, to say goodbye to her. She would never know peace. That was another unimaginable loss.

The razor was being dragged over my scalp carefully and I fought back the furious tears that filled my eyes. I would not cry. I would not give these women the satisfaction.

I would channel all my hurt, my loss, my suffering, my pain into anger.

Vengeance.

I would find the eye of the goddess, rebuild my nation, save my sister, and then I would come back here and burn this entire city to the ground.

My lungs seemed to grow tighter and tighter until I could no longer breathe. I fell forward, the world going black before I passed out.

◆ ◆ ◆

I woke up with a start, reaching for my weapon.

It wasn't there.

Everything came rushing back, crashing into me like a giant wave. Pain lanced through me, striking every extremity.

Quynh was gone. I had made it to the temple and forced them to keep me even though they hadn't wanted to.

I raised my wrist and felt a rush of relief that her bracelet was still there.

Then I reached up to run my fingers along my scalp.

There was just stubble, rough against my fingertips. They'd made sure to finish the job even though I'd fainted.

"Good morning," an entirely too happy voice said to me.

Again I found myself reaching for my sword. A girl stood at the foot of my bed. She was short and wore her dark hair pinned up. She had light brown eyes, light brown skin, and pink cheeks. She wore a pale green tunic.

Even though her physical resemblance to Quynh was only slight, there was something that reminded me of my sister. Something that felt familiar and right, as if I'd met this girl before.

As if my sister had sent her to me.

Which was confirmed when I heard a voice inside me whisper, *You need to trust her*, and it sounded just like Quynh.

My heart clenched in response.

"I'm Iolanthe," the girl said. "But everyone calls me Io."

"Lia," I offered.

"Welcome to the temple. Is there anything I can get for you?"

My instinct was to accept what the voice had said and believe that she was a nice person who wanted to help, but the wary nature Demaratus had nurtured inside me hadn't gone anywhere. Just a short time ago, the priestesses had been ready to kick me out, and when they'd been forced to accept me, they had done their best to make sure that I knew I wouldn't be one of them.

Why was this Io being so kind to me?

"Water." My throat felt like it was on fire.

She hurried over to a table, where I saw a pitcher and cups. She filled one for me and brought it over.

I took it eagerly, the cool liquid slipping past my lips, but then I immediately spat it out.

"What is that?" I asked. There had been a strange metallic taste that I didn't recognize.

Io looked confused. "What do you mean?"

"Is this poisoned?" Was that the way the priestesses had decided to deal with me? Using subterfuge to kill me?

171

"No. May I?" She reached for my cup and I gave it back to her. She took a big drink before returning it to me. She waited for a few beats and then held up both of her hands. "See? Not poisoned."

"Why does it taste like that?"

"We get our water from a special fountain and that's just the taste. You'll get used to it," she said, pulling a chair over to the side of my bed. "I understand your suspicion, though."

"You do?"

"It's a long and complicated story that isn't worth sharing," she said with a nod, leaving me to wonder what circumstances she had been in where being poisoned was an actual possibility. Io paused, looking down at her hands. As if it were difficult for her to make eye contact. "I heard that you weren't exactly welcomed when you arrived."

Ha. She was definitely understating it. "They weren't friendly, no."

"And they . . ." Her words trailed off as she pointed at my head.

I touched my scalp, self-conscious. "They did. Did they do this to you, too?"

"No."

So it was special treatment reserved only for Locrian maidens, then.

"I've been here for a few months," she added, and it seemed like she was trying to change the course of our conversation.

I realized that I didn't know how Ilionian women joined the temple. "What is the process for you to become a priestess? Do they chase you, too?"

She looked embarrassed and ducked her head slightly. "First, I'm only an acolyte. Like you. It takes a long time to become a priestess. Second, we run, but we aren't chased. We can, however, do whatever it takes to reach the temple first. Including fighting with other competitors."

Io must have seen the incredulous look on my face because she smiled. "I know I must not seem like the sort of person who would win that kind of ultra-competitive race. Acolytes are taken every six months, and they take as many as are necessary to replace priestesses that have died since the last race."

"What if no one dies?"

"Then there are no races. When I participated, they took two. The six months prior to that, they took two as well."

That was concerning. Why were priestesses dying so quickly?

"Of old age," Io added, correctly interpreting my expression. "We serve our entire lives. Now this will be your home until you die."

I didn't bother to correct her. There wasn't a point. But even if it was from natural causes, that still seemed like a significant number.

She leaned in, her eyes twinkling. "Can I tell you a secret?"

Part of me wanted to warn her that anything she shared with me I'd use to further my own ends, but I couldn't risk failure. It might mean that I'd have to betray people, pretend to be their friend, earn their confidence.

It bothered me, and I heard Demaratus's voice in my head telling me that it shouldn't.

"Yes," I said, pushing those concerns aside.

"I shouldn't be here. It's believed that only the strongest and fastest should be allowed to serve the goddess. I cheated."

"You did?"

She nodded, her eyes dancing. "I have worshipped the goddess and her creations since I was a little girl. The only thing I have ever wanted was to serve her in her temple. I knew I'd never win the race. I'm too small and I'm not very fast. So I hid near the end and waited. After Suri crossed the threshold, I immediately followed her."

Her confession made me uneasy. This seemed like information that could get her tossed out of the temple. Why would she tell it to me, an enemy, someone the priestess had wanted to offer to the hunters last night?

Was it a test? To see where my allegiances might lie?

Or was she just as she appeared? Kind, generous, trusting?

Not able to help myself, I vocalized my concern. "Why would you share that kind of confidence with me?"

She tilted her head and looked at me as if I'd just asked a foolish question. "Because now you are my sister. And we have been waiting for you."

CHAPTER
TWENTY-FOUR

"Waiting for me?" I asked, not understanding what she meant.

Io nodded and then stood. "I am to take you on a tour of the temple grounds and then there will be a ceremony for you because it's the fifth day."

She didn't clarify what she'd meant when she said they'd been waiting for me and instead began to speak about something different. I felt like I was struggling to keep up, my questions overwhelming me.

"The fifth day of what?" I knew for a fact it was not the fifth day of the month.

"The fifth day since you arrived."

I sat straight up in my bed and realized that I wasn't in any physical pain. I tested all of my limbs, holding my arms out in front of me, pressing my fingers against my ribs. Had I really been here for five days?

"Do you have healers with magic?" I asked. My grandmother's book had mentioned life mages with a special type of magic that could mend bones, stop bleeding, or wipe away any sickness.

"There hasn't been someone with that sort of ability in a very long time," she said.

Perhaps the mages had drained too much power from their shards?

"Daphne tended to you, which is why you feel better. You most likely met her the night you arrived. She's an older woman and wears her hair in one long braid?" Io said as she offered me her hand. "She is a master of potions and remedies. She always knows the best ways to combine various plants and herbs to help others. She's teaching me how to do it, too."

I waved her extended hand away. I didn't need any assistance. I was more than capable of standing up on my own. I noticed that I was wearing a black tunic, but it seemed different from the one I'd been given initially.

My feet hit the ground with a thud, like I'd almost forgotten how to walk. I quickly leaned against the bed as Io tried to hide her smile, but she didn't succeed. It took a few seconds, but I regained control of my legs. She pointed at a pair of leather sandals, and I quickly slid them on and tied the straps around my ankles.

"This way," she said as we passed through the open door. "Obviously we were just in the infirmary, and it is situated not too far from the dormitories." We walked down a long, covered patio with white marble columns along the outer edge. "The dormitories are arranged by age. The older priestesses apparently don't like sharing their sleeping quarters with the newer acolytes."

The inner wall was covered with foreign shields—relics of battles past. I assumed that they were from wars Ilion had won. Were there Locrian shields on display? I didn't see any.

And why would they hang them here in the temple, and not in the barracks?

More questions I wanted answers to. I started to ask about it, but we turned a corner and I couldn't help but let out a small gasp. There were women of various ages everywhere. Dozens of them. Hundreds. And that was just the women within my eyeline.

No wonder so many of them passed on within a short period of time.

And I could feel every single pair of their eyes on me as we headed toward one of the dormitories. I wondered what made them stare. That I was new? The black tunic? The shaved head?

Or that I was a Locrian maiden?

While Io seemed so welcoming, none of the women who glared at me did.

I wished I had my sword with me.

"How many Locrian women are here?" I asked.

I already knew the answer but a part of me hoped she might respond differently.

"None. You are the first to ever make it to the temple."

In a thousand years, the first and only. Another thing I couldn't dwell on—those two thousand girls who had lost their lives for a crime they hadn't committed.

My heart clenched as I again thought of Quynh.

As I avoided the gazes of the women surrounding us, I couldn't help but take in the greenery. Grass in the open areas. Trees overhead, their leaves swaying gently in a breeze while shading the path. Bushes lining the walkways. So much green, so much life.

We entered one of the dormitories and climbed the stairs to the second floor. We walked down a long hallway until we reached the last door on the left. "This is our room," Io said as she opened the door and let me in. It was larger than I would have imagined, big enough to fit five beds. "We have three sisters that you'll meet later. Your bed is over there, along with your things."

The bed she'd pointed to was closest to the window and I rushed over to find my pack. My throwing knives were there, my dagger, the two bags of salt, the tunic that I'd borrowed, my sheath, and my xiphos. Everything had been cleaned and polished. If I'd been alone, I would have kissed my sword. I'd thought I would never see it again.

"That's a beautiful weapon." Io's voice was tinged with envy, which seemed strange. Why would an acolyte of the earth goddess care about my xiphos?

"Thank you." I debated whether I should put it on or leave it here. I figured I wouldn't have any need of it within the temple complex, and given that it had been waiting for me on my bed for the last five days, I was probably safe to leave it.

There was a pouch with a long strap attached to it. "What's this for?"

"For whatever you'd like to carry. Everyone here wears one." I glanced at Io and saw that she had hers about her waist. "I find it convenient for keeping snacks for between meals."

When I didn't smile at her jest, she added, "You may want to put your bracelet in there. Jewelry is not permitted at the temple."

The idea of taking off Quynh's bracelet made me ill, but it didn't seem that I had much of a choice. The temple priestesses already wanted to throw me out—I wouldn't visibly defy them by breaking their rule.

My stomach rolled and protested as I undid the knot Quynh had made. I quickly put the bracelet into the pouch and then tied the straps around my waist.

"Are you ready to see the rest?" she asked when I finished, and I nodded.

She showed me the dining hall, which was attached to the kitchens and storage rooms, and it wasn't far from the administrative building. I made a mental note—that might potentially have documents that could prove helpful.

"Do you have a library?" I asked. That would be the best place for me to start my search. The eye could be anywhere and I needed to gather as much information as I could.

"No."

That surprised me. Even my family still had a library, and we'd had to sell off most of our books.

Thinking of the palace led my thoughts quickly to Quynh again and that ever-present white-hot pain of losing her, just as sharp and bright as it had been the moment she'd dropped.

Would it ever not hurt as much?

My body might have been healed, but my heart had not and I was afraid it never would.

Io was still talking and I forced myself to pay attention. "There's no reason for the temple to have a library. No one here can read."

Another stunning revelation. In Locris basic education was given to all women, regardless of rank. Although I probably shouldn't have been surprised that a city that hunted women for sport wouldn't worry too much about whether girls could read.

How long had things been this way? My grandmother had taught me that wisdom had always been passed down through the written word—through the stories told, through songs that were sung, through poems read aloud. If women couldn't read, they couldn't access that information. They would never know what the women before them had done. How they had been heroines and overcome trials and obstacles.

I supposed I couldn't be too outraged over it—my own nation had banned the goddess stories, songs, and poetry entirely.

"No women in Ilion can read? Not even the daughters of nobles?" I clarified.

"The daughters of royals and nobles are not allowed to join the temple."

A loud warning bell sounded inside me. This felt like treading over dangerous ground. Another reason to hide my identity—it might give the priestesses an excuse to expel me. "Why not?"

"I suspect that it's because those kinds of women are expected to make marriages of alliance for their families, but what we're officially told is that the goddess should only be served by those who have lived lives of hardship, who will know what it takes to sacrifice and to serve, and so those raised in homes of luxury don't qualify."

That certainly wasn't true. I'd had more than my fair share of obstacles and heartache.

I knew what it meant to sacrifice and serve.

I was closely acquainted with adversity and loss.

Quynh's face rose up in my mind's eye and I had to tamp down my feelings again. I wanted to stuff them into a wooden box where I could close the lid and hide them away. I feared I wouldn't be able to function otherwise.

Io said, "There might be some books in the head priestess's office, but she always keeps that locked."

Useful information for a later date. Who had the keys? And how would I get my hands on them?

"Over there is the treasury," she said, pointing at a large square building.

Of everything we'd viewed so far, that sounded the most promising. Trying to keep my voice even, I asked, "Does everyone have access to it?"

I bit back a curse word. I sounded so obvious with my intentions. I might as well have asked her if the eye of the goddess was being held in that building and how I could get inside to steal it.

But Io didn't seem to notice. "That's always locked as well and only the high priestess, Theano, is allowed to go in."

I thought of my welcoming committee, of the woman who had commanded the others and had tried to throw me out. "Is she the one who wears the veil?"

"Yes."

"Does she always wear it?"

"I've never seen her without it," Io said. "And there's a lot of speculation as to why she has it. Some think she's been disfigured or burned. Some have guessed that she's so beautiful that she hides her face away so the gods will not be jealous of her or try to steal her. Others that Theano is the earth goddess herself and must cover her face so that we won't be incinerated by her glory."

I hoped Theano wasn't the goddess, because I got the distinct impression she wouldn't be very sympathetic to my cause.

"Or that it's a rite associated with her office that none of us know about because we're not the high priestess," she finished. "But I do know that wearing and keeping the keys of the temple is part of her responsibilities. Something she sometimes shares with the Chosen."

"Chosen?" I echoed.

"The Chosen are the five acolytes who are performing best at the temple, and they're given specific responsibilities. Water bearer, key bearer, washing the statue of the goddess, creating sacred clothes for her, that sort of thing."

There would be so much for me to learn. There was no way I could break into Theano's office or the treasury, given how terrible I was with locks. Demaratus had known what I'd be up against and my dismissing lock picking as not important had again come back to bite me. I sighed. I'd have to get the keys, to find a way to steal them without anyone noticing.

I didn't know how possible that would be. So if that plan didn't work out, I would have to become one of these Chosen so that I might just be handed the keys I needed. I wondered how much time that would take.

We walked past the front courtyard, the one I'd dashed across to reach the steps of the temple. It was full of women, but they were wearing more neutral colors—no green.

"Are those all priestesses, too?" I asked.

"No, those are the women of the city who have come to beg the goddess for favors or to honor her with a sacrifice. It's mostly younger women who wish to be married or to become pregnant, as the goddess oversees both of those things."

I nodded, watching the women as they knelt in prayer and supplication, laying sacrifices of fruits and vegetables at a small stone altar that I hadn't noticed before.

"Only priestesses and acolytes may go into the temple proper, but women can enter the courtyard and temple grounds," she said. "Men are completely forbidden from all of it."

I opened my mouth to ask why but shut it quickly. I knew why.

My ancestor, Ajax, and what he had done to a temple priestess.

That was also why all the men hunting me had not gone past the archway.

"You've seen all the important buildings, but there's something special I wanted to show you," she said. "Come with me."

I trailed along behind her and reached up to brush my fingers across the leaves of the closest tree. I'd never felt a leaf before—it was softer than I'd imagined, with veins underneath that looked a bit like the ones in my wrists.

And for the briefest of moments, it felt like the leaves were responding to my touch. Calling to me.

Euthalia.

I dropped my hand and put the thought out of my mind, drawing in a shaky breath as I hurried to catch up to Io.

CHAPTER
TWENTY-FIVE

We walked around a building and I saw a fenced-off area, the stone wall coming up as high as my head. Io pushed at an iron gate that opened easily and waved me inside. "Here we are. The flower garden."

I took a step in and then came to a complete halt. Stretched out in front of me was the most unbelievable sight. As if a master artist had painted it. Like a giant hand had pulled a rainbow from the sky and shattered it into a thousand pieces.

The garden was a cascade of flowers in every size and color. I had seen illustrations of flowers before. Life mages made a single flower bloom in front of us every year. My brother had brought me back a pressed flower from one of his trips, and for a long time it had been my most prized possession.

That faded, flat, dried-up flower was nothing compared to this. I'd had no idea that this kind of vibrant beauty existed in the world.

And the fragrance? It was otherworldly and it was everywhere, surrounding me. I'd never smelled anything so good.

I reached out to touch the petals of the nearest flower and the texture was unbelievable. Soft as silk.

My heart lodged itself in my throat. More than anything I wished that Quynh were here to see this. She would have loved it.

Io stood nearby, watching me. "I've heard that you don't have flowers in Locris."

I nodded.

"That's called a rose."

Something gently flew up into the air, surprising me. "What is that?"

"A butterfly. They like to land on flowers. Daphne says they help things to grow. There are a lot of birds and insects that do so."

Butterfly. That wasn't something I'd ever heard of before. It was blue and delicate looking, flitting around in the air near my head. Like it was dancing.

The color of the butterfly made me think of Jason and his blue tunic.

Before I had a chance to ponder where that thought had come from and why, Io was talking. "Let me introduce you to everyone."

She told me the names as we walked—anemone, carnation, pansy, hyacinth, peony, daffodil, violet, delphinium, crocus, lily, larkspur. The names were magical and beautiful and Io spoke about them almost like they were people, as if she knew and cared about each one. She watched indulgently as I stopped to smell and touch everything. I couldn't get over the variety and brilliance of it all. Purples and pinks and blues and yellows and whites and reds and oranges in so many different shades.

"This is a sunflower," she said. "The blossoms actually turn and follow the sun."

There was a feeling of familiarity because it was just like the one I'd seen in my dream on the ship. My heart pounded in my chest as I reached out to touch this flower as well.

Was this some kind of sign?

"You have to come over here and see this one. It's called an iris and it's special. This is the goddess's favorite flower."

It was a bluish purple and shaped differently than the other flowers I'd already seen. "Why is this her favorite?"

"I'm not actually sure," she said. "There are so many medicinal usages for it. It's always the incense they use in the temple."

"They do?" I sniffed but there didn't seem to be much of a scent. The blossom had three opened petals with a yellow heart in the center and I had expected it to smell more strongly, like the violets had.

"The fragrance comes from the roots instead of the petals. It's one of the only flowers we do that with." There was a clay pot on a bench and she ran over to retrieve it, bringing it back to me. "Here, smell."

The recognition was instant and immediate. The back of my neck prickled. It was exactly the same scent I'd smelled in the dream with the sunflowers. The one coming from the goddess's robes.

I detected a mixture of notes—floral, sweet, a bit like fennel, but also earthy, woody, with a slight hint of mineral.

As if it featured everything that encapsulated the goddess.

"What do you think?" Io asked.

It felt like everything was whirling around me, and there were answers to my questions but when I stuck my hand out, trying to catch even one in an attempt to make sense of my situation, they stayed frustratingly beyond my grasp.

When I didn't answer, she filled in the silence. "We dry the roots and then we grind them up. Daphne says that the longer you let the roots dry, the better. She has some that have been drying for the last five years. We add them to resin or oil, depending on whether we're going to use them for the scent or for medicine."

She finally took a breath, glancing up at the sky. "This is one of my favorite gardens to work in."

"'Gardens'? As in plural?" It was hard to imagine that there could be more beyond what I was seeing.

"Yes, we have orchards and vegetable gardens and herb gardens. We tend to all the plants here. It's our responsibility to care for them, nurture them. Daphne is the best at it. I've even traveled with her to work on burned olive trees."

So many questions, such as who had burned the trees, but I settled on, "Why would you waste time trying to save something that is destined to die?"

Again, she gave me that smile, as if she were indulging me. "Olive trees are nearly impossible to kill. If they are burned, they will still bear fruit the next year. You can freeze them and they persevere. Even if you cut them down, a new tree will grow from the roots. It's why it's the symbol of Ilion—even when we are burned, frozen, cut down, we grow back."

I clamped my teeth together so that I wouldn't respond. Because Locris was imprisoned thanks to Ilion's ability to quickly return to full power.

It was becoming clear that Io didn't like silence as she added, "We still have a bit of time and I thought you might like to help me."

"Do what?" I asked.

"There are some bulbs I need to plant. They come from a kingdom far north of Thrace and supposedly they won't bloom until spring next year."

"I don't know how."

"It's easy. I'll show you," she said. "There's a reason that gardening is my favorite thing. Putting your hands in newly dug earth? Coaxing life to grow from nothing but soil, water, and sun? There's something so healing about that. It can mend hearts and souls. It helps you to realize that even a desolate land can be healed and made green again."

The restoration of a desolate land was the deepest desire of my heart, but I tried not to react to her statement as she handed me a small spade and a pot full of water. She did as she promised and showed me exactly how to make a hole and where to put the bulbs, how to cover them up with dirt and water them.

She was right. Very simple. I felt a bit foolish. Io moved a few feet away and began digging.

I started my own hole and something strange was happening. There was a humming in the ground, a vibration I could feel. Was this the healing she had spoken of? This sensation that seemed to travel up through my fingers and spread throughout all my limbs? Or was it something else?

It was as if there were a pool just beyond my fingertips. A reservoir of power. Or magic. I didn't know how else to describe it, but it waited for me. Although no matter how deep I dug, it continued to stay frustratingly out of reach.

I placed both of my palms against the black soil and the feeling intensified. Like if I could only figure out how to harness it, direct it, I would be able to do magic myself.

While I was doing this, Io had kept up a monologue, talking about the kind of work she did with plants, that I only half listened to. Something about weeding and fertilizing and making sure that there wasn't any blight or rot or too many predatory bugs.

Given how caught up I was in trying to figure out what was happening with the dirt, it took me a moment to register that Io had fallen suspiciously quiet. I pulled up my hands and lifted my head and saw that three women had entered the gardens.

Every instinct inside me screamed that they were enemies.

They wore green tunics that were a slightly darker shade than Io's. I'd figured out the oldest priestesses wore the darkest green and the acolytes the lightest. These three women were a bit older than us and looked like most of the people I'd come across since leaving Locris. Light brown skin, dark brown hair.

I reminded myself that I was new here and didn't know everything. They might be friends with Io.

The woman in the center bent slightly at the waist and said to Io, "Are you enjoying digging your dung?" The other two girls laughed cruelly.

Not friends.

Io was on her hands and knees and ignored the trio.

"I'm speaking to you," the leader sneered and kicked at Io, knocking her down.

"Stop!" I said, getting up, my head spinning. I didn't know what kind of medicines they'd administered to me in the infirmary, but it felt as if they hadn't cleared my system yet. I was a bit woozy and weak and in no state to fight.

The woman whirled on me. "And who's going to stop me? You?"

I balled my hands into fists. I hated people who preyed on those weaker than them. Hitting someone might help with this overwhelming rage and sadness I was feeling. Even if I wasn't at full strength yet, I at least had the benefit of training to assist me.

"Yes, me."

She smiled with amusement. "You must be the Locrian. Nice haircut."

Her cohorts laughed again and I tightened my fists.

The woman came over and walked in a wide circle around me. "You're the first Locrian I've ever seen." When she finished she stopped directly in front of me and said conspiratorially, "It's amazing you survived. I've heard that the captured maidens are cut up into pieces and sold off, to be used in potions."

A weight settled hard against my chest. That couldn't be true. I wouldn't allow it to be. "You're lying."

"Am I?" she mocked.

"Artemisia," Io said to the woman tormenting me in an attempt to come to my aid, but the other girls grabbed her, pulling her up and holding her arms behind her back so that she couldn't move.

Io did not deserve to be treated this way. "Tell them to stop."

This Artemisia glanced over her shoulder. "No, I don't think I will."

"I will make them," I said, threatening all three. They were nearly as tall as me, but I had fought much taller and stronger people. I wasn't worried about taking on some flower-loving acolytes.

Artemisia grinned and drew a sword from its sheath. How had I missed that she was carrying a weapon? "Come and stop us, then," she challenged.

I swore under my breath, furious that I'd left my xiphos back in my room. "I'm unarmed."

She threw her sword to the ground. "I don't need a weapon to beat you." She raised both of her fists in front of her face.

I tried not to smile. Artemisia had no idea what she was going up against. Boxing had been a regular part of my regimen, in large part to help build up my muscles and reflexes. This almost seemed unfair.

And I believed in my own superiority clear up until the moment when her fist connected to my face, sending me whirling back. She went to hit me with her other fist and I was able to throw up my arm, blocking the shot.

But she was relentless. She drove into me and I wasn't able to defend against every blow, my body not responding the way I needed it to. She got in far too many hits and my head was throbbing as I tried to hold her off.

"Who taught you to fight?" she asked incredulously.

I realized that I hadn't been taught to fight. I'd been taught to avoid the fight. To escape situations like this. Artemisia had clearly been trained differently than I had—she went on the offensive and never let up.

Who had trained *her*?

And her hits were powerful. How was she so strong? I attributed it to me only recently being healed and lying in bed for five days. There was no other way to explain why she hit harder than any of the men from my regiment.

Io made a sound and it distracted me, which Artemisia took advantage of. She walloped me, knocking me to the ground.

A voice called out. "Enough!" My vision was unclear for a moment, my head ringing and dizzy, but then I saw the older woman from the first night. Daphne. "Stop, Artemisia. I just fixed her up—I don't need you to break her apart again. That is not how you treat a sister. You took an oath."

Artemisia stared down at me for a few beats and I could see in her eyes that she wanted to finish the job. To beat me into oblivion, or worse.

I was going to have to watch my back.

She called to her companions, who released Io. Io rushed over to me. "Are you all right?"

My cheek felt bruised and I reached up to my lip, realizing that it had been split open and was bleeding.

I had honestly believed that once I reached the temple of the goddess, I would be safe.

That it would be a sanctuary.

I had never once considered the danger that waited here for me.

CHAPTER TWENTY-SIX

Io had to repeat her question. "Lia, are you all right?"

"I've had worse," I said as I sat up, spitting blood out of my mouth.

Daphne joined us, peering down at me.

"This is Daphne," Io offered unnecessarily, and it was easy to hear the admiration in her tone.

"We've met," I said and hoped that I was disguising my bitterness.

But apparently I wasn't doing a very good job of it. Daphne said, "Just so you know, I didn't agree with what Theano wanted to do. You made it here and have earned the right to serve the goddess alongside the rest of us, no matter where you come from."

That did mollify me slightly and I felt some of my anger toward her slipping away.

Then Daphne turned toward Io and said, "Shouldn't you be in the temple by now?"

Io's eyes went wide and she again glanced up at the sun. "Yes! I lost track of the time."

Daphne gave her a kind smile. "You often do. Hurry along!"

"Come on," Io said and again offered me her hand to help me up, but I didn't need it. I'd only been punched a few times. I was fine and got up on my own.

We walked through the garden and Io shut the gate behind us. As we went along the path toward the temple, she said, "You know what Artemisia said about the maidens being cut up? That was a lie."

I was glad to have it confirmed because my mind had created such gory, horrific images.

"She only said it to hurt you," she added.

"Who is Artemisia?" I asked, feeling like there was more to the story that I wasn't aware of.

Io turned her gaze away, as if to confirm my suspicions. "She has been here for a few years. They say that she killed six girls during her race to join the temple."

"Is that typical?" I asked, horrified.

"No. I know of no other priestess who eliminated fellow racers, even though the law allows for it."

Why slaughter people if you didn't have to? A pit started forming in my stomach. Artemisia was definitely dangerous and I was going to do my best to steer clear of her.

I did not intend to end up as one of her victims.

We entered the main room of the temple, the one I had dropped into five nights ago. I glanced up at the ceiling, but the hole had already been repaired.

As if it had never happened.

And I was sure that there were people in this temple who wished for exactly that—that I'd never joined them.

Io led me over to a back staircase. It was located in exactly the same spot as the one in the Locrian temple and my heartbeat sped up.

The goddess statue should be downstairs. This could be it. I would see if she had the eye and then it would just be a matter of planning how to grab it and escape without alerting anyone.

But we didn't go down. "Wait here," Io said, and she opened a door to a room I hadn't noticed before. I reached out to touch the wall closest to me. There was no question that it had been built from Pyronean marble. It was a pure, translucent white with a fine grain and sparkling veins of silver.

Io returned with three girls behind her. Two of them were obviously related. They were nearly as tall as me and had dark brown skin with dark brown, braided hair that reached down to their waists. One had ribbons intertwined with some of her braids.

The third girl had medium brown skin and black hair that looked so much like Quynh's I felt my heart twist in pain.

All three were in the same pale green tunic that Io wore and looked to be close in age to me. Eighteen, nineteen maybe.

"This way. Maia is waiting for us," Io said, and I was surprised that she wasn't going to make an introduction. I wondered if I should, but all four of them went down the stairs. I sucked in a deep breath and followed.

"Who is Maia?" I asked from the back and Io stopped, letting the other three pass her while she waited for me to catch up.

"She's been here for ten years. Maia is our instructor and mentor and is so kind. Much kinder than Theano." Her eyebrows shot up her forehead, as if she'd only just realized what she'd admitted. "I shouldn't have said that."

One of the girls with braids shook her head. "You should always speak the truth. And that is the truth."

I wanted to ask what was happening but got the impression that I was about to find out.

We entered the lower room, and again, I recognized the woman waiting for us by the goddess. She had been the third person with Theano the night I'd come to the temple. The one who had gone from the room to find people to get my tunic and bring in a razor.

I reached up to feel my stubble again and tried to tamp down the anger welling up inside me.

Stupid girl! Look around you! Stop focusing on your petty grievances and search for the eye!

The room was lit by torches that hung from sconces. The walls were constructed from the same Pyronean marble, and in the center of it was the statue of the goddess, although unlike the one in Locris, it was intact and at least ten feet high.

The statue stood in a pool of dark, iridescent oil, and the colors of the rainbow on the surface seemed to shift and bend under the torchlight.

Then I noticed that the goddess was veiled with a cloth, like the high priestess. Her body was turned toward the east.

I couldn't see her face.

So I took a step forward. If I stood on my tiptoes, I could reach the veil and lift it up to check.

But Io's hand went onto my upper arm, holding me back. "You're not allowed to approach the goddess yet," she said. "That won't happen until much later."

How much later? I didn't have time to wait.

Maia had a bag in her hands and smiled at us. "Welcome, everyone. And a special welcome to you . . ." She let her voice trail off as she glanced at Io.

"This is Lia," Io said.

"Lia. I'm glad to meet you."

It seemed inappropriate to acknowledge, as I had with Daphne, that we had already met.

Then she said, "I'm Maia. Would you all follow me?"

She took us to a spot that faced the goddess but was still a good distance from her. I wondered what the goddess might do if I got closer to her statue.

Because that was going to happen. I just had to hope she wouldn't call a lightning bolt down on me or something equally terrible.

Maia gave everyone instructions on where to sit. The other four girls formed a square, each sitting at a corner, and Maia told me to sit in the middle.

"As it is the fifth day since Lia's arrival, this is the time when you will take your vows. Your sisters are going to bear witness, to be able to testify that you have become a true part of those who serve the goddess."

Four witnesses seemed unnecessary, but I held my tongue.

There was a small wooden table in the corner and Maia retrieved it, putting her bag on top of it. She undid the knot and opened the bag, taking out items and placing them on the table. She pulled out some logs of wood and I noticed for the first time that there was a firepit in the floor next to where she stood. She stacked the logs and then covered them in some kind of liquid so that when she took a stone and flint to them, a fire immediately roared to life, lighting up every dark corner.

There was also a small brazier on the table that she lit with a stick she took from the fire, and the room filled with the scent of irises.

Once that was finished, she faced me.

"Lia, here in the presence of the goddess, you must take vows. Vows that you will always keep or face her divine wrath and punishment."

My country was already suffering from her last divine wrath and punishment, and I had no desire to risk further destruction.

I was concerned, though, about taking vows. They were very serious things, and one did not enter into them lightly. Perhaps if I hadn't lost those five days, I could have spent them searching for the eye, maybe even found it and been on my way back home before reaching this point.

Where I would take vows and make promises.

I let out a deep breath, knowing there was no choice. I would have to agree to whatever they asked of me so that I could stay. I'd given up so much to be here and I had no intention of returning home empty-handed.

Maia continued, "The first vow that you must take is a promise to serve the goddess all of your days, to do her bidding and obey her laws and commandments. Do you swear to do this?"

Everyone was looking at me and I wasn't sure how I was supposed to respond. Io leaned forward and whispered, "Say, 'Yes, I swear it.'"

"Yes, I swear it," I repeated, and Maia looked satisfied.

"You must also vow to protect this temple and all of your sisters. Do you swear to do this?"

That seemed simple enough. "Yes, I swear it."

I wondered if Artemisia had taken the same vows as me, but then remembered that I hadn't yet been an acolyte when she'd attacked me, so she was probably technically clear from breaking that oath.

"And the last vow is a vow of celibacy. You must swear to never have sexual intercourse. You will never give your devotion to another—not a spouse, nor a child. You must devote your entire heart and body to the goddess. Do you swear to do this?"

This was the one that made me falter and my heart drop down to my toes, to reconsider what I was doing. If I promised this, it meant I would never be a mother. Would never marry, never have a love of my own or a companion by my side.

I would always be alone.

Which was not the future I had pictured for myself. I had always imagined that I would get married and have children. I didn't realize how much I'd hoped for that until someone said I wasn't allowed to have it.

But if it meant that I would save all of Locris . . . it was an acceptable sacrifice.

One for many.

"Yes, I swear it," I said, but the words felt difficult to get out.

"Come forward and bind your words with your body," Maia said, and my first instinct was to run, not knowing what she meant by it, but I had already proven to myself that I could withstand a great deal of pain. I got to my feet and stood in a spot close to her and the fire.

Maia held up a dagger and it glinted in the firelight. "When the earth began, the goddess cut her palm with her golden sword and from the drops of her blood came all the plants, all the trees, the rocky, desolate ground turning fertile. So too we cut our palms to make our vows. We bond our words by blood, by life."

Then she set down the dagger and took a large fresh leaf and a small glass container and lifted them up. She poured the contents of the container onto the leaf. It was thick and came out slowly. "We use the sap of a tree, the goddess's lifeblood, sweet and sustaining, to symbolize how she blesses these vows, and seals her words with her own blood."

When she had put enough sap on the leaf, she put the container back and kept the leaf up, careful not to spill. "The leaf is the symbol of the goddess because the leaf symbolizes all that is good about her—fertility, hope, growth, rebirth, life, abundance, peace, revival."

Maia put the leaf back onto the table and took the dagger again, reaching for my hand. I gave it to her and she held my palm up and quickly sliced along the surface, causing blood to gush up.

"Let your blood drip onto the leaf, mixing with the blood of the goddess."

I did as she instructed, turning my hand so that the drops would fall onto the sap on top of the leaf.

Maia picked up something else and it took me a moment to realize that it was one of the braids that they'd shaved from my head. She used the dagger to cut off a piece and gave it to me.

"Place your hair onto the blood and throw the leaf into the fire. That will seal your words, your blood, your vows, to the goddess as an offering. You must promise in your mind to never break these vows."

There was only a moment of hesitation as I considered what I was promising. There was nothing in any of my vows that would prevent me from traveling back to Locris. I would serve the goddess by restoring the land she'd abandoned, reinstating the worship of her there. I didn't have to live in this temple to follow her.

I threw everything onto the fire and watched as the edges of the leaf caught fire and began to burn, and the room filled with the smell of a strange mixture of sweetness and burning hair. Smoke rose from the leaf.

I promise to keep these vows, I thought.

"The goddess accepts your offering and now you are bound to her, as she is bound to you."

An unmistakable soft whisper somehow thundered inside me.

Euthalia.

I glanced around, wondering if anyone else had heard it, but nobody reacted.

And I should have felt nervous about a goddess calling my name, but I was filled with a strange kind of peace and comfort. I let that wash over me, let it lessen the overwhelming emotional pain I'd felt since I'd woken up today.

I also felt love. A kind of love I'd never experienced before. As if I were precious and important. Cared for. I put my hand over my chest and closed my eyes.

The goddess knew me. She offered me her protection and love. Those words were not spoken, but I felt them all the same.

I knew that I could never break the vows I'd just made.

We stood there quietly for several minutes, until I finally asked, "Is that it?"

Maia smiled broadly at me. "No. There is more."

CHAPTER
TWENTY-SEVEN

What more could there be?

"You are about to join a special sisterhood," Maia said, and I was confused. Wasn't that what I'd just done? "Please retake your seat."

I walked back over to the center of the square and sat down again.

"Five is a special number to the goddess. There are five elements, earth, water, air, fire, and aether; there are five fingers on our hands, five toes on our feet; your head, arms, and legs are five limbs; we have five senses, touch, sight, hearing, smell, and taste, which we use to experience life and all the blessings the goddess gives us."

And there were five acolytes.

"This is why you take your vows on the fifth day after your arrival. And your new sisters have been waiting for you so that you could form an adelphia."

At my quizzical expression Maia explained, "Your adelphia is made up of five sisters. It is an even higher bond and deeper vow than the one you share with other acolytes and priestesses of the temple. Your adelphia will perform your religious ceremonies together, learn together, train together. You are required to provide protection to one another, and you are legally and spiritually bound as a unit. Do you all agree to join as an adelphia?"

I said yes along with the others. Again this did not feel like something I could disagree with—it seemed that it was necessary in order for me to stay at the temple. I had already made so many vows, what was one more?

If I had to put on an act and pretend to belong, to be a sister in their adelphia, then it's what I would do.

"Step forward." Maia took out more leaves, more sap, and handed me another chunk of hair from my braid. The other girls all cut a lock from their own hair and placed it on the leaf in front of them. Maia passed the dagger around and we each cut our palms to put blood on our leaves. I winced as I reopened the slash Maia had made earlier.

"Grab your sister's wrist with your cut palm," Maia said. I reached out for Io's wrist and she gave me a brief smile. She took the arm of the dark-haired woman next to her and the two others did the same, one of them holding on to me. We were in a tight circle, our bodies pressed together.

Maia said, "This is your sacred sisterhood, your adelphia. You are bonded by blood, by life, willing to sacrifice your own to save your sisters'. Where one goes, so go the others. This bond is never to be broken, even in death. Do you swear this?"

It struck me as a bit silly that I didn't even know the names of most of the women in this circle, but I was about to promise to lay down my life for theirs.

"Yes, I swear it," we all said.

"Place your leaves in the fire to seal your vows."

We released one another and took turns putting our leaves, blood, and hair into the fire. I wasn't sure if it was only my imagination, but as my leaf went in, it seemed to turn the flames around it green.

That humming, buzzing feeling I'd had in the flower garden returned and my body felt light, as if I could float away.

"Go back to your dormitory and get cleaned up," Maia said after we stood there for a couple of minutes in silence, me trying to figure out what was happening, why I'd been experiencing so many strange sensations ever since the ceremony had begun.

Then she turned her gaze on me and smiled so kindly that I could see why Io liked her. "Lia, I know this was probably quite a bit to take in. Usually acolytes have several days to prepare before the vow ceremony and you didn't get that opportunity."

"In my own way I've been preparing for this for a long time," I told her.

"It is customary after an adelphia ceremony for the sisterhood to eat alone in private, so dinner will be brought to you in your room tonight. It is important for you to get to know each other since you haven't had that chance yet. You're a special kind of sister to one another now."

The other girls headed for the stairs and I turned to take in the goddess one last time. I would have to come back here the first chance I got to see if she had the eye.

"Do you need anything else?" Maia asked and I shook my head, worried that my lingering might have aroused her suspicion. "Then enjoy your meal and get some rest. Tomorrow, the hard part begins."

I wanted to ask her what she meant by that, but she'd turned her back to me to put out the fire. I headed up the stairs to find Io hanging back, waiting for me. She didn't say anything until we were outside the temple.

"Did you hear the goddess speak to you?" she asked in a low voice.

"What do you mean?"

She clasped her hands together. "Did she call your name?"

"I think so." Either that or I had imagined it.

"Sometimes it's hard to tell if she's speaking to you or if it's your own inner voice," she observed. "I'm glad it happened to you, though. It usually does, but not always."

I had become accustomed to hearing voices of my own making in my head, usually Demaratus's, so it probably was easier for me to distinguish. If the goddess did call me by name, what did that mean?

Io was making it sound as if it were something every woman here had experienced, so it must have meant that it wasn't that special.

Even though I hadn't been able to compare my experience to anyone else's, it felt like it was different. Like the feelings I'd had, the connection I'd felt, the strange things I'd heard and seen, were unique. I'd always believed in the goddess, in the ability of an object she'd blessed being able to restore Locris, and it was a relief to discover that it all seemed to be true.

We passed by the courtyard, still filled with women asking the goddess for favors. Something struck me—I'd just sworn an oath of celibacy. "Didn't you say earlier that the goddess oversees marriage and birth?" I asked Io.

"Yes."

"Then why did I take a vow not to do those things?"

"Because we need to keep our focus on the goddess, to serve her without giving our attention and devotion to another," she said.

It echoed what Maia had said earlier, but it didn't make sense to me, and I'd never liked things that didn't make sense.

I observed the other priestesses and acolytes as we walked by them. I asked, "Is everyone here in an adelphia?"

"Yes, and it's grouped by arrival date. We had to wait for you to be our fifth. There are hundreds of adelphias here. A larger sisterhood comprised of tiny sisterhoods. Like one tree that helps make a forest."

"I've never seen a forest." I'd seen many trees since I'd arrived, but not any clumped together.

"I'll take you the next time I go to the orchard," she offered. "It's similar."

"Thank you." I paused and then said, "So that means even Artemisia is in an adelphia."

She nodded. "And I can't imagine that it would be very pleasant, but we're fortunate. I promise you will like everyone in our group."

Her using the word "promise" made me think of my vows again and how the oath I'd taken didn't match up to the women of Troas in the temple courtyard seeking the goddess's favor in marriage and giving birth. "What happens to the priestesses who break their vows of celibacy?"

Io playfully nudged me with her elbow. "Why? Is there someone you want to break it with?"

Jason's face flashed in my mind, but I pushed the image away. "No. I was only curious."

"I've heard they bury the woman alive. And if the goddess chooses to save her, she can."

My chest constricted and I had to put a hand over my stomach. Being buried alive—I had to imagine that it was like drowning, something that had always scared me ever since I was a little girl.

When we reached our room, a table covered in food had been set up in the middle, along with five chairs. The aroma was incredible and as I walked around taking in all the different kinds of dishes, I wondered if this was a special occasion or if this was how they ate all the time.

"Before we eat, should we introduce ourselves to Lia?" Io asked.

"That might be good, given that we are now bound together by blood," I said, and the others laughed.

"I'm Zalira," one of the girls with braids said.

"And I'm Ahyana. You might have already guessed that I'm Zalira's sister. Well, we're all sisters, but she's my sister by birth." Another fact I'd already guessed. Ahyana was the one who had ribbons intertwined with her braids. Their faces were very similar—they had the same large brown eyes, matching high cheekbones.

"And that's Suri," Io said, pointing to the girl who had hair like Quynh's. Suri nodded, but she didn't say anything. Her eyes were nearly black they were so dark, and I noticed some tattoos around the edge of her tunic's neckline.

There was a flapping sound, and then a bird with midnight-colored feathers hopped onto the windowsill and squawked.

"That's Kunguru," Ahyana said. She held her finger out and he flew over, landing on it. When she lifted her hand, he rubbed his head against her cheek. "He knew it was dinnertime. He's a greedy little monster."

There was nothing but pure affection in her voice. She gave him a piece of bread that he snatched and ate so quickly I was impressed.

"She has a literal army of ravens," Zalira told me in a conspiratorial tone. "They're excellent thieves."

That was interesting. I was about to ask her to explain when she added, "It's a good thing he arrived when he did. It's about to start raining."

I looked out the window, and even though the sun had started to set, I could see that there wasn't a cloud in the sky.

But not a moment later, thunder boomed, making the plates on our table slightly rattle. It was a few seconds more before the rain began to pour down.

"How did you know?" I asked, incredulous.

"Zalira always knows when it's about to rain," Ahyana said.

Before I could ask her to explain, Io said, "Should we sit?"

The others pulled their chairs out, the wood scraping against the stone. I did the same. Io stayed at the head of the table, while we took the other four spots. I was seated across from the sisters and Suri was on my right.

"I'll say the prayer." Io held her arms out, pointing them down toward the ground. They all bowed their heads and after a moment I did the same.

She began to speak. "We greet you, great earth goddess, and beg you to hear us. You have listened in the past as we have prayed, and now we thank you for this food and for all the bounty that you provide. We thank you for the opportunity to serve and ask that you bless all of our endeavors and accept them. We eagerly await the day when your savior will appear to protect all of Ilion. We will remember you in words and actions."

Then each of the women took the cup in front of her and poured some of the wine onto the ground. Flummoxed, I did the same.

"We pour out a bit of our wine to the goddess as a small gift," Zalira said by way of explanation.

There was so much I didn't know. I'd never been part of a prayer before. Did they work? Was that how I was supposed to speak to the goddess? Should I pray and ask for her help with my plan? Would that be all right, or would she find it offensive that I wanted to undo the punishment that Locris was under?

Did she already know about my plans?

Or would I have to tell her?

Ahyana was seated directly across from me and she picked up a wooden platter with a flatbread on it that had a light covering of sea salt.

"You're the newest member of the sisterhood, so you should be served first," she said. Kunguru was perched on the back of her chair, next to her shoulder, and he cawed, as if he agreed.

There was no way any of them would understand what it would mean for me to have this meal with them. "Where I'm from, when you eat together, we call it sharing salt with one another."

It was a stronger promise to me than the vows I'd made earlier. This would be taking a quiet oath that carried weight among my people.

It meant these members of my adelphia would be under my protection, and that I would come to their aid whenever they called. I was pledged to them.

And I would never turn against them.

Understanding lit up Ahyana's eyes, as if she knew what it meant without me explaining. "Then would you like some bread?"

There would be no turning back from this, no technicalities or loopholes to release me from this bond. I took a deep breath.

"Yes," I said, and accepted the food she offered me.

CHAPTER TWENTY-EIGHT

"What is Locris like?" Zalira asked and I did my best to explain without giving away too much about my past. I couldn't let them know that I was a princess—I would be thrown out of the temple.

"As you might imagine. Dusty, desolate. Devoid of plants, most insects, and animals. We have to import everything we need." I didn't tell them how little hope we had there, how we were holding on without any relief in sight.

"I can't even picture it," Io said, shaking her head. "To live without flowers and trees? I'm not certain I could do it."

Now that I had been here, I didn't think I'd be able to return to that life, either. How could I accept such a barren wasteland when I had seen the most incredible green and vibrant beauty firsthand? I had to succeed so that Locris could look like Ilion again, as it was meant to.

"What about your family?" Ahyana asked.

I took some of the chicken from the tray she offered me. "Fairly typical. Parents, siblings."

"How many?" Io asked.

"Parents? Just the two."

She smiled at my joke. "Siblings."

My throat closed in on me as tears burned behind my eyes. Regardless of the promises we'd all made each other, I wasn't ready to share this part of myself yet. "I only have one sister still alive."

That caused a hush to fall over the table. I could see from their expressions that they wanted to question me about it, but they didn't.

"It's just Ahyana and me now," Zalira said. "Both of our parents died."

"My mother died when I was young and my father remarried and so now I have too many half brothers," Io chimed in. "More than any one woman should be forced to endure."

That made me smile slightly.

"Is it all right if I speak for you?" Io asked Suri, and she nodded. "From what I understand Suri is an only child and an orphan."

I wondered why Suri didn't say so herself, but I sensed that I shouldn't ask. Maybe it was something I could speak to Io about later. I didn't think she'd have any problem sharing that story with me.

"Do you have any birthmarks?" Io asked, interrupting my thoughts.

That was an odd question. "No. Do you?"

"I don't," she said with a sigh full of regret. "None of us do."

Why did birthmarks matter? Maybe they were special in Ilion.

"What is your father's profession?" Ahyana asked me.

I paused. I probably should have spent time coming up with a backstory. Demaratus had spoken to us about how important spies were in wars and that in order to move freely among the enemy, you had to have your lies all sorted. He'd said that sticking as close to the truth as possible would make that easier.

"My father was a magistrate." That seemed like a good enough answer. "What about you?"

"Our father was a trader from Alodia."

"Alodia?" I repeated, hurrying to swallow the food in my mouth as quickly as possible so that I could speak. "Where they have stone pyramids, the Great Library, and elephants?"

Demaratus had traveled to Alodia as a young man and had once tried to draw a picture in the dirt to show me what elephants looked like. I'd laughed so hard he'd erased the entire thing out of frustration. Even his description had sounded made-up. A creature with a snake on its face that it used like an arm, larger than a man, with massive ears and ivory swords attached to its mouth.

Zalira nodded. "Yes, but we've never been. Our father traveled from Alodia to Ilion to trade gold and papyrus, until he took one look at our Ilionian mother and fell in love."

Ahyana sighed happily, as if this were a memory for her instead of something she'd been told. "They married right away and had Zalira a year later, me a year after that. My father settled down here and opened a shop near the docks. We were so happy."

But then her face fell. "Our mother passed away from a fever when I was twelve. And two years later, our father followed her to the underworld."

"Our mother's brother was supposed to take custody of us, but he did not. He gave us to an orphanage and kept all our parents' possessions. Our birthright," Zalira said, sounding furious. A boom of thunder accompanied her anger. "And we had no recourse, no way to stop it from happening."

"The orphanage was given two obols a day to care for us by the government, but we weren't fed. That was when I met Kunguru. He started bringing us food and then money. I always told him to only take from the rich, but I don't know if he listened." Ahyana pet the top of her raven's head and he closed his eyes. "He and his family took care of us. And then when I turned eighteen and we were going to be put out of the orphanage with no money, no prospects, nowhere to live, Zalira and I decided to race so that we could join the temple."

"No one will ever be able to decide our fates again except for us," her sister said. A bolt of lightning streaked across the sky, lighting the room so brightly that it was almost like daytime.

"My stepmother planned on marrying me off," Io said. "To a disgusting man old enough to be my grandfather. She wanted me out of the way and said it was my duty to obey her." It was the first time I'd heard her sound bitter. "But it had always been my dream to serve in the temple and I decided to do that instead."

There was a mischievous look in her eyes and I remembered her telling me about how she had cheated to get her position. Did the other girls know?

"By cheating," Ahyana added with a laugh, answering my question.

It seemed that Io really wasn't the sort of person who could keep a secret. I would need to remember that.

"Suri made it on her own merit," Io said. "She is one of the fastest and strongest people I know. There is no one better at finding lost items than her and you can't ask for a better friend. But people here don't always treat her kindly."

"Why not?" I felt a bit guilty speaking about Suri as if she weren't even in the room, but she didn't seem to mind.

"She's Sasanian."

I glanced at Suri's right wrist and saw the edges of the same tattoo that Mahtab, the hetaera who had helped me, bore. It wasn't clear initially because Suri had wrapped lengths of cloth on her arms, covering them.

A Sasanian fashion?

"Why does anyone care?" I asked. "That war took place hundreds of years ago."

The irony that I was the one to ask was not lost on me—I was hated for something that had happened even further back than that.

"Most don't, but there are some that still do," Io said.

Artemisia was probably one of the ones who cared.

"You came here all the way from Sasania?" I asked Suri, but she shook her head.

"There's a neighborhood in Troas with a large Sasanian population," Io said.

I took a sip of my wine. It was diluted, but it was still sweet and delicious. I felt warm inside, which I'd initially blamed on my drink. I realized that it had nothing to do with the alcohol, but the company I was keeping.

Demaratus had told me once that dogs who were fed together formed bonds and became attached to one another, which was why I'd always had breakfast and lunch with my regiment.

The same thing had already started to happen here.

Despite my resolution to keep these women at arm's length, to play along with whatever the priestesses demanded, to do as they wanted so that I could get my hands on the eye of the goddess, I found myself not wanting to shut out my adelphia.

They would understand what you're doing, a voice whispered inside me, and this time it sounded like my mother. *They might even help you.*

It could be true. They had all suffered the loss of loved ones, had been put into impossible situations where racing for the temple had been their only option, and they believed in the goddess and the old stories. I realized that I had more in common with them than almost everyone else from my former life.

As the evening progressed, I discovered that my adelphia were funny and kind and warm and welcoming. I felt included. Like I was already part of their sisterhood, despite the fact that I'd only just met them. Being with them felt like coming home.

That concerned me.

I couldn't afford to get too close to them. Maybe they'd help me, or maybe they'd actively try to stop me if they knew what I was after.

Our dinner continued and we exchanged more stories about our lives. I was careful to steer away from any possibly identifying information and thankfully no one seemed to notice that my answers were a bit vague.

Their personalities became clearer as the evening went on. Ahyana was playful and mischievous with an irrepressible and generous spirit. Her raven clearly adored her. Zalira was protective and fierce, with a gentle and kind heart. Despite her toughness on the outside, it was obvious that she was soft as a down pillow inside.

Suri was a bit harder to get to know because she didn't talk, but she smiled and nodded or shook her head throughout the meal. I sensed strength and that she was a steadying, calming influence. It was obvious the other women cared a great deal about her, and I found myself wanting to know more.

I'd never been able to resist a mystery.

Io had been so completely herself from the first moment I met her that it felt like there wasn't anything new to discover about her. She was talkative and happy, positive and determined to do what was right. She was dedicated in her service to the goddess and to her sisters, attentive and tuned in to everyone's needs.

I shouldn't have been feeling this way. I needed to keep my defensive walls intact. These women were supposed to be my enemies. They were Ilionian in whole or in part. They had grown up here—this was their land, their customs, their people, their goddess.

But somehow they didn't feel like enemies and were quickly becoming new friends.

There was a lot of laughter and teasing around the table. I'd forgotten what that was like. My brother's death had cast a permanent pall over our family and now with Quynh—

I realized that a couple of hours had passed and I hadn't thought of Quynh once in that entire time.

At first I felt guilty, until I reminded myself that I had been down this path before and knew that this was the way of grief—that it would come and go in waves, surprising with its overwhelming intensity in a moment where you thought yourself past it, imagined you'd become accustomed to the constant pain. Walking along the shore as the water harmlessly lapped at your feet until a wave came along that knocked you over and dragged you back into the ocean, drowning you in sorrow.

But even when you made it back to shore, that grief would continue to flow and ebb and there would be moments where you felt like your old self again.

Like tonight.

"Are you all right?" Io asked. I nodded but a silence descended over the table.

As if they knew I wasn't telling the truth.

Zalira exchanged a glance with Ahyana and then asked, "How did you survive the race?"

What could I share with them? How I'd cheated and bribed an official to make certain that I'd be selected? That I'd trained and prepared for the event? I had to keep my true background quiet.

"There was someone in my life who used to be a great warrior. He helped to train me in case I was chosen," I finally said. There were Ilionian men I'd only injured who would be able to tell the tale of the Locrian maiden who had fought back. I couldn't keep that part a secret.

And although I'd never had a problem lying to people before, the words felt heavy on my tongue, like they were burning on the way out.

I didn't want to lie to them. I felt a compulsion to confess everything.

"Did you have to fight?" Ahyana asked.

"Yes."

"And won." Zalira nodded with satisfaction, like she was proud of me.

"Wasn't there another maiden?" Io looked at me sympathetically, as if she somehow already knew that this would be the hardest question for me.

To my horror, tears began to spill down my face. I did my best to get myself under control, but I couldn't. "My best friend. My sister. Quynh. She sacrificed herself so that I could live."

Those words knocked down a wall inside me, letting all my sorrow and heartache pour out. Great heaving sobs racked my body and I crossed my arms over my chest, like I could stop it from happening.

My throat ached, my chest burned, my heart broke.

The pain was nearly unbearable.

Io got to me first and wrapped her arms around me. "Sometimes it has to hurt before it can heal," she said.

I felt more arms until all my adelphia stood in a circle around me, protecting me as I cried my pain and anger out.

And while I wanted to blame the wine, I knew that wasn't the reason that I could finally cry.

It was because for the first time since I'd stepped foot onto the *Nikos*, I felt safe.

211

CHAPTER
TWENTY-NINE

I was asleep until I felt a large, warm hand on my shoulder, turning me over. I reached under my pillow, my fingers wrapping around the handle of my sword. My eyes flew open as I brought my weapon up.

"Jason?" I asked, shocked, my voice still sleepy.

"Did you miss me?" he asked, his voice low and intoxicating. He took my xiphos from me in one swift, easy movement, letting it fall to the floor. His gaze was on mine and it was somehow both lazy and predatory, making me shiver in response.

"You can't be here," I hissed at him, but he just smiled, and somehow my concern and anger instantly faded away.

"You're the one in my bedroom," he said, and I sat up to look around.

He was right. We were not in the room I now shared with four other people, but how had I come to be in Jason's bedroom? I didn't know where he lived.

Before I could ask, he leaned down and his mouth was on mine, urgent and needy, and I immediately melted into his kiss. His feverish passion pulsed through my body so that even my toes were aching with want.

He parted my lips with his so that his kiss was all I could taste, all I could feel, all I could think about. He set a smooth, insistent, fiery rhythm that had me gasping against him, reaching up to pull him down to me.

With a low growl of pleasure, he broke off the kiss and I softly protested. He knelt on the floor in front of me, grabbing the backs of my knees and pulling me against him, hard. I wrapped my legs around him, trapping him right where I wanted him.

He knotted his fingers in my hair. "So beautiful, so soft," he whispered against my mouth before capturing it again, sweeping me into the undertow of his desperate fervor.

His kisses burned my lips, branding them like hot coals.

Lightning flashed outside his window, but there was a bolt of lightning living inside me. The energy of it crackled, and every nerve ending inside me felt alive, sparking with heat. It overwhelmed my heart, making it pulse unevenly in my chest.

I was flushed with a thick and heavy desire that dulled my ability to think. His clever fingers ran up and down my bare calves, sending waves of heat skating across my skin. The butterflies I'd seen in the flower garden had now taken up residence in my stomach, and their wings fluttered and flapped, hollowing me out.

I wanted him so much.

His lips moved from my mouth to the column of my throat and I let out a sigh of pleasure.

"Why won't you give in?" he asked, and the desire in his voice burned a destructive path through me, intent on getting me to surrender.

"I took a vow."

"Vows are made to be broken," he said, and I shook my head hard. No.

But my hands were still on the back of his head, holding him in place while he continued to kiss my neck.

"When I give my word, I mean it," I breathed.

Almost like a punishment, he wrenched his mouth away from mine. He gazed deep into my eyes.

"As do I. And I give you my word that you will never know pleasure like you would with me."

My insides quivered at his words, my core melting, my heart pounding hard against my chest, as if it meant to break free and give itself to him.

I believed him.

Without taking his eyes from mine, he began to push the hem of my tunic up my legs, exposing more of my skin, until he had it all the way to the tops of my thighs. I held my breath as his strong, warm fingers pressed into the skin there and everything went up in flames.

He bent down and kissed the inside of my right knee, and all the bones in my legs turned to liquid.

"Lia, let me love you," he pleaded.

"I can't." But my words were weak. I didn't mean them and he could tell.

Because his mouth was back on my leg, working his way up my thigh, and I started panting. I didn't know what he intended to do, but I was desperate to find out.

"Tell me to stop." His clean-shaven face was soft against my inner thigh as he left hot, consuming kisses there. "Tell me to stop, and I will."

I couldn't have even told him my own name, let alone ordered him to stop. I had no more will left to resist him.

"Jason," I begged. His name I still remembered.

"Lia," he groaned my name into my sensitized skin and I dug my fingers into his scalp.

"Lia!"

My eyes opened and I saw Io standing over me with a silly grin on her face. In a loud whisper she asked, "Who is Jason?"

I felt my cheeks going up in flames and I pressed my hands over them. "How much did you hear?"

"Enough to know this Jason must be handsome and a very good kisser." Somehow her grin got even bigger.

I wanted to bury my face in my pillow. "He's someone I met back home." The last thing I should do was tell her that Jason was somewhere here in Ilion. I guessed that the teasing would be constant if I did so.

And I didn't even know if he was still in the city. He probably was back at sea.

"Is he worth getting buried alive for?" Io asked.

"No!"

"Shh," she said, putting a finger to her lips. "The other girls are still sleeping. You need to get up so that I can show you what your responsibilities will be in the morning."

"What time is it?"

"Just before dawn," she said. "I'll meet you out front when you're ready."

With a yawn, I nodded and sat up. I had intended to sneak out last night and go into the temple to check the statue of the goddess, but I'd been so exhausted that I had fallen asleep the moment I'd lain down.

The second floor of the dormitory had a special shared washroom for cleansing ourselves and toilets to use. Cold water came out of metal pipes in the wall when a handle was turned.

"Aqueducts," Io had said when I'd marveled over it, as if that explained everything.

After I relieved myself, I came into the main room to wash my teeth and face. My eyes ached and felt puffy from crying so much the night before. It had been cathartic, though. Cleansing.

As I thought of Quynh, I realized that the pain of losing her had subtly lessened. Instead of a continual feeling of being stabbed over and over again, it had become more like a dull ache. Always there, but more manageable now that I'd had the chance to grieve her loss.

I reached behind my neck, as if to brush my hair away, forgetting that it wasn't there.

Thinking of my long hair reminded me of the dream I'd woken up from and my cheeks turned hot again. I'd had many dreams before, but none this vivid or detailed. None that had ever felt like real life. As if I were really there, and it was all actually happening to me.

In that dream I'd had my old hair. Was that supposed to mean something? Or was it just that I couldn't picture myself any other way because I'd never seen myself with a shaved head?

I wished that we had mirrors so that I could properly take in my reflection, absorb my new physical appearance, but Io had said there were no mirrors at all in the temple because they encouraged vanity. "We're supposed to focus on the goddess and our sisters, not on ourselves."

It was a convenience I had taken for granted my entire life and now I missed it.

After I finished up, I found Io waiting for me just outside the main entrance to the dormitory, as she'd promised. She was holding two brooms and a large, empty pot, which she handed to me.

"We're going to the temple. Part of your duties will be to clean the first floor and the patio and steps near the front doors."

My pulse quickened. "What about the bottom floor? Do I clean that as well?"

She squashed my hope. "No, an older priestess takes care of that. You're not allowed down there. I haven't even been back to worship her yet—just my own vow ceremony and then the adelphia with you yesterday."

That hope surged back to life. Because despite her telling me that I couldn't go into the room where the goddess was, there was a reason why it was off-limits. Why keep acolytes out unless there was something important, valuable, on the statue?

Maybe there would be a chance to sneak down there today while Io was busy with something else and I could see for myself what was under that veil.

We stopped at the fountain in the courtyard and Io said, "After we sweep, we take this water and sprinkle it onto the ground, purifying our work."

In Locris that would have just led to a lot of mud. She handed me a pitcher and we both started drawing the water out, filling up the pot.

"So we have water on demand in our dormitories, but not the temple?" I asked.

"I suppose they want the acolytes to do things the old way, as they've always been done."

After the pot was mostly filled, we covered it with fresh vine leaves. Io held one of them up and smiled. "This is exactly what the symbol of the goddess looks like."

I nodded—I'd seen that particular motif all over the buildings since yesterday.

"We put the leaves on top of the water to keep it cool and to protect it from dust and dirt." She took one of the handles and I took the other and we carried it over to the steps.

"You start sweeping at the bottom, I'll start at the top," she said.

"Why are you the one showing me how to do everything?" I asked. "Weren't you the last one here before I arrived? Shouldn't someone with more experience be the one to teach me?"

"It has always fallen to the newest acolyte to teach the others. Zalira taught Suri and me when we arrived. If the race is run in a few months, you will be the one to show the newest member or members how to acclimate."

I wondered if I would even be here. I'd promised Kallisto I'd be home in six months.

"Last night . . ." Io's voice trailed off, and by the goddess, if she brought up Jason again I was going to dump that pot of water over her head. "You cried a lot."

Feeling immediately chastened for my unkind thought, I nodded. "I think I needed it."

"You've had to deal with a lot of difficult things."

She phrased it not as a question, but as a statement of fact.

"Yes," I agreed.

She was quiet for a little while, which seemed very unlike her. Then she said, "Have you ever seen a plant where part of it is dying?"

"Before I came to Ilion, I'd never seen a plant at all." I wasn't sure the olive tree in the palace or the flowers the life mage had briefly created counted.

I had a flash where I remembered kissing Jason against that tree, but I shoved it away.

"Sometimes you'll have a healthy plant where a stem or leaves have died. The plant's instinct is to divert all of its energy to restoring the lost parts, which inhibits its growth. And so, as the gardener, you have to cut those pieces away so that there can be new leaves, new flowers, new life. Sometimes you have to brush away the parts of your life that no longer serve you so that you can move forward."

There was a reason I'd resisted crying for so long. I wanted to hold on to those missing parts of myself, those loved ones who had been ripped away, my land that needed my help, the anger I had over how my nation had been treated. "I'm not sure I'm ready to do that."

She nodded, her face somber. "I understand. But I also know what it's like to be so caught up in bitterness and anger and sorrow that you miss out on the good things surrounding you. There can be a lot of joy waiting for you here. If you do what they ask and fulfill your obligations, this temple should be as much a sanctuary for you as it has been for the rest of us."

Io walked farther away, letting her words sink into my heart while she cleaned another part of the porch. I had a hard time imagining her being bitter or angry or sad. She was the opposite of that.

It was the same advice Demaratus had given me, just phrased differently. I needed to get a handle on my emotions, to pay attention to what was happening now, to behave with honor and follow the law—but with one marked difference.

The battle to save Locris wasn't over, so I couldn't leave the battlefield or my fellow soldiers behind.

CHAPTER THIRTY

Between the two of us we quickly cleaned the patio and the steps. She showed me how to sprinkle the water and I didn't protest that it seemed like a waste of time and did as she asked.

"Let's go inside," she said. We got the pot and carried it between us as we headed toward the massive bronze doors that had been closed to me the night of the race. I was about to ask her whether she had a key, but she pushed against the door and it easily swung open.

"Not locked?" I asked in surprise.

"These doors are never locked. There's no need for them to be."

Other than the statue downstairs that none of us were allowed to go near? "They were locked the night I arrived. I had to climb onto the roof and create a hole to get in."

The expressions shifted rapidly across her face. At first she was confused and then shocked. "That's not possible. They would never keep an acolyte out."

"They would a Locrian one. And they did."

For a second it seemed that I had overwhelmed Io and she appeared unsure as we walked into the temple's main room.

"Did you really make a hole in the roof to get inside?" she asked, her eyes flickering upward.

"Yes. If I hadn't, someone would have eventually killed me with an arrow."

She shuddered slightly. "I'm sorry you went through that. I abhor violence."

There was an older woman, probably close to my mother's age, standing next to the top of the stairs. Her sharp gaze followed us as we walked in. I noticed that a sword hung at her side.

"Is she making sure we do our chores?" I asked under my breath.

"No, she's not here for us." Io said it like it was foolish for me to even think it. "She's protecting the statue."

Excitement bubbled up inside me. There was only one reason to post a guard.

The eye had to be downstairs.

It was so frustrating to be this close but not able to do anything about it. A part of me fantasized about running past the guard, sprinting down the stairs, grabbing the eye, and being out of the temple complex before anyone could catch me.

But what if the eye wasn't there? I couldn't take the risk of breaking a rule that had been communicated to me multiple times and being expelled from the temple.

I would have to bide my time.

We put the pot on the ground. "I thought she was here just to keep an eye specifically on me."

I bit down a groan. Why had I used that as my phrasing? I might as well have painted my plan on my forehead where everyone could see it. My guilty conscience was getting the better of me.

"Why would she need to keep an eye on you?" Io asked, as oblivious as ever.

Grateful that she didn't have a devious mind, I said, "Because I'm Locrian."

"That doesn't matter." Io began brushing along the doorframe and little motes of dust danced in the early-morning sun, the beams shining through the open doors.

A pang of homesickness made my heart twist. I had seen the same thing every morning as I'd trekked over to the barracks, ready to begin my day. Dust bits sparkling in the light.

"Why don't you hate me?" I asked.

She stopped sweeping to stare at me in disbelief. "Why would I hate you?"

"As we've established, because I come from Locris."

"No Locrian has ever done anything to me," she said. "You can't help where you were born any more than I can, and either way, it doesn't matter. All that matters is who you are."

There was a lot that Io didn't know. "I might be a terrible person."

She smiled while shaking her head, then resumed sweeping. "You're not a terrible person, and before you object, I'm an excellent judge of character. You made it to the temple. That speaks to your determination, fortitude, and strength. Your ability to persevere. We already have a reason to admire you."

Io was including the rest of the adelphia in her statement, making me wonder if they'd spoken about me after I'd fallen asleep. "Or my terrible nature is the only thing that made it possible for me to get here."

"I don't believe that, and there's nothing you can say that will convince me otherwise." Her tone reminded me of Quynh, and how stubborn my sister could be about certain things.

Like forcing me to take her bracelet. I felt the outline of it in my pouch. I was grateful to still have this piece of her.

"Don't forget that you fought Artemisia to protect me. Again, that tells me you're a good person." She took a few more long, sure strokes with her broom before she added, "It's the sort of thing Suri would have done, had she been there."

Curiosity filled me and I found myself saying, "What happened to her?"

I understood that it was none of my business, but I really wanted to know. Suddenly some kind of tiny monster dropped down right in front of my face, hanging by an almost invisible thread. I yelped, preparing to swat it away.

"Don't!" Io called out, hurrying over. She reached up carefully and let the creature climb into her hand and I watched in horror as she carried it outside, putting it on the ground and letting it go.

"What was that?" I asked.

"A spider."

"Why does it have so many legs?" I demanded.

"It's just how the goddess made it," she said. "I don't know why some people are scared of spiders."

While she made it sound irrational, it didn't feel that way to me. That spider had been ugly and threatening and deserved to be swatted away. I hoped to never see one again. "Why did you let it go outside?"

"Because all life is sacred," she continued. "I serve in the temple because I want to help create and preserve life, not take it away."

"What if you didn't have a choice? What if someone you cared about was in danger?" Would she judge me for having done that? Look at me differently?

"Even then, I still don't think I could."

It was easy to make that kind of decision when it was purely theoretical and had never been tested. I swallowed my annoyance and went back to sweeping.

Io seemed to pick up on my shift in mood. "What were we talking about before? Suri?"

A petty part of me wanted to tell her we should just finish up our work, but my curiosity was too strong. "Yes."

"You already know that Suri and I ran at the same time. She was first and I came in right after her. She was covered in bruises, both her eyes blackened. At first I thought one of the other racers had done it to her, but the bruises weren't fresh. They were yellow and green, as if they'd happened weeks earlier."

I stopped what I was doing. "Someone hurt her?"

She nodded. "That's our guess. But I don't know anything other than that to share. Suri doesn't speak."

I'd noticed how quiet she was last night, and how Io had spoken for her, but I'd just assumed she was really shy and reserved. "Ever?"

"Never. I don't know if she can't or if she won't. I suspect the latter because I tried to communicate with her using signs, but she stopped me. We only know about her being an orphan because the orphanage reached out to the temple when she joined."

Bile rose in the back of my throat. How bad had things been for Suri that she didn't want to speak at all now—not with her voice or her hands? "That's terrible."

"It makes me glad that she's here. We have protection and sisterhood and freedom from the outside world. Once you're inside these walls, you are a servant of the goddess and safe. You become one of us. Even if you are a Locrian."

"Someone should tell Artemisia that," I said and Io laughed. Then she glanced at the open doors. "We should hurry. It's getting late and we still have a lot to do. I'm just so glad that starting tomorrow this will be your sole responsibility and I finally get to sleep in!"

"I am going to do this alone every day?" I asked. That might offer some interesting possibilities. There might not be a guard posted at the stairs every morning, allowing me to sneak down.

"Yes. It's always the job of the newest acolyte. When the sun rises to greet the goddess, it will be in a clean temple."

The statue was downstairs with no windows. I didn't understand how she would be able to "see" the sun, but figured it wasn't worth arguing about it.

It was also a good thing that Demaratus had insisted on early mornings for so long. I'd always preferred staying up late and rising midmorning, but his schedule hadn't allowed for it and my body had reset. Now I was accustomed to getting up early, so it shouldn't be too difficult.

When Io and I had come over to the main building, the temple complex had been almost completely empty. Early mornings might be my chance to explore without interruption. To test locks and doors, to uncover the location of the eye.

After we had swept everything up, we finished by sprinkling the floor with water. Then we poured the remaining water out in the courtyard. The city was slowly coming to life, as were the women of the temple.

"I'm supposed to take you to see Maia," Io said as she took the broom from me.

"More vows?"

"No," she said with a grin. "That part is done."

We entered the administration building and the first things I noticed were several musical brass horns hanging on hooks just inside the doorway. There was a stairway past the instruments and I wondered if it led up to Theano's office. Io went left and took me into a large room that looked as if it had once been a theater—we entered at the top and walked down the stairs. There were long stone benches for seating and a raised dais in the center of the bottom level.

The theater in Naryx was open air. I'd never seen one enclosed like this.

Maia waited for us with a happy smile. It was easy to see why Io had such an affinity for her—they seemed to be the same kind of person.

"Thank you for delivering Lia!" Maia said.

Io nodded. "I'll find you later."

She left and I gave Maia my full attention and told her, "I'm almost afraid to ask why you wanted to see me."

"There is nothing to worry about. Come, sit." She indicated two chairs facing one another and I sat in one of them.

Maia took the other and folded her hands in her lap. Her expression was open, and she seemed to be searching for the right words. "I understand that your religious education may be . . . lacking."

I wasn't going to tell her what I already knew, about the book my grandmother had entrusted to me. But there was truth to what she was saying.

"We know almost nothing of the goddess in Locris, other than she requires tribute." Not a complete lie.

Maia nodded. "That's what I suspected. You will have private lessons with me in the mornings after you sweep the temple floor so that I can help you to catch up. This will be necessary in your preparation to become a priestess. You cannot be responsible for the higher vows unless you have all the necessary knowledge."

"Higher vows?" I'd been joking with Io earlier. I hadn't seriously thought that there could be additional vows. "What more can I promise than I already have?"

"Oh, no. There's nothing else. It applies to the higher calling as a priestess, where you will have a new position and new responsibilities, such as teaching the acolytes, preparing clothing for the statue, washing the floor in her room—that sort of thing. It is the office itself that is higher. The promises you've already made remain the same but become more meaningful."

That was good. I didn't want to be backed into a corner where I would have to speak a promise that I wouldn't be able to keep.

"What do you do with an acolyte who can't say the vows?" I asked.

"Suri?" she correctly surmised. When I nodded she said, "The goddess knows the intent of our hearts. Suri promised in her heart, then sealed that promise with her blood and hair, just like everyone else."

Maia was saying the goddess could read minds. A strange, sickly flapping started in my stomach. If the intent of my heart was to steal and leave, did the goddess already know that? I had spoken my vows aloud, so would I be condemned for saying one thing while plotting another?

Should I try to explain myself to the goddess?

"It seems like something is troubling you," Maia said.

"I . . . I don't know how to talk to the goddess. To pray. Io did it last night before our meal."

"That's simple enough." She beamed at me, as if proud that I was taking our instruction seriously. "The first is that you must call on the goddess. You may mention how you have served or worshipped her before. You can thank her and petition her for things that you need. If you have made her an offering or sacrifice, you can remind her of that so she will look more favorably upon your request. And then you promise to remember her in your words and actions. But I think anything that you say out loud to her, with real intent, will make it through even if you don't follow the format."

I nodded.

She added, "The important thing to remember is that you must turn your will over to the goddess. Let her decide and take comfort in her wisdom."

"How will I know what she wants?" What if what I was going to do was contrary to her wishes?

"There are many ways. The high priestess can speak for her. Sometimes the goddess will speak words to you, but that is rare for most. Some priestesses and acolytes have reported the goddess communicating through their dreams—telling them things that we wouldn't hear when we're awake."

Since I'd gotten on that ship, my dreams had been primarily about Jason. Were those supposed to be messages? If so, what did they mean?

Or did they only represent a longing for something that I now knew I could never have?

CHAPTER
THIRTY-ONE

But given the vows both Maia and I had taken, it seemed inappropriate to ask her to interpret my dreams for me. Instead I asked if any of the priestesses had magic, even though I knew what the answer would be.

"Only men wield magic," Maia said.

Honestly, I had hoped that there would be one or two women at the temple who would be life mages. It would have made it much easier for me to find someone to bring back with me to Locris. I had no idea where the life mages were located in Troas or if they could be bribed.

Ignoring my disappointment, I asked, "Then why do only women serve in the temple?"

Discomfort flitted across her face and I wasn't sure why. Was it because she didn't have the answer, or was the answer the same as always—because of the crime Ajax the Locrian had committed?

"You should return to your room." She handed me a small bundle. "There's breakfast in there, so eat on your way back. Io will meet you there to show you where your classes will be."

"Classes?" I repeated. "Like a school?"

"This is so much more than school. I think there are going to be a lot of surprises for you today. Will you be able to find your way to the dormitory?"

I nodded because I had committed this place to memory during my tour with Io.

Maia promised to see me later, and I took the bundle she offered. Once I was outside the building, I opened it to find honeyed bars of dried fruit. This was like dessert in Locris, and they just served it as breakfast here. I didn't know if I would ever get used to having such a variety of food.

When I returned to my room, the door was slightly ajar and I heard the sound of a wooden stool being knocked over.

I pushed the door all the way open to find Suri alone. She was trying to put on one of her cloth bands, but I could see that it was slipping. Frustration was etched onto her face as it fell from her grasp and onto the floor.

Hurrying over, I picked up the band and held it out to her. "Can I help you?"

Suri looked panicked, hiding her bare right arm behind her body.

Something very important was happening in this moment, and I didn't know what it was. I let the bundle I carried drop onto her bed. "We're sisters now, remember? I will stay quiet if that is your wish."

Her indecision was obvious as she fidgeted for several moments before finally offering me her arm.

Old, deep scars covered all of her skin. "Did someone do this to you?" I demanded.

She shook her head.

"Are you a warrior? A soldier?" Did they have female warriors in Ilion?

Again, a no.

Understanding dawned on me as I realized that the scars were in a row. As if they'd been done methodically. Deliberately.

Suri had done this to herself and she hid it from everyone. That was why she wrapped her arms.

"Oh," I breathed. "You're a survivor."

The unshed tears in her eyes were bright as she nodded. I wished she could tell me who had hurt her so that I could track him down. I decided that every man in Ilion should be shoved into a bonfire.

I took the cloth band and helped wrap it around her arm, tying it off at the end. I could see that it had probably been very difficult for her to do on her own every day, having to use her nondominant hand to tie it shut. "If you ever need help with this again, I would be happy to do it."

Suri nodded and let her arm drop.

"Do the others know?" I asked.

No.

"I know it isn't my place to say anything, given that I just got here, but I think you could trust them with this. They wouldn't judge you. You don't have to cover up if you don't want to."

She pressed her lips together and looked down at the floor. My heart went out to her. Then I heard Demaratus's voice in my head telling me that they were trying to deceive me, to wear me down in order to get information, lure me in with a false sense of security by befriending me, but that was inane. Why would they? What information did I have that they would want? They had no reason to use me, because as far as they knew, I had nothing to offer them.

"They love you," I added. That much was obvious—how the four girls had already bonded to each other long before we'd taken vows as a group. "And I can see how much you care about them. I know that you would do anything to protect them."

Yes. Then she pointed a finger at me, as if questioning whether I would do the same.

My intent yesterday had been to use these girls if necessary to achieve my own ends. Betray them if I had to. But in a single day, everything had completely changed and I wasn't exactly sure why.

"I already have," I told her. I had defended Io when Artemisia verbally attacked her, and I would do it again. I would place myself in the line of danger for any member of my adelphia.

Satisfied, she nodded.

"Do you still do it?" I asked.

No.

That was good. I was glad she wasn't hurting herself any longer.

"I won't tell anyone unless you give me permission," I said.

Her face was very expressive and easy to read. Although she didn't say the words, it was obvious she was grateful.

"I'm here if you want to talk . . ." I let my voice trail off as I realized how strange my offer sounded. "Well, I suppose you won't want to talk things through."

A slight smile.

"But if you ever want someone to sit with you in silence, I'm here. And if you want someone to jabber at you relentlessly, I can go get Io."

She rewarded me with a real smile, the first I'd gotten from her since yesterday. It spread, lighting up all of her features.

I had gotten through to her. My plan would have worked. I could have worn them all down, convinced them to trust me, and then discarded them when I no longer needed them.

But that wasn't going to happen.

Again that feeling that I could trust them crashed into me.

Io entered the room. "Good morning, Suri and Lia! Did you enjoy your tutorial with Maia?"

She had a knapsack and dumped the contents onto her bed. Several scrolls fell out and one kept rolling right off the bed and over to my feet. I picked it up and turned it over and saw a wax seal with a leaf imprint on one side.

The symbol of the goddess.

Interesting. "What is this?"

Io held out her hand and I gave her back the scroll. "I've been promoted. Letter bearer. It's now my responsibility to collect the letters every morning from Theano and deliver them to the messenger in a few hours."

"Do you go into her office to get them?" I asked. Did I sound casual? Bored? It was what I was aiming for.

Because even if my instincts were pushing me to bring my sisters in on my plan, I couldn't do it. I couldn't risk being wrong and having one of them betray me out of loyalty to the temple.

"No. They're kept in a basket outside of her office."

Her words were at first disappointing, and then confusing. "Wait, Theano can read and write?" Wasn't that forbidden here?

"It's obviously necessary for the high priestess. She has to run the entire complex."

"Who taught her?"

Io shrugged. "She's been here a long time. She could have brought in a tutor to learn."

"How long has she been high priestess?"

"I'm not certain. I could ask." Io let out a little laugh. "Do you always question everything?"

"Yes. It's my nature."

She was still smiling as she told me, "You don't have to have all the answers."

"I'm afraid that I do."

Io was laughing at my reply as Zalira and Ahyana came into the room. Kunguru landed on the windowsill and announced his presence before flying over to settle on Ahyana's shoulder.

The others began to greet and chat with one another and I thought about the fact that Io was in charge of sending letters. I had no idea what information my parents had been given, what sorts of lies, half truths, and gossip had already reached the Locrian shore. Did they think both Quynh and I were alive? Both dead? Did they know that one of us had made it? Would they know which one?

I supposed that part didn't matter. They would be destroyed either way.

My heart ached so hard that I put a hand over my chest. Not only for the loss of my sister, but for the pain that the rest of my family was currently feeling.

And would continue to feel for a long time.

I wanted to get word to them that I had lived. That might bring them some comfort. But I had no idea how to do it.

Io's new position had initially made me think that maybe I could take advantage of it—sneak a letter in with the others.

But there would be too many risks there. Io might notice. I did not have wax or a seal—it would stand out.

And if it was addressed to the royal palace in Locris? I might as well paint a giant sign on the side of the temple announcing my lineage to the entire world.

Especially since Theano was the one who hired the messenger. It would be obvious where his loyalties would lie.

No, the best course of action for getting in touch with my parents would be to travel back to the docks and find a Locrian sailor that I could entrust with a message. Nothing could be written down where it might possibly be traced back to me.

"Do you ever go into the city?" I asked abruptly, interrupting the conversation where Ahyana and Zalira had been teasing Io about her new job.

"Why would we?" Ahyana asked. "It isn't safe."

"But you said that you went out with Daphne to work on some burned trees," I said directly to Io. Was I misremembering that?

"That's different. We were in a very large group and only went under Theano's specific direction. Like Ahyana said, Troas isn't safe. Not like the temple."

I stifled a groan. If there were no approved excursions, I was going to have to sneak out and risk getting caught.

Tonight. After the others had gone to bed, I would find my way to the docks.

All I would have to do was what Jason had sung and follow the blue lines on the labyrinth walls.

More images of him from my dreams filled my mind, him dragging his lower lip along my thigh, questing for—

"Lia?" Io said. "Did you hear me?"

Letting out a shaky breath, I said, "No. I'm sorry. What were you saying?"

"That you need to get changed."

"From one black tunic to another?" I glanced down at myself. "Why? I didn't get that dirty today."

Io went over to the large wooden cabinet where everyone hung their spare tunics and cloaks. "For what's next. Here, I hemmed this for you this morning."

I took the black tunic from her and held it up. It was extremely short, which surprised me. "What is this for?"

"Training," Io replied.

I was confused. "Do I need to be taught the correct way to lay down fertilizer for the flowers?"

Suri grinned at me while Zalira rubbed her hands together with delight. "It's not that kind of training."

CHAPTER THIRTY-TWO

Despite my repeated requests, they refused to give me any further details and seemed to be enjoying the fact that they knew something I didn't.

They all changed into similarly short tunics and we walked across the complex together. In my outfit this felt so eerily similar to going to work with Demaratus in the morning that I again felt homesick. I listened as they bantered back and forth, looking beyond the temple toward the labyrinth walls, trying to remember where the southern entrance was so that I could use it.

Zalira looked over her shoulder at me and announced, "We heard all about Jason."

Oh no. Now they were going to turn their teasing on me. "You told them?" I said to Io.

She shrugged innocently and said, "We don't keep secrets."

Suri's gaze turned guilty and she looked away. There was at least some comfort in knowing I wasn't the only one holding back.

"Yes, and we would like all the details," Ahyana added, her eyes sparkling.

"There are no details," I said.

All four of them managed to exchange knowing glances.

"No one here believes you," Io said in a singsong voice.

"It was nothing!" I protested.

Suri shook her head and Zalira said, "Again, we don't believe you."

In exasperation I threw my hands up. "Fine. I kissed him once."

There were too many voices and questions for me to keep track of and try to respond to.

"Was it good?"

"Did you enjoy it?"

"What was it like?"

Suri waggled her eyebrows at me suggestively.

"Was it a long kiss or a short kiss?"

"How did you meet him? Was he someone you grew up with?"

"Where is he now?"

In my dreams. I wondered how they'd respond if I gave that answer. I suspected the inquiries and teasing would amplify, so I stayed quiet.

We entered the gymnasium and I came to a stop so quickly that Zalira smacked into me. I apologized and she stepped around me while I took in the massive room.

It reminded me of the temple, with twenty-foot-high ceilings supported by large wooden beams, but that wasn't what had surprised me.

There were women of various ages engaging in combat. Some were doing hand-to-hand fighting, boxing, wrestling, and there were others practicing battles with all sorts of weapons. Staves, swords, spears, axes, knives. I heard wood hitting wood, metal clanging against metal, grunts and shouts as fists hit flesh. It smelled like sweat, which wasn't surprising, given how hard the women were working and that it seemed hotter in here than it did outside.

They moved like my regiment back home. None of these women were novices.

No wonder Artemisia had defeated me so quickly.

As if I'd summoned her, she smacked her shoulder into mine, hard.

"Stay out of the way," Artemisia growled as she entered the gym with her laughing friends.

Most likely her own adelphia.

I internally thanked the goddess for giving me such decent and kind people to become sisters with.

There was a large dais against the farthest wall and I watched as Theano entered the room flanked by Daphne and Maia. I caught Maia's gaze and she smiled at me with her eyes. A fourth woman was with them. She had fair skin and very light brown hair that was shaved on both sides and longer on top, where she had a series of intricate braids interwoven to make one giant braid that hung down her back. Her face was scarred and she wore a leather breastplate that had obviously been designed for her, given how well it fit.

"Who is that?" I whispered to Io, feeling a bit awed.

"Antiope. She's the battle master. Others say she used to be a Scythian." At my quizzical expression she elaborated. "They were a race of warrior women who ruled themselves."

"Why would she come here?" I asked. Ilion did not seem like a good place for women.

"Probably for the same reasons that so many of us have. I've never asked and I never would. She's too scary for a conversation."

I already liked Antiope. She reminded me of Demaratus with the confident way she held herself.

Theano stepped forward and held her hands aloft, meaning to gain our attention.

All the battles ceased and the room quieted.

"Kneel," she said, and almost as one, the entire body got to their knees. I was a beat behind, copying them. Then they prostrated themselves on the ground, hands in front of them, faces nearly touching the floor. I did the same so as to not draw attention to myself, but it felt strange.

Theano's voice boomed above me. "We kneel before you now in humility to honor and worship you, who is above all other beings! We dedicate ourselves to you, to your eternal cause of vengeance. We ask for you to send your savior to wreak your punishment upon those that deserve it."

Although I couldn't see her face—not only because of the veil but because I was face down—it felt like that last comment had been directed specifically at me.

"Ilion has become hard-hearted against you and your ways, and the only way to clear out the blasphemy is for your savior to rain down terror upon those who would deny you and your laws. The time is nigh and we ask for the strength to carry out your furious and terrible will."

After a beat, the people around me started to stand up. I did the same, but I was very confused. The high priestess hadn't followed the format Maia had just taught me that morning, and the prayer Theano had offered had been so unlike Io's I wasn't sure what to think.

When Maia and Io spoke of the goddess, their words were filled with talk of love and peace and kindness.

But the image Theano had just painted?

It was of a bloodthirsty deity who hungered for more carnage.

I supposed it wasn't entirely inaccurate, given that the furious and vengeful goddess had cursed my own lands.

"Who is the savior?" I asked Io.

"No one knows. There's an ancient prophecy about Ilion turning their backs on the goddess and that it would put us in danger. It says that a savior would rise up to protect the Ilionians and restore the goddess's glory. And that we will know the savior because they will be flame-kissed and bear the mark of the goddess."

She pointed to a spot against a far wall of the gymnasium to indicate where we were going, and I followed her. "What do those two attributes mean?"

"Again, no one is quite sure. There's lots of guesses, though. The flame part—maybe someone who has been burned in a fire? Perhaps a metalworker or swordsmith, who works with intense flames? Someone infected with a fever? A person with red hair?"

Fury grabbed me by the throat. I'd only ever seen one person with red hair. The man who had pulled Quynh out of my arms. "Are there many Ilionians with red hair?"

237

After I'd secured the eye and my life mage and restored Locris, I would return to Ilion with the sole intention of tracking that man down and making him die slowly.

"There is a kingdom north of here called Thrace, and many Thracians have red hair and fair skin. Some move here and marry."

A Thracian. But there might be many with the same heritage. That didn't narrow things down for me, but that was a problem for a later date. "But why flame? Why not earth-kissed?"

"Fire gives new life. It burns away old undergrowth, creating ashes that nourish the soil, and makes it possible for new things to grow."

I nodded. There was still so much that I didn't know. "What about the mark?"

"Again, there is only speculation. The general consensus seems to be that it means a birthmark."

"Which is why you asked me if I had one," I said.

Io nodded. "Every child in Ilion is carefully checked when they are born."

"Maybe it could be a tattoo," I said.

"Perhaps," she agreed. "We're all just conjecturing. The only thing we all agree on is that the savior will come. I've prayed for that every day of my life."

It seemed silly now that she had asked me whether I had a birthmark. Why would an Ilionian savior be born in Locris?

And what Locrian would agree to fill that role?

My adelphia gathered against the wall as Antiope stepped forward. Her voice boomed out of her, echoing against the walls. "Women of the temple, what do we say to the outside world?"

"Never again!" everyone around me yelled back, the sound overwhelming as every priestess and acolyte said the words in unison.

"Why do we train?" Antiope demanded.

"Never again!"

"Why do we prepare?"

"Never again!"

"Why do we fight?"

"Never again!"

"Never again!" Antiope roared the words back. "Never again will a priestess of this temple be defiled, taken captive as a plaything for men! Never again will any woman here cower to a man because of his strength! You are warriors, capable of vanquishing any foe!"

Everyone in the gymnasium began to stamp their feet as quickly as they could, hooting and hollering their agreement.

Even I was caught up in it. I made myself a vow. *Never again.*

Never again would I allow a Locrian maiden to run that race. I would find a way to stop it.

No more sacrifices.

"Let our training begin!" Antiope declared.

She jumped down into the crowd and started directing the women closest to her. "Keep your shield up! If you were in a true phalanx, you would be responsible for breaking the line."

Daphne and Maia also left the dais and I saw Maia walking toward us. Theano stayed put, sitting in a chair and watching the room.

"Does she always do that?" I asked Io.

She followed my gaze. "Theano usually observes training, yes."

There was something intimidating and unlikable about the high priestess. "Doesn't she have more important duties to attend to?"

Io shrugged and then let out a sigh as Maia came closer. "I hate training. I don't want to accidentally hurt someone."

"Then why did you admire my sword?" I asked.

"Just because I loathe violence doesn't mean I can't appreciate a beautiful piece of craftsmanship," she countered. "My father loves collecting swords. He had so many while I was growing up. I used to watch my brothers practice with them for hours. They fought so well. It was like a dance."

"A dance where one of them dies at the end."

She smiled. "I love the way your sword is shaped like a leaf. It's beautiful."

I agreed with her. I wondered whether I should have brought it with me today.

Maia joined our group. "Zalira against Suri to start us off, fighting with staves. First one to three points wins."

As Zalira and Suri retrieved their weapons, Io told me, "You get points for pushing your opponent out of the ring, or for rendering them immobile. And for slipping past their defenses and making bodily contact."

"Some people are using swords and axes," I said, a bit alarmed.

"The points are different for more dangerous weapons."

That was a relief, at least. I'd hate to lose an ear because somebody was overeager to win.

"They keep track of the best warriors over on that wall," she continued. "The top five fighters are always the Chosen."

Io had mentioned earlier that the Chosen were selected due to their abilities. I just hadn't realized that it had included hand-to-hand combat.

Artemisia was the top ranked, which didn't surprise me in the least. She was aggressive and seemed dangerous, and I personally knew how strong she was. I wished that I could challenge her and secure that top spot for myself, but I had to consider my situation.

If I walked into the ring and won my very first fight against the best acolyte here, the women around me might get suspicious about my background. I was sure they would realize that only someone from a royal or noble family would have the resources to be trained in fighting.

Despite my determination to become one of the Chosen, I was going to have to give it some time in order to avoid questions. I would have to slowly "improve" and work my way up the list eventually.

Although patience had never been my strong suit.

"Begin!" Maia called out.

Suri and Zalira sprang to life, their staves whacking into each other over and over again.

Ahyana and Io were calling out encouragement while Maia gave them tips. "Watch your opening! Protect your left side! Better!"

The fighting here was different. I had been taught to harm, maim, and to get away. To deflect and defend and escape. But this was almost entirely offensive and I didn't understand why they trained for combat. They wouldn't be fighting other women outside the temple. And if they were attacked by a group of men, they'd be able to take a few of them out, but with this fighting style they would eventually be overwhelmed.

They would lose.

You didn't, a voice whispered inside me, but I brushed it aside. That had been different. I'd been in situations where I had been able to face them one at a time. The priestesses and acolytes were training for war.

Zalira had just jabbed the end of her staff into Suri's gut when a high-pitched scream rent the air.

It had come from outside. All the fighting ceased and an uneasy silence settled over the room. The scream came again. We were close to an exit and we ran out into the courtyard to see what was happening.

A woman with a torn dress and wild hair was running toward the temple grounds, screaming as she went.

She was being chased by nearly a dozen men.

"Help me! Someone help me!"

CHAPTER THIRTY-THREE

"Sanctuary!" the woman called out as she burst through the archway and collapsed in a heap in front of the fountain. "I claim sanctuary!"

Antiope shoved her way through the crowd. All the women from the gymnasium were lined up on the outer edges of the courtyard. No one moved to help the woman. I took a step forward but Io put a hand on my forearm, keeping me in place.

"Close the gates!" Maia called out. There were two iron doors on either side of the archway that could be swung into place and locked together.

"No!" Antiope yelled back, pointing her sword at the oncoming men. "Leave them open!"

The men drew closer and the disheveled woman got to her feet and rushed up the steps but stayed on the patio, not entering the temple. The men pursuing her stopped at the archway, not crossing over.

"Return her to us!" one of the men yelled.

"She has claimed sanctuary, and by law, we will protect her," Antiope replied. "Men may not enter this sacred ground."

One of the men took his helmet off, throwing it to the ground. "I do not believe in superstition, and that woman belongs to me."

"She belongs to herself!" someone in the crowd called back, and there were several murmurs of agreement.

"I will not ask again! Return her to me now!"

"Come and claim her, then." Antiope gave a terrible grin as the man entered the courtyard. I realized that she had ordered the gate to be left open because she wanted the men to break the rules. Half the men followed the first.

Io turned, burying her face in Suri's shoulder, as if she knew what was about to happen.

"Stay back," Antiope said to all the women lined up to watch. "Do not interfere."

Then she approached the men alone, sword at her side. "It is against the law of the goddess for you to be here. Leave now or face the consequences."

"What do you think you're going to do?" That first man laughed, as did his companions who had joined him.

"You have made your choice, and now you will pay with your life," she said.

There was a new round of laughter from the men.

With a war cry Antiope quickly swung her blade and removed the first man's head from his neck with a single stroke. There was a stunned silence when his head fell onto the courtyard with a sickening thud.

Then the other men attacked Antiope, all at the same time. Not one of them could reach her, though. She not only defended herself from every oncoming stroke but found openings to slice and stick and stab.

She moved so quickly and surely, never missing a step as the sound of metal clanging filled the air around us. She whirled and spun, hitting away every weapon extended toward her. The men were shouting, some yelling in pain, their expressions serious and angry.

But Antiope bore a ferocious smile on her face, delighting in the carnage, like she lived for this kind of thing and wanted more of it.

Three men collapsed to the ground in heaps, clearly dead. The three left alive ran back to those waiting at the archway, limping and clutching their sides.

"Would anyone else like a one-way voyage to the underworld?" she taunted as she pointed her sword at the men, streaks of blood across her face.

They all fled as quickly as they could.

I was in shock over what had occurred. And that shock was increased by the fact that no one else seemed very concerned that our battle master had just slaughtered four men.

Although to be fair, she had given them ample warning.

Someone handed Antiope a rag and she cleaned her sword, and then her face. Several older priestesses, led by Daphne, went over to the woman who had asked for sanctuary. Daphne put a cloak around her shoulders as they helped her up. Their small group began walking with her toward the infirmary.

Acolytes near me were speaking in low voices to one another.

"The courtyard will have to be cleansed and blessed."

"At least they didn't enter any buildings. Can you imagine?"

"What would happen if they did?"

"I don't know and I don't want to find out."

Maia stood a few feet away with a sword gripped in her hand. I wanted to ask her about the consequences if men entered the buildings, but I sensed now was not the time.

I was surprised by the lack of reaction to what we'd all just witnessed. No one was crying or screaming or seemed upset. These women were battle hardened. Even Io, who had turned her head away the entire time. She had stayed calm.

What had these women experienced?

"Back inside," Maia said, and the members of my adelphia moved to obey, with Io still pointing her gaze at the ground, away from the men who had just died.

I envied Antiope and her skills. I wished that I could be more like her. I hesitated a moment and then approached her.

When she acknowledged me with a slight nod, I said, "I want to fight like you."

She studied me for a moment while cleaning her neck. "Dedicate yourself to your training, do what I say, and you will."

"Lia!" Maia called, and I hurried to catch up with the rest of my group. I wasn't sure what had compelled me to approach Antiope—the absolute ferocity and strength I'd witnessed from her had been a marvel.

I wanted that for myself.

Not only because of my mission to retrieve the eye, but because I never again wanted to be in a position where I wouldn't be able to defend myself or my loved ones.

My heart ached as it again mourned for Quynh, but I swallowed my sadness back and instead mentally replayed the fight I'd just witnessed.

Antiope had to be goddess-blessed. A warrior who was chosen by the goddess and given supernatural strength and speed. How else could I explain what I'd watched? I'd always assumed that only men were goddess-blessed, but I'd just seen that it wasn't true.

One thing was certain—I was not goddess-blessed. I wished that I were—I would have given anything to be so. If I had been, I might have been able to keep my sister alive.

Thinking about Antiope's skills reminded me of when I had seen Jason fight, when he had protected us from those pirates on the *Nikos*. His abilities had been both exhilarating and terrifying. *Attractive.*

I internally sighed. Why did my thoughts continually turn to him? I wasn't ever going to see him again. Our brief adventure together was over. He was traveling out at sea and I was here.

Maybe it was because he'd helped me, even though I hadn't realized it. He had given me the clue I needed to find my way through the labyrinth.

It wasn't as if he were the only person who had ever been nice to me, though. That single act didn't warrant my mind's devotion.

Maybe it was because he was the only man I'd ever kissed—and most likely always would be, now that I had taken a vow of celibacy.

I reentered the gymnasium and noticed that Theano had stayed in her seat. She had not come out to watch the fight that had occurred. She was still, unmoving. Like a statue.

"That poor woman," Io said behind me.

At first I thought she meant Theano, but I realized she meant the woman who had claimed sanctuary. "What will happen to her?"

"There are safe houses that are funded by the temple. Worshippers bring monetary and food gifts here to the goddess, which we use to provide for ourselves and to assist women who are being mistreated and ask us for help."

I supposed something like that would be necessary in a society where men hurt women. It was not the Locrian way.

Why had things changed in my nation and not here? Maybe it was in response to Ajax's actions and the repercussions. It might have caused the men to choose to be and do better. Or perhaps the Locrian women had demanded the change so that we wouldn't be cursed even worse.

Ahyana waved at the ceiling and I glanced up, seeing Kunguru watching us from the rafters.

Antiope approached our group and there was a tiny flicker of excitement in my stomach. Would my training start now?

"Tell your bird to leave," she said to Ahyana. "He needs to stay outside."

It made me wonder how many times Kunguru had attended their sessions.

With a small frown Ahyana cupped her hand next to her mouth and said, "Kunguru, you have to go outside. I don't want you to go, but Antiope says you must."

He cocked his head, as if he understood. Which was silly because birds couldn't speak. And even if they could, there was no way he would have been able to hear over all the noise of the priestesses and acolytes still feverishly discussing what had just taken place in the courtyard.

Kunguru flew from the rafter to a windowsill. His black feathers gleamed in the sunlight, and it was almost like he was taunting Antiope by mostly following her orders. Technically, most of him was outside, while his feet and head remained inside the building.

The battle master shook her head in annoyance and then climbed up on the dais. She knelt before Theano and they seemed to be speaking to one another. I wished I could hear what they were saying.

Then Antiope got to her feet and yelled, "Silence!"

The gymnasium fell quiet, with only a few murmurings here and there. It didn't surprise me that people were so quick to obey her after what I'd just seen. I wondered if Antiope was going to address how the men had entered the temple grounds. Remind us that there was a reason why we trained so hard.

But she didn't do that. "It is time for the weekly matchups to determine rankings! And our first fight will be between Artemisia . . ."

Artemisia walked over to the center ring and smirked at the crowd, some women patting her on the back as she passed by.

"And Lia of Locris."

My adrenaline spiked at the announcement. What? Why?

Had this been Theano's choice or Antiope's? And what was the intention here? To embarrass me?

"She's not trained!" Maia called back, which surprised me. I knew she was my adelphia's mentor and charged with watching over us, but she seemed quiet and meek. Not the type to openly defy Antiope. "It isn't fair."

If Antiope was bothered by Maia speaking up, she didn't show it. "What better way is there for the novice to learn than to fight the best? Come into the center ring, Lia."

Zalira clapped me on the shoulder. "She usually tries to sweep the feet. Watch out for that."

I didn't tell her that I had personal experience already with that particular move of Artemisia's.

My heart was thudding slowly as I walked toward the ring. I didn't know how to play this. I wanted to protect myself, to keep from getting too hurt. I also wanted to inflict some damage on Artemisia as payback.

There was another part of me that wanted to impress Antiope. To show her that I was someone worth investing her time in.

None of that would be possible, though. I couldn't let any of them suspect that my background was royal because of the temple rules. I considered whether I should pretend to know absolutely nothing about fighting, but I figured that might also seem suspect, given that I'd survived the race and being chased by armed men.

Somehow I was going to have to walk a path in the middle.

I was obviously going to have to lose.

Antiope handed me a staff. It wasn't something I'd ever trained very much with, as Demaratus had preferred things that were pointy.

"Try not to get hit," she said as I entered the ring.

I hoped I could put on a good enough show. The task seemed impossible.

Artemisia whirled her staff around in lazy circles as she observed me. The deadly look in her eyes was unmistakable.

She would kill me if the opportunity presented itself. And was there more of an opportunity than being engaged in combat?

I knew, without being told, that she had other weapons on her. I would have to start carrying my own and keep an eye on her during sparring.

Antiope explained the rules, and they were exactly the same as what Io had shared earlier. There would be points awarded for contact and if one opponent pushed the other out of the ring.

My heartbeat grew louder in my own ears as I prepared myself.

"Ready?" Antiope verified, and when we both nodded, she said, "Begin!"

CHAPTER THIRTY-FOUR

I braced, expecting an onslaught. Like what had happened in the flower garden—for Artemisia to attack immediately.

She didn't do that, though. She continued to twirl her staff in a circle, pacing back and forth. Was she waiting for me to strike first? I wasn't going to.

"Quit toying with your prey!" someone yelled from behind me, and it caused Artemisia's smirk to widen.

She feinted at me and I instinctually responded, bringing my staff up to meet where hers would have been if she'd carried through with her jab.

She wasn't just delaying. She was going to test me. She wanted to see where my weaknesses were, my reaction time.

"Hit her!" another person yelled, and I wasn't sure which one of us they were talking to.

Although considering how they felt about Locrians, I assumed it was meant as encouragement for Artemisia.

"Keep your hands up, Lia!" That was definitely Zalira's voice, and it was nice to know that I had my sisters supporting me.

Artemisia swiped at me and I reacted, again bringing my own staff up to prevent her from making contact with my body. Her eyes narrowed, absorbing this information.

Was I accidentally betraying my previous training? I glanced at Antiope, but her face remained passive.

Yesterday in the garden I had felt groggy and slow, whatever remedies administered to me by Daphne and Io still in my system.

That was not the situation today. I felt extremely alert, and that earlier attack had only heightened my senses, preparing me for a fight. I was ready.

And I couldn't show that to anyone.

Artemisia stepped forward with her right foot and swung at me on my left side before quickly switching to my right.

I blocked her both times. I clenched my teeth. Demaratus had trained me too well.

She spun to her left and I could see the incoming blow, but I closed my eyes and held my own staff straight up while I waited, allowing her to land her strike.

"Oof," I breathed out as her staff whacked me on my right shoulder. She hit really hard, much harder than I'd anticipated. That was definitely going to bruise.

"Point for Artemisia!" Antiope called out.

Would they separate us, have us start over? Apparently not, considering that Artemisia was again swiping at me and I instinctively jerked to my right to avoid the hit.

Should I try to strike her? Would it seem too unrealistic if I didn't at least make the attempt?

I again heard my adelphia cheering for me and I was struck with a desire to not let them down.

But I didn't have that option. Glancing down, I deliberately stepped out of bounds while trying to make it seem accidental.

"Point for Artemisia!"

One more point to go and this would be over.

Artemisia lifted her staff over her head, indicating her next move, and I raised my staff to meet hers, wood smacking into wood. Then she dropped it low, intending to hit my exposed left side.

But I met her staff there, too.

Her eyes widened slightly, surprised.

It let me know that I had pushed things too far. It was time to let her win.

She again raised her staff, but her body told me that she was going low with her feet. And she did exactly what I thought she would, using her weapon as a distraction while she swept me to the ground. As I fell I turned slightly to my left so that my shoulder would take the brunt, lessening the impact on my chest. It made it so that the wind wasn't knocked from my lungs.

Artemisia could have easily tapped me with her staff and won the point, but instead she threw it to the side and was on top of me, a knife pressed up against my throat.

"What are you playing at?" she demanded, and I felt a drop of blood trailing down my neck. Her tunic slipped slightly and I saw the edges of a reddish-brown tattoo.

"I don't know what you mean." Did I sound convincing? Or like I was tormenting her?

The tip of her knife dug deeper into my throat. "I beat you, Locrian. I will always beat you."

We'll see. The words were on the edge of my tongue, but I didn't get a chance to say them as Antiope had grabbed Artemisia by the back of her practice tunic and was hauling her off me.

"Enough!" she yelled. "You know better than to pull an unauthorized weapon on one of your sisters! If you do another stunt like that again, I will ban you from the gymnasium for an entire month. Go outside and run ten laps around the complex."

Artemisia gave Antiope a look of pure hatred but did as she was commanded. The battle master offered me her hand and helped me to my feet.

"You did extremely well for a beginner," she said. "You have excellent instincts, which we can easily build from. You have the potential to be one of the best fighters here."

I tried not to preen under her compliments but feared I was failing to stay humble.

She went over the mistakes I'd made, outlining what I should have done instead. I already knew all of it, but I nodded and listened as we walked back to my adelphia. Another priestess took over the main matches in the center ring and some women watched, while others had returned to their own smaller rings to continue sparring.

Zalira and Suri were fighting again, resuming the battle that had been interrupted earlier. Antiope had a running commentary on what they were doing, pointing out their strengths and weaknesses and what she thought they should have done better.

I noticed that Zalira was stronger and technically more skilled, but that Suri was relentless. She didn't want to give up, even when she'd lost a point.

"I've had to yell at that one more than once to get her to stop," Antiope said in an indulgent tone, like she enjoyed that part of Suri's personality.

Zalira won all three rounds but not for lack of Suri trying. Maia said that Io and Ahyana were up next.

It was easy to see how uncomfortable all of this made Io. Ahyana even went easy on her, despite Antiope barking at her to not do so.

"Are you going to hold back when you face a real enemy?" Antiope yelled. "Hit her, Ahyana! And Io, defend yourself!"

Io had tears in her eyes and it took everything in me not to interfere. While Io understood the techniques, there was no will or want to fight. She simply wasn't built for it.

Fortunately, Ahyana scored all three points quickly.

I was put into the ring with Zalira, and Antiope talked me through the battle, telling me how to stand, what to watch for. This all felt so comfortable and familiar but, at the same time, strange and different. She was teaching me offensive fighting and correcting my stance. It was easy to pick up as it was similar to the things I'd already learned.

At the end of the training session, we had a quick lunch break in the dining hall. I felt completely energized and ravenous and Zalira teased me about the amount of food I was eating. I couldn't remember the last time I'd felt so hungry.

After lunch we went to our afternoon class, along with the other acolytes who had been there for three years or less. It was in the same big room where I'd met with Maia earlier that morning.

"We have to sit up front because Io wants to be the favorite," Ahyana told me in a loud whisper that had Io mock glaring at her.

"It's so we can hear better," she corrected.

"What is this class for?"

"General religious education," Zalira said. "There is a lot of repetition. We have to know everything inside and out. Apparently there is a test we have to pass in order to become a priestess, and recitation of certain stories and rules is part of that."

It didn't surprise me that they would have to study the same things over and over again. Not being able to write it down or read books about the topic must have made it more difficult to retain.

Maia was the instructor for the class and I was glad. She must have really loved teaching to be doing it so often. She had a pack with her and set it down on a podium. When she opened it, some cylindrical objects of various colors fell out and rolled away. Maia gathered them up, but apparently one was still missing.

"My white chalk! Did anyone see where it went?" She hunted around. I leaned forward but didn't see it. So many had fallen at once.

Suri got up and stuck her hand under the far corner of the dais and pulled out the chalk, handing it to Maia.

"Thank you, Suri. Everyone take your seats and we'll begin!" Maia glanced up at the doors. "Hurry up, Artemisia."

Her run must have finally finished. She definitely looked sweaty and tired. She glared at me and I was the one who looked away first.

I knew she wasn't allowed to hurt me but that she would probably think of another way to pay me back.

"Today we are talking about the different aspects of the goddess," Maia said, and she was immediately interrupted by Artemisia.

"Why are we going over something so basic? We all know this. Is it because of the Locrian?" The disdain in her voice was evident.

Antiope probably would have made her run more laps. I thought someone as sweet as Maia might wither under that kind of disrespect, but she said, "It never hurts to review material. If you have a problem with the way I run my lectures, you are welcome to leave."

I half expected Artemisia to storm out, but she crossed her arms and leaned back.

"As I was saying, the goddess has various aspects. Like faces that she shows her followers. Or different parts of her personality. Different things that she has control or dominion over."

"Like plants," Io said.

"Yes, we know the love the goddess has for all things that grow. She controls the crops, their fertility and abundance, the rain that ensures their survival. She oversees gifts and hidden treasures, the animals and insects that aid plants. She oversees the law, marriage, the birth of children, healing of the sick. She is mistress of the very earth itself. Here in the temple we learn to appreciate all of the aspects of the goddess and can devote ourselves to serving one particular aspect over the others."

I already knew what Io's choice would be. She grinned back at me, as if she knew exactly what I was thinking.

Was there an aspect of the goddess devoted to vengeance? I wouldn't mind dedicating myself to that.

Maia spent the rest of the hour talking about each area that the goddess had dominion over and then dismissed us to return to our rooms.

When we got there, Io took her satchel of scrolls and left while the rest of us washed up and changed our tunics.

I asked Zalira to show me the combination she'd used to catch Suri unaware during their third round, and while she was walking me through it step-by-step, Io returned with a broad smile on her face and carrying something large that she set down on my bed.

"There is a delivery for you, Lia. It's heavy."

"For me?" Who could have sent me something? I was thoroughly bewildered. Had my parents done this? I didn't think so. Not only had enough time not passed but they knew not to send me something as it would risk exposing my background.

I unwrapped the bundle and my breath caught when I realized that it was the pot of Locrian soil I'd left on the *Nikos*. The one I'd asked Jason to bring to the temple if I survived.

There was no note, but given the lack of education in Ilion, that wasn't too surprising. I did find myself wishing that he had included one, though. I'd been thinking of him more than I wanted to—it would have been nice to know that he was suffering from the same affliction.

Although I supposed his delivering the pot here was an indication that he hadn't forgotten about me. I wondered why it had taken him so long—nearly a whole week. Maybe he'd been traveling and couldn't until now?

Did that mean he was in Troas? My pulse beat a bit faster at the thought.

"Is that dirt?" Io asked, sticking her hand into the pot.

"Yes. I wanted to have a piece of home with me," I said, putting the pot on the floor next to my bed.

"And who sent it? Was it Good Kisser Jason?" Ahyana teased with a mischievous glint in her eye.

"He's not important to me." I didn't deny that he was the sender, though.

A fact they seemed to pick up on.

"He is the one who sent it! That must be why you're blushing right now," Io declared.

"I . . . never mind."

That made everyone break into peals of laughter and I couldn't help but smile, too. I could deny him all I wanted, but there had to be a reason I thought of him as often as I did.

◆ ◆ ◆

"You can't stop thinking about me," Jason murmured into my hair. My back was pressed against his chest and he held me against him tightly. He nuzzled my hair, then dropped a kiss on the top of my ear.

"It's you who can't stop thinking about me," I countered, running my fingernails along the tops of his forearms.

I could hear the smile in his voice. "In the light of day you can protest all you want, pretend like nothing is happening between us. Now we're here alone, under the cover of darkness, in my bed. Can we attempt to be honest with one another?"

Then he lifted my hair, brushing it over my left shoulder. His other hand was splayed against my stomach, holding me in place. He began to kiss the back of my neck with hot, little, delicate brushes of his full lips and I collapsed against him, my entire body aching for him.

"Lia, what is it you want?" he asked, kissing along my shoulder. "Tell me."

There was a nagging feeling at the back of my mind that I had to stop this, but I couldn't remember why. There was no room for rational thought—just pure need.

"I want to touch you. To see you," I said.

He released me and I shifted away from him, turning around so that we faced one another. Jason got up on his knees and my stomach pulsated with want as he reached up to unpin the top of his tunic.

I sucked in a sharp breath when the top fell away, exposing his chest. Liquid heat gathered along my spine, spreading out to my limbs, and I got up on my knees and moved closer.

He was more beautiful than any statue I'd ever seen. I reached out cautiously, almost afraid that my fingers might catch flame when I touched him. Now he was the one with stuttering breath as I put my palm flat against his broad chest.

There was such an addictive warmth in his skin, a strength and hardness to his muscles that were a sharp contrast to my own body.

I let my fingers drift down, tracing the outlines of the fascinating ridges and planes of his torso. I watched his stomach contract sharply when I made contact, heard how harsh his breathing had become, felt the way he shuddered from my touch.

"Perfection," I said and leaned forward to kiss his pectoral muscles. His hand went to the back of my head, his fingers flexing against my scalp before he pulled me back.

"My turn," he said, his eyes molten pools of desire.

Now I was the one shivering. This was new territory but I trusted him. I trusted Jason more than anyone else in the entire world.

His hands went to the belt at my tunic and my breathing became unstable. It was too loud and too fast but I didn't want him to stop.

"May I?" he asked.

I was struck by a giddy urge to laugh uncontrollably. He could do whatever he wanted to me and I would thank him for it.

But I saw that he wanted my assent. "Yes."

He undid the belt that cinched my tunic in at the waist and held the fabric in place, letting the belt drop onto the bed. Without breaking eye contact he pulled the tunic up over my head and I felt the cold air hitting my skin.

With a loud gasp I sat up in my own bed. Dreaming again. I bit off a groan. I had wanted to see his face and reaction to my body, to feel my skin against his, and then I was embarrassed that I had been so amenable to something I knew I could never have.

And I had kicked my blanket off in the process. No wonder I was cold. How was it possible to feel chilled and overheated at the same time?

I had drifted off, and I had not intended to. I had planned to wait until my adelphia had fallen asleep and then sneak out to the docks to try and get a message to my parents.

There was a rustling sound and I looked at the window. Kunguru was on the windowsill, watching me.

I was worried he might call out, but he didn't. The nearly full moon outside made it easier to pack up my knapsack. I took one of the bags of salt and left the other behind.

For a moment I felt like I was being watched. I whirled around and could have sworn that I saw Suri's eyes open. I held still, waiting, as my heart thundered in my chest. But her breathing was steady and even, and I figured I was imagining things.

With my xiphos strapped to my thigh, I crept over to the door. I opened it slowly, cringing each time it softly squeaked. Was it this loud during the daytime?

At long last I got it open and hurried down the hallway and the stairs, then through the front door.

I got six feet from the dormitory before I heard a voice holler, "Halt!"

CHAPTER
THIRTY-FIVE

A woman in her thirties was striding toward me, her sword drawn as she approached. A guard? Had she been posted solely because of me? Had someone guessed at my intentions and shared them with someone in charge? Was I about to be expelled?

Given that I didn't know exactly what was happening, I considered my options—I could run and hope that I didn't get caught or say a fervent prayer to the goddess that I would only be punished and not tossed into the street for trying to sneak out.

"Where are you going?" she asked, and I ran through possible excuses in my head.

I couldn't use the obvious one, that I needed to relieve myself, because the toilets were inside. I finally settled on, "What time is it? I'm supposed to go clean the temple."

At that the guard sheathed her sword and I let out a tiny sigh of relief. "Not for a few more hours. You need to go back to bed. There is a curfew and you can't be out here at night."

"Oh. I didn't know." And that was the truth. No one had told me about a curfew. Most likely because they didn't expect me to try and sneak out in the middle of the night.

"There is." I saw three other women gathering behind her, ready to offer support if she needed it.

How many guards were there keeping watch?

I felt foolish for not even considering this as a possibility. Of course someone like Antiope would make certain that the temple grounds were being watched over at all hours.

"I'm sorry. I suppose I was just excited to serve."

The guard smiled slightly. "I understand. Go on. Back to bed."

I nodded. "Yes. I'm sorry." I wasn't sure why I felt compelled to tack on another apology. I hurried back into the dormitory. That could have gone so much worse.

With a sigh I realized that sneaking out was going to take a lot more planning than I'd initially thought.

The next morning I arose before dawn, still sleepy, and still able to feel the phantom imprint of Jason's lips on mine, his hands on my body. I had dreamed of him again.

After I got ready and gathered my tools, I went down to the temple. The guard on duty outside the dormitory nodded to me and I noticed that it was someone different from the night before. I wondered what time they changed shifts. That would be helpful information to know.

The courtyard in front of the temple had been diligently scrubbed, but the stones were still stained with blood. It would take a long time for the sun to bleach the stains away.

I heard a buzzing sound and turned my gaze to the archway. The bodies of the men who had dared to broach the temple grounds and had been killed by Antiope were mounted on pikes. Some kind of loud insect hovered near their bodies. My stomach turned at the sight but I supposed that was the point. It was a gruesome warning to anyone who would dare to break the goddess's laws or question the resolve of her servants.

After I cleaned the steps and patio, I went into the temple and held my breath, hoping that I would be alone.

But there was a guard stationed at the top of the stairs. I let out a sigh of frustration. How was I ever going to be able to investigate the statue?

Creating detailed battle strategies had never been a particular skill of mine. In the past I made a general plan and then just hoped that I'd be fast enough and strong enough to find a way to reach my goal.

It had served me fairly well so far.

At some point the statue guard would make a mistake. They would fall ill or need to use the toilet or there would be a miscommunication about who was supposed to be on duty.

And I would have to wait until an opening presented itself. What else could I do? I had just discovered that there were guards everywhere, both day and night.

The only thing I could do was to learn their patrols, what times they changed shifts, and use that to my advantage.

Which meant more waiting.

I went about my new normal day. A private session and breakfast with Maia in the morning, then off to training, lunch, afternoon classes, chores, dinner, and bed.

In our acolyte classes, Maia was teaching us about the relationship between the earth goddess and the sun god.

"The sun god fell in love with the earth goddess, bathing her in the light and warmth of his devotion. They were joined and had twins—a boy and a girl. But the sun god began to suspect that the goddess had fallen in love with another, and his jealousy and bitterness consumed him. The goddess banished him back to the sky, where he circles around her day after day, burning with hatred and envy of all that he has lost."

I supposed my teacher wouldn't be interested to hear that the theory that the sun circled the earth was incorrect. It was better to keep my mouth shut.

"When the sun god comes too close, scorching the earth, the goddess will call forth storm clouds to block his view, and send rain to soothe the ground. The goddess's silver daughter inherited her father's light, glowing like the stars in the heavens, made of aether. The goddess's bronze son took after his mother, having many of the same abilities, along with dominion over the metals of the earth. He rebelled against his mother, rejecting her and her ways. Even now he seeks to usurp her, to remove her from her throne. The goddess had to banish him and he took the earth dragons with him when he left, which is why they haven't been seen in centuries. What did the son do that caused the goddess to send him away?"

Someone behind me raised her hand and Maia called on her. "He captured his sister and forced her into marriage with a god of war."

"Yes! The goddess didn't know what happened. The sun hid himself away for three days to hinder her search. With a torch in hand, she scoured the whole earth for her child. When she couldn't find her, she went into a deep, dark cave to lament her loss. The moon goddess had witnessed the bargain and traveled to the cave to tell the earth goddess. The earth goddess went to the war god's home, demanding her daughter's return. A council of gods, including the earth goddess's parents, determined that the war god had done nothing wrong, being unaware of the son's treachery. They ruled that for four months of the year, the daughter was to remain with her husband but would spend the remaining eight with her mother. That is why wars are always fought after the harvest, when the war god has been separated from his wife for too long and riles up the hearts of men to go to war because of his own grief. When she returns to him, he is soothed and mortal men go back to their lives. But when the daughter rejoins her husband, the earth goddess laments her loss and doesn't allow anything to grow while her beloved daughter is gone."

I wished I could write this down. My grandmother's book had not mentioned the goddess's children at all and I didn't understand why, as it seemed very important. Why had it been excluded?

Maia was still speaking. "It's why we allow women the right to choose whether or not to marry. They cannot be forced or sold into it.

The goddess will not permit what happened to her daughter to happen to any other daughters."

We were released shortly after that to attend to our chores. Io explained that the chores would change on a weekly basis and this week we were responsible for tending to the flower garden and assisting with gathering the annual harvest of the honey from the temple's private beehives.

I wasn't worried about the bees until one of them stung Zalira. She cursed as she swatted at her arm.

"Are you all right?" I asked.

"It really hurts," she said with clenched teeth. She didn't seem to be the sort of person who would complain about pain, so I knew it had to be bad.

"I saw a woman die from a beesting once," Io said, sounding as worried as I was starting to feel. Bees could kill someone? "Her face and throat swelled up until she couldn't breathe."

It would just be the height of irony if I had survived everything that I had so far only to lose my life to a tiny yellow-and-black-striped menace.

"You just have to be calm and unafraid," Ahyana said. "They can sense fear and view it as a threat."

"That is the opposite of how I'm feeling right now," I confessed, and we hung back as Ahyana did most of the work. The bees didn't even seem to notice that she was there.

"What did you think of class today?" Io asked, her gaze also on Ahyana as she stood in the midst of bees, unharmed.

I couldn't help but be honest about it. "I found it utterly fascinating. I've never heard any of those stories. I'm still trying to comprehend the fact that there are more deities than just the goddess."

"Of course. There are so many. And she has parents and children, just as we do. Mortal lives are patterned after the gods' lives."

"Except for the children part," I reminded her.

She shrugged. "Maybe with the sorrow and grief her own son has brought her, she's trying to prevent her servants from suffering the same fate."

That couldn't be completely true. "I know there can be heartache from being part of a family, but there is also a great deal of joy."

"Yes." Io had a faraway look in her eyes, like she was remembering something. "I used to have that kind of happiness in my life. My youngest half brother was born when I was six years old. I adored him and we were so close, until my stepmother drove a wedge between us. He hates me now."

I had a hard time imagining that anyone could hate her. And I privately wished for a painful accident for her stepmother, a woman so horrible that she would try to hurt someone as sweet as Io.

After Ahyana finished with the honey, we went to the dining hall. The prayer at dinner that night was disconcerting. The priestess offering it was long-winded and the entire thing was focused on Theano's greatness. Again going against the structure Maia had taught me.

There was no way to tell what Theano thought of it with her face covered. It was almost like the priestess worshipped Theano instead of the goddess.

"What is happening?" I asked, but Zalira just shook her head, indicating that I should remain quiet.

Perhaps the high priestess was being given this kind of honor because she was the goddess's mouthpiece.

"The goddess must hold her in high esteem," Ahyana added in a whisper, as if she had heard my thoughts. "And so it seems that the other priestesses believe that we should also treat Theano with the same kind of respect."

Her words made me think that my adelphia didn't like the high priestess any better than I did.

Theano shifted in her seat and there was the unmistakable clanking of metal against metal. The keys. She always wore them around her waist. Io had told me there was a key bearer, but so far, each time I'd seen Theano, she'd had the keys on her person.

Including the night I'd fallen through the roof.

I had come up with a number of ridiculous scenarios for how to get my hands on the keys. Sneaking into Theano's room late at night and stealing them. Although that wouldn't work with the patrols. I'd get caught long before I even got close to her bedroom. If she ever did give the keys over to a key bearer, maybe I could bribe them to loan them to me briefly. But I was fairly certain that whoever I asked would immediately turn me in.

I considered asking Ahyana to train Kunguru and his associates to steal keys and getting them to go to Theano's room for me. But I would somehow have to buy a key from a metalsmith or locksmith and I would have to tell Ahyana what I was up to and why I needed her help. Not to mention that the ravens might be completely uncooperative.

Ahyana's allegiance was to the temple and the goddess. The same was true for all my new sisters. I couldn't ask for their help.

The only other path I saw was to be selected a Chosen, to become someone the high priestess trusted. A person who would have access to her office and possibly her keys. The eye was somewhere in this complex, or there had to be information about how to find it. But to become one of the Chosen would mean excelling in both training and my studies. Something that would take time.

The problem was that it felt like I was trapped inside a giant hourglass and time was slipping away from me far too quickly.

CHAPTER THIRTY-SIX

That desperate, panicky feeling that time was passing too fast only got worse as the days went on. For two weeks straight my routine remained unchanged.

On the morning of the fourteenth day, I woke from a dream in which I'd been lying face down on a bed, unclothed, while Jason kissed and stroked my bare back, murmuring unintelligible words against my skin that made me shiver and ache.

I cleaned the outer patio and steps and then entered the temple, expecting to exchange a nod with the guard.

Only she wasn't there. For the very first time, I was alone in the temple.

My heart pounded, my blood rushing in my ears, as I evaluated my situation. What had happened? Where was the guard? Should I wait to see if she showed up? Or take advantage of her absence? If I went downstairs, what would I do if someone caught me?

What if this was a test? And by going downstairs, I would fail?

I had to risk it. I didn't know when I'd have this opportunity again. I threw my broom down to the base of the stairs. It would be my excuse if I was apprehended.

With my heart in my throat, I crept down the stairs, listening for any sound that would indicate someone was coming. The lower floor felt cooler than the top. Only two torches were lit, casting most of the room in darkness.

I hesitated at the bottom step, waiting. Making certain that no one lurked in those shadows. As my eyes adjusted, I saw that the room was empty of everything but the statue. I pulled in a deep, fortifying breath and began walking toward it.

Was I going to be struck down by lightning? Would the floor beneath me open up and swallow me whole for my blasphemy? I considered all the ways the goddess might punish me before I ever reached her.

Hesitating, I wondered if she would see this as another act of Locrian aggression. Would she be angry with me for wanting to heal a land she had cursed? Upset that I was violating her rules?

I glanced over at the stairs. I didn't have time to spare. Regardless of the outcome, I had to do this now.

Resolved, I approached her statue, eyes darting left and right, still listening. Total silence. I climbed up on the ledge at the base of the statue and reached for the veil.

This was it. I might finally have what I'd come here for.

My hand was shaking, my heartbeat so loud I was sure the entire temple complex would be able to hear it. I forced myself to push through and lifted the veil away from her face.

Nothing.

The socket was empty.

The eye wasn't there.

Disappointment flooded my limbs and I let go of the veil, taking a step down.

I had been so hopeful.

They had posted a guard not because there was anything valuable in this room, but for the sole purpose of keeping acolytes like me away. I'd heard other girls whispering about wanting to visit the statue. Their reasons were different from my own, but it was enough of a problem to explain the security they'd instituted.

Not because she had the eye.

I took a couple of steps back and looked at the statue. That humming feeling I'd felt in the flower garden returned. Maybe there was a value here that I couldn't see. I got on my knees.

"Oh great goddess." I whispered the words, afraid that I might be overheard. I tried to remember the correct way to do this. I sighed, worried I would mess it up.

"I'm not sure what to say," I continued on. "You probably see me as a thief. Or a usurper. But I'm here because I do believe in you. I need the eye to take it back to Locris, to save my people. I know you were angry, and you had every right to be. But it was a thousand years ago. And there are people paying the price who have never trespassed against you. I'm asking for your forgiveness. And your help."

Was that too presumptuous? Were we supposed to speak to the goddess this way? Should I be humbler, or use more flowery language? I only knew how to speak from my heart and I had to hope that it would be enough.

"I have to find the eye. I think it's at the temple somewhere, but I don't know where." I swallowed the lump in my throat, fighting off tears. I was so frustrated and worried and everything seemed hard.

Then I remembered that I was supposed to tell her what I had sacrificed for her when asking for a boon. "I gave you my sister. There's nothing more precious to me that I could have offered to you as a sacrifice. You know what it's like to be parted from someone you love. Don't let her death be meaningless. Please let me save my land and restore your worship there. If I've ever pleased you, I beg of you to grant me this."

I waited several beats in the quiet. I wasn't sure what I was expecting, but I was a bit dismayed that there wasn't some kind of response. While gazing at the statue, I saw a glimmer on her arm. Curious, I stood and walked over. Maybe I'd imagined it. No, it was definitely bright. I scratched at the spot and flakes of ivory paint fell away, revealing gold.

I tried to find a spot that wouldn't be immediately noticeable. I lifted the cloth tunic that they'd draped over her. The statue also had a carved tunic underneath the cloth one, and on one of the green painted folds, I scratched. More gold.

With a gasp I let the cloth tunic drop. She was plated in a layer of gold under the paint. There was a literal fortune on this statue. More than a king's ransom.

This was why they had the guard.

I briefly considered returning here and retrieving enough gold to help my nation after I found the eye, but I immediately felt sick to my stomach. That would be wrong. Selfish and greedy. I rejected the notion.

Feeling as if I should say something, I managed, "I'm sorry for scraping off the paint. I'm sure someone will fix it. And . . . thank you for listening."

I began walking toward the stairs when a wave of emotion hit me, hard in my chest.

A love so pure and shining that I put my hand over my heart and turned back to the statue.

Euthalia.

The voice echoed loudly inside my head, unmistakably coming from someone else. Then everything dissipated and it was just me in an empty room again. I grabbed the broom and hurried up the stairs, starting to sweep. What had that meant? Why was she saying my name? Was she answering my request? Approving of it? I wanted to take things that way, but I couldn't be certain.

And there was no one I could ask.

During my morning tutorial with Maia, I questioned her about why life mages weren't allowed in the temple considering that they performed the goddess's magic, and that seemed to completely befuddle her.

I wanted to ask her about the goddess. The words were burning my tongue because I was so desperate to say them. But I focused my attention on something else.

Because I didn't honestly care whether life mages could enter the temple. Why was the statue covered in gold? Why did I get these feelings, hear someone speaking my name? What did it mean?

Instead we talked about things that didn't seem to matter. Much of what Maia shared with me I already knew or had heard from Io. Io had been an excellent teacher and was careful to impart everything she thought might be important. I could see her taking over Maia's role someday.

It made me a little sad that I wouldn't be here to see it.

As I went about the rest of my day, it felt like someone had painted giant letters on my black tunic, announcing what I'd done, and people would only have to look at me to know that I had broken a rule.

But no one said anything to me. No guards rushed into the dining hall to seize me and drag me off to Theano for punishment.

No one knew.

My small success made me even more determined to sneak out into the city to get my parents a message and then find a way to break into the temple treasury.

One of the major issues was that there was no predictable pattern to the guard patrols. The shift changes didn't take place at the same times, either. For the last two weeks, I'd gotten up every night after my sisters went to bed, watching out our window. I made mental notes and was so frustrated that I didn't have any papyrus or lead to write down my observations.

The night after I'd approached the statue, Ahyana surprised me by joining me at my watch. I was apprehensive, but she didn't ask me what I was doing. She stood next to me, her gaze pointed the same direction as mine.

"Have you ever observed ants?" she asked me in a soft voice.

It was such an odd question that I couldn't even formulate a response.

"They always have a path. Humans might not be able to see it, but the ants know exactly which way to go. The guard patrols might seem random, but the path is there even if it feels like it isn't. The pattern resets, depending on the individual priestess. It will become clear if you know what to look for."

My mouth hung slightly open as Ahyana went back to her bed. Why had she helped me? She must have realized that I intended to break some rules, but she still wanted to assist me.

I didn't have to ask. I knew why.

Because I was her sister.

Ignoring the guilt I felt, I marveled at the fact that Antiope had created security that would have been impossible for an outsider to penetrate. Only a member of the temple would recognize the individual guards and be able to keep track of the routes they chose.

Not even Demaratus had instituted such a strong protection system. It seemed like a shame that I couldn't introduce him to Antiope. I was fairly certain it would be love at first sight for him.

Ahyana's counsel was correct. It took me a couple more weeks but I was finally able to come up with an accurate mental map of the routes each individual guard would take.

I kept trying to refine my plans. I was no closer to earning a spot as a Chosen. I certainly made a valiant effort, though. I got into the highest rankings, making sure that I always stayed near the bottom of the top five. I deliberately lost every fight with Artemisia so that she could retain her top slot. It was difficult, though. I wanted so badly to beat her into the ground but always restrained myself. I still wanted to keep people from questioning where I had learned to fight before coming to the temple, and I was also hopeful that Artemisia might pay less attention to me if she could dismiss me as a potential rival. Unfortunately, every fight we had made her angrier and angrier, as she seemed to intuit what I was doing.

It also made Antiope wildly frustrated. The battle master sensed what I was capable of and yelled at me constantly to do better. It reminded me so much of home that it was very hard not to smile while being lectured.

Despite doing well in all my classes, I was never picked as one of the Chosen. I decided to keep working toward that goal because, at some point, other people would start to notice that I was being deliberately excluded. I planned on making it so overwhelmingly obvious that I should be selected that the high priestess would have no choice but to make it so.

I was also still refining strategies on how to sneak out. It worried me that I didn't know which way to go, but I was capable of figuring it out now that I knew the trick to the labyrinth. At some point, while eating with my adelphia in the dining hall, I realized that my sisters had all grown up in Troas. They could help me.

At every meal I coaxed more information from them about the city. What directions the docks were from our location, whether there was a public library (there was), and where one could find the scribes' and booksellers' shops (not far from the library, which made sense). I felt guilty about secretly wheedling this information from them and I didn't like the way Suri would look at me as if she knew exactly what I was doing.

I worried that Ahyana might confront me about watching the guards, but she didn't. And as far as I could tell, she hadn't shared my nighttime observations with anyone else.

I thought of how when I'd first arrived, I had planned to use these women to get what I wanted. To befriend them and take the information that I needed. But they had offered me everything that I wanted and more. These women were my sisters, my friends. The rest of the priestesses and acolytes might have hated me, but not my adelphia.

Time began to feel like a sword hanging over my head by a very thin rope and I constantly felt anxious about it. I ate, studied, cleaned, and trained. Day in and day out. I'd asked Kallisto to give me half a year and now I'd been at the temple for more than a month. It was like I was stuck in place, as if I were swimming through deep mud. Kicking hard with my feet, stroking with my arms, but holding still and never making progress.

The only thing that made the passage of time easier was my dreams. Jason was always there, waiting for me. Physically things would reach a certain point and then stop, which was entirely frustrating. Was it because I didn't know what would happen next, so I couldn't imagine it?

It didn't feel that way, though—it was more like someone putting up a wall to separate us the moment things got too intense. Deliberately keeping us apart.

There were other nights where he and I only talked. He would ask me about my day and would listen attentively while I shared my routine with him. He told me about his voyages at sea, the freedom of traveling wherever the wind and waves carried him, never knowing what adventure the next day would bring.

Our kissing and our conversations made me feel so connected to him. Like an unseen hand was stitching our souls together, making us one.

I found myself looking forward to falling asleep, to being able to temporarily escape my fears and worries.

Jason wasn't the only person I dreamed of. Demaratus was often there, yelling at me while I trained.

The Demaratus dreams were always the same. I was running as fast as I could through the labyrinth in Locris. He was up on the wall, looking down at me.

"Stupid girl! You can't run forever! Stand still and do what needs to be done!"

I never knew what to make of his advice. It was the opposite of everything he'd ever told me.

I finally did as he said and stood still, my hands on my hips while I waited. The ground beneath my feet gave way and I was sucked down into an abyss.

"Oof." My lungs quickly expelled air when I landed. I sat up and looked around. I was in the field of wildflowers again.

The goddess was waiting for me, looking just as she had in my first dream. Her rippling golden hair, beaming face, the smell of irises coming from her green robes. I was afraid to approach her.

Euthalia. I heard her voice inside my head, but her lips didn't move.

She came closer to me and then held out a fist. She turned her hand over and opened it. A massive green gem lay against her palm.

The eye.

She held it out to me. Was she offering it to me?

Was this some kind of sign or just my own wishful thinking? It was impossible to tell.

It is time.

"Time for what?" I asked and then clamped a hand over my mouth. If I wasn't even allowed to approach her statue, it seemed completely blasphemous to be questioning her. Would I offend her?

I waited, my limbs trembling.

Instead she gave me a slight smile.

Time for things to change.

CHAPTER
THIRTY-SEVEN

"What things?" I asked, but then she disappeared and I woke with a start, disoriented.

But despite what felt like a prophetic dream, the day was like any other. I didn't know what was supposed to change or how. Would the goddess reveal it to me? Or was I supposed to figure it out on my own?

I hated that I didn't know and that I couldn't ask anyone.

Her words ran through my head, distracting me during training. Fortunately we were doing rhythmic movements as a group, teaching our bodies to naturally move as a warrior's would so that if we were in a fight we could respond fluidly, without thinking.

We never knew when we entered the gymnasium what we would be doing that day—Antiope seemed to pride herself on keeping us on our toes. Some days we would run; others we would lift heavy objects repetitively to strengthen our muscles. One-on-one sparring was common, but we were also taught to fight groups of attackers.

Artemisia in particular took far too much pleasure in laying out every opponent who challenged her.

When I had trained with Demaratus, he'd emphasized my limits and weaknesses. Antiope, in contrast, saw only potential and encouraged me to think beyond my limitations.

That I was stronger and faster and better than anyone believed, myself included.

"Any Locrian maiden who survives the run is someone to be reckoned with," she had said to me on more than one occasion as she encouraged me, praised me.

It was an entirely different style of teaching, and I found myself blossoming under her guidance.

After the training session ended, Suri put her hand on my shoulder and pointed toward the river that ran through the temple grounds. It wasn't unusual for the priestesses and acolytes to cool off in the slow-moving waters.

I nodded and walked with her in silence to the riverbank. The water made a calm, soothing sound as it glided over the rocks in its bed. Suri sat down on the grass and I took the spot next to her.

She hadn't ever attempted to spend time alone with me before, and I wondered why she had chosen today. Io and Suri were close, which I understood. Not only because they'd arrived at the same time, but because Io did all the talking.

I wondered if Suri ever felt left out. Her face was so expressive that even though she didn't say words, she still participated in our conversations. I felt like I had come to know her.

There was a cawing above me and then Kunguru swooped down, coming to a stop near my hand. He cocked his head to the right. I knew what he wanted. I opened the pouch at my waist to get him some stale breadcrumbs. I saw Quynh's bracelet and sadly smiled. She would have loved this bird.

He made a happy, trilling sound and moved closer, eating the crumbs off my palm. It was easy to see why Ahyana liked him so much. He was a good companion and I had become very attached to him. His only demands were to be fed and told how pretty he was.

He was also an excellent listener. I could share my secrets with him and he didn't judge me or share them with anyone else.

Kunguru had taken a dislike to Artemisia and had swooped at her head a few times until Ahyana had told him to stop because she was afraid the other girl might shoot him out of the sky.

Suri tipped her face up, soaking in the sun's warmth. I placed my hand against the grass, feeling that familiar hum.

I realized that Suri had turned her gaze toward me. She pointed at the ground and then laid her hand against it.

"Yes, I feel it," I said.

She nodded, satisfied. Did she know what it meant? Or was she just as mystified as I was and wanting someone to commiserate with?

Like Kunguru, Suri was someone I could confide in. I knew she wouldn't share my secrets. Her allegiance was to the temple and her sisters, but her silence made her an ally.

"Do you have vivid dreams?" I asked her.

Yes.

"Do you dream of your former life?"

No.

Given what I suspected she'd gone through, I wasn't going to ask her if she dreamed about kissing anyone. I settled on, "What about the goddess? Do you dream of her?"

Yes.

My heart thumped loudly. "Does she speak to you?"

Yes.

"What does she say?" I realized a beat too late that Suri couldn't answer that question. "Did you dream of her last night?"

Yes.

Just as I had. I wasn't the only one. Did she appear to everyone in the temple? Was this something that happened regularly and I was just unaware of it?

Why hadn't anyone said anything to me about it?

Was that my fault? I was the one keeping everyone at arm's length, not sharing all of myself with them, not opening up about why I was really here. I didn't invite their confidences.

The goddess's words repeated in my head. *Time for things to change.* Had she meant my relationships with my sisters?

The rest of our adelphia approached, laughing over something Io had said. It must have been time for lunch, and then we would go to our afternoon class. Several butterflies were fluttering around Ahyana's head and she grinned up at them, holding out her finger. A bright orange one landed, gently flapping her tiny wings.

Suri tapped me on the shoulder and I turned to look at her. Then she did something utterly shocking. She opened her mouth slightly, as if to speak, and then touched her lips with her fingers. She moved her hand to gesture at our sisters.

It took me a moment to understand what she was trying to communicate. "Tell them?" I asked.

Yes.

Suri had never signed like that with me before. She had pointed, moved her head to indicate yes or no, but not this. It felt important and significant.

What had the goddess told her?

It was difficult to listen in our afternoon class, with both the goddess's words and Suri's unspoken ones running around in my mind, and the only reason Maia managed to grab my focus was because she said, "Jason."

"That got Lia to pay attention," Zalira said with a grin.

"Did they say Jason?" Ahyana whispered. "I'm fairly certain I heard the name Jason."

"Stop it," I told them under my breath, but this seemed to make things worse.

Io leaned forward and I expected her to tell us to be quiet. Instead she said, "I thought we'd decided Jason was stupid."

"What?" I asked, confused.

"You talk in your dreams, but you always say the same two words. 'Jason' and 'stupid,'" Io said. "What did he do to make you call him names?"

"Can we please listen?" I asked. I knew exactly why I'd said what I did. Those were the things I dreamed about—Jason kissing me interspersed with Demaratus calling me stupid.

"You know it's dire when Lia's the one telling us to be quiet," Zalira said, and I made a shushing noise as Io and Ahyana started to giggle, Suri grinning.

They finally stopped, but I knew my cheeks were red. As far as I could tell, I was the only one who had ever had any type of romantic relationship and all my sisters wanted to live vicariously through me. I kept trying to tell them that I'd only had the one brief experience, but it didn't seem to matter.

Maia spoke about a great warrior named Jason, who had been tasked with finding and destroying a horrific beast. A creature that had the head and body of a woman, but the lower half of a dragon.

Every time she said the name Jason, I could feel my sisters' eyes on me. I was going to be teased relentlessly later on, I already knew it.

The lesson was not only about him, but about other heroic warriors who were celebrated in word and song for having hunted down and destroyed other monsters. Creatures who could turn men to stone with a touch, or unhinge their jaws to devour men whole. Ones who had poison in their veins and instantly killed anyone who tried to mate with them. Beasts who kidnapped children in the middle of the night, breathing fire on those who tried to reclaim them. A chimera who had a hundred heads and would grow two more if you cut off one.

"What do all of these monsters of mythology have in common?" Maia asked.

The room was silent. Finally a second-year acolyte raised her hand. "They all eat people?"

"They're all female," Artemisia said from the back of the room, cutting through the first answer like a knife.

"Yes." Maia nodded. "In the stories, the beasts that must be vanquished are always female. Have you ever wondered why? It is because men have always feared women's destructive potential. Knowledge gives us power. Your power is a threat. Especially the women in this room."

My breath caught. Was this why Ilion kept their women ignorant? I raised my hand. I needed to know more.

A priestess entered the room, obviously out of breath. "The king is dead!"

Maia's face fell. "Class dismissed!"

She raced up the stairs, grabbed the messenger priestess, and exited with her. The entire class broke into a noisy uproar.

While it was sad that the king had died, I didn't understand the confusion.

"What's going on?" I asked.

"This is going to cause total chaos," Ahyana said, her face grim. It wasn't an expression I'd ever seen on her face before.

Now I was even more bewildered. "Why?"

"A new king must be selected," Zalira said.

"Won't it be his oldest son?" There should be a line of succession. It was how things worked in Locris.

"No," Zalira said with a shake of her head. "There is a council of elders for the city and they will determine the king in three months' time. They will choose from the king's sons."

"How do they choose?"

Ahyana said, "My father once told me that the king was chosen over his brothers because he was already married with an heir."

That made my breath catch and solidify in my chest. I couldn't breathe.

As far as I knew, none of the king's sons were married.

And only one of them was betrothed.

Prince Alexandros.

To me.

My mind quickly followed the logical outcome of this situation. If the prince had to be married in order to be chosen as king, he would press the betrothal. He would demand that I be brought to him and our contract fulfilled.

How much time did I have? Two weeks? Two months? I didn't know. Panicked dread made my limbs feel shaky and I had to stand up.

The journey across the Acheron Sea took less than a week. There would only be so many times that my father could put the prince off before he grew suspicious. What would he do if he discovered what I had done? That I was sworn to the temple and the goddess's service?

I'd known from the start that my actions might put Locris in danger, and now that day had arrived.

Everything had changed. I had to get a message to my parents.

I would have to sneak out of the temple tonight.

CHAPTER THIRTY-EIGHT

"We should return to our room," Io said in a low, urgent voice.

Everyone else got up and we all followed her out of the auditorium. We had chores, but I had the feeling the rules and standards were going to be a bit loose today. It seemed as if everyone needed the chance to regroup.

Outside there were scattered pockets of women standing around talking to one another in raised voices. The shift of power in Ilion wasn't a predictable one and everybody was worried.

What would the prince do to claim his kingship? The pit in my stomach deepened and I focused on putting one foot in front of the other.

Eventually he would find out what I had done. Would he respect the vows that I had taken? Or would he insist that the signed, contracted betrothal that predated my entering the temple took precedence?

It didn't matter. Contract or no, the law still granted me the right to refuse him and marriage. I wouldn't even consider saying yes until I had healed the lands of Locris.

After we filed into our room, Suri shut the door behind us. There was a flapping of wings and Kunguru landed on the windowsill, as if he'd been following us. He flew across the room to perch on Ahyana's shoulder.

Io came over to me and took my hands in hers. "Are you all right? What's wrong?"

She looked so upset. She was the most empathetic out of all of us and I felt bad that my anxiety and worry were affecting her.

I had to send a message to my family. Now. No more delaying. No more waiting for opportunities, like I had with the statue. I was going to have to take fate into my own hands and make something happen. Change my circumstances, my situation, my relationships if necessary.

I needed to let my sisters know what I had planned.

Taking in a deep breath, I announced, "I need to sneak out of the temple tonight."

There. Too late to take it back or undo it.

It was a relief to finally say the words aloud. To show them more of my true self.

"Why?" Zalira asked.

I couldn't bring myself to tell them about my personal quest to find the eye, but I could share part of the reason why I had to find a way out.

"My parents don't know that I'm still alive. I have to get word to them. I'm going to find a sailor down at the docks to carry a message for me."

Ahyana nodded. "I can see how the king's death would push you to send word. It also reminded me that life is very short."

That wasn't at all the reason, but if I said so, it would just create a lot of questions I wasn't ready to answer. It was easier to go along with her assumption. I nodded.

"You've been planning this for a while, haven't you? Is that why you've been asking us about the locations of specific buildings?" Zalira folded her arms. It didn't surprise me that she would be the one to immediately connect those two things.

"Yes. I wasn't sure how to get back to the docks."

Io released my hands and an expression that looked like she felt betrayed flashed across her face briefly. "You could have told us. We would have understood."

"She's telling us now," Ahyana said.

"I don't want you to sneak out," Io said, directing her words to me. "It's not safe. It worries me."

"You always worry," I told her.

"Because all of you give me a reason to!" she said with an indignant huff.

This was unlike her typically warm and sunny personality and I found myself wanting to ease her mind. "I will be fine. If anyone is foolish enough to approach me, Antiope has made certain I can defend myself."

Suri patted Io on the back, comforting her.

"That's true," Zalira acknowledged. "Lia can take any of us in a fight."

"We should go with her," Io said.

"No!" I shouted and lowered my voice to a more moderate tone. "No. I'm not going to let anyone else get in trouble for my actions."

"That's what we do," Zalira reminded me. "We're sisters."

I shook my head, hard. They all kept telling me the city wasn't safe. I wasn't going to put any of their lives at risk. I would never do that again. "No. I will do this on my own."

"Will you be able to get past the patrols without getting caught?" Ahyana asked.

Thanks to her, yes. "I think so."

Io just shook her head. "We need to get to the courtyard. Someone will come looking for us."

Right. Our chores.

We walked in a strange silence and I felt guilty. Io was obviously upset and I didn't want to be the cause of it. Even Kunguru seemed uneasy. He flew away from us, off into the distance.

Io led us over to the stone altar. "We're supposed to replace the fruits and vegetables that have been left here, and then tidy up the courtyard. Zalira and Ahyana, can you go to the kitchen storage and get new ones? And Suri, could you get the brooms? Lia and I will get rid of the older food."

The others left and Io was quiet while she began to gather the fruits and vegetables.

"Why are these here?" I knew the answer but wanted to get her talking again. I wanted things to be all right between us.

"They were brought in as sacrifices to honor the goddess. These offerings are to remain fresh all throughout the harvest season. The citizens count it as a miracle that they are continually preserved."

I hadn't known the last part. It seemed a little dishonest to me, but I knew that now was not the time to press that particular issue. "Can't the goddess keep them fresh?"

"Why should the goddess do anything when we are available to do her work in her stead? It could be worse. I have heard that there are some bloodthirsty gods who demand the sacrifice of animals." She shuddered. "Our peaceful goddess only asks for the first fruits of the plants she has grown for us to be returned to her."

Although I should have controlled my anger at her statement, it was too difficult for me to let her words pass unchallenged. "'Peaceful'? In my home, her need for vengeance has nearly destroyed us."

Io paused her work, looking at me. "Sacrilege cannot be treated like other crimes. The whole community inherits the guilt from one generation to the next."

That seemed incredibly unfair. When I managed to steal the eye, would my children be punished for my actions?

Then, with a sinking feeling, I remembered that it wouldn't be an issue. I could commit all the sacrilege I liked because there would be no one to follow after me.

"Should we quiz one another?" she asked, and she still had that strange tone in her voice that made me concerned. But Io routinely tested us to make certain that we were retaining the things we were taught in our classes.

"Yes. What should we start with?"

"Do you remember yesterday's lesson?"

I helped her push all the food into a pile at the center of the altar. "It was only yesterday," I said with a smile, teasing in an attempt to restore her typical good mood. "So, yes. We spoke about shape-shifters."

She nodded.

"Do you think they're real?" I asked.

"I don't know," she admitted. "It's hard to tell sometimes what's been made up to illustrate a specific point and what's fact. Are there really creatures with a scorpion's tail, the head of a dog, and the body of a lion? Possibly? As I said, I don't know."

"It's just hard to imagine that someone can be human one moment and then an animal the next. But I've seen a water dragon in real life, so who am I to question whether or not strange monsters exist?"

A bird called out. Io's back stiffened and then she suddenly turned, depositing a big armful of squashes and melons into my arms. "Would you mind taking those to the refuse pile?"

I nodded and carried them to the pile located not far from the kitchens. I spotted Zalira and Ahyana in one of the storage rooms throwing bits of food at each other, laughing. I shook my head and smiled as I returned to the courtyard.

When I got there, I saw Suri studiously sweeping at the far end, but Io was gone. I approached Suri and asked if she knew where Io was.

No.

I crossed the length of the courtyard and found Io on the opposite end, on the side of the temple. She was standing on a bench next to the stone fence, peering over the top.

"Io?"

She startled and then whirled around. "Lia! You scared me."

"What are you doing?"

"Nothing." She quickly climbed down. "I thought I saw a bird."

And she had climbed up onto a bench to look at it? A flower I might have believed, but not a bird.

"We should get back to work," she said. She hurried off, and even though I berated myself for being far too suspicious, I still climbed up on the bench to look over the wall.

The alley was empty in both directions. There wasn't anyone there.

But my instincts warned me that I was being watched. I continued to scan the buildings across the way, the rooftops. Nothing.

Uneasy, I jumped down and headed for the courtyard.

It reminded me that I wasn't the only one keeping secrets.

◆ ◆ ◆

My adelphia stayed up with me long past curfew. Kunguru joined us while we kept watch at the window.

I started muttering the names of the guards that I saw. "Isidora. Megiste. Phaedre. Cybele. Metis." I knew exactly which routes they would take.

My pulse beat quickly in my wrists but I had to admit that a part of me was secretly excited. I'd wanted this for so long and I was finally going to be able to let my family know that I had survived.

I had already decided that I wouldn't tell them anything about Quynh yet. I wanted to deliver that devastating news in person. Not to mention that her heritage and name were unique enough that if the wrong person intercepted my messenger, they might be able to piece together my true identity.

My heart twisted as I thought of my sister. The passing of time had helped some, but not nearly enough. I still missed her every single day.

"When?" Zalira asked in a whisper, rapidly shifting her weight back and forth on the balls of her feet. She was excited, too. Like she was the one sneaking out instead of me.

"Soon."

Another guard came into view, but I didn't know her. She had never patrolled before. I let out a groan.

"What is it?" Io asked, still exuding anxiety and concern.

"A new guard. I don't know what her path will be." I wanted to kick something. I was out of time. I had to let my family know right away to delay the prince as long as possible.

"I could contact your parents," Io said. "I'll speak to the temple messenger and ask him to write a letter on your behalf. I would just need their names and where your home is located."

I nearly choked at her suggestion. "Thank you, but this is my responsibility and I can handle it myself. I wouldn't want you to get in trouble."

Although that hadn't been specifically spelled out to me as a rule, I saw from her face that it was. It meant a lot that Io was willing to break rules for me. I squeezed her shoulder to let her know.

She patted my hand and then I released her.

With a sigh I realized that I had gotten prepared for nothing. I had all of my weapons on, my knapsack with a small bag of salt, and a hooded, black cloak. *I should just go to bed.*

Isidora passed by our window again. "If I was going to still go, now would be the time."

Ahyana's face lit up. "You need a distraction!"

She rushed out of our room. I called after her as quietly as I could, but she didn't come back.

Zalira took me by the hand and we raced together to the front door of the dormitory. We waited several seconds and then I heard someone yell, "Fire!"

I bit back a groan. Was Ahyana going to burn down the complex just to allow me to sneak out?

"Go!" Zalira said with a grin, as caught up in the thrill of this as I was.

I smiled back and then ran out into the night.

CHAPTER THIRTY-NINE

It was a bit different running this time—no one was chasing me and trying to kill me. It didn't mean that I didn't have to worry, because I knew what would happen if someone in the temple caught me.

What it might mean for my sisters if they were implicated.

I ran around to the side of the dormitory, peering out to make sure the way was clear. There were raised voices rushing toward where I assumed Ahyana had started the fire. I hoped she was able to sneak back into our room, undetected.

Ducking down, I kept my body low to the ground so that I would be less noticeable.

My heart was beating so loudly in my ears that it made it a bit difficult to hear. I tried to calm my trembling legs and my ragged breathing but couldn't. I made it to the edge of the temple and was about to round the corner into the courtyard when I heard Kunguru loudly cawing.

He was just above me, on the temple's roof. I flattened myself against the wall, and two seconds later a guard rushed past me, on her way to the fire.

The raven had just saved me from being discovered. I was going to reward him with extra treats tomorrow.

Running through the courtyard was the scariest part, as it was the most open. There was nowhere for me to hide, no building I could duck behind.

I was exposed.

But I made it safely past the archway, and once I was out in the street, I pressed myself against the stone wall, waiting to see if I'd been noticed.

I waited two whole minutes, where each second was an agonizing torment.

All quiet.

No one had seen me; I wasn't being followed.

I headed south, doing my best to keep to the shadows. I seemed to be the only person on the street. I was heading past well-lit establishments and could hear singing and lively conversation.

While I'd initially planned on avoiding this area, wanting to go around it, I quickly realized that would be foolish. It was a straight shot to the labyrinth exit I needed.

But it was the exact neighborhood where I'd lost Quynh. I slowed down when I reached the street where she'd been taken from me. My instinct was to hurry past but I couldn't do it. I had to stand in the spot where she'd had her last moments.

It wasn't hard to find it. It was forever seared into my mind. The image of her dangling over this very street would never leave me.

I swallowed down the heartache and soul-destroying sorrow I felt and knelt on the cobblestones. I ran my fingers across them. She'd been right here. There weren't any bloodstains, though. The citizens must have been more diligent about cleaning them than the temple workers.

Or she'd been suffocated instead of stabbed.

"Quynh. I miss you. I think of you every day," I said softly. I hoped that she could hear me.

A door suddenly burst open not far from me and half a dozen men spilled out into the street, obviously drunk.

"Get out!" a woman's voice called. "Go destroy someone else's business and leave mine alone!"

I hesitated for a moment too long. I should have immediately run or found a hiding place. But I was in the midst of honoring my sister and had naively hoped the men would leave me alone.

They did not.

"What do we have here?" one of them said. He was large and already had a black eye.

Someone who didn't mind getting into a scrape.

"You shouldn't be out here all alone. You never know what kind of men you might come across," another said, and the whole group laughed.

I knew the best way to end a fight was to not engage in one to begin with. They were drunk, which would give me an advantage, but they were large men. From their swagger and muscled arms, they might have even been professional soldiers.

Time for me to go. I turned around but the man who had spoken grabbed my cloak and yanked me back toward him. "I asked you a question!"

I quickly assessed the situation I was in. Their looks were predatory, instantly telling me their intentions. Nothing good was about to happen. As confirmation they began to spread themselves out. I couldn't allow them to do that.

When you have multiple attackers, keep them in a line so that you only have to fight them one at a time! Use their bodies to create distance and keep the other combatants at bay! Antiope's voice was the one filling my head at the moment.

I knew what to do. I had literally trained for this.

I'd just never expected that those skills would become necessary.

The leader tugged me closer. "Come here and give us a kiss."

When he leaned in, I used the front part of my skull to headbutt him and was rewarded with a sickening crunch when I broke his nose.

He swore and then said, "Get her!"

I twirled around to jerk my cloak from his grasp and withdrew my xiphos at the same time. I backed up, taking small, quick steps, forcing them to follow. It prevented them from being able to surround me.

Because if they did, I was done for.

This was an area full of taverns and brothels. I was sure no one paid any attention to a woman screaming for help here.

I would have to deal with this on my own.

And I had to attack first so that I could control the situation. I wouldn't be able to defend myself from multiple directions.

There's no such thing as a fair fight, Antiope reminded me. *When your life is on the line, anything goes.*

A calm settled into my limbs. I knew what to do. My breathing slowed, my body ready.

I feinted at the closest man and he responded the way I'd hoped—he lurched forward, intent on grabbing me, and I used the element of surprise against him. I reared back and kicked him square in the chest, right into the attacker behind him.

Another man reached for me and I slashed at his forearms, making contact and dragging my blade through his flesh. He yelled in pain and I kicked at his left knee, knocking him to the ground. I punched him hard in the face and he fell back, unmoving.

One down, five more to go.

Always know where all of your attackers are, that Antiope voice said.

Blood pumped through my veins quickly as I continued my nimble steps to stay on the edge of their group, not letting them flank me. But one of my attackers darted to the right and moved past me at the same moment that his companion went to hit me in the face.

Raising my left arm, I easily blocked his shot, gritting my teeth against the impact. I turned slightly, elbowing the face of the man behind me before carrying the swing through to the attacker in front.

The man to my rear regained his balance and I felt him surging toward me. I ducked down, twisting myself out of the way so that his punch landed on the man who had been directly in front of me. I kicked out at the two entangled men and they went sprawling.

An attacker moved out of the way so that he wouldn't be caught up by his falling companions and lunged at me with his sword, thrusting forward. I veered left, grabbing his hand and turning his wrist hard so that he had to drop his weapon, and then I shoved him into his friends.

I spotted a narrow alley nearby and I blocked the incoming strikes from the other two men with my sword or my arm, keeping all of them at bay while I worked my way toward it.

When I found the alley, I backed into it. They wouldn't be able to swing their swords here, and it would ensure I only had to deal with one fighter at a time.

The first man tried to hit me, but his inebriation prevented him from realizing that he couldn't arc his arm around at me, and I took advantage of his confusion to hit him hard in the middle of his neck. He grabbed at his throat, making a choking sound, and I kicked him in the groin. He fell to his knees, letting out a loud moan of pain.

The attacker behind him jumped over his fallen friend and stabbed at me with his sword. I met his blade, turning it aside. He growled and tried again, but no matter how many times he came after me, I parried every one of his thrusts. He was breathing hard from the exertion but I didn't feel the least bit tired.

I continued moving down the alley while we fought. I landed one of my strikes, piercing him in the gut. He looked down in surprise as blood rushed from the wound.

He slumped against one of the walls, holding his stomach, but there was another man waiting to take his place.

As I emerged from the end of the alley, I had an overwhelming moment of panic as I realized that I had lost track of the leader. A second later that man came up behind me, trapping me in place. He had gone around to surprise me. He pressed his thick forearm against my neck and began to squeeze. He hadn't bothered to disarm me.

His mistake.

"Not so tough now, are you?" he taunted.

I clamped my teeth down onto his arm while stabbing him in the right thigh. He howled and shoved me away. I surveyed my immediate area, registering everything that could be used as a weapon, the places where I could position myself to have an advantage.

Another attacker swung out and I ducked and then reached up to grab his extended arm and shoved him into the leader. I held my weapon up and waited. There were three men left and all of them were bleeding.

They tried to fan out again, to triangulate around me so that they could attack at once. I wasn't going to allow that.

This needed to end.

Because the longer this went on, the greater the risk to me.

I went after the man on my left and, before he realized what was happening, stabbed him in the thigh. As he fell to his knees, I swung out a fist to connect with the side of his head, knocking him out.

The leader hung back, sending his last companion after me. That one rushed at me with his sword held over his head. I turned sharply to the left as he tried to hit me and pushed him into a nearby wall. He hit his head and slumped to the ground.

"I am going to make you suffer and watch as the life ebbs from your eyes," the leader said, spitting a mouthful of blood on the ground.

Adrenaline was still coursing through me, giving me a rush. I smiled. "You are not the first Ilionian who's threatened me that way and yet here I am."

I turned my body sideways to present less of a target and the leader roared as he rushed toward me.

When he got close enough, I dropped down and hooked my foot around his left ankle, using Artemisia's move to get him on the ground.

He fell and I grabbed a clay pot near the wall and hit him over the head, smashing it against his skull. He went limp.

I realized that I was breathing hard. I smiled again. I should have been worn out. I should have been sore and aching, exhausted. Instead

I was completely exhilarated. It was like I'd been made just for this purpose.

How had this fight been so easy? As much as I wanted to give the credit to Antiope and her methods, this hadn't been only because of my training. I had been equal to these men in strength and speed. Because they were drunk? I wasn't sure. All I did know was that it had been different from any other fight I'd had against men before.

And I was primed to keep going.

Then I felt a pair of hands on my shoulders and I ducked down and turned, grabbing the man's tunic and throwing him against the wall, holding him in place with my left forearm, putting my xiphos to his throat.

"I'm pleased to see your old blade again."

"Jason?"

CHAPTER FORTY

I blinked several times, making sure I wasn't imagining this. Had one of those drunken louts knocked me out and I was actually lying in the street dreaming of Jason?

"Good evening, Lia. Have you tried to feed yourself to any dragons lately?"

I pushed the tip of the blade a tiny bit into his skin. "What are you doing here? How did you find me?"

He smirked at me. "I just followed the blood and screaming and it led me straight to you."

"You're not funny."

"Disagree."

His eyes glittered in the low light, full of intensity and heat and want. I felt sweat breaking out along my hairline, my lips tingling, my stomach throbbing. Seeing him again, it was like I was back in a dream, delirious from all the wicked things he did to me with his mouth and fingers.

This moment didn't feel real.

"You seem stronger," he observed, echoing my own observations from a few moments ago.

"Would you like to see how strong?" I asked, letting the point of my sword further pierce his skin. He didn't even flinch when a tiny drop of blood appeared.

He took my measure and then leaned gently toward me. He was harming himself, the forward motion causing the point of my sword to dig deeper into his neck. He didn't seem to care, though. He kissed me, briefly, shockingly. My body turned liquid, loose.

"As weak as any other woman when it comes to that," he murmured.

Angry, both with him and myself, I tightened my grip on his tunic and reminded him of my blade against his throat. The drop of the blood had turned into a tiny trickle. "Never do that again."

"Never?" he repeated playfully, his eyebrows raised. "Never is a long time, Lia. You might get lonely in your temple."

I ordered my lips to stop aching, but they did not obey.

"Did you not want me to kiss you?" he asked softly. "I thought that you did."

It didn't matter whether I had wanted it. Yes, I had been desperate for his mouth on mine, more than anything, but there was no point.

He reached up and touched my hair. "Did you do this?"

My hair had grown half an inch in the last month, but I still felt extremely self-conscious about it. But he wasn't looking at me like he found my short hair unattractive. "No, it was done to me."

"Why?"

"To humiliate and degrade me. To make it so I wouldn't forget that I didn't belong."

"Who did it?" he demanded in a tone that implied he was going to hunt those people down and make them suffer.

A thrill rang through me at his unspoken threat.

"It doesn't matter," I said.

He was still running his fingers along the edges of my hair when I heard a loud groan behind us. For a single moment I was afraid that I was the one who had made it because he was touching me.

"We should get off the street before a patrol happens by or those men come to," he said. "I don't imagine they're very pleased with you. And I would prefer you not slip and accidentally cut my throat."

I had forgotten I had my sword still pressed against his neck. I took a step back and released him.

"There's somewhere I can go. I was planning on stopping by there, anyway. You should go back to your ship," I said. "I don't need your help."

"I can see that," he said. "But if I get caught, I'll be accused of being your accomplice. We should stay together. Just in case."

That was a nonsensical reason, but I didn't actually want him to leave. "Fine. I suppose you can tag along if you'd like."

"Thank you," he said gallantly while wiping his throat with the edge of his cloak. For a moment I was struck by the urge to apologize for doing anything to maim his perfect skin but brushed it off.

We walked away from the mess I'd made, with him staying a step behind me. When we passed by the leader of the group who had attacked me, it took all my willpower not to kick him in the ribs.

"Why are you in this neighborhood tonight? Were you hoping to get robbed and murdered?" Jason asked in a conversational tone.

"What are you doing here?" I countered. He had to know as well as I did the kinds of services they offered in this area. "Looking for the nearest warm body?"

"Are you offering?"

I glared at him and he laughed.

"Were you the one who was planning to rob or murder me?" I asked.

"If I was going to do either one, I would have done it already."

He was stronger than me. I knew that for a fact. I very clearly remembered how much I had struggled to get up when he had held me down in the courtyard in my palace—how had I been able to pin him against the wall?

Had he just allowed me to do it?

"So, have you missed me?" he asked.

There was no chance I was going to tell him the truth. I knew what he would do if I told him I dreamed of him every night, in very explicit ways. "It's been a month. I forgot you existed."

He placed both of his hands over his chest. "You wound me!"

I peered over my shoulder at him. "I can, if you'd like."

That wicked, delicious glint in his eye nearly made me trip over my own feet. Fortunately, we had arrived at the building I'd been searching for. It was a bit different locating it at night.

I raised my hand to knock and Jason unnecessarily announced, "This is a brothel."

"I know."

"What business do you have at a brothel?" He sounded both intrigued and confused.

"It is none of your concern." I knocked and a younger hetaera answered the door.

"I'm here to see Mahtab," I told her.

"Give me a moment," she said, closing the door.

"Are you really not going to tell me?" he asked and I ignored him.

The front door opened again. The hetaera's gaze darted over to Jason's face and a smile lit up her features. "Come right in."

"Stay here," I told him as we entered the house. I didn't want Jason to know what I was up to.

"Mahtab is upstairs," the young woman told me. "The first room on your right."

I thanked her and pulled the edges of my cloak down to shield my face. I couldn't risk anyone being able to identify me later. Seeing a temple acolyte in a hetaera house would be gossip too good not to share.

When I reached the room, I knocked on the door.

"Enter."

Mahtab was sitting in a chair near the window. Her eyebrows shot up. "It's you."

"Yes. I wanted to make sure that you and your house weren't affected by what I did the night of the race." If they had suffered in some way, I would have to make reparations. This was the last place I'd spent time with Quynh and I wanted to honor that.

"We weren't affected in any way," she said gently. She walked across the room. "How is your friend?"

Her words were like an arrow straight to my gut. "She didn't make it."

"That was the rumor we'd heard, but I'd hoped it was wrong. I am so sorry for your loss."

"Thank you."

"And please know that the very generous gift you left has made it possible for me to help many of the women here. So thank you for that."

I nodded. When I thought of that night, losing Quynh was the thing that stood out, but the idea that I might have put the women in this house in danger had always bothered me.

"I'm glad," I said.

"If you should ever need anything in the future, please don't hesitate to call on me," she said.

While I couldn't imagine a situation in which I would need her assistance, I thanked her. It was a kind gesture.

"And the same for me." Again, there didn't seem to be any scenario where Mahtab might need my help, but it seemed right to offer after what she'd done. She had given me precious hours with my sister that I wouldn't have had otherwise.

The hetaera came over and took both of my hands in hers, squeezing. "I wish you the best of luck. You are a very brave young woman."

I briefly considered asking to see the storage room where Quynh and I had hidden, but it felt like too much. Maybe there would be a day in the future when I could sit in there and think of my last moments with my sister without wanting to double over from the pain.

My sorrow was steadily increasing and I worried that if I stayed here it might engulf me entirely.

I said my goodbyes to Mahtab and went back downstairs. Jason was in the main room and the hetaerae were draping themselves all over him. He seemed to be greatly enjoying himself.

He had just kissed me a few minutes ago and now he was entertaining the advances of so many different women. I knew what he was. Why was I surprised? Swallowing the disgust I felt, I said, "Time to go."

"I thought we were staying off the street," he said, and the woman on his right let out a giggle as he squeezed her shoulders.

"I haven't heard an alarm being raised or patrols calling out," I countered. "I'm going to leave."

It wasn't as if a gambling sailor could afford their rates. But given how attractive he was . . . it wouldn't have surprised me if someone here would have been willing to offer him a steep discount.

"Perhaps I'll stay," he said as the hetaera to his left snuggled in closer to him.

"Do as you wish," I said, jealousy roaring inside me like a dragon. Why was I envious? I couldn't have him. I didn't even want him.

That's a lie.

Yes, that was a lie. It didn't matter, though. He was free to consort with whomever he wished, as often as he wished. I opened the front door and let myself out and back onto the street.

I heard him rushing to catch up. "What did you do upstairs?"

"As I said, it's none of your concern."

"You do realize that by being mysterious, it only makes you more intriguing? I'm curious as to what a temple priestess, sworn to safeguard her virginity, would be doing at a hetaera house."

I came to a sudden halt, spinning on my heels. He towered over me, nearly crashing into me. "Speaking of intrigue, how did you find me?"

He gave me a half smile. "I told you, I only had to follow—"

"No." I held my hand up. "I remember what you said. But I don't believe in coincidences."

Jason folded his arms across his broad chest. "They do happen."

"In a city this size, you didn't stumble across me by accident."

"Perhaps I sensed that you needed me."

"We both know that didn't happen, either." Maybe I shouldn't have been so quick to dismiss the connection he was hinting at. I'd certainly felt it when I was dreaming.

If he were in trouble, would I know it?

A mischievous grin lit up his face. "What if I said a little bird told me?"

CHAPTER FORTY-ONE

My heart stopped completely before it began beating too hard and too fast. Was he being literal? For a brief moment I wondered whether Kunguru was also keeping secrets from me. Could he speak? But that was impossible and ridiculous. I immediately dismissed that possibility.

But I was going to ask Ahyana about it later, just to be certain.

"You have your secrets, and I have mine," Jason said. I wouldn't tell him why I'd come to the hetaera house, so he was going to keep how he'd tracked me down to himself.

Had he been watching the temple? Hired someone else to do it?

If he had, why? It made no sense.

Maybe it really had been just a coincidence. Or perhaps the goddess had decided I needed to be punished for approaching her statue without permission and had sent him as a plague to vex me.

If I shared something of why I'd come, would he do the same?

"The owner asked about what happened to my sister," I said. Truthful, but not the entire story.

Jason frowned slightly, seemingly lost. But then he realized that I was answering his earlier question about what I'd been doing upstairs. The frown stayed put, though. "I'm sorry about what happened to Quynh."

A Tribute of Fire

I hadn't heard her name out loud in so long that it was like he'd punched an open, gaping wound with all his might. My head felt light and I bent slightly at my waist, needing to catch my breath.

What had the Ilionians done with her? Had her death been quick or slow? Had she suffered? Had her captors triumphantly paraded her lifeless body through their streets before they set her on fire? I squeezed my eyelids shut. I couldn't think about these kinds of things or I would curl up into a ball and never move again.

His fingers brushed lightly against my arm, as if he intended to hold me. Like he planned to put his hands on my shoulders and then pull me in close. I could have used a hug. It had been so long since I'd had one. I missed that kind of close physical contact.

But he didn't follow through, dropping his hands away from me. I didn't know whether to be sad or relieved. I groaned internally. I had to stop being pathetic like this, hoping for some affection from a man willing to offer it to anyone who looked his way. I didn't have time for Jason. I had something I needed to get done before the sun rose.

Opening my eyes back up, I resumed my determined march toward the docks. Despite how quickly I was moving, he had no issues keeping up with me.

"Do you blame me?" he asked.

His question surprised me. "Why would I blame you for what happened to Quynh?"

"You did on the *Nikos*."

That was true. I had blamed him and the entire crew for taking us to Ilion and putting our lives in danger. It wasn't his fault, though. He wasn't the one who had ripped her out of my arms. I renewed my internal vow to someday find that redheaded man and stab him repeatedly.

"I hope you know that she's not dead because of me," he added unnecessarily.

With a shake of my head, I said, "I know that. And I don't blame you."

"That feels like progress."

I was about to tell him to take it any way he wished, but given the kind of person Jason was, I knew he would find some way to take advantage of my statement. Better to stay silent.

But he couldn't let the conversation falter. "You're not at all worried that you might be recognized?"

"By who?"

"After your run, you became quite the legend. There are many who would still kill you just for the opportunity to brag about having done so. You did a fair amount of damage. You even killed some men."

I would not feel bad about that. "They tried to kill me first."

"You misunderstand me. I wasn't accusing you—I was admiring you."

"That's a strange thing to admire."

He jogged slightly ahead of me and started walking backward so that he could make eye contact with me. "I've always admired women willing to deal a little death when crossed."

"I would be happy to cut your throat open," I offered.

He came to a sudden stop and I wasn't fast enough to keep myself from crashing into him.

Or I had been looking for an excuse to get close to him again and took advantage when the opportunity presented itself.

His hands went to my shoulders, holding me in place now that I was pressed firmly against him.

Our chests moved against one another as we breathed in and out.

"I'll only agree to it on the condition that you promise to throw me up against a wall again, pressing your body to mine just like this."

His lips lightly brushed against my forehead. Soft as feathers.

My whole body flushed with heat. I hoped he hadn't noticed the way that I was shivering under his touch.

The look in his eye told me that he hadn't missed a thing.

With a sound of disgust, I wrenched myself away from him. How could he be expressing condolences over the loss of Quynh in one moment and using his masculine wiles to seduce me in the next?

Even worse, how could I be so weak as to respond to it? Just a few minutes ago he'd been focusing all of his energy on courtesans. And they had been clinging to him, happy with what little attention he had deigned to give them.

That would never be me.

I wouldn't permit it.

"So I'm supposing that means you would say no to my marriage proposal." The teasing in his voice was unmistakable.

Why did he think himself so clever? "I'd sooner marry Prince Alexandros." And I had no intention of marrying that man at all.

Jason let out a scoffing noise. "What does he have that I don't?"

"Money? Power? A kingdom? Servants to do his bidding? Knowing where his next meal is coming from? Not being indebted to every gambling house between here and Locris? Women he doesn't have to pay for?"

"All right, all right," he said with a laugh. "I see your point. I wouldn't trade lives with him, though. I prefer the freedom of going wherever I wish, whenever I wish."

I had heard him say that exact same sentence before. *I prefer the freedom of going wherever I wish, whenever I wish.*

Only he'd said it to me in a dream. That caused a chill to settle into my spine, spreading slowly through me.

I'd told him I didn't believe in coincidences.

So what did it mean that he was saying things in real life that he'd said to me only in my imagination?

"Where are we going?" he asked.

"To the docks," I said. It was so much easier traversing the city now that I knew the correct ways to go. I kept my gaze forward, avoiding looking at the labyrinth walls as much as I possibly could. They all made me think of Quynh and the sheer terror I'd felt racing through here the first time.

"Do you know how dangerous the docks are?" Now he sounded slightly angry.

"In my experience every part of Troas is dangerous."

He stayed quiet at my retort, silently acknowledging the truth of my statement before he said, "The docks are worse. Especially this time of night."

"I can take care of myself."

"Yes, I saw. But at some point you might get overwhelmed with numbers. Not even you can fight an army."

His words pierced my heart with a hot, flaming spear. Quynh had said the very same thing to me.

There was no way that Jason could have known that, though.

It felt like some sort of sign, but I didn't have the time to ponder it or examine it. I had to focus on putting one foot in front of the other, to keep moving so that I wouldn't be crushed under the weight of my memories and sorrows.

He tried a different tactic. "Is it your plan to be out all night, then? Won't you be tired tomorrow?"

Like he was my older brother or father, trying to use reason to convince me that it was in my best interest to go back. It just annoyed me. "Haven't you ever stayed up all night before?"

"Yes, but I wasn't wandering around the city."

"What were you doing?" I asked, and then immediately wanted to take it back because I understood what he had been doing.

My cheeks felt hot and I wished I could melt into the shadows. He made me feel so naive. I never felt that way when I dreamed of him, but I was quickly discovering that real life wasn't living up to those fantasies my mind spun when I was fast asleep.

And how many reminders did I need about the kind of man he was? He couldn't have made it any clearer.

Why was I attracted to him?

Sighing, I tried to pay attention to where I was going. I had taken a more circuitous route when I'd first arrived and my adelphia had told me a quicker way to get to the docks.

Given that Jason wasn't trying to correct me, I figured it had to be the best path.

"Have you ever thought about leaving the temple?" he asked.

Had I? Every day since I'd arrived. It was an odd question. He seemed to be saying whatever thought popped into his head tonight. I wondered if he'd been drinking and if that was the reason for the lack of a filter.

"Why would you ask me that?" I glanced over at him and saw him shrug.

"If you want to go, I can smuggle you out. Just say the word and I'll get you on a ship back to Locris."

Of course a part of me was tempted. It would be wonderful to just board a boat and see my family in a few days. I would have given almost anything to be reunited with them again.

But I wouldn't leave until I'd gotten what I came here for.

"I'm staying in Troas. In the temple." For now.

He accepted my answer with a nod and then added, "Didn't you say you wanted to go to the docks?"

"Yes."

"You're going the wrong way."

I glanced up at the walls and it was nearly impossible to make out the faded colors in the dark. Had I taken a wrong turn?

I was so distracted by his presence that I was making mistakes. Frustration built up inside me and I had to refrain from kicking the closest wall.

"Which way do I go then?" I asked, coming to a halt. It was difficult to ask because I knew he would lord it over me.

He stood in front of me, his broad frame practically blocking out the moon, casting him into shadow. "I still don't think you should go there."

"That's not your decision," I told him.

"I could show you the correct path . . ." His words trailed off. "If you would pay the toll."

Crossing my arms I asked, "And what is your price?"

I couldn't see his face, but I heard the desire in his voice when he answered, "A kiss."

A kiss? I should have been disgusted. Or infuriated. I should have kicked him in the groin for that kind of demand.

Instead my lips tingled with anticipation, my heart beat as quickly as Kunguru's wings, and my knees threatened to stop functioning.

I should not be tempted.

But I was.

"I already paid my toll earlier when I didn't cut out your Ilionian heart and show it to you on a silver platter."

His response surprised me. He laughed. So loudly that it echoed off the walls surrounding us.

When his laughter finally subsided, he said, "I have missed you, Lia."

My stomach hollowed out at his words, but I refused to be swayed.

He took a step closer to me. "You're right, though. When you kiss me, it will be because you choose to, not because I tricked you into it."

I felt his words against my skin, like he was touching me. I straightened my back and moved away from him. I noted his word choice. "When," not "if." Clearing my throat I said, "Either take me somewhere that I can find a Locrian sailor or get out of my way."

His face was still cloaked in shadows, but I felt his gaze upon me. "Fine. I'll show you. But I won't be held accountable for whatever happens next."

Jason walked away and it took me a second to follow.

He had been speaking about thieves and ruffians and drunken sailors and the kind of danger they might present to me.

I was far more concerned about what might happen next with him.

CHAPTER FORTY-TWO

"Why do you need a Locrian sailor if you don't intend to leave?" he asked.

This night was going to drag on so slowly if I kept avoiding his questions. I'd seen him fight—he wasn't the kind to give up. He might also prove useful in helping me locate the right messenger. He knew the docks far better than I did. In this instance I should share with him.

"I want to send a message to Locris to let my parents know that I'm alive. So I have to find someone I can trust, who will get there quickly."

"You could trust me. I would deliver your message for you."

Not able to help myself, I let out a short bark of laughter. "I barely know you."

"You won't know this sailor you choose at all."

"Yes, but he will be Locrian, which automatically makes him more trustworthy than you."

"You already know me almost as well as anyone in this city. But if you feel that you don't, then you should get to know me," he offered. "Ask me any question and I'll answer."

I had so many questions I wanted to ask him, but there had been one in particular that had plagued me since it had happened. "When we were on the *Nikos*, why did the pirates throw red dirt onto the deck?"

"I don't know why. I don't know who they were."

Was he telling me the truth? I couldn't be certain. I stole a glance at his face. "Why are you smiling like that?"

"Because if it were not for your insatiable curiosity, I think that you might never speak to me again."

"You're right." Jason was only a means to an end. He was not someone that I would seek out for any other reason.

Even if my body currently had a thousand reasons why I should do just that.

"Then I am thankful that the goddess gifted you with a fine intellect and a desire to understand exactly what things mean and why they happen. It makes me think I should hide things from you, just so that you'll seek me out."

"That is not a good plan," I told him. "I'd rather suffer in ignorance than deliberately choose to spend time in your presence."

He held his arms wide, as if to say that I was doing just that—deliberately choosing to be with him.

Only so that you can show me the way to the docks, I wanted to protest but stayed quiet.

"And by the way, I meant you should ask me a personal question and I'll answer it," he said.

"There's nothing I want to know about you." Another lie.

"As I've just pointed out, that's untrue. Your curiosity won't allow it."

I pressed my lips together, in an attempt to hold my tongue, but he was right. I couldn't do it. "How did you get that scar?"

He reached up with the fingers of his right hand and traced the outline of the scar from his eye down to his chin. I found myself wanting to do it, too, and balled my hands into fists so that I wouldn't accidentally reach for him.

"Last year I was involved with a woman who had a spiteful lover."

Was he serious? Or teasing me? It was impossible to tell. His words hadn't been intended to wound me, but they did. My response infuriated me. I didn't want to be jealous where he was concerned, but it kept happening.

I recognized the main entrance of the city and again I was forced to repress the memories that came rushing at me. We crossed the open field and I wouldn't let myself think of Quynh and me lining up here, the hope I'd had that we would both make it.

"Do you want to try one of the docked ships?" Jason asked, and I was grateful that he was there, that he could help me to focus on what had to be done.

"No. Let's go to a tavern." A man out having a good time with his fellow crew members would be easier to convince than a sober man bitter about having to stay at his post.

Jason stopped and folded his arms, widening his stance. "I won't take you into a tavern at this time of night. Someone will insult your honor and then I'll be forced to take his life as retribution and I'm too tired."

"I can protect my own honor."

He nodded. "I know. I saw. But taverns and inns are disreputable and the people who frequent them are not the kind a temple acolyte should consort with."

"Don't you go to places like that?"

"Exactly," he answered with a grin.

"I'll find a sailor on my own," I announced. "You can go."

I felt his hand wrap around my forearm, tugging me back. I tried to ignore the way my skin burst into flame everywhere that his fingers made contact. "Fine. If this is what you are going to do and I can't talk you out of it, I'll help you. I think the Golden Lamb is going to be our best bet. Follow me."

Jason released my arm and I found myself missing and craving his touch. The sooner he went on his way, the faster I would regain my peace of mind.

At least until tomorrow night, when I fell asleep again.

We came upon a tavern that seemed to be leaning, as if the sea winds had blown against it for so long that it could no longer stay upright. The building was weathered, the edges of the roof frayed where the salt had eaten it away. The sign hanging above the door had a gold sheep painted on it. Firelight illuminated the open windows and someone was speaking loudly.

Jason reached over to me and pulled the hood up over my head. I held my breath while he put it into place. "Keep yourself covered up. I will find a reasonably sober Locrian for you."

"Why can't I—"

He put one finger over my lips and I was struck with the urge to draw it into my mouth. It did have the intended effect of quieting me. "If the very drunk men in this room see how beautiful you are, you will receive a great deal of unwanted attention. While I know we can fight our way clear, tonight we should try to allow everyone to keep their blood inside their bodies, where it belongs. And the best way for that to happen is for you to wait for me in the back. Can you do that?"

I nodded, my pulse thrumming inside me. He left his finger on my sensitized lips for a moment longer, briefly tracing the outer edge of my top lip before he seemed to remember himself and withdrew his hand.

Again I was left aching for him.

We went into the tavern, and I noticed an older man standing on a stool near the fireplace as he told a story to the enthralled crowd.

There were only male patrons in the tavern, and as Jason had predicted, they seemed very drunk. The whole place reeked of sweat, dirt, sea, and alcohol. I put my hand up to my nose, hoping to block out some of the smell.

He found us a table near the door and had me sit in the farthest corner, mostly cloaked in shadows. He sat down next to me, acting like a giant shield. I let my hood fall farther forward so that no part of my face would be visible.

"Aren't you going to find a Locrian?" I asked.

"When the bard is done," he said.

"What's a bard?"

"A storyteller. Many people can't read and someone has to carry on the stories. A bard travels the cities and the countryside, sharing his tales so that we don't forget. We need to wait for him to finish or else we're going to be dealing with a lot of very angry, inebriated men upset about their entertainment being interrupted."

A woman in a tunic so light that it left little to the imagination came over with two glasses of something that smelled sour. She held out her hand for payment while giving Jason an appraising look. He handed her a small silver coin from the pouch at his side.

"I'll be done with work in two hours if you'd like to meet me out back," she told him, and I found myself angrily tightening my fingers around the handle of my xiphos.

He just smiled at her and she went off to serve other customers.

"Are you going to meet up with her?" I hadn't meant to ask him that, especially given his knowing smirk.

"Pay attention to the bard. You might learn something."

The man on the stool said, "When the Great War was over, many men fled from Ilion after their defeat by the Achaeans." Several patrons booed and started naming off individual nations who had fought, including Locris.

I tried to move even farther into the shadows.

"Those Ilionians, deprived of their homeland, traveled south to Caria. They were starving, thirsty. They claimed hospitality rights but they were turned away. In their righteous anger, they laid siege to the city. The Ilionians easily tunneled under the walls and overwhelmed the Carians. After they defeated the men, they forced the Carian women into marriage and started new families."

"Against their will?" someone called out.

"Yes!" the bard said. "Which displeased the goddess greatly."

I understood that. Those poor women, compelled to marry the men who had slaughtered their husbands, fathers, sons, and brothers. I hoped the goddess took vengeance on those Ilionians.

313

"The Carians did not share the faith of the Ilionians and tried to erase their beliefs. But the men were steadfast and would not forsake their goddess. Ten years passed away, and the Ilionians missed their previous home. Most of them abandoned their new families and returned, rightly guessing that the Achaeans had left and they could rebuild. They made the walls of Troas even higher and stronger, expanding the labyrinth so that no invader could do what they themselves had done in Caria. It is why no man may enter the temple of the goddess today. She is still angry with them for their treatment of the Carian women. And the Ilionian men's superior fighting skills and engineering capabilities are why, within a single decade, the entire nation of Caria was wiped out. We speak of them now only in stories."

I swallowed back the bile that rose up in my throat. That was going to happen to Locris if I didn't find a way to restore it. We would be nothing but a story for some bard to share in a tavern.

The bard got off the stool and began begging the crowd for money.

I wished I could get drunk, but I needed my wits about me. I sniffed the drink the barmaid had left us. "What is this?"

"Beer."

"Why does it smell like that? Like rotting bread?"

"I don't know how to answer that question. It just does. Stay here, I'll be back." I watched as he got up and started speaking to groups of men, clapping them on the back, buying them drinks, charming everyone he came into contact with.

Sitting here in the dark, I had to admit what I kept trying to reject. He was so desperately attractive. I wanted his mouth on mine, his fingers exploring my skin, his weight pressing down on me. A wave of desire crested up inside me and I wrapped my hands around my drink to steady myself.

I wondered why it was so important to the goddess that I not lie with a man if she let me have these kinds of feelings for one.

Expelling a shaky breath, I tried to stop myself from following his every movement, but it wasn't working. Everything he did was utterly fascinating. The way his mouth formed words, how his muscles flexed in the firelight, the sheer delight in his laughter.

Why was he helping me? Did he feel guilty about what had happened with Quynh and the inadvertent role he'd played in it? My mind wanted to be suspicious, but I couldn't think of what he had to gain from assisting me.

The one thing I might have to offer, he couldn't have.

Thanks to his jest earlier, I knew that he was aware of the vows that the goddess required. And he might have been a gambling philanderer, but I sensed that there was at least a tiny shard of morality in him. I suspected that he would honor my promises.

Especially given that he was aware of how capable I was of defending myself.

Although I would not want to try hand-to-hand combat against him. I would most likely lose.

I was not goddess-blessed. My skills had been acquired through practice and training, and his came naturally.

It was unfair.

But I had learned a long time ago that life generally wasn't kind.

Jason approached the table with another man and, with a broad smile, announced, "I have found you a Locrian."

CHAPTER FORTY-THREE

"Shall we take this outside?" Jason asked. He waited for me to stand up and then followed me out with the sailor.

When we exited through the front door, Jason said, "This is Simos. He said he can carry a message for you."

I was going to tell Jason to give us a moment alone but there was no reason to do so. I had hopefully crafted a message that would withstand scrutiny and not give anything away about my background.

"If the price is right," Simos added.

I opened my knapsack and took out the smaller portioned bag of salt that I'd brought with me. I handed it to him and his eyes widened.

"Will that suffice?" I asked, knowing that it would.

"Yes. What is your message?"

"There is a soldier in the palace named Demaratus. I need you to find him and tell him that his daughter lives." Demaratus would know that I intended for him to pass the message along to my parents.

"That's all?" Simos asked.

"Yes." I thought short and simple would be my best bet. "It is important that this message be delivered as quickly as possible."

"Simos told me that his ship is setting sail tomorrow," Jason offered.

"We are." The other man nodded.

"That's good. Swear to me that you will deliver this message right away."

Simos put his hand over his heart. "I swear it. I will make certain that I find your Demaratus as soon as we land and I will tell him his daughter lives." I was glad he repeated the message back to me, showing that he would remember it. He tucked the bag of salt into his belt. "It was a pleasure doing business with you."

I nodded. I was so very relieved. Finally, I had managed to accomplish something. I would be able to get word sent back to my parents. They would delay the prince, giving me more time to find the eye. I was no longer treading water—I had surged forward.

Simos pulled open the door to the tavern and loudly announced, "Drinks are on me!"

A loud cheer broke out and I made eye contact with a man I recognized.

It was the witness for the selection. The one who had made sure Quynh and I got on the ship and not some substitute Locrian maidens. Alarms sounded inside me, my breath quickening. Something was off about him being here.

About him watching me.

The door swung shut but I yanked it open again.

"What are you doing?" Jason asked.

I scanned the room quickly but I didn't see the man. As my breathing evened out, I figured that my overly anxious imagination had created it.

It didn't stop the dark and creepy sensation currently crawling up my back, though.

"Nothing," I said to Jason. "I thought I saw something, but I was wrong."

He looked concerned but only said, "You paid Simos too much."

"It's worth that and more to me." I had enough left to hire a life mage and book us passage back home. If the mage required more compensation, I would offer him his weight in salt when we reached

Locris, if he wanted. Jason didn't know the lengths I was willing to go to.

If anything, I would argue that I'd given Simos just enough to ensure his loyalty and make certain that the message was delivered.

Now, if Jason had told me that I'd paid Mahtab too much, he would have been right. But I would have given her all three bags of salt to have had that extra time with my sister.

Regardless, how I spent my resources wasn't any of his business. Our time together was at an end. I wasn't sure how to communicate that to him effectively. I settled on, "I have to be going." My mother would have insisted that I thank him for his help, but given that he had annoyed me tonight more than he'd helped, I decided my farewell was enough.

"Where?"

"The library." I grimaced. Again, I hadn't intended to share that with him. It had just slipped out.

"You should go during the day. When it's open to the public."

"That's not really something I can do."

"Why? Oh. You're breaking the rules by being out this late," he said, not waiting for my answer. "I'll come with you."

"You don't have to—"

He held up a hand, cutting me off. "Let's not have this argument again. I'll accompany you. Besides, I have to come. My toll has not yet been paid."

I narrowed my eyes at him. "And it won't be."

"We'll see." His arrogance was infuriating.

Biting back a growl I asked, "Do you know where the library is? And can you take me there?" If he was going to shadow me, I should at least take advantage of his knowledge.

"Yes. And yes."

With that confirmation I headed for the main gates to enter the city, trusting that he would tell me what direction I should head. Or that he would take the lead and I could follow quietly behind him.

But when he caught up, he walked alongside me. Forcing me to keep an eye on him so that I could see which way to go.

"Why are we going to the library?" he asked as he headed into one of the northeastern paths, the opposite of the ones leading to the temple.

"Libraries have information."

"What kind of information do you need?"

I let out a big sigh. "You say that I'm the one with the insatiable curiosity, but I think you're even worse than me."

He placed his hands against his chest. "Is it my fault that you're so fascinating that I have to understand everything about you?"

My breath stumbled. It was the kind of thing he would have said to me in my dreams. So much so that for a moment I didn't believe he'd actually said it out loud. I wasn't going to let myself get caught up in some foolish fantasy, though. "I can't fault you for your curiosity because it would make me a hypocrite. But if you're going to play at being my bodyguard, we have to get one thing straight between us. I will not be telling you what I'm looking for. You can either accept that or go meet your barmaid."

A part of me expected him to say his goodbyes and travel back to the Golden Lamb so that he could fully enjoy the attention of the beautiful and willing barmaid.

"I accept." And while he didn't say it, I could see on his face how amused he was by my demand.

Because he thought I was jealous.

Which I was *not*.

We walked in a comfortable silence for a few minutes with him leading me through the labyrinth.

"If you're looking for information, you'd be better served searching the palace library. I've heard they have a great number of collections," he said.

"Yes, I'm sure it's very easy to break into the palace so that I can search through their scrolls and books," I said sarcastically.

"Fair point. But the library will be worse. It's heavily guarded."

That was disappointing. There had to be a way inside or else he wouldn't bother leading me there. If Jason didn't have a plan, I would come up with something. It wouldn't be the first time tonight that I'd sneaked through a heavily guarded location.

We had entered a pocket of businesses and apartments, and we passed by a tavern serving something delicious. The scent of roasting meat hung in the air and I let out a small groan.

"Hungry?" he asked, and I couldn't deny it.

"Always." I should have packed myself something to snack on.

"It's one of the things I like best about you," he said. His words felt like they were loaded with meaning but I didn't understand what he was trying to actually say. "Wait a moment. I have something for you."

There was a stone half wall running along the sidewalk, and he took a knapsack from his back and placed it on that wall. I hadn't even realized that he'd been carrying one. So much for my powers of observation. Both Antiope and Demaratus would have been mad at me.

Jason began digging around inside it while I sat on the wall. Someone was playing a flute nearby and the melody was sad and haunting. I was caught up in the music when I noticed something fluttering out of the corner of my eye.

I turned to see a bright yellow feather floating down and landing on the wall next to me.

My lungs constricted so tightly I could barely breathe. I reached for the feather, holding it aloft. I realized that it had come from Jason's bag.

"It's here, I swear it," he mumbled.

When I stood up, still holding the feather, he finally ceased his search and looked at me, confused. "What's wrong?"

I held the feather out accusatorily. "Is this yours?"

Memories raced into my mind, piling on top of each other. I remembered when Quynh had been hit by that bola, knocked off her feet. How I'd been so focused on reaching her, helping her, that I had forgotten my surroundings. Leaving myself utterly defenseless.

That man standing over me with his sword, about to strike. Realizing that my life was at an end. My mouth flooded with the taste of metal as I perfectly recalled the terror and panic I'd felt in that moment.

But then he'd been struck in the chest with an arrow.

An arrow with bright yellow feathers.

It took Jason a moment to drag his focus away from his knapsack to look at the feather in my fingers. "What? Oh, yes. That's mine."

He didn't seem to realize what he'd just admitted to.

"You shot that man."

"Which man? You'll have to be more specific," he said as he returned his gaze to his bag.

"The one that nearly killed me."

He finally seemed to pick up on the tone in my voice and gave me his full attention. His face revealed nothing, keeping his secrets, and he didn't respond to my accusation.

"You protected me." My voice caught. "More importantly, you protected Quynh." From this day forward, no matter how annoying I found him, I would always be grateful to him for that.

Still, he said nothing.

"I thought it was against the law to help a Locrian maiden." I felt desperate. I had to know why he had done it. To understand why he would risk breaking the laws of the goddess to help me.

It felt extremely important.

The guarded expression fell off his face and the teasing charmer returned. "I didn't break any laws. I was aiming for you. Am I to blame for being a poor shot?"

He was not going to dissuade me. "You saved my life."

"I would disagree."

"You gave me the clue I needed to navigate the labyrinth," I tried again.

Jason shrugged nonchalantly. "I did no such thing. I was only singing a song."

The fact that he knew how the clue had been conveyed to me meant that he had done it deliberately, no matter how he attempted to deny it.

Pieces started to fall into place and I realized all that he had done that day. He must have been watching over us. He hadn't acted on my behalf until he'd shot the arrow and he'd only done it because I'd been about to die.

"The ambush waiting outside the temple," I said, remembering how I'd expected a trap and instead found a bunch of unconscious men on the ground. "You fought them."

"That had nothing to do with you. Those men owed me money."

"All of them?" I asked incredulously.

"Yes. It was fortunate for me that they all gathered themselves together in one spot like that so that I could demand payment. And if they were there for you, well, it hardly seems sporting to lie in wait like that."

"I expected a trap." It was important to me that he knew I hadn't run into that situation without realizing what the outcome would be. That I had understood what I would be up against.

With a shake of his head, he said, "You wouldn't have gotten past them."

I frowned. "You did."

"I'm me," he said with a grin.

Yes, he was. The one blessed with an incredible otherworldly fighting talent that he wasted in taverns and on ships.

And he had used that gift to save my life. To help me get into the temple.

"The spear?" I asked.

"I'm not much of a spear thrower, either. Again, I was aiming for you but I missed you on the wall."

He must have been an incredible shot. I remembered how precisely that spear had been placed, exactly where I needed it. How it had buried itself deep in a rock wall, speaking to Jason's strength. "You gave me the additional hand- and foothold I needed to climb."

"That's not how I remember it," he said. "But it was very clever of you to go down through the roof after you found the doors locked."

Had he been keeping pace with me the entire time? Watching over me, protecting me?

"Why?" I asked. I needed to understand this, more than I had ever needed to understand anything.

"You know why, Lia," he said quietly.

I did know why. Even if I couldn't have said the words, I felt the reason in my soul.

The defensive walls I'd built up around my heart shattered with that realization, leaving a pile of rubble behind and no way for me to protect myself against him and his charm. I was afraid that I wouldn't be able to keep him out any longer.

Everything else faded away. My fears, my sorrows, my worries. All I could concentrate on was Jason and what he'd done.

If I managed to save Locris, it would be because he had saved me first.

Without thinking I stepped forward and pressed my lips against his.

CHAPTER FORTY-FOUR

His first response was shock. His body stiffened, his lips unmoving against mine.

"I told you that you'd kiss me," he said with a smile against my mouth.

It was enough to break the spell that he'd put me under and I stepped back. I shouldn't have kissed him. It had been a mistake. My heart was pounding, my head dizzy. Our lips had barely even touched and I felt as if I might faint.

"Not that I'm complaining, but what was that for?" he asked.

The kiss had happened because I'd wanted to do it ever since I'd pushed him up against that wall, my xiphos at his throat. Thanks to my vivid dreams, I had spent the last month desperately aching for him, even if I hadn't been able to admit it.

Not even to myself.

I had kissed him because if I hadn't, my entire body would have been engulfed in flames and I would have combusted, burning down to ash and floating away. The problem was kissing him had only made those feelings intensify.

More fire, more unbearable lightness.

"It was a thank-you, nothing more," I said, hoping the tone of my voice wasn't giving away my true reaction.

He obviously didn't believe me but was polite enough not to mention it. "Then I'll have to endeavor to win your favor again if that is the reward."

My whole body felt heavy. I recognized that I shouldn't have opened that door, even slightly. I needed to rebuild my walls.

But broken rubble wasn't meant to be put back together, and I couldn't construct a strong enough defense to shove him out. I had to steel my heart against him. Remind myself that he was nothing more than a distraction. A tempting, delicious distraction, but one nonetheless.

"I would also like to point out that I led you to the docks, found you a Locrian sailor, and am now leading you to the library, if you'd like to thank me some more."

Oh, I was still very much in the mood to thank him. But if I kissed him again, I worried that I wouldn't stop.

"Where is the library?" I asked, ignoring his teasing words.

He pointed east of our current location and I began heading in that direction.

"Never was much shorter than I would have imagined," he said. I could feel my cheeks flaming in response while I tried to ignore him and his soft laughter. It was humiliating that I hadn't even made it a couple of hours after I'd told him that I would never kiss him again.

He continued speaking. "I also hope you don't think my toll has been paid. I would hardly consider that a kiss. Not in the way that I know you're capable of."

Now my whole body was aflame from his words, from the kind of exhilarating imagery I was easily able to conjure up. Most of it was directly supplied from my dreams, but I knew exactly what he was capable of in real life as well. A part of my brain called me a fool for not taking advantage of what he was offering while I had the chance.

"Is your father the reason why you have your position in the palace?" he asked.

My father? I was so busy imagining all the different ways that I would like to break rules with Jason that at first I didn't understand what he was saying. I was confused. Obviously my father was the reason I was a princess, but then I realized that he was talking about the message that I'd entrusted to Simos and that he'd been speaking about Demaratus. Because when Jason and I had first met, he had assumed I was a maidservant.

"Yes, he helped me to secure my place." Not in the way that Jason would understand it, but it was true. Well, adjacent to the truth while still obscuring what I needed to cover up.

"Did he train you as well?"

Should I say yes? If someone started asking questions in Locris about a girl Demaratus had trained, there were enough people in the palace who knew that it was me and I would risk exposure.

My regiment had been sworn to secrecy, but my mother had taught me long ago that everyone had a price.

"All you have to do is find the right incentive," she had said.

I'd never forgotten it.

"Here. I found what I was looking for." Jason offered me a wrapped bundle from his knapsack, eliminating the need for me to answer about Demaratus training me.

I took it, careful not to make contact with his fingers. When I opened it I let out a soft sigh. "Pasteli."

"One never knows when they might run into a Locrian maiden who loves it," he said. I would not be charmed by his smile. I refused.

"And that's another thing you can feel free to thank me for later," he added.

I shouldn't eat it. Accepting his food was like making an agreement with him. But I was really hungry. All that fighting had taken it out of me.

Glancing at him, I saw that heated, wanting look in his gaze that made my abdomen clench. I was glad we were walking. If I had been seated across from him, unable to escape his expression, I wasn't sure what I might have done.

And I should not be provoking fate now, but it was like I couldn't help myself. "Why did you say that you liked that I was always hungry?"

His voice was low, sensual. "Because a woman who has an appetite for one thing often has a healthy appetite for others."

Suddenly I couldn't swallow the pasteli down. The rich honey seemed to melt onto my tongue and I wished it were him instead. I gulped, letting the honey leave a sweet trail along the inside of my throat. "Like what?" I whispered, already knowing but wanting him to say it.

"Like the physicality that exists between us. How you can't get your fill of my kisses," he said in that same hypnotic tone that made me lose all feeling in my legs.

"That's not true," I weakly protested.

"It is. I could spend hours kissing you and you would demand more."

I suspected that he was right, again.

But I would never admit that to him. I focused on eating all the pasteli that he'd given me. It wasn't something we were fed in the temple and I wanted to enjoy every last bite.

I also had to ignore my body urging me to try savoring Jason instead.

We approached a large building and he sneaked over to a column, hiding behind it. I found myself admiring both his stealth and speed. I finished up the last bit of pasteli and joined him.

He was so close that I could smell him, and he was an intriguing combination of leather, honey, salt, and something else. It might have been my fevered brain, but I would have sworn that I detected the faint scent of irises.

Like the goddess had marked him just for me.

Jason noticed how still I had gone and his expression practically smoldered at me. His gaze shifted to my lips and I parted them, ready for his kiss.

Completely forgetting all of my very recent resolutions to myself.

And not even counting what I'd promised the goddess.

He moved a step closer and I stopped breathing altogether as I swayed toward him. He lifted his hand, as if he intended to cup my face with it. I waited in what felt like agony for him to make contact, but he didn't.

"There's the library," he said, pointing across the street. Back to business. How could he do that? Turn his feelings off and on, as the situation demanded?

I was still lightheaded and standing too close to him. It was probably due to experience—his overabundance of it and my total lack.

Taking a step away from him, I attempted to steady my breathing and remember why I was here. Why was I so weak where he was concerned? I spent most of my time building up my strength. But every bit of it seemed to flee just because he existed.

Letting go of a deep breath, I studied the library. It was massive and impressive. There seemed to be engraved artwork that was probably stunning during daylight hours, but I couldn't make much of it out. The building was painted in reds and blues, and like the temple, it had a large patio and a grand staircase leading up to the entrance.

There was one thing I couldn't find. "I thought you said it was heavily guarded."

"It is."

"I don't see any guards."

He leaned against the column and grinned. "Not any human ones."

"What do you mean?"

"The library is guarded by geese."

I'd heard that word before, although I'd never seen one. "That's a bird, isn't it?"

"So they claim."

Who would leave a bird to protect an important resource? It made me question the intelligence of the people who ran security for the library. "I've been around birds before," I said confidently.

"Not like this, you haven't."

I dismissed his claim. Kunguru was delightful. I still had some crumbs of the pasteli in the cloth Jason had given me. Surely the geese could be bribed. "I'm not worried."

He grinned. "You're going to regret saying that."

There had been a lot of things I'd done tonight that I was regretting, but having confidence in myself and my abilities would not be one of them. "I'll feed them. And if they're unruly, I'll just . . . I don't know, kick them."

"Good luck with that." He was treating this like he was sending me off to my doom.

Was he trying to intimidate me? Why? Was he afraid of what I might find in the library? That couldn't be it. If his goal was to prevent me from finding information, he could have just refused to bring me here. Or he could have yelled for the patrol, alerted them to our location.

No, it was something else.

Maybe it really was just the geese.

His reaction still seemed silly to me, though. "I'll be fine."

Jason folded his arms against his chest and leaned against the column. "Do you want me to come with you?"

I didn't want him to see what I would discover. The problem was that I didn't know what I was looking for, and given the size of the library, I had no idea where to even start. Maybe he would, but I doubted it. He didn't strike me as the reading sort. This was probably the first time he'd ever been near the library.

"No."

"I'll stay here and keep watch," he offered. It was kind of him. He could have left me, and if a patrol had appeared, I would have been on my own. Stuck fighting my way through another group of angry men. It would be better to avoid that sort of situation, and his acting as lookout would help.

I put my hand on the column, peering out into the darkness of the street, ready to dart out when his voice stopped me.

"If I were a gambling man, which I am, I would wager that you're going to lose this fight."

"With the goose?" I clarified, not knowing if he meant my internal struggle to stay away from him.

He nodded.

I made a scoffing sound. "You don't know me at all."

"Oh, I know how capable you are. How intelligent and clever. But you are severely underestimating your opponent."

"Fine, gambling man, why don't we make a bet?" I was seething that he thought me so inadequate a fighter that I would be taken down by a bird. Why was my pride so wounded? I suspected that it was because his opinion mattered to me.

It shouldn't have, but it did.

"What do you want from me if you're successful?" he asked, and my blood sang in response, telling me precisely what sort of boon I should require.

"If I defeat the geese, I get that dagger you carry in your belt." It was a beautiful piece, well crafted. I assumed he'd won it in some gambling den from a nobleman.

"Done," he said.

But he didn't say what he wanted in return. "And if you win?"

A slow smile spread across his face. He moved closer to me, his face moving down to be a whisper away from mine. His lips were so close, but not quite touching. A feverish longing filled me.

"My terms have not changed. You know what I want."

CHAPTER FORTY-FIVE

I did know what Jason wanted. It was the same thing I wanted.

My body ordered me to close the gap between us. To give him his boon, pay his toll, thank him, whatever excuse I could come up with, just so that I could be kissing him again. The kiss of gratitude I'd given him hadn't been nearly enough. It had been the smallest taste of what I was missing out on.

Like starving and sitting down to the greatest feast imaginable and eating only a single morsel of bread. It wouldn't fill me up. I was too greedy for that, just like he'd noted. I wanted everything.

But I'd made a vow.

I swallowed down the desire I felt for him and crossed the street. I climbed the stairs to the front doors and pushed slightly. Unlocked.

Frowning, I opened the door enough to let myself through. Jason had made it sound like they were so concerned about security, but they hadn't even bothered to lock the doors. Why?

My steps seemed unnecessarily loud as I traveled down a long stone hallway. The end of the hallway emptied into a massive room, even bigger than the auditorium that we studied in at the temple. There were wooden shelves everywhere, set up in perfect rows. So many scrolls and books and papers.

I didn't even know where to begin, how it was arranged. If it was organized. It might not have been. I went into the middle of the room and turned in a small circle. I had to make a choice.

My grandmother's book was very old. Maybe that was a good starting point—to locate the oldest documents. Was there a vault? A special room with a collection of religious texts? There was too much to search through. I felt a bit panicky as I realized that I could spend the rest of the night here and not find anything helpful.

The only thing I had left was my instinct. I decided to walk through the shelves and see if anything called out to me. I realized how foolish that decision was, but I didn't know what else to do.

I went to the shelves farthest from the entrance. If I'd been in charge of the library, that was where I would have put important documents. Where they would be the least likely to be handled by patrons and scholars.

As I went down the aisle, I let my fingers brush against the scrolls and books. I wondered if I was the first woman who had entered this room, given that most Ilionian women couldn't read. I reached the end and turned the corner, intending to walk down the next one.

But a very large white bird waited for me. He was half my height. He looked like a large duck with a long, curved neck, and he was bobbing his head up and down. He spread his wings out, shaking them. His wingspan was enormous.

"Would you like some treats?" I asked the bird softly, reaching into the cloth that held the leftover pasteli. I took out the crumbs and threw them toward the goose.

This seemed to alarm him. Where Kunguru would have hunted down every single scrap, this goose made a strange hissing sound.

I didn't know birds could make a noise like that.

He continued to bob his feather-ridged head as he slowly moved toward me. It was a threatening move, and I responded by backing away slowly. Maybe if I just returned to my own row he would leave me alone.

But when I went around the corner, he continued to follow me. It was concerning. I should just grab some books and run.

The second my hand made contact with the nearest one, the hissing sound got louder.

A warning.

I raised both of my hands.

This didn't seem to placate the creature. He honked, a loud trill that I felt in my bones.

It seemed ridiculous, but I knew I was in danger.

Stupid girl! It's only a bird!

Demaratus didn't know what he was talking about. I reached the center of the room and judged the distance between myself and the door.

The goose came closer, hissing as he went. He darted out and his ridged bill clamped onto my forearm, pinching my skin. He twisted his neck to inflict the highest amount of damage.

"Ow!" I called out as he withdrew. It had really hurt, my skin was throbbing.

"I'm going," I told him, again trying to placate him. He honked loudly and it suddenly occurred to me that he might be calling for reinforcements.

The last thing I wanted was to deal with an entire flock of these snake-duck hybrids. Like the monsters out of one of Maia's stories.

Then without warning, the goose launched himself at me, hitting me hard with one of his wings. It was like being hit by a stave. He snapped at my face with that strange beak, lifted both of his feet, and kicked at me. He had short claws and I felt them drag across the skin of my right arm, which I'd brought up to deflect his attack.

Enough.

Turning, I ran for the door and felt him behind me, flying at my head, all white feathers and fury. It was unlike any other opponent I'd ever faced, where I could predict where they would be from one moment to the next. He didn't stay in one spot but came at me from different angles, flying in the air one moment, rushing at me on the ground the next. I'd never dealt with an enemy who could attack me from above before. There was no way to anticipate his next move.

I was a fast runner, but the goose stayed with me.

When I reached the entrance, I squeezed through the opening I'd left for myself and turned to pull the door shut, but the goose was faster. I took several steps back and the goose rose in the air, aiming for my head.

Without thinking I threw my fist and punched the goose in its chest, knocking it down. That seemed to momentarily stun the creature, and I took advantage of his confusion to run across the street and hide behind a column.

The goose regained his equilibrium and honked several times into the night air, as if to tell me that he had won. Which I was willing to concede since I was the one currently hiding from him.

He waddled back inside the library and I felt my body relax.

Until I turned my head to see Jason doubled over in laughter.

"Why are you laughing?" I demanded.

"You . . . punching a goose . . . I will never forget it." He could barely get the words out.

"It wasn't funny," I insisted but surprised myself by laughing along with him.

"You'll stare down a dragon but you're afraid of a goose?" he said, and he started laughing all over again.

It had been a very long time since I'd laughed like this, felt this light and free. It was probably before my brother died. He had taken a piece of me with him, as had Quynh.

My laughter finally died down and I leaned against the column, studying Jason. He was so handsome and the lightness of his expression made him even more so. I liked seeing him this way. I felt my heart rise up, causing a warm feeling to spread along my veins.

His eyes were dancing with delight as he realized that I was watching him. I averted my gaze as a pang of longing struck me so powerfully that it was all I could do to resist it.

"About our bet . . ."

A flash of anger punched me in the gut. "Oh no, I didn't lose anything, because that wasn't a goose. That was a demon. You lured me into the library under false pretenses."

"No, you chose to go in. This was your idea. You were not lured. If I was luring you, you would know it."

I was sure that I would. A pulse of desire began to throb at the base of my neck. The anger quickly faded, even though I was trying desperately to hang on to it. It was the only way I could stop from throwing myself at him.

"That goose had been altered by magic. It was like a small horse."

"I saw it. It was a standard-sized goose."

"No. It was like something out of a nightmare. Which makes this all unfair," I said. The bet, the situation I was currently finding myself in, the undeniable attraction I had for him. All of it. "I didn't know what I was agreeing to."

"If I throw dice, after I lose I can't suddenly claim that I didn't know what I was agreeing to."

My body was upset with me. This seemed like a perfect solution—I had no choice. I had to keep my word. We had made a bet that I had very obviously lost, especially since I'd left the library empty-handed. I hadn't managed to grab even a single scrap of papyrus. I could give in and I wouldn't be at fault.

As if he knew what I was thinking, he said, "An honorable woman would pay her debts."

"We both know I'm not honorable." I was here with him, already breaking rules that I'd promised to abide by.

"I wish that were true," he said under his breath.

That frenzied urge to kiss him attacked me like that goose had. From every direction, all at once, so that I didn't know which way was up and which was down. Driving out my reason and logic so that all I wanted to do was launch myself at him.

"I didn't have all the facts," I protested, but didn't mean it. Part of me hoped he would insist I do what I'd said I would.

"Geese are relentless," he said, as if agreeing with me that I had walked in unaware of what I would face.

"I noticed," I said, rubbing my hand along my arm. "That thing bit me. Or whatever it is that they do with their beaks."

"Are you all right?" he asked, walking over and taking my injured arm in both of his hands. My arm looked so small in comparison to the size of his hands that I sucked in a sharp breath at the difference. He was searching my arm for marks or cuts, and the top of his head was so close to my mouth that I could have kissed him and he might not have even noticed.

"I will be fine," I told him.

Then he leaned in and pressed his lips onto my arm, setting all my skin afire.

"What are you doing?" I asked, alarmed.

"Kissing it better. Didn't your mother ever do this?" He murmured the words just above my arm. I curled my fingers toward my palm as tiny bumps rose along my forearm.

My mother had done that when I was little, but that had been an entirely different experience from this.

Apparently satisfied that no serious damage was done, he released my arm and it fell to my side, useless and heavy.

He said, "I once saw a goose break a man's arm with his wing because they hit so hard. There's a lot of force behind that motion."

"And you let me go in by myself?" I asked, my feelings swinging back to anger.

"I offered to accompany you, but you insisted on going alone."

This wasn't about me. This was about him wanting to win the bet. Knowing that he would. That was why he hadn't helped me.

Or I was just being so obstinate and headstrong that he'd let me do something reckless just so that I could learn my lesson the hard way.

And he understood me well enough to know that it was the only choice he could have made.

That bothered me in a way I didn't want to examine. "You should have been more persistent," I tried to argue, knowing that I was losing.

The corner of his lips hitched up. "You like persistence. Duly noted."

"That's not what I—" I sighed. "The point is you shouldn't have sent me into a situation where there wasn't any opportunity for a peaceful solution. You can't reason with a goose."

"I know the feeling. You can't reason with you, either."

"I am entirely rational!" I told him and he laughed again.

When he finished he asked, "A peaceful solution? That sounds unlike you. I'm a little surprised you didn't stab the goose."

To be honest, drawing my weapon hadn't even occurred to me. "One of my sisters is very opposed to harming animals and I suppose she's influenced me."

"We should be grateful that you only encountered the one goose and not the entire guardian flock. Then I would have had to come to your rescue."

While I was very capable of rescuing myself, there was something thrilling about the idea of him battling snake-bird monsters in order to save me. I was sure that it would have been quite an exciting sight to behold.

The goose honked inside the library again and I couldn't help but smile. I turned to Jason and he was doing the same, and I liked sharing this moment with him.

There were responsive honks from other geese. He toyed with the sword at his side. "Do you want me to go in there with you and stab some geese?"

I knew that he would if I asked him to, but I was going to have to figure out a way past the geese besides massacring the entire lot. Io would never forgive me. "Not tonight."

Which meant finding another potential source of information.

"We will have to leave soon. A patrol will eventually show up and they'll go in to see why the geese are honking. Are you going back to the temple?" he asked.

"Not yet. Is there a records or an administrative building nearby?" I didn't think it would be as helpful as the library, but it might be something. Just so long as there weren't any resident geese.

"There is. I suppose you're expecting me to take you there."

"I can find it by myself if you're too busy."

"No, it's just customary to pay people for assisting you," he said. "It's all right. I'll just add it to the list. It's getting rather long, though, the things you owe me."

"Let's just go. And I'm not kissing you," I told him, but it was more like a personal reminder.

"I've heard that before," he countered with a bold wink before he set off for our next destination.

Trying not to sigh, I followed after him, and although I told myself he wasn't right, I feared that he was.

CHAPTER FORTY-SIX

"What's wrong?" Jason asked, misinterpreting my sigh.

"I'm just worried that I'm going to have to do battle with more wildlife," I told him.

"You won't. The administrative offices have human guards."

That was an odd tidbit of information. "How do you know the different types of guards at various public buildings?"

He raised both of his eyebrows playfully and I realized what he was communicating.

"You're a thief?" I asked, discouraged. Not that I had much room to talk, given that I was doing all this so that I could steal the eye of the goddess, but that was for a noble reason. Stealing at this level was just selfishness.

"Sailing doesn't pay nearly enough to support my . . . habits."

I grimaced. "Don't you mean your vices?"

"You say 'vices,' I say 'a good time,'" he responded. Jason was so obviously wrong for me in every regard. In background and upbringing, in current lifestyle choices, in what we thought constituted an enjoyable evening.

It didn't stop me from being drawn to him, even though it should have.

"You won't have to worry about the guards. They're rather elderly and easy to sneak around. People don't usually want to break into the records offices."

I was one of those people who didn't want to break into the administrative building, but this was my only option at the moment. I was going to have to find a way past those geese in the library. I either needed to bring a stave long enough to keep them at bay or figure out how to eliminate them as a threat. I wondered if Io could create something for me that might put them to sleep. I would need a big batch, as I didn't know how many of them lived inside the library.

Which meant I was going to have to sneak out again. Preferably in a manner that wouldn't include Ahyana having to set another fire.

And if I did sneak out, would I see Jason again?

That in and of itself might be reason enough to attempt it.

"There are other ways to make money," I told him. Not that things could change between us but it might be more palatable to me to be attracted to him if I at least knew he was earning an honest living.

"Such as?"

"I've seen you fight. You could hire yourself out as a mercenary."

"Lia! That almost sounded like a compliment. I am quite overwhelmed." His teasing was just like the rest of him—annoying in a way I couldn't explain while also being endearing.

I did not want him to be playful with me. It made him harder to resist. "There are houses here." Expensive ones. Nobles must have lived in this neighborhood.

Thankfully he didn't mention what an inane comment it was, how much I had veered us away from the direction our conversation had been headed.

"There are houses all over Troas," he countered.

"Yes, but these are costly. Is this where the life mages live?" It was a shot in the dark, but perhaps it might prove fruitful.

"All of the life mages live in the palace. There's not many of them left and they are highly regulated and kept track of," he said.

I frowned. That was going to put a definite wrinkle in my plans. How would I sneak into the palace to find a life mage?

It wasn't somewhere I should go. The prince was there and I didn't want to put myself in a position where he could capture and imprison me and try to force me to honor our betrothal. Not that he would have any reason to, as he didn't know who I was, but if the witness had seen me with my parents at the selection and realized who they were, then there was at least one person in Ilion who knew my true identity.

The witness couldn't share his knowledge with anyone else because he couldn't speak, but it still felt dangerous that the possibility existed. And that I had thought I'd seen him earlier tonight at the Golden Lamb. Like it was some kind of omen or warning.

"Here it is," Jason said. This building was not nearly as grand as the library and looked much older. We also had a records building back in Locris. It was the place where all the boring bureaucratic documents were kept. Taxes paid and collected, lawsuits and their verdicts, census lists documenting every citizen, businesses opened and operating, architectural plans for buildings and roads, past public announcements, minutes of government and royal meetings, official sets of weights and measurements for the marketplaces.

I didn't know why I thought any of that would be helpful but I hoped there would be something that might lead me in the right direction.

"This way." Jason whispered the words and I followed him as we entered the administrative building. We crept through hallways past multiple sets of doors. I wanted to ask him where he was going but stayed quiet. He seemed to have somewhere specific in mind.

He stopped in front of a door that was unmarked. "This is the chief recordkeeper's office," he said.

There was no lock and he opened it for me. After I went inside he checked both directions of the hallway and then also came in, gently closing the door.

Fortunately for me, everything was labeled. I only had to search for a few seconds before I found a drawer marked "Temple."

Perfect. I slid the drawer open and started sorting through the papers. I wanted to grab everything and bring it back with me but that might arouse suspicion. It was better to do what I'd planned on in the library—find the oldest set of documents and hope that they contained useful information.

I took a bound book that looked very weathered and aged, located underneath tax documents and financial records for the temple—which included significant donations made by noble families and the royals. I saw a salary listed for the high priestess and my eyebrows lifted in surprise.

Theano was doing well for herself.

There was another flat papyrus marked as "Inventory of the Temple Treasury" dated from this year. That could prove useful. I took that, as well.

I slipped the book and the papyrus into my knapsack and closed the drawer quietly.

"Did you find what you were looking for?" Jason asked, again whispering.

I nodded.

"Are you finished or do you need to keep searching?"

"I'm done," I said softly. I didn't want to tempt fate by staying here longer than was necessary.

Jason pressed his ear against the door. "I think the way is clear. Let's go."

We had only gone about ten feet when there was a sound somewhere off to our left that was clearly footsteps. Jason grabbed me by the arm and opened the closest door.

It turned out to be an incredibly small storage closet. There wasn't really enough room for both of us, but he squeezed in next to me and closed the door.

We were pressed completely against each other and my mind forgot how to function. I probably should have been listening for the guard but instead all I could think about was the way Jason's body was hard against mine, the way both of our chests were rapidly expanding and contracting, coming into contact with one another over and over again.

I glanced up at him from under my eyelashes but he wasn't looking at me. His gaze was trained on the door, listening.

Did he not feel this? This sparking energy between us, like lightning was flashing and filling the entire room with heat and light? Overwhelming and terrifying all at the same time?

My mouth had gone completely dry and I knew that I was trembling against him. My blood was thundering inside me, blocking out sound, as heat swirled in my gut.

We fit together so well. As if we'd been made for one another.

The guard must have left because Jason smiled down at me. "I think he's gone. Good thing he wasn't a goose."

I could only nod, unable to speak. He slowly pushed the door open and stuck his head out to survey the hallway.

"All clear," he said. He easily disengaged from me and I had to put a hand out on the cold stone wall in an attempt to center myself back in reality. My heart was beating so hard it felt like I might expire.

He raised his eyebrows, questioning. I shook my head at him and came out into the hallway. I had fought through worse battles than this. I could control my rebelling body.

We made our way out of the building with no other close calls, and after we'd put a few streets between ourselves and the offices, Jason said, "I suppose you're not going to tell me what you took."

"I wasn't planning on it," I said.

"Is there anywhere else you'd like to trespass? The palace, perhaps? There might be a royal vault where you can steal the queen's jewels," he said.

Although he was teasing, his suggestion gave me pause. What if the eye of the goddess had been mistaken for a simple gem? What if it really was among the jewels the queen kept for herself?

It was something worth considering.

But the hour was growing late and the morning was approaching. "I should return to the temple."

As we started our trek west, something flew up in front of me and lit up. "What's that?" I asked.

"A firefly."

"It's on fire?"

"No," he said with an indulgent smile. "It only lights up, like a tiny fire."

"How?"

"No one knows. It is a bit late in the year for fireflies, though. This one is a straggler. Out past her curfew," he said with a knowing look.

The light reappeared before blinking away. "It's like magic," I said, completely awed.

"I like how ordinary things seem special through your eyes."

While he had spent the night saying things intended to inflame my physical passions, this was entirely different. It was sweet and warm and made me feel like he had wrapped me up in a thick blanket.

Jason seemed intent on inflaming my emotional passions, too.

Somehow that seemed even more dangerous. I kept reminding myself why this was a very bad idea. Oblivious to my internal struggle, Jason shared the details of his latest voyage to a city called Sestos, within the Thracian borders, and how he'd won enough money to clear his debts in Troas.

I was only half listening and instead was internally listing all the reasons why I needed to keep my distance.

It was an argument I was losing with myself.

We were close to the temple, only a street away, when he suddenly slammed me up against a wall, his body covering mine, pressing into me.

Out of instinct I drew my sword and held it against him. "Unless you want to become a eunuch, I suggest you move back."

"That would be your loss," he said as he glanced down at my xiphos. "And I'm not trying to take advantage of you. I'm hiding us."

"From what?"

"Shh," he responded. "Patrol."

It was like earlier in the closet at the records building. He was close, touching every part of my body with his, so that every breath I took was also his.

I should not have been as excited as I was.

The patrol passed by, but I wasn't paying any attention to them. All I could think about was the incredible sensations Jason was causing inside me. How he could create a spark with only a glance and with this much contact. I was a raging inferno, desperate to be set loose.

It was as if dreaming of this with him so often had prepared me for it, making it more likely to happen. It would be so easy to give in.

"They're gone." He breathed the words against my ear and I shuddered at the hot, surging feeling.

The still-working part of my mind thought he might step back, but he stayed where he was.

My xiphos slipped from my hand and I heard it land with a clank against the sidewalk.

"Thank you for allowing me to keep all of my appendages," he said in a teasing tone as his nose grazed mine. My breathing hitched as my nerves quivered from his nearness.

"You're welcome," I breathed.

He reached up and began running his fingers through my hair. The sensation was utterly divine and I was going to turn completely liquid and wind up as a pool at his feet. "Have I told you how much I like the red? It suits you."

"What red?" I asked, confused.

"Your hair."

"My hair is not red," I told him. "It's light brown." He knew that. He had seen me in Locris when it was still long.

He looked at me like I was seriously confused. "No, it isn't. You've been dyeing it red."

It was such a ridiculous and odd thing to say. Was he lying? Making it up to torment me?

But then his fingers were stroking the back of my neck and I couldn't recall anything he'd just said. My entire body was vibrating with desire and awareness. Even my earlobes were throbbing with want.

"What is it?" he asked, even though I was fairly certain he knew exactly what was happening to me.

That he had caused it deliberately.

I was past caring about any of that. I forgot everything and everyone else. I shifted my gaze up to his lips.

"I always pay my debts," I told him.

CHAPTER
FORTY-SEVEN

His eyes lit up with understanding. "Oh? Does that include outstanding tolls, unpaid bets, and debts of gratitude as well?"

How could he joke at a time like this? "Yes."

"Interesting." Now he was ghosting his lips along my forehead, down over my eyelids, across my cheekbones. His warm breath fanned over my skin, causing prickles of heat. "Although I don't know if out here on the street is the proper place for you to thank me."

He was teasing me, tormenting me. Nearly offering me what I wanted but staying just out of reach.

Why was he behaving this way?

Stupid girl, because he likes you!

I quickly pushed Demaratus out of my head. I did not want him here while this was happening.

Maybe Jason withheld his kisses in some misguided attempt to wear me down. He didn't know that I was already worn down. My resistance was so thin it was like a spider's web, easily pushed aside with the tiniest amount of pressure.

He kissed my cheek. "Perhaps I'll sneak into your room in the temple one night and surprise you. That would be a better place for you to thank me."

His words sent an illicit thrill through me. "You wouldn't dare cross onto the temple grounds."

Lips brushing against my forehead, he said, "It would depend on who was waiting for me on the other side. And how willing she might be."

If he were anyone else, I probably would have punched him for his implication that I was willing and waiting.

But when Jason said it?

There was no one more willing than me.

And I was tired of waiting.

His arms were on either side of me, enclosing me against the wall. It was a terrible defensive position. He could have easily overpowered me.

I didn't care. I liked how it felt.

Now his fingertips had replaced his lips and he was tracing the outline of my face, creating little pools of fire everywhere he touched.

"You are so soft." It sounded as if he hadn't meant to say the words aloud. "What do you bathe in that makes your skin so soft?"

"Water," I responded without thinking and was rewarded with his grin.

"Soft, and so, so sweet."

"I am not sweet."

"You are. The sweetest thing I have ever tasted."

He kissed along the column of my throat and I felt the tip of his tongue flicker out to taste my skin. I arched against him in response and he made a sound at the back of his throat at my movement.

I realized then that he wasn't going to kiss me. I was the one who had lost the bet. He had asked for a kiss as his reward—he hadn't offered one.

He pulled his head back so that he could look down at me, our gazes locked. He was waiting.

"You want me to kiss you." It was a statement, not a question.

A smile hovered just above his lips. "That's very bold of you. You didn't even ask my permission."

"I didn't think I needed to."

"You don't."

Satisfied, I wrapped my arms around his neck. We had done this before but it still felt like the very first time, like it was all fresh and new. I was equal parts anxious and eager.

Not to mention that during our last kiss he had been the one kissing me. I let my fingers drift up into his hair, and the dark, silken strands caressed my hand. I wasn't the only one who was soft.

But his hair was the only part of him that I was touching that felt soft. His broad body was pure muscle. Firm. Hard. I brought my hand around so that I could explore the stubble along his jaw, the texture rough against my fingertips. He expelled a sharp breath and let his eyes drift shut.

I trailed my fingers down over his jaw and then farther south. I touched where my xiphos had pressed into his neck hours ago. He swallowed.

"I'm sorry I cut you," I said. And I was. I had committed a crime by marring such beauty.

"It was worth it." His words were rough, full of longing.

Perhaps it was my turn to kiss him better. I pushed forward so that my lips pressed against his throat. I was rewarded with the sound of his breath catching.

Not as indifferent as he'd pretended earlier.

Although that act might have been nothing more than a ploy to trick me.

He'd said I would know when he was luring me. And it seemed that was exactly what he'd been doing.

Luring me in.

I didn't mind being trapped, though.

"Lia." My name on his lips was both a whisper and a warning that I didn't quite understand. Perhaps he was telling me that if I wanted to change my mind, now was the time to do so.

My stomach tightened in anticipation. I didn't want to stop.

My pulse beat slow and thick as I brought my mouth up to his and carefully, oh so carefully, fitted our lips together. I let out a moan of pleasure. It was everything that I'd remembered, everything that I'd wanted, everything that I'd been dreaming of for the past month.

Glorious.

He quickly took control of the kiss, leaving me gasping. One of his large hands cupped the base of my skull, cradling me while he parted my lips and deepened the kiss. His other hand stole around my waist, somehow pulling me even closer.

I'd never craved anything the way I did his mouth. My lips were frantic. I needed more. I demanded it. He made me feel like a ravenous beast.

And he was every bit as hungry and desperate as I was.

His lips meeting mine, his tongue against my own, it felt like a kind of battle. Like swords clanging against one another, caressing as they pulled apart and reengaged.

"Why does kissing you always feel like swordplay?" I asked against his mouth, sighing the words.

"And we haven't even involved my sword yet." He grinned back.

Then I was the one plunging us back into battle. It really was like combat—he would thrust, I parried. He advanced and I was there, ready to engage him in return. He retreated and I coaxed him back into the fight.

He had somehow completely disarmed me and I had permitted it.

Everything happening between us was so visceral and intimate. He was devouring me, kissing me into oblivion. The crushing heat of his lips against mine burned through my entire body, consuming me.

It felt like there were massive, flapping geese in my stomach, their wings beating so hard and so quickly that I was going to take flight.

How could everything feel new and surprising but also like something that had happened a million times before? As if we already knew each other's bodies perfectly?

The way that Jason could tilt his head, or slightly change the pressure of his kiss, or dig his fingers into my back and have me panting against him, practically begging him for more, was beyond my comprehension.

As if he instinctively understood every single way to make me respond, to make me melt, to turn me mindless with need for him.

Only him.

Fire raced up and down my veins, engulfing me. Jason seemed to burn just as brightly, just as hotly. His breathing was harsh, rapid. I clung to him, as if I were out at sea during a wicked storm, my boat destroyed, and all I could do was hold on to a piece of driftwood to keep breathing while the seas and skies raged all around me.

"Jason," I breathed. It felt as if I would go mad. As if the sensations and feelings he created were too much for any one person to bear. They couldn't be contained within my mortal and weak body.

He was like magic.

I slowly became aware of something warm and bright. I mistakenly attributed it to the way he was kissing me, but then I opened my eyes to see that the sun was rising over the horizon.

With a gasp I pulled away from him. "I have to go." It was difficult to form words, my overly sensitized lips aching for him, my body screaming at me to keep kissing him.

"What? Why?" He seemed every bit as disoriented as I was.

"The sun is up." My brain began to function again and I realized how bad this could be for me. "They're going to realize that I'm missing."

It might have already been too late.

I cursed myself for being so intoxicated by him that I had potentially risked my place at the temple. I disentangled myself from him with every part of me protesting.

"Wait, one last kiss," he said. He reached out to cup my face with his hands and I meant to tell him no, that I was late, but instead I leaned into the kiss, which quickly escalated.

Stupid girl, time to leave!

I had to reluctantly break it off again. "I really have to go."

"Thank you for repaying your debt. As Simos said, it was a pleasure doing business with you."

It took every bit of willpower I had to walk away from him. I reached down to get my sword and returned it to its sheath.

"Please remember that if you want to go home to Locris, I can arrange it for you. All you have to do is ask," he said.

"I wonder what it would cost me if you sailed me across the ocean."

He grinned. "I would be happy to set up some sort of repayment plan with you."

My entire body ached from the mental images that put into my head. I began walking toward the temple, worried that if I didn't make myself leave right then I was going to change my mind and take him up on his offer.

Sail home, convince him to stay with me in Locris, and find a different way to save my nation.

It suddenly didn't sound so bad. And if I were already married to Jason, there would be little the Ilionian prince could do about it.

But I knew it wasn't realistic.

Not to mention that Jason had never once seriously brought up the subject of marriage and I felt like he was the sort of man who would run away screaming into the night if I said something about it.

We reached the corner where the next turn would lead to the front of the temple. The same place where he had destroyed an entire ambush for my sake. That rush of warm emotions filled me again. I didn't want this night to end. I wanted to stay with him.

Although I knew I couldn't.

"Thank you for sending the soil," I said suddenly as I realized that I'd never thanked him for that.

"Thank you for the kiss," he said.

It felt like I should be the one thanking him. As if I should be composing epic poems to express how incredible it had been, how good he was at it.

Not knowing what else to say, I nodded and started forward. Before I could take a step, his hand was on my arm.

"Lia, if you're going to sneak out again, send for me."

That wasn't going to happen. I would leave the temple again, but there was no way that I would deliberately involve him in doing so. I knew that whatever we shared, whatever this was, had to be over.

Even if I didn't want it to be.

I nodded, though. As if I agreed.

He gave me one fleeting, quick kiss and then I ran for the archway. I pressed myself against it, looking into the courtyard. I didn't see anyone. I risked glancing over my shoulder one last time, but he wasn't there.

It ended up being easy enough to sneak back in. I ran for the temple and no one noticed. No alarm was raised. I reached the temple patio and leaned against one of the columns to catch my breath.

I was safe. I had made it. It was time for me to clean the temple. I had a reason to be out of my bedroom and no one would question what I was doing.

There was sweat on my forehead and I brushed it away with the back of my hand. Had that been from running over here, or had it been Jason's doing?

That made me remember something he had said and I took my sword and reached up to the side of my head and cut off a chunk of my hair. I was probably leaving a gaping hole behind but I didn't care.

I held the hair up in the blooming sunlight.

Red.

It was definitely a dark red.

What did that mean?

CHAPTER
FORTY-EIGHT

I couldn't get over the fact that my hair had changed color. It was so bizarre that it made my heart race and my hands shake. How had that happened?

It was a deeper red than that of the man who had taken Quynh. Perhaps that was why the goddess had done it—she had marked me with the hair of my enemy so that I wouldn't forget to take my vengeance against him.

We didn't have mirrors in the temple, so I hadn't realized. It felt very strange to have something fundamental, something you knew to be true, change about yourself and to not even have been aware of it.

I tried distracting myself, using my time alone to look over the documents I had taken. It was a good choice because it made me forget all about my hair. The first thing I read over was the temple inventory. I ran through it twice and didn't see any mention of the eye.

But there was an entry for "various, unspecified gems."

That seemed promising. It meant that I was going to have to figure out a way to get into the vault and search through those various, unspecified gems and find the eye.

No one had been chosen as key bearer since I'd arrived more than a month ago. Theano still wore them on her belt.

But I would bet that she had extra keys to the vault. She didn't strike me as the type of person to not have a backup plan. What if something happened to her? Or the keys were lost? She had to have a spare.

Her locked office seemed like the perfect spot to keep it.

That was the plan, then. I would figure out a way to break into her office and search for the spare key.

While avoiding the guards and not getting caught.

Easy, I thought sarcastically.

I let out a sigh and continued to flip through pages. There were a bunch of entries about court cases where priestesses were called to testify, about festivals planned and paid for by the king, list after list of supplies provided to the temple. All boring and useless information.

It was the very last page that caught my attention. The first entry stated:

Danae, priestess, married to Solon, dowry provided by the temple of the goddess, 60 minae

That made no sense. A priestess was married and the temple had provided a dowry? A significant one at that.

The next entry was just like the first.

Arsinoe, priestess, married to Theophanes, dowry provided by the temple of the goddess, 60 minae

That was a fortune. Given the treasury inventory I'd seen, it didn't surprise me that the temple had those kind of resources, only that they were provided to priestesses as dowries.

When we were sworn to celibacy.

The rest of the page was the same—priestesses listed by name and the men they'd married and the substantial dowry given to each one.

Priestesses used to get married? How old was this book? And when had things changed to the way they were now?

Why had they changed?

I was so confused.

"What do you think you're doing? Why aren't you working?"

I nearly dropped the book when the guard assigned to watch over the stairs in the temple came out to scold me.

"I'm sorry," I said, sliding the book back into my knapsack. If she took it from me, I would be in a horrific amount of trouble. She hadn't seemed to notice the book, though—her attention was focused more on the fact that I wasn't sweeping. "I forgot my broom."

"Go and get it then."

I nodded and hurried toward my dormitory. I wanted to tell someone what I'd discovered, but who could I trust with this information?

When I got to my room, all my sisters were gone. They must have been at breakfast. Kunguru was in the window and cawed at me. I took the book out of my bag and slid it underneath my bed. No one here stole—I probably could have left it out on my table without having to worry about it being taken.

But I did have to worry about someone finding it and the questions I didn't want to answer. I'd been trained to be suspicious. What if there were inspections of rooms that took place while we were out? I didn't want an older priestess accidentally coming across it.

When I was done, I went over to pet Kunguru. He made a happy sound at me.

"Watch over the book," I told him.

He hopped around on the windowsill. Almost like he was patrolling.

I bent down and caught his eye. He cocked his head to the side to look at me more properly.

"Can you talk?" I asked him.

I half expected him to answer. It wouldn't have surprised me if he did.

Instead he just squawked. I let out a sigh of disgust. It was a foolish whim. I grabbed my broom and headed back to the temple.

But I did think about Jason and how he'd said a little bird had told him of my plans.

Too many things were happening at once. I couldn't properly evaluate each separate incident in order to come up with reasonable explanations. I was just more and more confused. I hated that there were so many things I didn't understand and couldn't puzzle out.

During my tutorial that morning with Maia, all I could think of was all the questions I had that I couldn't say out loud. I only half listened to everything she was saying while the unanswerable issues I'd discovered swirled around in my head.

Dowries? Marriage? There had been no mistaking what I'd seen.

"Was there ever a time when temple priestesses got married?" I asked, interrupting her.

"Of course not." She sounded scandalized. "Why would you think that?"

"I heard something during dinner the other day. Another acolyte, I think."

"That's not possible. It didn't happen. Someone is making up lies," she said.

Frustrated, I slunk down in my seat. I knew it wasn't a lie. I had an official government document that proved otherwise.

Maia apparently felt as if she had failed my education in some way due to my erroneous belief, and it caused her to launch into more extensive, detailed explanations that made our session go long. I tried to force myself to pay attention but it was a losing battle.

Because of the delay, I had to hurry from my tutorial to the gymnasium. I was no closer to understanding what I had uncovered.

Zalira was sparring with Ahyana. Suri saw me first and nodded. I nodded back at her. She made the same hand motions she had yesterday when we'd sat on the riverbank.

Tell them.

It surprised me. What did she know? How did she always seem to intuit that I was keeping secrets when everyone else was oblivious?

Maybe the goddess spoke to her more often than I thought.

"How did things go?" Io asked anxiously when I came to stand next to her.

"Fine." It was an inadequate explanation for what had occurred over the last few hours. I could still feel the phantom imprint of Jason's body against mine.

Strangely enough, even though I'd just seen him, I missed him.

"I found out that my hair is red. Why didn't you tell me?" I asked.

"We thought you knew!" Zalira said, surprised.

"It used to be light brown." Now all my adelphia looked shocked.

Ahyana spoke first. "That happened to a woman in our old neighborhood. Remember, Zalira? Her family got lice and she had to shave all their heads to get rid of it. She'd had straight hair but then it grew back in curly."

Even if they'd seen this type of thing before, I never had because no women in Locris cut their hair. It had been such an important part of my identity that I felt a little betrayed that it was growing back in differently.

I didn't think anyone here would understand that, though.

"Who told you that your hair was red?" Io asked, her eyes narrowing at me. I knew that my sneaking out had been hard on her because of how much she cared about me. I'd expected her to be teasing and laughing with me this morning but she was being particularly somber.

I glanced over her shoulder and saw Suri, standing behind Io. Even though I hadn't said Jason's name, it was like Suri knew. My chest tightened. Was she going to find a way to communicate that to everyone else? How did she know?

What should I say? I didn't want to lie. "No one important. It was just when he said—"

"He? It was a man?" Zalira immediately asked.

"Was it Jason?" Ahyana batted her eyes and then laughed.

"Don't be ridiculous," I said. It wasn't a denial because I didn't want to do that. To say it wasn't him would be like denying what had passed between us and I couldn't do that.

Suri's knowing expression made me feel guilty about keeping secrets from them, but I wasn't going to tell them about what had happened with me and Jason. It was too special to share with other people. I didn't want to invite their opinions or their judgments, their gentle teasing. I would keep it between him and me.

My lips tingled as I thought of him and I couldn't help but reach up to brush them with my own fingertips, though it was an extremely poor substitute. I wanted to kiss him again, especially given how fantastic he was at it.

I reminded myself that he was so good at kissing because he had extensive experience. I somehow always forgot about that when I was with him. I should have remembered it. I should keep it in the forefront of my mind to recall if I ever saw him in person again. Because the sort of man who flitted from one woman to the next like a honeybee with a garden full of flowers was not the right type for me.

My parents were utterly devoted to each other. Haemon and Doria had been the same way. I expected total fidelity and adoration in a relationship.

Jason had shown me repeatedly that he was not the faithful type.

I swallowed back a groan of annoyance. Why did I keep thinking about this? None of it mattered. He wasn't going to be anything in my life. Yes, he had kissed me so thoroughly that every other man would have paled in comparison if I hadn't taken my vows, but we wouldn't end up together.

Despite understanding the reality of my situation, I found myself thinking of how he'd helped me.

To be fair, he had done more than just help me. He had saved Quynh's life. My life. Had made it possible for me to join the temple. He had helped me break into government buildings. Assisted me in getting a message to my parents.

He would do all of it again, and more, if I but asked. I knew that.

I thought about him saying that I should reach out to him if I planned on sneaking out again. It was so tempting to wait a few days and then send him a note and ask him to meet up with me. Although I wasn't exactly sure how I would get in contact with him. Presumably if I addressed something to the *Nikos* he would receive it, but then someone in the temple would be sure to notice that I'd written a letter.

It didn't matter either way. I had to push those impulses down and keep them buried. Things between us had to be at an end.

"That doesn't sound like a no to me," Ahyana said to Zalira, and they both smiled.

I sensed that they were going to push the issue further but Io spoke up. "Did you get your message sent to your parents?"

"Yes, I did." I was very grateful for the change in subject. I got the feeling I would eventually break and tell them every detail if they kept asking me about it.

"I'm so glad," she said and her relief was evident. "Now that they know you're safe, this is over. We can all go back to the way things were."

That wasn't true, though. Suri frowned at me.

Tell them.

I knew exactly what she meant. She was talking about my plans to break into the treasury. I wasn't sure how she'd figured it out. Had I talked about it in my sleep?

Or had the goddess appeared to her and told her?

There wasn't going to be an answer for me either way. Suri would stay silent.

Why would Suri or the goddess want me to tell our adelphia about it? Was that even fair to them? Wouldn't it be better to keep them in the dark, to not risk their place here at the temple by making them feel obligated to either help me or keep my secret? Although I was keeping so many secrets that it would be nice to have one less to worry about.

The words formed on my tongue, as if they wanted me to speak them into existence. The urge to do so was overwhelming.

Zalira and Ahyana resumed sparring with their fists.

Io said, "No more sneaking around. No more breaking rules. Everything is going to be calm and peaceful."

I had to do it. "Not quite. I need to break into the temple treasury."

CHAPTER
FORTY-NINE

"What?" Zalira demanded, looking away from Ahyana, who accidentally punched her hard in the jaw since Zalira had dropped her defense.

Ahyana apologized to her sister as she helped Zalira get back to her feet and then turned to face me. "Say that again," she said.

"I have to break into the treasury." I glanced around to make certain that no one could overhear us.

"Why?" Io asked.

"There's something specific that I'm looking for that is in the vault."

"Tell us what it is," Zalira said.

I shook my head. "I don't want you to have to lie for me. If I'm caught, I don't want any of you to be in trouble. You can honestly tell them that you didn't know what I was searching for."

Ahyana and Zalira exchanged a look communicating their displeasure, Suri angrily crossed her arms over her chest, and Io looked like she was about to faint.

I tried to reassure them. "It will be fine. I went out last night and nobody noticed. I can do this without getting caught. I just wanted to be honest with you about what I'm planning."

Io pushed away from the wall. "Well, obviously we're going to help you."

That was the last thing I had expected any of them to say. "What?"

"We are bound to you," Ahyana said. "Where you go, we go. If you're going to break into the vault, we're breaking in with you."

"You're our sister," Io added.

My breath caught and I felt tears burning my eyes. If they got caught, they would be thrown out of the temple, too. Where would they all go if their home was taken from them?

It was one thing for them to help me sneak out for a reason they understood—to send a message to my parents. This was an entirely different situation and yet they were still willing to be there for me. "No. I can't ask that of you."

"You didn't ask," Zalira said. "We're offering."

Suri nodded her agreement.

If they were willing to take this risk, maybe they should have all of the information. "You should at least know why—"

But Zalira interrupted me. "We don't need to know why. The only thing that matters is that you need help."

"When?" Io asked.

"As soon as possible," I said, stunned and touched that they wanted to help me. The Jason distraction aside, I was still on a deadline. I only had so much time before the Ilionian prince sent for me in Locris. I had to find the eye first.

Ahyana nodded. "What's the first step?"

"I think that it might be easier to break into Theano's office. I'm theorizing that she may keep a spare key in there."

"That sounds logical," Zalira said. "Can anyone pick a lock?"

My hopes lifted momentarily but were immediately dashed when nobody responded.

"We'll figure it out when we get there," I said.

"Do you ever have an actual plan?" Ahyana teased, and I smiled back at her.

"Were you going to try tonight?" Io asked.

"Not tonight." The exhaustion hadn't caught up with me, but I knew that it would eventually. At the very least I wanted a good night's rest before I attempted something as dangerous and foolish as breaking into the high priestess's personal office.

"Tomorrow night, then," Zalira said with Suri nodding.

"Tomorrow night," I agreed.

"Maia's looking at us," Ahyana said. "Let's get back to work."

I stepped into the ring with Ahyana so that we could spar. I couldn't keep the grin off my face. My mouth actually hurt.

I had started out this morning thinking that I was completely alone. It was such a relief to discover that my sisters were ready and willing to stand by my side.

◆ ◆ ◆

What I wanted to do was return to our room so that we could try to stitch together some sort of plan on how to break into Theano's office. Instead we had to attend our afternoon class, where Maia was again instructing on the different aspects of the goddess.

"When you become a priestess, you will choose an aspect to specialize in," she said. I'd now officially been at the temple long enough that she had started to repeat her lessons. Io had warned me that would happen, but it felt excruciating to hear recycled information, given that I was so desperate to talk to my sisters.

Maia began listing the different aspects and I realized that I hadn't ever really worried about choosing one because I didn't plan on being in the temple long enough to do so.

It was easy to see what my adelphia would pick to honor the goddess. Io loved new life and plants. Zalira had an instinct about storms and when rain would fall. Ahyana surrounded herself with insects and animals that helped things grow. Suri was drawn to uncovering secrets, like the types hidden in the deep earth.

I was the only one in our immediate group who hadn't shown some kind of affinity or interest. The thought bothered me. I might even be the only one in the room who hadn't picked a specialization.

Artemisia might not have chosen one yet, either. And probably wouldn't, unless the goddess had a murderous, destroying aspect that I was unaware of. I'd spent the last month keeping clear of Artemisia, who continued to lash out at the other acolytes every chance she could. She was careful to not ever cross the line to where she would officially be hurting someone and running afoul of her vows but came as close as she possibly could.

There was something truly awful deep in her core and I wondered why the priestesses couldn't see it and continued to reward her by making her a Chosen, week after week. An honor still denied to me, no matter how well I did.

Like Theano had some kind of personal vendetta against me.

Our class finally ended and we headed over to the courtyard to take care of our weekly chores.

"Is there a possibility of getting the vault key some other way?" Zalira asked. "Without having to break into a locked room?"

"I've been trying to figure out how to do that since I arrived. Theano wears them all the time. I thought maybe I could become a Chosen and offer to be a key bearer, but as far as I can tell, she doesn't let anyone else have that responsibility."

"You're right," Io said with a nod. "She doesn't. She always wears those keys."

"I don't remember anyone being given the role of key bearer when I was a Chosen, either." Zalira had been a Chosen for two weeks a few months ago, before she'd been pushed out of the rankings.

I turned toward Ahyana. "I even thought about asking you if we could train Kunguru to retrieve keys and maybe he could steal them for us. She must take them off at some point. To bathe or to sleep."

"It wouldn't take him that long to learn how to do it. He's very smart. Maybe a week?"

That wouldn't work. I didn't have that kind of time. "He doesn't speak, does he?"

I was rewarded with a bunch of strange looks and Ahyana's laughter. "Of course not. Why would you think that?"

"It would just make things easier if he could," I mumbled, feeling foolish.

"Oh, I agree. It absolutely would." Ahyana was trying to make me feel better but it wasn't working.

We performed our tasks and continued trying to formulate a plan together. It was quickly decided that two people should remain behind because the smaller the group, the better. Ahyana and Zalira were going to stay back. Initially they had volunteered to accompany me, but Io said she wanted to go.

It surprised everyone.

"I can do this," she said. It was like she insisted on coming because she had something to prove to herself.

Which I understood.

Suri was also going to come along and keep watch near the administrative building. Ahyana would stand guard outside the entrance to our dormitory, promising to send Kunguru if something went wrong or if one of the guards changed her nightly path. Zalira would remain in our room in case the guards came to check on us. They did that from time to time. It wasn't a constant or a given, but we had to be prepared.

I still didn't know how I was going to get Theano's office door opened and hoped a solution would present itself when I got there.

It was foolish to go without knowing exactly how I would accomplish my goal, but there was no other option and nobody else had a suggestion on what I should do, either.

I also had to consider the possibility that I might not be able to get into her office. That despite my best attempts and efforts, I could still be kept out. Or even if I did succeed, find a spare key, and open the vault, the gem might not be there. It might mean I would have to investigate other paths.

Like returning to the public library.

Which could mean seeing Jason again.

While sweeping alongside Io, I asked her, "Is there something you could create that would put a goose to sleep?"

"Why would you want to put a goose to sleep?" She didn't sound surprised, only curious. I think at this point my sisters expected me to say bizarre things to them.

"So that I won't have to kill it."

She accepted this as an explanation and paused. "I think so. I could combine some poppy powder with valerian root. The problem would be having it work and then immediately dissipating so that the person who threw it wouldn't fall asleep as well."

Io began mumbling to herself, brainstorming a formula out loud.

A wave of exhaustion hit me and I sat down on one of the temple steps.

Zalira saw me and wagged one of her fingers at me. "We have to make sure the courtyard is spotless for the festival."

I nodded. There was some annual festival that was set to take place in a few days. It had been mentioned frequently but I'd mostly been ignoring the details as it was unimportant to me. Again, I hoped I wouldn't still be here when the festival took place. I knew almost nothing about it—just that it was something that only women participated in here on the temple grounds and in the surrounding neighborhood. Men were not allowed to attend.

Maia had said something about harvest and fertility and that the festival would ensure good fortune for the next season by celebrating and thanking the goddess, if I remembered correctly.

I yawned.

"You should skip dinner and go to bed," Zalira said.

"Maybe I will." It wasn't like me to miss out on a meal, but I would probably fall asleep halfway through.

She reached for my broom. "Go now. We have this."

I thanked her and headed for our room. I used the washroom and then crashed onto my bed. Kunguru was waiting in the windowsill and called out to me. I reached under my bed and felt the edges of the book against my fingers. He seemed to have done as I'd asked and watched over it.

"Good boy," I called out to him right before I passed out.

◆ ◆ ◆

"Who's a good boy?" Jason asked me.

Blinking, it took me a few beats to take in my surroundings. I was back in Jason's room, with him on his bed. We were sitting up, facing one another. I had my legs over his so that the backs of my knees were on top of his strong thighs.

I was running my fingers through his midnight-black hair and he was turning his head so that he could lean into my touch.

"Kunguru is a good boy," I told him. "I was talking to him before I got here. Your hair reminds me of his feathers."

"You like him."

"I do. He's usually quiet. Unlike you."

Jason grinned. "I can be quiet."

"Only when my lips are on yours. And you're not very quiet then, either."

"That's true." His hands were around my waist and he pulled me a bit closer to him. "Should I be jealous?"

"Of a bird?" I asked with a laugh. "No."

It was different when we were here together. I wasn't ever as angry with him or as annoyed. We could be playful. Tease. Laugh.

Or, more accurately, I could. He was always like that.

Which was where the annoyance came in.

"I am jealous of him, you know," he said.

"Why?"

"He gets to be with you as often as he would like. He can fly in and see you and touch you and be near you and I would give anything to have that."

I kissed his forehead. His words were so sweet, so romantic. "Now I know that I'm dreaming."

"Why would you say that?"

"Because you aren't vulnerable like this with me when we're awake. I wish that you would be." I kissed his face in between my words, still running my fingers along his scalp.

He released my waist and reached up for my wrists, pulling them away from his head. He put them on top of my legs and then reached up to frame my face with his hands. "Lia, don't you know how I feel about you?"

CHAPTER FIFTY

My breath stilled in my lungs. "No."

He kissed me and I went pliant against him, reaching out to grab his tunic so that I would have something to hold on to. We kissed until we were both having difficulty breathing. I felt his heart galloping under my hand.

Jason pulled back and rubbed his nose against mine, such a familiar and sweet gesture that I was melting all over again.

"I pledge to you my whole heart. My entire soul. Every part of my being already belongs to you. Ask for anything and it is yours."

It was simultaneously the most wonderful and the worst thing I'd ever heard.

Wonderful, because it was everything I'd ever wanted from him.

Terrible, because I knew he didn't mean it.

This wasn't real. He wasn't here. I was only imagining his words.

He didn't speak actual words of love.

And if we had been awake and he'd said it, I wouldn't have believed him then, either. He wasn't the sort of man who could be faithful to just one woman.

It was what I wanted him to say, but it was not how the real Jason actually felt.

"We were made for each other," he said. "Can't you feel it? The goddess herself blesses us."

Imaginary Jason had taken it one step too far. "No. She doesn't. She has made me promise to stay away from you. And with good reason. You would break my heart, shatter my soul, if I allowed myself to return the feelings you claim to have."

He drew back, his hands falling away from me, even though our legs were still intertwined. "Do you really believe that?"

"Of course I do. I sealed my vow to her with my blood and fire." He was missing the point, though. "But even if I hadn't made an oath, I could never be with a man like you."

While I thought he might be offended, instead his handsome face broke into a smile. "A man like me? Why not?" He sounded both delighted and confused.

I imagined not many women refused him the way that I just had. Especially not after he'd made that sort of emotional confession. "Because you're a philanderer."

His eyes danced. "What makes you say that?"

"You do. With your own words."

He shrugged one shoulder, as if it were unimportant. "The past doesn't matter. Only here and now. And there hasn't been any other woman for me since I first laid eyes on you."

Oh, how I wanted to believe him. How I wanted to push him back against his bed and kiss him until the entire world faded away.

Then, as if he knew exactly what I had been thinking about, Jason pulled his legs away from me while tugging me toward him. I went flat onto my back and he loomed over me.

His expression was serious but soft. He reached up to stroke my face. "I pledge you my sword, my body, my blood. I will protect you and keep you safe."

I put my arms around him, tugging him closer, but he wouldn't budge. "You would lay down your life for me?"

"Without hesitation."

He continued to stare down at me, and then he said, "I'm glad that you finally stopped wasting time."

"What do you mean?" I asked while tracing the column of his neck with my fingertips.

"You've been delaying the inevitable."

"With you?"

"No, not with me. With what you came to Ilion to accomplish."

That made my fingers still. "You know about that?"

He rolled to my right side and propped up his head with his arm. "Lia, no one knows you the way that I do. I know the things that make you smile, what makes you angry, what I can do to coax those soft, excited noises out of you that I so adore."

His words went straight to my gut, setting me on fire. He reached down to kiss me and I rose up eagerly to meet him.

"Does anyone else know you the way that I do?" he asked against my mouth.

"Only you," I breathed.

"It's time for things to change."

Now his words had the opposite effect, as if someone had doused me in cold water. It was the same thing the goddess had told me. "What?"

His eyes stared into mine with an intensity that I had never seen from him before. "When the time comes, you need to say yes."

"I don't know what you mean."

"You will," he promised.

"Why are you being so mysterious?" I had enough frustration in my regular life. I didn't need it here.

"Isn't that the way of dreams? Open to interpretation?"

Jason had never mentioned that we were in a dream before. I was about to tell him that, but he kissed me again until I was mindless with need for him.

He went still against me and then said, "Be ready. And remember that you love me."

When I awoke with a start, Ahyana was sitting on her bed adding a new ribbon to one of her braids. "How's Jason?" she asked.

I groaned. My heart was pounding, my body aching with frustration and need for him.

"Still in love?" she asked.

Had I said his words aloud? His claim that I loved him?

Did I?

I turned on my side and contemplated what both he and Ahyana had suggested. Was I in love with Jason?

I'd never been in love before. Never felt anything even close to it. I had no experience with it at all.

But I did feel something overwhelming and powerful for him. I missed him. I wanted to see him again. My dreams were just exercises in frustration. There, but not there. Not real.

I thought of him often, wondered what he was doing. If he was out at sea, what kind of places he was visiting.

The various women he was probably consorting with.

At least I could identify that burning feeling as jealousy. Women were probably throwing themselves at him and I couldn't even blame them. I thought of how they weren't bound by lifelong vows and were free to be with him in any way that they chose and it made me feel physically ill.

It was so unfair. Why would he think of me when he could have anyone else?

My jealousy had to mean something, didn't it? Was it an indication of love? I wished that I could speak to my mother about it. I was sure that she would have had very wise insight into my situation.

I tried to imagine what she might ask me. She would ask me to qualify the feelings I did understand. I knew that I cared about him and his well-being. I wanted him to be safe. I looked forward to going to sleep because I knew he'd be there.

With a sigh I told myself that this was the absolute last thing I should be worried about. I couldn't let him consume my waking thoughts as well as my sleeping ones.

We had an office to raid tonight. That should be my focus.

Keeping myself and my sisters safe.

Not fixating on the fact that Jason had pledged himself to me, willing to lay down his own life for me.

With a wave of sadness, I realized that even if he hadn't declared his love, it was the closest I would ever come to it.

◆ ◆ ◆

"Are you ready?" Ahyana asked me, Kunguru perched on her shoulder. It was approximately three o'clock in the morning and the four of us were standing in the doorway of the dormitory. Zalira was back in our room, where she had used extra blankets to make it seem as if we were all still sleeping soundly in our beds.

"Yes." My toes were tingling, my heart thumping, my nerves shaking. I was excited. Ready to go. It felt so good to be taking action. Dream Jason had been correct—I'd been wasting my time. I'd thought I was being cautious, gathering information, but I shouldn't have waited for so long.

There was too much at stake.

This was going to work. It had to.

After Calliope passed by us, Ahyana whispered, "Go!"

Suri, Io, and I darted out into the night. It was a straight shot to the administrative building and Ahyana would be able to keep an eye on us while we ran. We had agreed for her to make a birdcall if she saw anything out of the ordinary.

We were about to enter the building when Suri yanked both of us against a wall. We heard several priestesses pass by, speaking to one another. It was a very odd hour for people to be out socializing, but they weren't guards. I wanted to peek out and see who it was, get closer to hear what they were talking about, but Suri put her hand on my chest and pushed me back.

I stayed put and we waited for the group to pass. When they did, Suri led the way and we reached the administrative building and ran inside. We waited several heartbeats, and when no one challenged us, Io said, "I'll keep watch at the door."

Suri nodded and then gestured toward the east. Zalira had given her the task of keeping a lookout for the guard that would be coming from that direction. It allowed us to triangulate our watch so that every angle would be covered.

"Let us know when you see her," I said. She nodded. She was going to throw a rock our direction against the wall. Something that wouldn't seem too alarming but would let us know.

Once Suri was gone, Io took her spot just inside the door. "Hurry."

I ran up the stairs and reached the office. I had brought a hardwood staff that I could hopefully use to pry open the door if necessary. It was because of something my father always used to say, quoting Archimedes: *Give me a lever long enough and a fulcrum on which to place it, and I shall move the world.*

I didn't need to move the world, just this door. It would be a last resort, though. Theano would certainly notice if I pried her door open. I set it down on the floor. I said a quick prayer to the goddess and used my throwing daggers to begin picking at the lock.

I had just inserted one when I was overwhelmed with a sense of dread. Something was wrong.

Io needs you.

I didn't know where the voice had come from, only that I felt compelled to listen.

Io hadn't called out or made a sound. A part of me thought I was being silly, imagining things. If she needed me, she would let me know.

That urge returned again, stronger. It was like someone had hooked my stomach and was pulling me away from the door.

This was ridiculous. I didn't have enough time to respond to my overactive imagination. But I sheathed my knives and went down the stairs. The dread in my gut increased with each step.

It reached a frenzied pitch when I realized that Io wasn't at her post.

My heart thudded low and hard as I went through the doorway and saw Io on the ground. An absolute giant of a man was kneeling on top of her, his meaty hands wrapped around her throat, squeezing the life from her.

For a second I was so shocked that I didn't react.

Then I threw one of my knives at him, but my aim was poor and it bounced off his breastplate. He turned to glare at me, a murderous gleam in his eyes.

"Leave her alone!" I said, hurriedly trying to calculate my next move. Io's face was turning purple. In the time it would take me to reach them, he could easily snap her neck. I had to get him away from her and to chase after me.

"Where's the Locrian?" he asked.

Only a tiny part of me registered panic at the notion that he was looking specifically for me. The rest of me was hysterical over Io's eyes rolling back into her head before her eyelids drifted shut.

He was going to kill her.

"I'm the Locrian," I taunted him. "Come and get me."

CHAPTER
FIFTY-ONE

My remaining throwing knife wouldn't be enough to keep this man at bay. Not only did I need to get him away from my sister but I had to find a longer weapon. Something that would keep him at arm's reach. I had one upstairs.

Thankfully he released Io, who was unmoving.

I didn't know if she was alive or not.

He pulled out a giant broadsword from his back. My heart twisted in my chest as I realized that it would cut the staff I'd left at the door of Theano's office into kindling. Maybe she had a weapon of some kind in that room.

It would be the only way I could hope to survive this.

I cursed myself for leaving my xiphos back in my bedroom. I turned and ran for the stairs and heard the man following behind me. I raced up, ducking as he swung out at me with his weapon. I heard his broadsword smash into the stone wall. I ran down the hallway, grabbed the staff, and tried the door handle.

Some part of me had secretly hoped that I'd miraculously managed to undo the lock earlier. How many times was this going to happen to me? Chased by killers, locked out from safety.

With a desperate yell I rammed my body against the door with all my might, and to my complete shock, it gave way. There was still a fire burning in the fireplace, giving me enough light to quickly search the room.

There was no weapon. It was only a workspace.

I turned with my staff in front of me, but without a sound, the man wrenched it out of my hands and knocked me down with his fist. I heard his broadsword drop to the ground while he climbed on top of me, straddling my hips. Everything was happening so quickly that before I knew it, he was on top of me, had pulled a knife from his belt, and was aiming it down at my throat.

I reached up and grabbed at his wrists and shoved with all my strength against him. I didn't know which one of us was more surprised that I was able to hold him off—him or me.

It shouldn't have been possible. The man was built of pure muscle. He should have been able to obliterate me within moments.

He growled and kept on pushing his knife at me. I couldn't shove him off or get myself free. I was stuck, my heart beating so fast it felt like it was going to burst out of my chest. I grit my teeth together, my entire body aching from trying to save my life.

I somehow managed to direct his blade to my left, slowly moving the pointed tip of the dagger away from the base of my neck and over toward my shoulder.

My strength began to falter and his weapon moved ever closer to my body. Moment by moment, inch by inch. I was shaking from the strain of trying to keep him from stabbing me.

The knife hovered just above me and I could feel the cold edge of it against my heated skin.

No, no, no.

This couldn't be it. Things couldn't end this way.

Please help me.

There was no answer.

I screamed when his dagger finally broke through my skin's surface, slowly plunging in through veins and nerves and muscle. White-hot pain radiated in my shoulder.

Then he twisted his blade, doing more damage.

Out of desperation I punched him in the face. His head reared back but he didn't release the dagger. I was panicking, terror digging its sharp teeth into me. I punched him again and heard the sound of his nose breaking.

Still he didn't let go and somehow managed to push the blade in farther.

He laughed as blood dripped down his face.

His laughter suddenly stopped and he gagged while the tip of his broadsword appeared through his throat.

I gasped and saw Io standing behind him.

She was the one who had plunged his own sword into the back of his neck.

My adrenaline crashed inside me, my fear fled, and now all I could focus on was the throbbing, shooting pain. The man slumped forward, nearly suffocating me. I tried to move but realized that he had pushed his dagger into me so hard that I was pinned into the wooden floor.

Io shoved at the man and he collapsed to the side and I could breathe again. Every breath I took made the pain radiate further and faster.

"What do I do? What do I do?" she asked, panicking.

I was about to tell her to go get a healer when she reached over and yanked the dagger out.

It was the worst possible thing she could have done.

Blood spurted from the wound, thick and hot.

I let out a moan.

My mind was frantically trying to recall what Demaratus had said about gushing wounds.

Stupid girl, you have to seal them shut!

I needed stitches or cauterizing. There was no time to sew me up. "You have to cauterize the wound," I told Io.

The pain was somehow intensifying.

"What?"

"Get something metal. Stick it in the fire." I wanted to tell her to get the knife that she'd pulled from my shoulder, but she ran over to Theano's desk and grabbed the first thing she saw.

The seal Theano used for the wax on her letters. Io ran over to the fire and put the metal seal into the flames.

I was feeling so woozy and lightheaded. I just wanted to go to sleep. My eyelids began to drift shut.

Stupid girl, stay awake! It's just blood. You have plenty—you can stand to lose some and still keep alert!

"Demaratus," I whispered. I wished he were here. He would know what to do. He would save me.

"The seal is hot," Io said. "Now what?"

Didn't she work in the infirmary? "Bring it over here and press it against my wound."

"What?" she exclaimed. "I can't do that!"

"You have to," I told her. It was getting harder and harder to hold on to my consciousness. "I can't do it myself, and if I tried, I might faint. Make sure you seal the skin shut. Don't stop, even if I scream. You have to stop the bleeding or I'll die."

The edges of my vision were blurring into black. I felt her pushing my tunic aside and then heard her take in a deep breath.

"I'm so sorry."

She pushed the heated seal into my skin and I screamed, the pain blocking out my ability to see or hear. My senses pinpointed to the excruciating burning on my shoulder and it utterly consumed me, ravaging my body with the worst, most intense pain I'd ever experienced.

It hurt worse than getting stabbed.

I couldn't breathe, couldn't think, couldn't move.

"The other side," I gasped after she took the seal away. The smell of burning flesh filled the high priestess's office. "You have to close the opening on my back, too."

Tears streamed down her face as she rolled me onto my side and, without hesitating, pressed the hot seal against the open wound there.

I screamed again, and then I must have passed out, because everything went black.

It seemed to have only been for a few moments because I awoke to see Io vomiting in the corner.

"I'm all right," I mumbled, trying to soothe her.

She shook her head. "I killed that man. I killed him. I took his life."

"You did it to protect me." It was getting easier to form words. Feeling was returning to my limbs, and even though my shoulder was screaming at me, I struggled to sit up. I couldn't do it. I was too dizzy from the pain. "You saved my life."

"I know, I know," she cried, wrapping her arms around her knees and curling up into a ball, rocking back and forth.

I'd spent months preparing to take a life while training with Demaratus, so it hadn't been an earth-shattering thing for me when it had happened.

But for Io? Who only wanted to protect all living things?

The only way I could think to help her in the moment was to spur her to action. To get her focusing on something else.

"We have to raise an alarm," I told her. "There might be others."

That seemed to reach her. "Yes. I'll go sound the horn. You're right. We have to warn everyone."

She ran out of the room and I screwed my eyes shut. This was my one chance. I had to get up. I had to search this room before the others arrived. I turned over onto my stomach, clenching my teeth against the pain. I wished I had something to bite down on. I crawled over to the wall and used it as leverage to push myself up.

I was breathing hard, sweating. My whole body was in pain, like it had radiated out from my shoulder and infested every part of me so that I was one giant ache. My head throbbed, my vision blurring.

A horn sounded, again and again. Io was letting the entire temple know that we had been invaded.

There was a movement at the door and my heart sank. I had lost my one opportunity.

With a sigh of relief, I realized that it was Suri.

She had a dagger drawn. She must have just missed Io. She raised both of her eyebrows at me, questioning whether I was all right.

"I'll live," I told her as I leaned against the wall, lacking the ability to step forward.

Her gaze fell upon the dead man.

"Io," I told her, and she looked so sad and concerned. "She did it to save me."

Suri nodded.

"I need you to look for me. I can't do it. Before anyone comes to check up on us. A key."

At that Suri's eyebrows climbed even higher up her forehead and then she made a face like she couldn't believe I was still going to search after what had just happened. She pointed in the direction of the infirmary.

I shook my head at her. "The guards will fight off whoever remains and then they'll scour the grounds to make sure they didn't miss any invaders, which means they'll be here soon. I'm running out of time. Please."

She frowned and then closed her eyes. She stood still for several moments and I became aware of how labored my breathing had become. I fought to keep my eyes open and my throat burned from thirst.

Suri opened her eyes again and headed straight for Theano's desk.

The edges were engraved with leaves, the symbol for the goddess. I watched as Suri ran her fingers along the leaves on the outer right side of the desk and came to a stop.

I couldn't see what she did. Everything looked exactly alike.

She pushed against a leaf and a little drawer popped out.

Containing a silver key.

Suri had done it. She had found the vault key. I let out a small pained laugh. I hadn't been stabbed for no reason. I had found what I'd come for.

But she turned her head toward me and my heart stopped beating entirely at her expression.

She wasn't going to let me have the key.

CHAPTER
FIFTY-TWO

Suri could have easily prevented me from taking the key if she wanted to. I was in no condition to retrieve it or to fight her for it. She took it out, pushed the drawer back into place, and then came to stand in front of me.

To my confusion, she offered it to me. I must have misinterpreted her earlier expression. She had looked upset about something, but what?

"Can you please put it in my pouch?" I asked. Again, she could have refused. She could have walked out of the room and buried it somewhere and I never would have found it.

But without hesitation she opened my pouch and slid the key inside.

There was relief despite the crushing pain. "Do you sense anything else hidden?"

No.

I supposed that would have made things far too easy, if the eye were in the office.

Although now I had no idea how I was going to break into the treasury. I thought of what Demaratus would have done if there had been an attempt made on my family's life. He would have doubled the guard.

Antiope would do the same. Or worse.

I might have had the key, but this attack had just complicated everything in my life. Not only in getting to the vault but in having to worry that someone specifically wanted me dead and might make another attempt.

Io's voice came from just outside the office. "We have to take Lia to the infirmary. Daphne needs to help her." She didn't come into the room and I couldn't blame her.

Suri came over to my right side and put my arm around her shoulders. I leaned against her heavily, but she easily held me up.

"Thank you," I told her. "You don't know what this means to me."

She nodded and we walked out into the hallway. I could see that Io wanted to assist us, but that would have meant going on my left side, where I'd been stabbed, and I didn't think I could bear the blinding pain. I held my left arm against my body and stumbled down the hallway, nearly tripping on the stairs.

But as we walked, I told Io our cover story. "We were up late talking. We heard something outside. We came out to investigate and were attacked. I led the man away from you."

She nodded and I saw her gulp. I hoped she would be able to lie effectively or else we were going to be in a lot of trouble. They couldn't know what I'd taken or everything would be ruined.

When we got outside I couldn't help but gasp and stop short. There were so many bodies. Some were being dragged out into the courtyard.

Men in full armor, but I also saw a priestess and a couple of acolytes. How many people had died?

"Come on," Io said, waving her hand and averting her gaze from the horrible scene. My mind felt foggy, but one of the things I noted was how easily the guards moved the bodies. Some of these men were thick and heavy and the women were dragging them like they weighed no more than a bird.

I also thought of what I had done that evening that I had no explanation for. How had I broken down Theano's door as easily as if it had been made of papyrus? I had managed to hold back a man twice my size with biceps larger than my legs. While I knew that people in stressful situations were capable of powerful things, panic and adrenaline could only account for so much.

Not to mention how I'd managed to hold off those men who had attacked me in the streets of Troas only a couple of days ago. Technique would not have been enough to keep me safe.

It was like I'd gotten stronger. A lot stronger.

And the same was true for all the women of the temple.

My head was pounding so hard that I stumbled. It hurt to think.

But I couldn't turn off my questions. Why had these men attacked us? This felt like the pirate raid on the *Nikos*. And the pirates had been specifically looking for me, just like the man who had chased me tonight.

Somebody wanted me dead.

Who?

Was it someone here in the temple? Theano? Artemisia? I wouldn't have been surprised by either one. But would they really be willing to commit sacrilege just to kill me? I couldn't imagine that they would go that far, but maybe they would.

Who else in Ilion would wish me harm? Why were they seeking me out? No one knew who I truly was, beyond being a tribute. My identity was a secret.

Why was this happening?

As I tried to think of who and why, I remembered that the pirates had thrown that red dirt before fighting. The man tonight had not done so. I didn't think they were the same people.

Which meant that there was more than one group of warriors trying to end my life.

That was terrifying.

Especially when I didn't know who was behind it.

They got me into the infirmary, where Daphne was helping another wounded acolyte, who was groaning with pain.

"Io!" Daphne said when she saw us. "I'm so glad you're here. I need you."

"Lia is hurt," she said, helping me onto one of the beds. "She was stabbed in her left shoulder and the blade went all the way through."

"Everyone is hurt," Daphne muttered under her breath, but she still came over to inspect me. "It was quick thinking to cauterize the wound."

"That was Lia," Io said. "She told me to do it."

"It probably saved your life." Daphne tested my limb and I let out a muffled moan, not able to hold back the sound. It was like she was torturing me. "Make a fist."

I did as she asked even though my hand protested in agony.

Daphne nodded, satisfied. "You still have full range of motion, which indicates that the blade didn't hit any tendons or arteries, for which you should be very grateful. You're lucky that it only went through muscle."

I didn't feel very lucky at the moment.

"We'll get you something for the pain, and after we've treated everyone, we'll create a salve to help soothe your skin and fight off infection. Then we'll bring you something to help you sleep. Io, with me," Daphne said. She went back to the patient she'd been treating when we arrived.

Io hovered over the bed, reaching for my right hand and squeezing it. "I would stay here with you if I could."

I squeezed her back. "I know. I need to thank you for earlier. I know that tonight was . . . difficult. But I want you to remember that you protected life. He would have killed me and others."

She released my hand and twisted her lips to the side, as if she were trying not to cry. "Deep down I understand that. I just . . . never thought I would be capable of doing it. I also know that you would have done the same for me, to save me."

"A thousand times over," I told her. It was then that I noticed that black-and-purple bruises in the shape of fingers had formed on her neck. It was a miracle that man hadn't crushed her windpipe. I was glad he was dead, or I would have gone back over to the administrative building to finish the job myself.

As Io went off to assist Daphne, I realized that Suri had disappeared. I lay in the bed, aching and exhausted, and ran my right hand over my pouch to feel the outline of the key. Still there, right next to Quynh's bracelet.

The key had to be for the vault. It had been hidden in a secret compartment that presumably no one but Theano knew about. Why would she do that unless it was important?

I should have paid closer attention to the keys that Theano carried on her belt so that I would be able to tell whether it was a match.

There was at least one good way to find out if it would open the vault.

Should I wait? There was no doubt in my mind that Antiope was going to immediately increase the number of guards patrolling. So perhaps it would work better in my favor to delay trying to break into the treasury.

Not to mention that I currently wasn't in the best physical condition to be attempting a break-in.

A few minutes later Zalira and Ahyana came into the infirmary with Suri. She had apparently gone to retrieve them, and I was relieved that she had. Zalira had the beginning of a black eye and Ahyana's lip had been busted open.

"Are you all right?" I asked them, at the exact moment that they said the same to me.

"We're fine," Zalira said. "Three men climbed into our window. I was able to call for Ahyana and we fought them off until the guards arrived to help us. I'm so glad we were awake and waiting for you. Can you imagine if we'd been asleep and unaware?" She shuddered.

The whole situation was so unnerving. "How did they get past the guards in the first place?"

"They must have observed the guards and figured out the pattern as well," Ahyana offered. "But instead of sneaking out, they were figuring out a way to sneak in."

"What were they after?" Zalira asked.

"I think me," I told them in a low voice. "The man who attacked Io said he was looking for 'the Locrian.'"

"Why?" Ahyana asked, and I could only shake my head. "Maybe they hate me for making it to the temple?"

Now Zalira was the one shaking her head. "That doesn't make any sense. Who would risk blaspheming against the goddess just because you're serving here?"

All questions, no answers.

"Do you think someone in the temple helped them?" I asked carefully, not sure what their reactions would be.

Suri's eyebrows rose as if this surprised her.

"Of course not!" Ahyana said. "We are sworn to each other."

Yes, we all vowed to protect one another, but that didn't mean somebody couldn't have used a third party as proxy to technically circumvent that rule.

Daphne approached and handed me a cup. "Drink this." Then she turned her attention to the other three. "All of you need to return to your room. It's late."

We told each other good night. They left and I could feel the pain medication doing its job.

Despite my body not hurting quite as much, I was filled with an uneasy feeling. I realized how badly things could have gone. If I'd been asleep, caught up in my nighttime fantasy world, those men would have come into our room and slaughtered us all.

I woke early the next morning, my body accustomed to rising at this hour.

It was the first night since I'd arrived that I hadn't dreamed of Jason, and it bothered me. I wanted to tell him about what had happened last night.

To be in a place where there wouldn't be any pain.

Maybe he would have insight that I didn't. Which was ridiculous because I was the one doing the dreaming. Anything that he offered would be something I'd already thought of.

The pain medication had long worn off but my head felt clearer and I was able to move. My shoulder still throbbed like I was being stabbed on a continual basis but I could sit up. The pain was bearable.

I got myself a drink of water, which was difficult to do with only one hand. When I had finished with the entire cup, Daphne came over to check on me. She felt the pulse in my left wrist and then looked into my eyes.

"How are you feeling?" she asked.

"Slightly better."

"Good. Now why aren't you sleeping? I would have thought that you'd sleep for a few more hours."

"I have to go clean the temple." I didn't imagine that my responsibilities were to be ignored just because I'd been stabbed.

"Not today you don't," she said. "The goddess can do without you. And it's a good thing you're an early riser. Especially since I think you will be needed elsewhere this morning."

"Where?"

An evasive look passed over her features. "There is a meeting that is going to take place in a few minutes in the gymnasium. All of the uninjured priestesses and acolytes will be gathered together to discuss last night's events. And I think you might want to attend."

That unsettled feeling returned, causing a pit in my stomach. Daphne didn't say anything else and left the infirmary. Io wasn't here, either. Several of the patients from last night were also gone.

It took me a bit longer than I would have liked to make my way over to the gymnasium. All of my limbs felt too stiff, unresponsive. I saw women entering the building and tried to quicken my steps, but I could only go so fast.

When I finally reached the gymnasium, I realized why Daphne had thought I should come.

I was being held responsible for the attack.

CHAPTER
FIFTY-THREE

Theano was sitting on the dais, flanked on either side by Daphne and Maia. She had a veil on, as she always did.

A priestess named Nysa was speaking. She was the mentor for Artemisia's adelphia, and she'd always made me uncomfortable. She was standing on the dais, addressing the triumvirate of priestesses along with the entire body gathered there.

"One priestess is dead, along with two acolytes," Nysa said. "That's not even counting those who were seriously injured."

Those men had wreaked a lot of damage before they were caught and stopped. They had certainly utilized the element of surprise to catch so many unawares.

I had been repeatedly told since I'd arrived how safe I was here in the temple, and now there was deadly evidence that it was entirely untrue.

"Maybe they were thieves!" someone called out.

"The Locrian brought this tragedy upon us," Nysa said, ignoring the suggestion. "While we have dealt with those who have dared to enter the courtyard, no man has breached the inner sanctums of the temple in a thousand years. Not until last night."

Some of the women nearby saw me standing there and began whispering to one another.

Was this only conjecture on Nysa's part? I hoped no one here knew that those men had been looking specifically for me. They already wanted to blame me—I wasn't going to add logs onto the fire of their indignation and accusations.

"We should throw the Locrian out," Artemisia said from the center of the room. "She doesn't belong here."

"She has taken the same vows as the rest of you," Maia interjected, angrily. "She has every right to serve."

Nysa spoke over the end of Maia's last sentence. "We pray daily for a savior, and yet we have opened our temple doors to a destroyer."

Ha. Those doors hadn't been opened to me. I'd had to fight my way in. I wondered if anyone else here knew that.

"Why would anyone want to kill us?" I couldn't see the priestess who was speaking, but her voice sounded familiar. "Were they soldiers? Mercenaries? Assassins? People seeking vengeance?"

The words made me think of the men who had chased the woman who'd claimed sanctuary. My sisters had told me that women had asked for protection many times before—maybe someone was angry about the priestesses' actions?

That wouldn't explain why they'd been looking for me, though.

Were there really people in Ilion who hated Locris so much that they would intentionally seek me out, committing blasphemy just for their hatred? It seemed far-fetched.

Or what if it actually had been my fault? I was the one who had gone out into the city a couple of nights ago. I thought of the men I had fought near the hetaera houses. What if they had come here solely to find and punish me?

Maybe I *was* to blame. I put my right hand over my stomach. I felt like I was going to be sick.

"They have no distinctive marks and do not bear the seals of any noble or royal families." Antiope sounded furious. I knew she would take each and every loss personally. "Their pockets were empty. There is no way to identify them or where they came from."

"Should we contact the government?" someone else asked.

"There is nothing they can do that we cannot do ourselves," Antiope said, immediately rejecting the notion. "We do not need their assistance."

"We should ask the Locrian. She is here," Nysa said, pointing at me. The women directly in front of me parted so that there was a clear opening between myself and the dais.

Maia looked concerned and Daphne just looked angry. The older woman stood. "We cannot hold Lia responsible for the actions of those men. She was severely harmed as well. None of us know what happened, and we cannot conjecture otherwise. We cannot turn our backs on one of our sisters."

When Daphne sat back down, Theano got to her feet. The murmurs and whispers around me died completely. She announced, "The Locrian will be questioned."

"I'll do it," Maia immediately offered.

"And I'll assist," Nysa said.

Theano nodded, her veil waving back and forth. "Maia will interrogate the Locrian with Nysa's assistance. If any of you have any information that might prove useful, you must share it with us. The safety of this temple must be upheld at all times. We have lost too many of our sisters and will not lose any others."

The women began to disperse and Maia headed straight toward me, with Nysa right behind her. My pulse beat unsteadily in my throat. Would they see through me? Would they think I was lying?

And if they did, what would they do with me? Three women were dead. This was not a situation that would end with extra cleaning duties.

Maia told me to follow her and led us to the auditorium. Nysa walked behind me, staring holes into the back of my head. I thought of Demaratus's advice to control my emotions. It was especially important now. I was so close to accomplishing my goal. I hoped I wasn't responsible for the attack, directly or indirectly.

There couldn't be any real way to tell.

Even if those men had been hunting me, their actions were not my fault. I shouldn't have to pay for their sins.

When we got to the auditorium, we walked down the stairs so that we could sit on the center dais. Both Maia and Nysa took chairs across from me. Nysa crossed her arms, while Maia leaned toward me with a kind smile on her face.

"What happened last night?" she asked.

I hated having to lie to her. Part of me knew that Maia might have real answers to some of my questions, but this was too big of a risk. Especially with Nysa here. Perhaps if we'd been alone I could have been more honest with her.

"Io and I were up late, unable to sleep. We heard a noise and went out to investigate. A man attacked Io, and I lured him away to protect her. We ended up in one of the offices upstairs because I was looking for a weapon. The man stabbed me with a knife and Io saved my life by putting his sword through his neck. She cauterized my wound and then she helped me get to the infirmary."

"That is the same story that Io and the rest of their adelphia told me," Maia said with a nod.

"Yes, it is very, very similar," Nysa said. It was obvious she didn't believe me. "It sounds rehearsed."

It was.

I wondered when they had questioned the other members of my adelphia. Late last night? Earlier this morning?

"You are always so suspicious," Maia said. Turning back to face me, she said, "You know how dangerous that was, don't you? You shouldn't have left your room. That's why we have guards. You aren't far enough along in your training to go against skilled warriors like that."

"Zalira and Ahyana said the men came into our bedroom, too." While I understood that Maia wanted to lecture me out of concern, we would have been in the midst of the fight either way.

"Yes, why is that?" Nysa asked. "Why would armed men enter your room specifically?"

A Tribute of Fire

"I don't know. When that man was stabbing me, he didn't confess his intentions to me." I knew I shouldn't be sarcastic, but as Daphne had pointed out, I wasn't responsible for other people's actions.

What had happened was a terrible tragedy, and I felt gutted that anyone had lost their lives. But I wasn't going to let Nysa or Artemisia eject me from the temple.

Not when so much was at stake.

And especially not now that I finally had the treasury key in my possession.

"I'm satisfied with her explanation," Maia said.

Before Nysa could object, Maia raised her hand. "Daphne has already told me that she will vote the way that I do, that Lia is not to blame for what occurred. Regardless of how Theano votes, we will have the majority."

Nysa glared at both of us and got up so quickly that she knocked her chair over. I wasn't sure what I had done to earn her anger, other than being born in a different land from her. She had no reason to hate me but she seemed to anyway.

She stormed out of the auditorium, and once she was gone, Maia's whole demeanor changed. She was furious.

"Do you have any idea how reckless you and Io were last night? Do you understand what could have happened? We have rules for a reason, Lia. You can't just disregard them out of curiosity!"

While I wanted to interject that I hadn't, now did not seem like the right time to say so.

Maia lectured me for a good half hour but she seemed to accept my story about what had happened. She even commended me for protecting Io but was angry at me for putting myself at risk.

I nodded and it didn't take much for me to look repentant. I did feel bad about the whole situation. I didn't know why those men had been targeting me specifically and I didn't want to be the reason that harm was brought to the women in the temple.

It seemed like the best thing to do would be to attempt to enter the treasury as soon as possible. If I found the eye, I could be on my way and then there wouldn't be any more attacks.

I was just going to have to convince my sisters to join me—given the condition I was in, I didn't think I'd be able to do it alone.

Maia finished and told me to go back to my room. I nodded meekly and did as she asked. Groups of varying sizes talked to one another as I exited the administrative building.

Their eyes were on me. It felt like the first day of being here all over again. Outcast and despised. Blamed for bringing death and destruction to the temple.

When I got back to my bedroom, my sisters weren't there. Were they at breakfast? Being questioned by somebody else?

The high priestess, maybe?

I let out a shaky breath. I wasn't sure that Io would be able to hold her own against Theano.

When I lay down on my bed, I turned to my side so that I could reach the edges of the book. *Various, unspecified gems,* I told myself.

But my fingers brushed against nothing. I stretched my hand out, thinking I must have pushed it back farther than I'd realized.

It wasn't there.

Starting to feel panicked, I stood up and, with my right hand, pulled the bed away from the wall completely.

The book was gone.

Like I'd never even had it.

Who had taken it?

My sisters would have told me if it had been them. I could see Zalira hiding it for safekeeping if she'd come across it during the struggle last night, but she hadn't said anything.

I would ask them when they returned.

The hollowed-out feeling in my gut only worsened. Somehow I knew that my adelphia didn't have the book.

It had been stolen.

I thought of the guard on watch who'd caught me reading it. I had assumed that she didn't notice it because she hadn't said anything, but what if I had been wrong? What if she had reported it to someone in charge?

Theano would want to keep that book a secret. She was the spokesperson for the goddess. She passed along the rules and regulations that we all followed. If there was proof that priestesses used to be married, that the temple had provided them dowries, she would be the first person who would want to destroy it.

It would go against what she was teaching us. What someone like Maia was so certain was true.

There were no written histories here in the temple that would contradict whatever Theano decided was doctrine. No religious texts that would say she was wrong. With a bitter taste in my mouth, I realized that she could make up any rule she wanted and there wouldn't be any way to countermand her.

She was the one the priestesses prayed to. The one treated like some living incarnation of the goddess. I couldn't imagine that she would want there to be anything out there that could undermine her authority.

But it couldn't have been someone from the temple who had found it. The book was a forbidden object, and I would already be out in the streets of Troas if someone here had found it. There were people just waiting for an excuse.

It must have been the men who had attacked us last night. Was this why they'd done it? Maybe they had come here not specifically to kill me but to retrieve the book that I'd stolen.

That seemed impossible, too. How would they even know?

My heart came to a complete halt as I realized that the only person who knew I had the book was Jason.

CHAPTER
FIFTY-FOUR

When my adelphia did finally return, I told them everything that had happened. The questions I'd been asked, the accusations. As I'd suspected, they had also been interrogated, but we'd all held to our version of events.

If they were risking themselves and their places here to help me, I was at least going to tell them as much of the truth as I could.

"There's something else," I told them. "When I was in the city, I went into the records office and found an old book about the temple. The last page was full of entries of priestesses getting married and the temple providing them a substantial dowry."

We were all seated on our own beds and everyone looked at me in utter astonishment.

"You can read?" Ahyana asked.

I'd been expecting this question. "All women in Locris are taught to read."

"Priestesses getting married? That can't be right," Io said, sounding extremely upset. I knew how important the temple and her faith were to her, and it made sense that she would be more sensitive to what I'd said than the others. "Abstaining from relationships and marriage is one of the fundamental vows of the goddess."

"I know what I saw," I told her.

"Maybe you misunderstood it," she said.

"I didn't. It was very clear."

"You said you didn't know how old the book was. Maybe it was from a really long time ago," Ahyana said with Suri nodding.

"No," Io interjected. "It can't be possible."

The attachment she felt to the goddess and the temple would make it nearly impossible for someone like her to believe me. I wished I still had the proof.

Part of me suspected that even if I could show her the book—and she could read it—she might not be swayed.

And that worried me. "I don't know what happened to the book or who took it. I'm guessing it was the men who attacked last night, but I don't know how they could have known about it or why they would want it."

Zalira tapped her fingers against her leg. "When we returned to our room after seeing you, I did notice that everything had been thrown around. I assumed it was because of the fighting, but now that I think on it . . ."

I felt bad, as if I were causing them to question everything the same way that I was. Making them more suspicious by nature.

"The mystery of the book aside, I am going to try and break into the treasury tonight." I held my breath, not certain what their response would be.

"You're injured," Ahyana observed.

"Which is actually a perfect cover. If someone realizes that the key is gone or that the treasury was broken into, who would suspect us? Especially me?"

"You know as well as we do that Antiope will increase the guard," Zalira pointed out.

I nodded. "I also know that everyone will be in a heightened state, expecting another attack. I think we can use it to our advantage. I have some ideas."

"I thought you didn't like plans," Ahyana teased.

"Tonight will be a special situation. We don't know exactly what we're walking into." At least before, with Theano's office, we'd known the general layout of the building and what we might expect. We had no such information for the treasury. None of us had ever entered the building.

Io let out a long, deep sigh. "Fine. We're going with you."

While I'd hoped they would help, I hadn't counted on it. I should have known better.

"Good. Thank you. Here's what I think we should do . . ."

Zalira stayed up and kept watch while the rest of us slept. I desperately needed it and had a deep and dreamless sleep until she shook me awake.

"It's time," she said.

She went around and woke the others and I strapped all my weapons on this time. I didn't ever want to find myself without them when I needed them again.

We had run over our plan multiple times throughout the day and had solidified what we would be doing. I probably should have given us more time but I felt everything closing in around me.

Like something was urging me to hurry.

When everyone was ready, we moved as a group to the front door of the dormitory. No one else in the building seemed to be awake. Ahyana had Kunguru on her shoulder and we crept stealthily outside.

The treasury was farther away than the administrative building and there would be quite a few opportunities to run into guards, including the new ones.

If I had done this alone and gotten caught, I could have easily explained that I had suffered a head injury and wasn't thinking clearly. Didn't know where I was. Lied my way out.

But with all of us? It was a massive risk.

Not to mention that it would be easier for us to be seen. I needed their help and special skill sets, but I felt guilty about it. There would be no explaining this away if we were apprehended in a group this size.

I'd tried to talk them into leaving a few of us behind, but no one would listen.

The bright, full moon beamed down from a clear sky. It lit up everything, erasing the shadows we'd been counting on to aid us.

We would be spotted.

"Oh no," I muttered.

"Give it a moment," Zalira said, looking up.

Sure enough, within a few heartbeats, the sky suddenly clouded over and blocked the moon completely. I was so grateful for her gift.

We got to the first intercept point and Zalira had a small bow and arrows that she had "borrowed" from the gymnasium during training today. Two guards were conversing not far from us. She raised the bow and shot wide, over their heads, so that it landed in a wooden post twenty feet away from them.

As we'd hoped, the guards immediately assumed that the temple might be under attack. They drew their swords and ran toward the arrow.

"Go!" I said and headed in the opposite direction. Io had told us about a large row of bushes that we could hide behind while more guards rushed past us to check out the arrow.

When it was clear we rose and continued our run toward the treasury. I wished the building weren't quite so far.

At the halfway point Ahyana told Kunguru to fly. He took off into the air, and a few moments later, he began to call loudly and repeatedly, causing a commotion. We heard more raised voices, more heavy footsteps following him. We were causing confusion everywhere we went, clearing a path.

I felt so many competing emotions—I was terrified that my adelphia might have to pay for what I was doing, excited that I was finally going to get my hands on the eye, anxious about making a mistake.

All those feelings propelled me forward. I told myself that I would succeed. This somehow seemed easier than the times I'd sneaked through the temple grounds before. Maybe because I'd done it so many times already.

And it felt like we were being watched over, protected. As if the goddess were blessing what we were doing.

Kunguru continued to call out as we reached the treasury. Two guards stood just inside the main door. We could see the spears they held.

Io said, "Let's hope this works."

She tossed a glass bottle into their midst and it shattered. The guards both immediately collapsed to the ground.

"You did it!" I told her. She'd spent the entire day coming up with the formulation, inspired by my goose request.

Her eyes shone brightly as we ran toward the treasury. "I don't know how long it will last. I was afraid of overdosing them, so I probably underdid it. We have to hurry."

I supposed some part of me assumed that if we got past the guards at the front door, we would see the vault immediately.

Instead there were three doors along each wall.

"False doors," Ahyana said. "Our father told us about this. The builders of the great pyramids deliberately created false doors to deceive and lead thieves away from the real door. The fake ones will lead to certain death."

"Which one do we pick?" Io breathed.

Suri confidently walked up to the third door on the right wall and put her hand against it. I trusted her instincts. I took the key over and fitted it into the lock. It felt a bit rusty and stuck a little but eventually it turned. Was that a good sign or a bad one? I pushed the door in and held my breath.

I'd read so many stories in my grandmother's book about monsters that would lie in wait in places like this, about traps that could end our lives. A rock slab sliding out from a hidden shelf above that would crush us. A floor that would give way when pressure was applied to it, impaling us on stakes below.

I took a few tentative steps forward, holding my breath.

Nothing happened.

A few more. Still safe.

"Hurry," Io reminded me.

Believing in my sister, I ventured farther into the hallway.

"Stay back. Wait until I make sure it's safe," I told them. If a trap was sprung, it would happen only to me. I held my breath as I traveled the darkened length of the hall. It almost felt like the stones in the walls around me were breathing and somehow getting closer together. As if they were going to close in on me.

After a sharp turn to the left, I found myself in the vault. The room was massive, with riches piled all the way to the ceiling. I saw ornate golden breastplates, steel swords with golden and bronze hilts, gilded furniture, helmets encrusted with gems and polished to a bright sheen. Vases of all sizes covered in various precious metals.

Multiple wooden tables were absolutely laden with jewelry—earrings, necklaces, crowns, bracelets, rings, shoulder pins, brooches. Piles and piles of gold and silver coins. Loose gems scattered throughout.

"There's too much." There was no way I could look through all of this. Even with all my sisters here, we had seconds, not hours.

Some part of my brain had fantasized that there would be a stone pedestal with the eye placed on a silk pillow, easy to find, waiting for me.

Suri had followed me into the vault first. I turned to her. "I'm looking for something called the eye of the goddess. It isn't an ordinary gem. It will have power. Like what we feel in the dirt."

She nodded.

Io came in after, followed by Zalira and Ahyana. She took one look around and gasped. "No one touch anything!"

"Why?" I asked.

"Do you not smell that? Everything here has been coated in fire dragon's blood."

"And?"

"It's poison!" she said. "We can't even be in this room for very long. We shouldn't be breathing it in. If I had known, I could have brought a remedy." Then she cursed in a very un-Io-like fashion.

That was bad but workable. When Suri found the eye I would make sure to use my cloak to grab it.

Suri walked the length and width of the room, back and forth. Two times. Three. She came back to me, looking defeated while shaking her head.

Bile rose in my throat, my stomach clenched, my hands started to shake.

"No. It has to be here." I began looking and quickly realized that not a single gem in this room was green. Every other color of the rainbow was represented, but not green.

The eye wasn't here.

I started to feel frantic and reached for the closest gold pile, intending to dig through it.

Io grabbed my arm and jerked it away. "No! Lia, we have to go. We're out of time."

Suri was with her, putting her hand against my chest. She looked me deep in the eye and shook her head.

No.

I didn't want it to be true. I had gone through so much, sacrificed everything, to come here and get the eye.

They had to push and pull me out of the vault. Zalira made sure to close the door while Ahyana was busy picking up the glass shards from Io's potion. Io went to help her, but Suri kept her hand on my right arm. I could tell that she didn't trust me to behave rationally.

The treasury guards had started to stir and we quietly ran out into the night. Kunguru was still calling and we were able to hurry back the way we'd come, hiding in all the same places, unseen.

All I could think about was that I had failed. I'd had my one chance and it had been for nothing. Quynh had died for nothing.

My throat burned and a sob that I couldn't let out formed in my chest. We had to stay quiet. When we got back to our room, everybody hurried to shed their cloaks and weapons, hiding them in the wardrobe.

Suri had to force me into my bed and pull a blanket over me. I felt like a child being directed by her mother. I was so devastated, so destroyed, that I couldn't act. The pain—physical, emotional, mental—overwhelmed me.

It was a good thing Suri had reacted so quickly because thirty seconds later a guard came into our room with a torch, checking on us. I held completely still, and after a few soul-destroying heartbeats, she left.

We had gotten away with it, but I was, once again, empty-handed.

CHAPTER
FIFTY-FIVE

I tossed and turned the rest of the night. My sisters quickly fell asleep, which I understood. It had been a long, taxing night. I heard when Kunguru came to the windowsill to watch over us. I might have slept, but if I did, I couldn't remember my dreams.

No Jason. It was ridiculous of me to want to confront a dream version of him. I had to speak to him in person. I needed answers as to who he might have told about the book. He was the only person who knew. It was such a betrayal that, if he'd done it, I wasn't sure I could ever speak to him again.

I could have been a great deal angrier but wasn't because a part of me believed he wouldn't do that to me.

But if not him, then who?

The next morning I got up to clean the temple. I still hurt but the salves and medicines that Daphne poured down my throat every few hours were helping. I could deal with the constant, dull, throbbing pain. The important thing was to stick to my routine. Those guards who had patrolled last night would talk, including the ones who had been drugged, but we had made sure not to leave any proof behind. I couldn't raise anyone's suspicions by deviating from what I was supposed to be doing this morning.

But when I got to the courtyard to fill my water vase, I discovered that the fountain was completely dry. I'd never seen that happen before, and I wouldn't be able to sprinkle water after I swept.

I wasn't sure what to do.

It seemed like something I should report. I decided Maia was my safest bet. I swept until it was time for my tutorial and headed over to the auditorium. She greeted me.

"The fountain in the courtyard has run dry," I told her, not bothering to return her greeting.

Her face paled and she stood up. "Are you certain?"

"Yes."

"Return to your room," she said.

I did as she asked. Obviously the fountain drying up wasn't a regular occurrence or she wouldn't have responded the way that she had. When I got back to my bedroom, I told my sisters what had happened. They were as confused as I was about Maia's reaction.

No one spoke of the night before. They all seemed afraid to bring it up. My devastation over my failure was obvious. They didn't ask what I'd been looking for and I didn't offer to tell them. It was the best way to keep them safe. If they were questioned, they wouldn't have to lie. They would be able to honestly say they didn't know what I'd been up to.

It was the only way that I could think of to protect them.

When we got to breakfast, nobody was eating. Instead the room was in an uproar. As I listened to the nearby conversations, it turned out the women were not only worried about the "attacks" the previous night that had resulted in a single arrow and two guards being knocked out, but were now tying those to the fountain drying up.

It was being taken as some kind of omen.

Again dirty looks and muttered voices were pointed in my direction.

I could only lay claim to half of the blame, though. I'd led the "attack" but hadn't done anything to the water.

405

The three lead priestesses were on the dais and Antiope had joined them. Maia turned in our direction and waved me over. It seemed she'd meant for only me to come but my sisters followed.

When we approached it was obvious the leaders were in a heated argument.

"Someone has to investigate the source and see what happened to the water," Daphne was saying.

"Send me," Antiope countered. "I will take a few guards with me. It should only be a day's travel there and back."

Theano said, "You are needed here."

"Lia is the one who alerted me," Maia told the group, and all of them turned to face me. I wondered why she had involved me. She probably wanted me to have some credit for informing her about the fountain, given all the accusations being tossed around the room.

In a time of crisis, people wanted someone to blame, someone to be responsible, so that the world would make sense again.

And the other priestesses apparently wanted that person to be me.

I was grateful that Maia was trying to help in her own way. I wished I could tell her it was unnecessary. Since last night I'd been wondering whether I had much of a future at the temple. The eye wasn't here. Was there even a reason to stay? I could send a message to Jason and have him help me return to Locris.

Then I thought of the vows I'd made. I'd been willing to break them to save my nation, but everything was different now. It was as if the oaths had more of a hold on me, rather than less. My word meant something to me. I'd made a promise to protect this temple and the people in it. If I ran home I wouldn't be doing that. I wouldn't be serving the goddess.

In my dreams Demaratus had told me that at some point I was going to have to stop running and face reality.

Maybe this was what he'd meant.

And it was time to stand still and do what I'd said I would do.

Then it seemed fate decided to put my resolution immediately to the test.

Antiope said, "The men who attacked us might have stopped our water supply. Maybe they're planning to lay siege."

Io had mentioned that the water from the river, which was also used in our washrooms, wasn't safe to drink. That it made people ill. If someone did plan a siege at our gates, being cut off from clean water might lead them to getting a quick surrender.

"Which is why you're needed here," Theano said to Antiope. The high priestess leaned her head slightly to the right and then announced, "We should send the Locrian and her sisters to investigate and report back their findings."

What?

Maia seemed to share in my surprise and concern. "Lia is not even fully healed yet!"

Not to mention that the temple had just been attacked. Of all the priestesses and acolytes she could have sent, Theano had chosen us? We were the youngest and had the least training.

Did she suspect what my sisters and I had done and meant to use this as a punishment?

Stupid girl, she wants to eliminate all of you while keeping her hands clean.

I hoped that wasn't true. I didn't want to be the reason the others might be put in harm's way.

I didn't have to see my adelphia's expressions to know that they were just as confused and astonished as I was.

"She'll be fine," Theano said with a wave of her hand, dismissing Maia's protest.

Antiope looked like she also wanted to object, but she stayed silent.

I could see that my mentor had much more to say but she followed the battle master's lead and kept quiet.

The high priestess apparently considered the matter closed. "Have them pack and leave immediately."

"I will get them a map," Antiope said with a nod and left.

Daphne brushed down a fold in her tunic. "I will fetch the salves and medication that Lia needs to take." I thought I sensed a note of disdain in her voice for what Theano had dictated.

"Come with me," Maia said to us. "We'll stop by the kitchen to load you up with supplies, and I will help you pack."

Although I couldn't see her face, I would have sworn that Theano's gaze was upon me.

If she hoped that this mission of hers would lead to our deaths, she was going to be bitterly disappointed.

◆ ◆ ◆

Everything happened so quickly. Maia helped us gather enough food and water for the next couple of days. She also made us change out of our tunics into basic beige ones so that we wouldn't draw attention to ourselves. Daphne came with my medication, giving instructions to Io on how to administer it. Antiope brought the map and showed us where the groundwater spring began that fed the aqueduct that led to our fountain.

As she'd mentioned earlier, it would only take us about a day to reach it and a day to return.

She also distributed weapons to each of us. "Stay off the roads," she said. "They won't be safe for you. And if someone is hunting for you, that's the first place they'll look."

Her warning did nothing to ease the large boulder that had taken up residence against my chest. She seemed to think it was inevitable that something would happen to us and that worried me.

Especially because I was not in my best physical condition. I didn't want Io to get in another fight. She still seemed traumatized from our last encounter. I'd caught her crying a few times over the last couple of days when she thought no one would notice. I didn't know how to ease her pain or how to help her other than keeping her out of harm's way.

I knew I could count on the rest of my adelphia if we got into a tough spot. I'd just make Io hide if we were attacked. Antiope and Maia walked us past the archway, into the street. It felt strange that they were allowing us to be here, outside of the temple, when all they'd done was tell us that we couldn't leave.

Maia smiled at us, but it didn't reach her eyes. "Watch over each other. Stay safe. Promise me."

"We promise," Io said, but her voice was a little shaky.

"All will be well," I told them both.

But our mentor didn't seem to believe me. "You have seen how dangerous the world can be beyond these walls."

I moved in closer so that only she would hear me. "I have seen how dangerous the world can be *within* these walls. I will bring them back to you. I swear it."

Her shoulders relaxed slightly. She nodded and bade us farewell.

Zalira and Ahyana led the way. They were the most familiar with the city and navigated the labyrinth with ease. No one paid us very much attention. There were so many people out on the street, and since we weren't in our temple colors, we didn't attract notice. We blended in.

It didn't take us long to exit the city to the south. I'd never been in this part of Ilion—the scenery was stunning. Trees and grass and bushes as far as the eye could see. An ocean of green.

It made me wonder if Locris had ever looked like this.

And if it ever would again.

"Let's do what Antiope suggested and get off the road," Zalira said. She headed into a nearby forest, and that was another brand-new experience for me. I'd been in groves of trees before, but those were orderly and planned. This was a riot of tree trunks and underbrush topped off by a canopy of leaves overhead. I could hear birds chirping and insects buzzing.

"I've never gone this far south," Ahyana said, worry creeping into her voice. "What if we get lost?"

"The sun rises in the east and sets in the west," I said. "As long as we can see the light, we'll know what direction we're headed."

It was a false comfort—we all knew stories of people who had gotten lost, gone missing, never returned home.

"I know which way to go," Zalira said. "Follow me."

"Maia seemed upset," Io observed to no one in particular.

"She did," Ahyana agreed. "I think she's worried that we're going into some kind of trap."

It echoed exactly what I had thought. "If we stay together, I think we'll be all right."

"If Maia thinks there might be a trap, that means it's not safe for us to leave the temple or the city," Io responded, ignoring my attempt to console her.

"I don't think the high priestess cares whether or not we'll be safe," Zalira said.

Io shook her head. "I don't understand why they would send us."

"I think because we're the newest and it makes us the most expendable if something happens. And I'm afraid it might." I hadn't meant to say the last part out loud, especially after I saw Io's face.

Ahyana frowned, pushing a branch away from her head. "I hope you're wrong."

So did I, but I got the distinct feeling that I wasn't.

CHAPTER FIFTY-SIX

"Do you think we'll miss the festival?" Io asked after we'd been walking for about two hours.

"We'll be back in time," Ahyana said.

I pushed back a sound of pain. I couldn't carry my knapsack on my left shoulder, and my right was aching from the weight of it.

Suri came up behind me and lifted it from my shoulder.

"I can carry that," I told her. She ignored me and put it on her front so that she had a knapsack on each side of her body.

"You can ask us for help," Zalira said, her eyes trained on the ground. She seemed to be following a path that only she could see.

"I'm not used to doing that."

"We noticed," Ahyana said with a teasing laugh.

They didn't understand. "I told you I was trained in fighting before I came to Ilion."

"Another thing we noticed," she responded.

"The man who taught me used to say 'one for many.' That it was my responsibility to defend myself and protect others and my country." I pressed my lips together, nearly admitting too much. "That I should do what I can on my own and not rely on others. That it was noble to sacrifice myself to save those I care about."

"That explains a lot," Zalira said as Io walked over to me. She put her hand on my right shoulder.

"You're here with us now," she said. "You don't have to do things alone anymore. My whole life I wanted a sister more than anything, and now I have four. You have us. We will always be here for you."

I nodded, biting my inner cheek so that I wouldn't cry. I knew she was right. I'd been learning that—instead of relying solely on myself, I'd needed my sisters to help me succeed.

That didn't make me weak or incapable. It just meant that we were stronger together.

Io let her hand drop. "How are you doing otherwise?"

It made sense that she would be the one to notice how I'd been feeling. "I'm a failure. Part of me feels numb. Disconnected. Hopeless."

"Whatever it is that you're looking for, will it hurt people?" Ahyana asked me.

"No!" I immediately replied. "It will save thousands of lives."

"Are you certain that it exists?"

"I think it does."

"Then it must be somewhere," Ahyana responded. "If not at the temple, then somewhere else. And if it's going to save so many, we will help you find it."

Again I was struck with the urge to tell them about the eye, but something prevented me. I wanted them to have plausible deniability if Theano questioned them. This was one burden I could carry alone to keep them safe.

"Just keep going," Io said. "One foot in front of another. We're all on this path together."

Now I couldn't help the single tear that escaped from each eye. I wiped them away with the back of my hand. I wanted to cry to let out my frustration and disappointment. I knew my sisters would let me and not judge, but now was not the time.

"You're right," I said, my voice catching. "I do have to keep going." There was no other option. I just didn't know what my next move would be because I had no idea where else to look.

The palace?

A return to the library to search for books that might have clues?

Theano's personal rooms?

"I have faith in you," Io said. "You'll regroup. You'll figure out your next steps."

Again, she was right. I would do that. I couldn't give up.

I was grateful I had a group of best friends who wouldn't let me.

◆ ◆ ◆

We stopped to eat and Io took the chance to put the salve on my still-healing wound.

She moved my tunic aside and said with wonderment, "Look at that. There's a leaf imprint on your shoulder."

"Because you used Theano's seal," I reminded her.

"Yes, but I thought it would go away. It's still there."

"A constant reminder," I said. It was too bad she hadn't used a flat blade instead, as that would have made the skin stay smooth. But beggars couldn't be choosers.

The irony that I was permanently scarred from retrieving a key that hadn't led me to the eye was not lost on me. I opened my pouch and took out the key, staring at it for a moment before I tossed it onto the ground. I wasn't going to need that again.

We continued on after finishing our meal and reached the groundwater of the spring just before night fell, with Zalira leading us directly to it.

It had been deliberately plugged up. We stood in a half circle around it. Rocks and mud had been packed into the spring.

And not just any mud.

Red-colored mud.

There was also red dirt on the ground all around us.

The hair on the back of my neck rose. I drew my sword and quickly observed the area.

My sisters immediately unsheathed their weapons as well.

"What is it?" Zalira asked.

"That red dirt. I've seen it before." I turned slowly, taking in everything around me, looking for any sign that we weren't alone.

"Where?"

"My ship was attacked by pirates. They told me that they had come specifically for me and my sister, the Locrians. And before they attacked, they threw this red dirt down on the floorboards." I wasn't sensing anything, but that wouldn't mean anything if the enemy had concealed themselves well enough.

"Why?" Io asked.

"I don't know. And—" I had almost said Jason's name, but now was not the time to bring him up. "No one on the *Nikos* knew what it meant. And when I went out that night in Troas to send the message to my parents, I took the chance to ask a sailor about the dirt, but still no answer. Have you heard of anything like that?"

All my sisters shook their heads. "No," Zalira added.

"The man who—" Io couldn't finish the sentence. "The one who was looking for you at the temple. He said he wanted the Locrian. Do you think it's the same people?"

"The men in the temple didn't throw down any red dirt." I didn't know if that was some kind of requirement for them, but considering the dirt here at the spring, it seemed important enough that if the men in the temple had been from the same group, I imagined they would have put down the dirt there, too.

"So there's more than one group of warriors trying to kill you?" Ahyana asked, her voice high-pitched.

"Apparently."

"I'm so glad we came out into the woods alone with you then," Zalira said with a slight smile and a shake of her head.

While I was glad she could joke, I couldn't turn off my fear that we were about to be attacked. Especially not after bringing up past fights that I'd been involved in.

After a few minutes passed, she said, "I think we're alone."

It seemed that way. The others had already put their weapons away and I finally put my xiphos back into its sheath.

"We should clear the rocks," Io said and Suri nodded.

The stones looked so big that I didn't know how we'd manage it. "I guess we could try lifting them together."

We gathered around the top one. Everybody got their hands underneath it, and I counted. "One, two, three."

It was so easy to lift the stone that it practically flew out of our hands. Like the rocks were as light as leaves.

"Have you ever noticed how strong we are?" I asked after we placed it off to the side.

Zalira and Ahyana exchanged glances and then Ahyana responded, "Other than just now? No."

"We fight men so easily," I said. "That's never been my experience before."

"Until the other night, none of us had ever fought men," Zalira said while Io's face fell. I saw the tears beginning to form in her eyes, but Suri was there, putting her arm around her.

"I have fought many men while training. And I was beaten every time. I could hold my own for a while, but eventually I would be defeated. They were always stronger than me. But now? Something is making us just as strong."

At first it was as if no one knew what to say in response. We easily moved the rest of the heavy rocks in silence, clearing away the mud as well.

Before long the spring had bubbled back up and was flowing again. We all washed our hands off and sat down at the edge of the spring to take a break.

Not that it was necessary. None of us were winded or tired.

"We should head back tonight," I said. I couldn't shake the sense that something was wrong, and the red dirt had only intensified that feeling.

"Agreed," Zalira said. "We should get as far away from here as we can."

"Don't you think we should make camp?" Io asked. "It's been a long journey. I would like to sleep."

It was true—we hadn't been sleeping very much over the last few days. But it seemed more important to put as much distance as we could between ourselves and the spring.

"Let's take a vote," Ahyana suggested. It was three to two—both Suri and Io wanted to make camp, though I suspected Suri only voted the way that she did so Io wouldn't feel alone.

Zalira took my knapsack this time and we began walking back in the direction that we'd come. It hadn't taken us very long to unplug the spring, and it was currently twilight.

Io walked alongside me. "I haven't been able to stop thinking about what you said before."

"About us being freakishly strong?"

"No, when we were speaking about how long Theano's been the high priestess of the temple. For some reason it stuck in my mind, and today when I was speaking to Daphne about your medicine, I asked her about it."

"And?"

"She said that Theano has been high priestess ever since Daphne arrived from her race, when she was eighteen. She's sixty-nine now."

My mind refused to accept this information. "Are you telling me that Theano has been high priestess of the temple for half a century?"

Io nodded, looking worried. "It takes years to achieve the lowest rank of priestess. I don't even know how long it would take someone to become a high priestess."

"That's not possible. Do you know how old that would make Theano?" While I'd heard of some people living to be in their eighties or nineties, it was extremely rare. "And shouldn't she, I don't know, sound older?"

To me she had the voice of a younger woman. She always seemed to move with ease, and nothing in her gait indicated that she might be older. The whole situation was unsettling.

"It's all confusing," Io said. "And today you gave us even more things to be confused about."

"I'm sorry about that," I said.

"Don't be. I would much rather know the truth than be living my life under a kindly meant lie."

"Speaking of lies of omission," Ahyana said, "are we going to tell the priestesses about the red dirt? Maybe they'd know what it means."

My heart rate slightly increased. "We can't. Because then I would have to tell them about the pirates and how people are trying to kill me and they'd kick me out of the temple for putting everyone in danger."

"They wouldn't do that," Io said, dismissively.

"They already tried. The night I arrived Theano wanted to put me out onto the street." I didn't tell them that the only reason she'd allowed me to stay was that I'd claimed the rights of the Aianteioi.

Io gasped angrily. "They what?"

"It's in the past," I told her. "It doesn't matter now."

"You told me about the locked door and I knew about the shaved head and the black tunic, but you never told me they tried to throw you out!" She stayed indignant on my behalf and talked about it for a long time. While the moon was bright overhead, the forest canopy blocked out the light. It had become so dark that it was difficult to see even our hands in front of our faces.

"I can still find the path," Zalira said, "but I'm afraid that we'll trip and hurt ourselves. We should make camp."

"Yes," Io agreed, her exhaustion evident. I felt bad because she was so much shorter than the rest of us that it made sense she would have a more difficult time keeping up with Zalira's long strides.

It still felt like a mistake, though. I wanted to keep marching all the way back to the temple. Something didn't feel quite right.

We gathered some branches and twigs while Ahyana took kindling out of her knapsack. Suri used a flint and stone to create a fire that Zalira breathed to life. It caught quickly and we all ate some fruit and honeyed nuts.

It made me think of the pasteli that Jason had deliberately packed for my benefit and I couldn't help but smile at the memory.

After we finished eating I volunteered to take the first watch. I sat on a fallen tree so that I could better survey the area. My sisters settled into their bedrolls and quickly fell asleep.

Except for Zalira. She came over to sit next to me on the log. "Not tired?" I asked.

"I am," she said. "Even more so than normally. Like tracking is somehow sapping my energy."

There was something I'd been wanting to ask her all day. "How is it that you know exactly the right way to go?"

The fire snapped when she fed it another log. "It's difficult to explain. In the ground, I can sense where the water used to be. There was an emptiness there earlier that was easy to follow. Now that it's flowing again, it's like I can hear and feel where it is."

"That's like magic," I said.

"Women don't have magic," she immediately responded.

"What if we do? What if we have magic that's different? Maybe we can't make a flower bloom on command but we can track underground water and talk to birds and make healing potions and find hidden things."

Zalira smiled slightly, as if she didn't accept my proposition. "What would your power be?"

"So far? Staying alive."

She laughed softly and then said, "I don't think it's magic. I think it's just what happens when you serve the goddess."

"Well, I think you all take it for granted but it's special. Although to be fair, someone told me recently that I see ordinary things and mistake them for magic."

"Jason's right."

"I didn't say . . . How did you know that?" I demanded.

Another smile. "I didn't for sure until you just confirmed it. Before Ahyana and I joined the temple, I had a boy that I was in love with. Stephanos." Her eyes took on a faraway expression, remembering. "We wanted to be married, but his parents wouldn't allow it, as I didn't have a dowry."

And now she had taken vows that would prevent her from ever being with him.

"Did you tell him? That you loved him?" It would have been a commitment she couldn't have been able to turn her back on.

"No. I didn't. And he never said it to me."

My heart ached for her.

She cleared her throat and then patted me on the knee. "All of that is to say I know what a well-kissed woman looks like when I see one. Good night."

Zalira got up and went over to her bedroll and curled up in her blanket, quickly falling asleep.

Leaving me to stare out into the darkness and think about everything that had happened recently—finding out how long Theano had been high priestess, the spring being plugged shut, the red dirt, that the eye was someplace else.

And my thoughts kept turning to Jason, especially after the story Zalira had shared with me.

It didn't help when I saw a pair of fireflies not far from where I was sitting, reminding me of when I'd first seen one with Jason. They seemed to be sitting on a low branch, unmoving, their golden lights slowly blinking.

They were mesmerizing.

A sudden high-pitched howl pierced the night air. It was eerie, chilling, sending a shiver down my back.

What was that?

All my adelphia immediately woke up at the sound. There was an answering howl even farther away, and Io gasped.

"What is going on?" I asked.

"Have you seen anything unusual?" she asked, sounding panicked.

"Just a couple of fireflies." I gestured in their direction. Her gaze followed where I pointed.

"Those aren't fireflies. They are eyes. Terawolves."

She started muttering the word "no" to herself over and over again and then said, "We have to go. Everyone pack up but don't make any sudden moves."

"What are terawolves?" I demanded.

Zalira grimaced as she said, "Lia, we're about to test whether or not you actually have a magical power of staying alive."

CHAPTER FIFTY-SEVEN

I packed my things, discreetly keeping those golden eyes within my line of vision. "Is somebody going to tell me what's going on?"

"Terawolves are part aether dragon, part wolf. They are the sacred animal of the goddess's son," Io said in a low voice. The son, the one who took after his mother and had dominion over earth and metals. "They were a gift to him from the war god. Once they choose their prey, they don't give up until they are dead."

The dread that had been building inside me since I'd heard the howl bubbled over, and I felt my back break out in a sweat.

"I only see one terawolf," I said. "We can handle that."

Io shook her head. "That's the scout. It is waiting for the others to arrive before they attack. They hunt in packs."

"So do we," I said more confidently than I was feeling. If we were going to survive, everyone was going to have to believe that it was an actual possibility. We couldn't have anyone giving up.

"Why are they hunting us?" Ahyana said, shoving her blanket into her knapsack.

"Were you looking for an answer besides 'in order to eat us'?" her older sister asked, quietly pulling out her dagger.

"They won't find us easy prey," I said.

Io was mumbling to herself. "Their bite is venomous. Slow acting."

"Are we going to fight our way clear?" I asked.

"No," Io said. "There's no way. We have to run but . . . oh! I remember now. When I read about them, it said that terawolves cannot cross water. If we can find a body of water, we'll be safe."

Zalira dropped to her knees, putting her hand flat against the earth and closing her eyes. "There's a fairly wide river not far from here."

It was probably the same one that fed into the temple grounds.

"I thought aether dragons weren't real," Ahyana said. "And that the terawolves were all dead."

"Apparently not," I said, taking my xiphos out and getting ready.

"We have to run for the river without stopping," Io said. "Just because we can't see them doesn't mean they're not there. They can turn invisible."

An enemy I couldn't even see? My heartbeat hammered in my chest. How was I supposed to fight that?

Stupid girl, if you can't see your enemy, listen!

Suri had been quietly gathering long branches, tying a strip of cloth at the top, and then dousing them in the fire. A light source so that we would be able to see in the darkened forest.

But it would also make it easier for the terawolves to follow us.

We didn't have a choice. We couldn't risk falling. I took the torch from her.

"Are we ready?" I asked. "On three, following Zalira." For the second time that day, I counted. "One, two, three!"

Zalira turned and sprinted and I kept back for a moment so that I would be the last one, making certain that Io didn't fall behind.

A few seconds later I heard something running in the bush behind our group, and heavy panting and the hurried footfalls of a large animal followed us. Terror churned in my stomach. I didn't know if we would be able to outrun them, but I wasn't in a condition to fight them all off.

I did as the voice in my head suggested and strained my ears to listen.

Another beast joined the hunt, and another, and another. I wondered how many there were, how many I couldn't hear because they were farther back.

There was a snarl to my right and then I felt the rush of something sweeping out at my legs. I immediately brought my xiphos down and was rewarded with a cry of pain as I made contact.

The next one came from the left in exactly the same way and I was ready for it as well.

This caused the terawolves to not attack again, but I felt them as close as ever. They were biding their time, waiting to corner us.

I knew from personal experience how dangerous it was to be cornered.

Io nearly stumbled and I reached out to grab at her and keep her upright. One of the terawolves seemed to see this as a weakness and it lunged for her.

"Go!" I told her. I had to sense where it was and stabbed my xiphos out, but I only swung at air.

The beast shimmered into sight. It was nearly as big as me, all dark fur with silver stripes, bright white teeth, and silver claws. It had curved silver horns on its head and its golden eyes stared at me. It seemed like it had appeared with the sole intent of terrifying me, and it was working. It growled and I tensed, prepared for it to make a move.

It didn't attack.

I realized that it was waiting for the rest of its pack so that they could overpower me together. I turned and started to run, feeling it right behind me.

If I ever saw Demaratus again, I was going to kiss his shaved head for forcing me to practice running so often.

The forest came to a sudden end and I broke into a clearing and could see again, the bright moon lighting my way. I threw my torch at the terawolf and heard it back off. There was the river! I saw Zalira, Ahyana, and Io were swimming across, but Suri was standing in the shallows closest to me. Was she waiting for me?

"I'm here! Let's go!" I told her and then ran past her into the water. I dived in and had gone a few strokes when I discovered that Suri hadn't followed. I swiveled my head to look at her and called for her to follow me.

From the frantic and panicked expression on her face, I realized that she couldn't swim.

Cursing, I immediately turned and rushed back, but before I could reach her, a terawolf tore out of the forest straight toward her.

"Suri!" I screamed. "Look out!" It was like I was moving in slow motion. The water was making it so I couldn't go quickly enough. I wasn't going to be able to reach her in time.

She slashed at the terawolf, but it evaded her blow and reached over to clamp its teeth around her other arm and pulled her to the ground. It started dragging her away.

I ran out of the water and plunged my xiphos into the back of its neck. It collapsed to the ground, its teeth still wrapped around Suri's forearm. I pried its jaws open and she quickly withdrew her shaking limb.

"Come on, I'll help you," I said. "In the water turn onto your back and I'll pull you." I was grateful that I had grown up next to the sea and had spent my entire life swimming and that my brother, Haemon, had taught me how to rescue someone who was struggling.

I also knew that if Suri panicked she could drown us both, and I couldn't imagine a worse death. Getting eaten might be preferable.

We ran into the river just as the rest of the pack came through the tree line, revealing themselves to us.

There were at least a dozen of them, all bristling fur over thick muscles and massive teeth, and they were the most horrifying things I had ever seen.

They came over to the riverbank and watched as I pulled Suri through the water. The cloak I wore was dragging us down, but I didn't have a way to remove it. Swimming like this was exhausting work and I was quickly tiring.

Despite my warning, Suri seemed to sense how I was failing, and she thrashed around, struggling within my grasp. I tried to warn her not to, but my arms gave out and we were both drifting down. Now I was the one utterly panicked. Drowning was my worst fear and I wasn't strong enough to save us both. I didn't know what to do. I kicked my legs out, but it was futile. I was too weak.

But then I felt hands on my arms, pulling me up. Zalira and Ahyana had come into the water and rescued both of us, taking us to safety.

We landed on the opposite shore, exhausted and breathing hard. We all collapsed and watched as the terawolves slowly disappeared, blinking out of sight until all we could see was their golden eyes. I heard the brush parting as they reentered the forest.

"They'll keep hunting us," Zalira said. "They will find a way around the river. We have to keep moving."

"Suri's hurt," I said. "One of them bit her."

Io was already moving, looking at the wound. She took off the cloth wrapping from Suri's arm and wrapped it tightly near Suri's elbow. Then she leaned down and wrapped her mouth around the bite mark, sucked, and then spat something out.

"What are you doing?"

"Sucking out as much of the venom as she can," Ahyana said as she started looking for some long branches. "We're going to need a litter for Suri. If she walks, her blood will pump faster and spread the venom."

Zalira went to help her, but I could only watch as Io tried to save our sister.

"Lia! Give us your cloak!" Ahyana said. I realized that I was the only one who still had mine. The cloak that had nearly drowned me was now going to help Suri. I quickly took it off and then handed it to Ahyana. She was using soaked ropes from her knapsack and tied the cloak to the wooden frame she and Zalira had constructed. I wondered why they hadn't used one of the blankets until I remembered that our cloaks had been coated in lanolin oil to make them somewhat waterproof. Our blankets would be drenched.

"That's all I can do," Io said as she wrapped the wound up with the cloth from Suri's other arm. "It is a slow venom and we have plenty of antivenin at the infirmary. We have time."

I hoped that was true.

After we secured Suri to the litter, we began pulling her with Io crying as she walked. We plunged back into the dark forest and again had a hard time seeing. I heard Zalira curse more than once as she tripped over something, but she managed to lead us safely through.

We found the main road, and despite Antiope's warning, we took it the rest of the way back. It was faster and felt safer than returning into the woods.

When Troas came into sight, Io suddenly collapsed. I called her name and rushed over to her.

"It's probably from sucking out the venom," Ahyana said. "She put herself at risk to save Suri." We put her onto the litter next to Suri and dragged it the rest of the way, trading off so that we wouldn't tire too quickly.

The streets were empty, but I kept my xiphos drawn the whole time just in case we ran into somebody we shouldn't. Urgency pushed us to hurry but I was so worried it wasn't fast enough.

Part of me wished that Jason would magically appear. I knew that he could have easily picked up Suri and Io and thrown them over his shoulders and run the rest of the way.

We reached the temple and the guards called out to each other in warning. "Intruders!"

"It's Zalira, Ahyana, and Lia!" Zalira told them. "We need healers! Suri and Io are hurt!"

The guards came to help, picking up our sisters and carrying them off to the infirmary for us. We followed.

I expected to see Daphne, but she wasn't there. Instead an older priestess I didn't recognize seemed to be in charge, directing the other healers.

"They need antivenin," I said, remembering what Io had said. "Terawolf bite."

The lead healer's eyebrows lifted in surprise, but she went to the cabinet to get what I'd requested and quickly administered it to Suri and Io.

I collapsed onto one of the beds. "Are they going to be all right?"

One healer was rinsing out Io's mouth while another studied the bite marks on Suri's arm and removed the tourniquet Io had made.

The head healer said, "Only time will tell. We will have to pray and hope."

There had to be something we could do besides just that. "Where is Daphne?" If anyone could help, it was her.

The three healers exchanged heavy glances.

Antiope and Maia rushed into the infirmary, clearly having just woken up. They were both asking what happened, speaking over one another, and we tried to answer as best we could but it was all confusion.

Zalira cut through the noise and repeated the question I'd asked earlier. "Where is Daphne?"

Maia looked very sad as she folded her hands in front of her and said, "I'm very sorry to have to tell you this, but Daphne passed away this afternoon."

CHAPTER FIFTY-EIGHT

"What?" I asked, unable to comprehend what she was telling me. We had just seen Daphne. She had seemed to be in perfect health to me.

"It happens sometimes with the elderly," Maia said, patting me on my right shoulder. "They can die suddenly and without warning."

Nothing about Daphne had ever seemed old to me. She'd moved and worked like a much younger woman. I glanced over at Io and my heart broke for her. She was going to be so devastated when she awoke. I knew how much she looked up to Daphne, how much she had learned from her.

"Are the rest of you hurt?" Antiope asked.

All three of us shook our heads.

"Then come with me. We need to know exactly what happened."

I briefly hesitated. Suri would be upset that her arms were exposed, but there was nothing I could do. The healers had to be able to access the wound.

We went with Antiope and Maia to the battle master's office in the gymnasium and it was just how I would have pictured it. Clean and pristine looking, but with weapons hanging upon every available inch of the walls.

"Start at the beginning and tell us everything that occurred," Antiope said after we'd all sat down.

Between Zalira, Ahyana, and me, we told them the whole story of all that had transpired within the last twenty-four hours.

When we finished, it didn't seem like the battle master believed us. "Terawolves are extinct," she said.

"Suri's arm would beg to differ," I responded more sharply than I'd intended.

Zalira joined in with her own sarcasm. "We probably should have told them they weren't real when they were trying to eat us."

I expected them to scold or lecture us for our rudeness.

But they didn't.

"What does this mean?" Maia asked Antiope as if we weren't even in the room.

"I don't know, and we can't even ask the high priestess." I got the feeling that Antiope wasn't often at a loss like this.

"Why can't you ask her?" Ahyana asked.

"Theano became very ill this afternoon and has been confined to her bed."

Hadn't Maia said that Daphne had died this afternoon? Was that timing coincidental? It had to be. How could one event affect another? My mind felt hazy. The exhaustion had finally set in now that we were back and had shared everything that was important to tell them.

We all left out the part about the red dirt.

"You three need to go back to your room and sleep. Tell no one of what you saw tonight," Antiope instructed. "I will tell Suri and Io the same thing when they wake up."

Again, I was left with a wealth of questions that I knew wouldn't be answered. And even worse? Two sisters who might be in danger of never waking up again.

◆ ◆ ◆

The next morning we were awoken by Nysa. She stood with Artemisia and the remaining members of her adelphia in our room. One of the acolytes who had been killed in the attack on the temple had been part of Artemisia's sisterhood. I wondered if they blamed me for it. I gripped my xiphos under my pillow, not sure what was happening.

"Get up," Nysa said. "Yesterday before she fell ill, Theano said one of her keys had been stolen. It opens the treasury vault. Nothing is missing from the vault and we intend for it to stay that way. She ordered me to conduct a search. We haven't found it so far and since you were the only ones who were gone yesterday . . ."

Her voice trailed off, but her implication was clear. She was sure we had it.

And if she had searched us yesterday, she would have been right.

But now it was lying in a forest south of Troas.

Artemisia smirked at us as she tore apart our room. They ripped open bedding, our pillows, and went through all our clothing, our pouches, our knapsacks. We had to sit quietly while everything we owned was tossed into the middle of the room or destroyed.

I was relieved that the book had been stolen. Without a doubt, they would have discovered it and I would have had no explanation.

"It's not here," Artemisia practically growled. She had expected to find the key.

I was so glad that I'd gotten rid of it. "Of course it isn't," I said.

She heard the secret in my voice, knew I had done something, but she had no way to prove it. The bitter and angry frustration was etched clearly into her features.

I stood up as she stalked over to me. If she wanted a fight, I was ready to provide her with one. She would probably be able to take me easily, given my left shoulder, but I would get in a few good hits before someone pried us apart.

"You will make a mistake," she said to me in a low voice. "And when you do, I will be there to expose you. You will lose."

Lose what?

"And I will make certain that you are removed from this temple. You have cost me a sister. You defile this place with your very presence and you put us all in danger," she hissed at me.

I couldn't even defend myself. She was right. "I'm sorry about your sister."

My pity seemed to just infuriate her further and she drew her sword.

"Artemisia!" Nysa called out. "Let's go."

The women left, with Artemisia glaring at me the entire way, and Zalira sighed. "Look at this mess."

"We should get it cleaned up before Suri and Io get back," Ahyana said, and I envied the easy optimism she seemed to have.

Kunguru flew into the window and Ahyana immediately rebuked him. "There you are, naughty boy! Where have you been? Terawolves tried to eat us. We could have used you as our warning system."

He cawed at her in response and came over to give her a drachma. She shook her head and took the silver coin. She usually kept them in a small wooden box by her bed, but Artemisia had dumped all the contents onto the floor.

I went over to help her clean it up while Zalira started putting our bedding back into place.

Io entered our room a few minutes later, shocking everyone.

We all rushed over to hug her.

"Are you all right?" I asked.

"I'm fine. I didn't get nearly as much venom in me as Suri did. She will be recovering for a while longer," she said. "What happened in here?"

"Nysa, Artemisia, and her adelphia came to look for the treasury key," I said.

"Did they find it?" she asked. There were dark bags under her eyes and fading red streaks around her mouth, and the purple-and-black finger bruises on her neck had started to turn yellow and green.

She looked like she'd been beaten up. She went over to sit on her bed and I was glad that Zalira had put that one back together first.

"No. I got rid of it in the forest on our way to the spring," I said.

Io nodded, looking relieved. "Good."

Ahyana went to sit next to her, taking her hand. "Did you hear?"

"About Daphne?" Tears instantly formed and began to slide down her cheeks. She sniffled. "I still can't believe that it's true. It doesn't seem real. We just saw her yesterday and she was fine. In perfect health."

"It can happen suddenly," I said, echoing Maia's words. "I'm really sorry. I know how close you were to her."

Zalira and Ahyana also told her they were sorry, with Ahyana hugging Io tightly.

"After the festival we were supposed to go out to a nearby farm to help with their olive trees. I don't know if that's still going to happen. I'm going to miss her so much," Io said.

We stayed silent for a long while, out of respect for Daphne and for Io's loss. Then I couldn't help myself—I had to ask the question that had been plaguing me. "Did anyone else think it was strange that Theano fell ill at the same time Daphne died?"

"You think the two events are connected?" Zalira attempted to clarify.

"I think it's a possibility. It seems too strange not to be."

"To what end?" Ahyana asked. "Do you think someone was trying to hurt them and it caused Daphne to die while Theano only became sick?"

I shrugged. "None of us know what happened yesterday. But who would attack them both?"

Zalira crossed her arms over her chest. "I think the more important question is why so many of these things are happening all at once. It feels like something is coming and each new thing brings us closer to a cataclysmic event."

I knew what she meant. I had felt that way ever since I'd stepped foot into Ilion.

Time was counting down, but I had no idea what would happen when it ran out completely.

◆ ◆ ◆

The next couple of days were filled with so much activity that there wasn't much chance for us to speculate as to the wild series of events we had been living through. There was endless cleaning that had to be done to prepare for the festival.

Some of the older priestesses made some noise about canceling the festival, given Theano's condition, but they were quickly overruled. The festival was too important to forgo for any one person.

Antiope was elected to the vacant leadership position left by Daphne's death. I had expected that there would be a funeral for Daphne, but they didn't have one. She was quietly buried in the earth with no fanfare.

"She was born of a woman, and to a woman she returns," Maia said. "To the bosom of the goddess of the earth."

Suri recovered quickly, and I figured it had to be due in part to Io staying down in the infirmary as much as she could to help concoct possible remedies. Combined with the antivenin, they seemed to work. We were all thrilled to have our sister returned to us, healthy and whole.

I wondered if she had the same red, fading streaks on her arm that Io had on her face, but Suri had returned to covering her arms. If my sisters had noticed her other scars, they didn't say so.

While I kept expecting Antiope or Maia to make an announcement about what we'd discovered at the headwater of the spring, nothing was said. And we were expected to go about our business pretending that we hadn't been attacked by creatures straight from a nightmare.

During my tutorial with Maia, I thought about what Ahyana had brought up—that someone at the temple might know about the red dirt. When Maia mentioned the ocean during a story she was sharing, I interrupted her to tell her a bit about my voyage over, where we'd been attacked by pirates and how they'd spread the red dirt.

"Have you ever heard of anything like that?" I asked. No one was more knowledgeable than Maia.

"No. That seems very strange."

Another dead end. I was getting tired of running into those, especially when I'd spent the past year training to avoid them.

I also hadn't dreamed of Jason the last two nights. Part of me thought I was just so exhausted in every way imaginable that my body was trying to recuperate, putting me into a sleep so deep that I didn't dream.

It didn't feel that way, though. It was more like he was being kept from me deliberately.

And I didn't like it.

We had to help in the kitchens before the festival began because so much food was being prepared for our guests.

Io described what would happen during the celebration. "There will be a parade that will start at the docks and make its way here. It will be led by the living goddess, the young woman selected by the people of Troas to be at the head of the procession. She will be given the honor of bringing a new tunic and veil for the statue."

She then explained about all the women of the city who would join in, carrying baskets filled with fruits and flowers, trays with wine and honey, incense burners that would fill the air with the scent of irises, olive branches to be offered as a sacrifice.

"They will wear irises in wreaths on their heads, their hair unbound, their feet unshod. They will sing and dance as they approach, great hymns to the goddess."

"Don't forget the horses," Ahyana said.

Io smiled. "Oh, yes. There will be five white horses in the parade, representing the goddess's daughter. They're her sacred animal."

That made me less interested in the horses. After the terawolves, I'd had my fill of sacred animals. "And there won't be any men involved at all?" I asked.

"No, this is a festival solely for women. Men who try to watch usually meet a bloody end," she said. I wondered who administered that punishment. Probably Antiope. "Along the way the procession will stop and dig five furrows into the ground to ensure fertility for next season."

"Five being sacred to the goddess."

She nodded. "It also has to do with the myth that the goddess lay with a mortal man in a recently plowed field with five furrows. Iasion was his name, if I recall correctly. He impregnated the goddess with a mortal child who became the first high priestess of her temple."

"Which is why some men talk about plowing women in a very crude way," Zalira said with a shake of her head.

I was curious as to why the goddess could take lovers and have children, but her priestesses were not permitted to do so.

"There will be a great bonfire in the courtyard, where sacrifices can be made," Zalira added. "After the fire burns out, those ashes are collected to sprinkle onto the fields for planting, as they will ensure a good harvest."

"And the wine!" Ahyana said, her eyes dancing. "There will be so much honeyed wine. The purest, sweetest thing you've ever tasted."

"Which none of you should drink because they add a mixture that includes pomegranate juice, saffron, and wild orchid powder to it," Io said with a wag of her finger.

"What does that do?" I asked, and my sisters laughed while Suri smiled.

"It gives the women a very strong desire to return to their homes and increase their own fertility with their husbands," Ahyana said with a wink.

"Does that actually work?" I asked.

Io just rolled her eyes at me. "Of course it does. A great number of children will be born nine months from now." Seemingly embarrassed, she directed the conversation to a more neutral topic.

The rest of the afternoon flew past and it was time for us to gather in the courtyard. Everyone had been given a new tunic in honor of the celebration. I supposed that I wouldn't receive one but Maia surprised me by handing me a light green tunic to match with my sisters'.

"Just for tonight," she said. I understood the message—I was to resume wearing my black tunic when Theano came back to rule over us.

We waited in silence and heard the far-off sounds of the processional.

"It has begun!" Ahyana said with undisguised glee.

Everything had been so difficult lately that I was looking forward to a night of revelry.

I couldn't wait to see what they were all so excited about.

CHAPTER
FIFTY-NINE

The music got louder as the women of Troas came closer, and I could hear them singing.

Io told me the words that I couldn't quite make out. "Sing, maidens and mothers, sing to the goddess, the lady of much bounty. Your daughter's five white horses convey us forward now as a symbol of you bringing spring and harvest to us. As we are unsandaled and our hair unbound as we walk through your city, so shall you bless our feet and heads to remain unharmed. As we bring you sacrifices, we ask for your glorious bounty in return. Grant us your fertility and gift of life. Hail, goddess, save this people with harmony and prosperity and bring us another great harvest!"

"That's beautiful," I said. It sounded more like a prayer than a song. I'd thought songs were supposed to rhyme.

The parade finally reached us and I was struck by the young woman leading them. She looked as if she could be the goddess herself. She was extremely beautiful, with long, golden hair and bright green eyes and delicate features. Her white tunic was embroidered with dark blue threads that probably spoke of the noble house she hailed from. She carried new clothing and a veil for the statue with a high degree of reverence and elegance as she entered the archway.

Maia went over to meet her and accept the gift of the tunic, presumably standing in for Theano.

"Chryseis, daughter of Ilion, you do us a great honor this day by acting as proxy for the goddess and by bringing such luxurious and fine clothing for her statue to wear. You honor us all with such a gift, and may the goddess bless you and your family."

I knew that name. Chryseis.

Then it came flooding back to me. That was the name of the girl that the prince of Ilion was in love with. The one Jason also liked. He'd told me about her back at the feast in the palace in Locris.

Sister to the man engaged to my sister.

Irrational hate and envy flared up inside me. I wanted to stab her perfect pale throat.

Then the other women from the processional began to put their offerings into the bonfire, causing it to increase in size with each new arrival.

I was off in a quiet corner of the courtyard with my sisters, watching the events unfold. To my surprise Suri approached with a skin of wine and held it aloft, her eyes questioning, wanting us to drink.

"What did I tell you about the wine?" Io asked, exasperated.

"That we should drink it because it is so delicious and it will be a bonding experience for our adelphia to share some?" Ahyana supplied hopefully and Io had to laugh.

"Don't say later that I didn't warn you," she said.

When the skin was passed to me, I took a long, deep drink. Ahyana was right—this was the most delicious wine I'd ever had. Undiluted and sweet. I immediately felt warmer and brighter.

"Good, isn't it?" Zalira asked, taking her turn.

"It's incredible," I told her.

We drank the skin until it was gone. Io immediately seemed tipsy and was grinning at us, telling us how much she loved us all.

I still felt like myself, but looser. More relaxed. As if all my troubles had been temporarily erased.

The women from the city also seemed to be having a great time and were wandering in and out of the temple grounds and into the surrounding neighborhood, where wine and food were made available to them, the streets cordoned off for their use.

Priestesses and acolytes were out in the neighborhood and no one seemed to care. The guards were there, but they were drinking and eating as well, laughing and chatting along with the rest of the crowd.

I wished that I'd known beforehand how lackadaisical things would be during the festival as I could have planned to sneak out again. I wouldn't have had any wine to drink. I still felt in control of myself but worried that my reaction time might be a bit slower, given what I'd had. I definitely wouldn't have gambled on my odds of winning against the library goose.

Ahyana and Suri were playing a dice game that Ahyana seemed to be winning, given her cheers.

"I didn't know it would be like this," I announced a bit loudly.

"We told you about the festival many times," Zalira countered, lying back on the ground so that she could look up at the sky. "Do you not have festivals in Locris?"

"No." We had parties but not citywide events like this to worship the goddess. All of that was gone.

Zalira made a sad face at me. "My father used to say a life without festivals is like a road without inns."

"Safe?" I asked, confused. Inns were terrible places full of murderers and thieves.

She laughed and then Io decided to drunkenly educate me. "Festivals are necessary because everyone here lives in constant fear of famine, so we have to pray and worship to make sure that next year will be bountiful." She stumbled over the last word several times before finally pronouncing it correctly.

"In a place like this?" I asked. That seemed unbelievable to me. I'd never been anywhere so full of life and greenery.

"It's happened before," she said. "The line between famine and surplus is a thin one."

Zalira put her hands behind her head and nodded her agreement. "It takes just one season without the right amount or type of rainstorms. The people here are constantly torn between anxiety and fear on the one hand and relief and gratitude on the other."

"My nation has been under a famine for the last thousand years." My announcement seemed to bring my sisters' moods down a bit and I felt bad about it. They were having fun and I didn't want to ruin that for them.

Musicians had set up and were playing festive, fast-tempo songs. Dancing began but it wasn't like any I had ever seen before. It wasn't polite and courtly, people weren't following steps. Instead it had a more primitive feel to it and the drumbeats and flutes called out to my soul, urging me to join them.

I couldn't let myself get lost in the music. With all the recent attempts on my life, I decided I should at least try to keep some of my wits about me. I instinctively understood that joining their dance would make everything worse.

"I'm going for a walk. I'll be back in a little while," I said. I worried for a moment that I might not be able to get up, but I was fine. I walked away from the crowds to let my head clear.

The priestesses and acolytes had also worn their hair down and gone barefoot. I noticed that being shoeless had the effect of making it so I could feel the power in the earth beneath my feet clearly. It was stronger, more present. Like it was about to burst up out of the soil and envelop me.

I bent down to put my fingers into the grass, laying my hand flat against the earth.

The humming sensation increased.

What I'd told Zalira the other night? About women having magic? I believed it. I didn't understand how it worked, but it had become evident to me that my sisters were special and their gifts were clearly goddess sent.

Although no one else seemed to believe me.

While crouching down I became aware of a particular sensation—as if I weren't alone. At first I thought that one of my sisters had followed to check on me but that wasn't it.

My breath caught when I realized who it was.

Jason. Jason was here.

He was waiting for me. I could feel him, as if everything surrounding me had changed because he was nearby.

I walked along the stone fence until I found a bench. I climbed up and easily pulled myself up to the top of the wall and then jumped down.

The alley was quiet—none of the revelers were down in this direction.

I was alone.

Had I imagined it?

Then I was being pulled back against a hard body, a hand going over my mouth, my heart flying up into my throat. As I'd predicted earlier, my reflexes were not at their best, and I couldn't think of what to do to break the hold I found myself in.

"Lia, it's me." Jason breathed his words against my skin.

My entire body sagged with relief. I was where I'd been longing to be—in his arms.

Then I remembered why I was supposed to be angry with him.

There was movement at the end of the alley, as if someone were passing by. He released me and I turned around, grabbed him by the front of his tunic, and pushed him behind a tree so that we wouldn't be visible. I leaned my head out slightly to make certain we hadn't been seen.

"If you wanted to kiss me, all you had to do was ask," he said with a teasing lilt. "You didn't have to shove me into a tree."

"I don't want . . ." My words trailed off as I looked at him. Really looked at him.

He was so, so, so handsome. Had he always been this attractive? I wanted to fan my overheated face with my hand but refrained.

My fingers relaxed so that they were flat against his strong chest. It was pleasurable to touch him, to be with him.

It reminded me of the time in training when Suri had sneaked past my defenses and slammed me flat on my back. I had struggled to pull air into my lungs, the wind knocked out of me.

I remembered what it had been like when I could finally draw a large, full breath in. That's what seeing him again was like—as if I'd been holding my breath for days and could only now breathe again.

"You shouldn't be here. Men who attempt to view the festival come to a bloody end. I learned that today."

"I'll take my chances," he said, sounding amused.

He had no idea what he would be up against. That despite how gifted he was with a blade, Antiope would certainly be a formidable opponent. She might even win.

"Did you miss me?" he asked as if he already knew the answer.

Yes, I had missed him.

Desperately. Completely. Totally.

His heart beat quickly under my hand while my own heart was trying to bruise itself against my rib cage.

"Because I've missed you," he said, and his words made my stomach knot up with pleasure.

Want for him beat through my blood, filling me up. My body felt like it was on fire just from standing close to him. I was desperate for him to touch me. I'd never craved physical contact before, but if he didn't put his hands on me soon, I was going to expire on the spot.

As if he knew exactly what I needed, he reached up with his thumb and ran it along my jawline. It was such a small gesture but it made the fire inside me reach dizzying heights. It shredded my nerves, this heady concoction of pleasure and yearning.

He moved his thumb over to drag it across my lips and sent bolts of desire from my mouth directly to my abdomen.

Jason touched me like he felt exactly the same way that I did.

Everything around me took on a soft, gentle sheen and he was the only thing I could see clearly.

He took his hand away and leaned his head forward, as if he intended to kiss me. "Thank you for not biting me."

"What?" I asked, very confused.

"When I put my hand over your mouth earlier. I apologize for doing it—I didn't want you to make a noise and draw attention to us." His lips ghosted over mine and I shivered in anticipation.

"Oh. You're welcome."

"There might be other parts of me that you want to bite later and I'm letting you know now that I won't mind at all," he said in a silky tone, and I didn't understand why it made me want to collapse against him.

Why would I bite him? That shouldn't have been arousing but for some reason it was.

Maybe because everything Jason said and did made me want him more.

My brain tried to remind me of something. Something important. But he was hovering his lips along the same path his thumb had taken earlier—along my jaw and over to my ear. The warm, wet heat of his breath against the outer shell of my earlobe was very nearly my undoing. I could actually taste my desire for him on the tip of my tongue.

"The book!" I said suddenly and then immediately turned all that lust into anger. I pushed against his chest, taking a step back.

He looked bewildered. "Book?" he repeated.

"Yes. Did you steal the book I took from the chief recordkeeper out of my room?"

CHAPTER SIXTY

He looked genuinely surprised. If he was acting, he was very believable. "No. Why would I help you steal the book and then take it from you later? As far as I know, it has no value to anyone but you."

And someone else, apparently. "Did you tell anyone about it? The book?"

"Who would I tell?"

"That's not an answer!" My body was angry at me for not being pressed up against his and I tried very hard to ignore it.

"I told no one," he said.

"Swear it. On your life."

"I swear it on my life," he said, putting one of his hands over his heart. "Even more meaningful, I swear it on your life."

Why would that be more meaningful to him? He wasn't making any sense. Or my anger and longing and his proximity were making it impossible for me to think clearly or to be rational.

His voice took on that low and intoxicating tone, the one more powerful and dangerous than any honeyed wine. "Trust me, if I broke into your room, it wouldn't be to steal a book."

His gaze traveled leisurely over my form, from head to foot, and it was like he was touching me even though we were standing several feet apart.

"Oh?" My voice was unsteady, just like my pulse.

He gave me a wicked smile, the one I saw in my dreams. "I can think of many, many other things I would enjoy doing first."

I wanted to ask him, "Like what?" but knew that whatever answer he gave me would wipe out the little self-control I had left.

The wine certainly wasn't helping with that, either.

Was he attempting to charm me so that I wouldn't question him further? "Why are you even out here?"

"I was worried you might try to sneak out tonight with the festival going on, and here we are. I thought you might need my help."

"It's not your concern." I hadn't even been planning on sneaking out. He didn't know me nearly as well as he seemed to think he did.

"I do know you," he responded, making me realize that I'd accidentally said the last part out loud.

That left me speechless, sputtering and trying to think of some kind of witty retort to impale him with.

"You shouldn't leave the temple grounds," he said while I floundered about without a suitable response. "It isn't safe."

"But you're the only person here," I said triumphantly, proud that I'd finally managed to say something. "Should I be worried about you?"

"Yes."

He'd said it seriously, like it was meant as a warning. Instead I was excited by the fact that he might be dangerous.

Maybe he was right and I wasn't safe here. I should have asked him to give me a boost so that I could climb back over the temple's fence. But I didn't want to do that. I both wanted to flee and to stay. I hated that he had this effect on my emotions, that with just one fiery look he could reduce me to ash and fill me with conflict.

He let out a short sigh. "Lia, Lia, Lia."

I liked the way his mouth moved as he caressed the syllables of my name.

"You know, I never asked you if Lia is a nickname."

Fear lacerated my heart and I fought to bring my face under control. "Why would you want to know that?"

"Names are important. They have power. Especially true names."

That caused me to think of when I'd dreamed about the goddess and when I'd heard her speak to me when I was awake. She always called me Euthalia. Never Thalia, never Lia.

"Do you know the name of the goddess?" I asked.

If he was surprised by my random question, he didn't show it. "Are you planning on controlling her?"

"What do you mean?"

"As I said, names have power. And when it comes to the gods, they're a bit like dogs. They only come when you call them by name."

In all the time that I'd been here in Ilion, I'd never once heard anyone refer to the goddess by any name. The same thing was true of my grandmother's book. "I don't know what her name is."

He hesitated for several long heartbeats before finally saying, "My mother always called her Damara."

Damara. I repeated it in my mind.

"Am I to expect something in return for such a valuable gift?" he asked in that teasing tone of his.

As if I would use my kisses as bargaining chips. Did they really mean so little to him? That I wanted to kiss him was beside the point. I grappled onto my anger as an anchor to keep me steady so that I wouldn't throw myself at him. "I saw your beloved tonight."

"Which one?" He laughed at my expression—his question, meant to provoke me, had so easily found its mark. "I don't know who you're talking about."

"Chryseis. The one you said every man in Ilion desires? The one the prince wants to marry?" Part of me still held out hope that Prince Alexandros would turn his attention to this woman and just wed her so that I would be free to do the things that I wished. Maybe he would do it after my parents rebuffed his requests multiple times.

"He's welcome to her," he said. "Just so long as it's not me trapped in the marriage net."

I grimaced. Of course he would be terrified of wedlock. "It's actually disappointing how typical you are for a man. Afraid of committing yourself to another."

His honey eyes shone with delight. The last time I'd been in his presence had been at night and I'd forgotten about their beautiful shade. I reminded myself that it bothered me that Jason wanted Chryseis and to hold on to that jealousy. "She is very beautiful," I admitted begrudgingly, almost daring him to contradict me.

To prove that I was the one he preferred.

I would understand if he didn't. She was everything I was not, had everything I didn't. Including all of her hair.

Jason took a step toward me. "I saw no other woman tonight."

"She was very hard to miss," I said. "They put her right in the front."

"Lia, I saw no other woman tonight."

Had he temporarily lost the ability to see? "The entire neighborhood and temple grounds are filled with nothing but women."

Another step. "I saw no other woman tonight but *you*."

It finally dawned on me what he was saying and my stomach swooped in response. He was right—he was dangerous.

My instincts were warning me that I was about to fall into a carefully constructed trap. "She's perfect."

"I don't want Chryseis," he said, so close now that we were nearly touching.

"Then who do you want?"

His answer was his mouth hot on mine, moving and sliding, pressing and pulling. He filled my senses so that he was all that existed—his taste, his heavy breathing, his salt and leather and iris scent, his touch making my eyelids drift shut.

The kiss was over as soon as it began, and he took a few steps back so that he was leaning against the tree. He sported a knowing smirk that I itched to wipe off his face.

"Why did you do that?" I demanded, my lips urging me to kiss him again.

"It's the best way I know to keep you quiet."

I walked over, determined to unleash my full wrath on him. "Of all the insufferable, arrogant, overbearing—"

But this time it was me who kissed him. Pressed our bodies together so that he was trapped against the tree. As soon as I realized what I was doing, I pulled away from him.

Wanting to break my vows seemed even more sacrilegious when I pushed him up against one of the goddess's trees.

"Are we sparring again?" He almost purred the words. "Is it my turn to lunge?"

I intended to tell him no, that this had all been a mistake and that I had to go back to the temple.

"Will you block my advance?" he asked as he approached.

No longer able to form words, I shook my head. My skin hummed in anticipation of his touch, my pulse slow and heavy.

He didn't kiss me. He stood so close that our breaths intermingled.

His right hand went to my waist and he dug his fingers into my hip bone. "What would the goddess say about this?"

I understood that he was giving me a chance to stop. To remember myself and the promises I had made, oaths that he was well aware of. "She told me it was time for things to change."

The corners of his mouth turned up. "The goddess speaks to you, does she?"

"Sometimes."

"What else does she say? Has she told you that she sees a tall, dark-haired, handsome, gentle, and patient man in your future?"

"She hasn't." Or had she? Was that the reason for the dreams I'd had since arriving? She'd obviously used dreams as a means of communication with me. What if she was sending me those interactions with Jason deliberately?

Maybe he was meant to have a bigger role in my life than I'd allowed. I kept dismissing him, pushing him away, telling myself that nothing could come of it.

What if he was destined to be something more?

Or was I just using what she had told me as rationale for my current behavior?

He tugged me forward so that I was flush against his muscled body. I tried not to sigh. "Are you sure you don't want to go back to Locris?"

While I'd decided to stay in Ilion at least until I'd exhausted every possibility of finding the eye, I had considered what it would be like to return home. "Would you take me?"

"Yes." He kissed my forehead softly.

I screwed up my courage and asked him the question I most wanted an answer to. "And would you stay there with me?"

He made me wait an agonizing amount of time. "My family is in Troas. My life is here. And at sea."

I couldn't believe how disappointed I felt. "Your life couldn't be in Locris?"

"You have no idea how much I want that." He murmured the words across my closed eyelids. "To go there with you. Start a life together."

My heart fluttered with happiness. Was that him saying yes? Agreeing to go with me?

There were female voices headed toward us. I shoved Jason between the wall and the tree, covering his body with my own.

I could see from his expression just how much he liked it.

The women revelers were clearly drunk and paid us no attention. They didn't even glance over their shoulders as they walked by.

"We're going to get caught," I said sadly as I backed up and let him out. This hadn't been nearly enough time with him, but the festivalgoers were spreading out all over the surrounding neighborhood. We would be found.

"As I've told you once before, we have to get off the street."

"I'm not going back to a hetaera house again." I was in no mood to watch them fall all over him.

He grinned. "No. I have an idea. Do you want to come with me?"

Jason held out his hand, offering it to me.

With no hesitation I laced my fingers with his. "Yes."

I was ready to follow wherever he wanted to go if it meant I would get to be with him.

Ignoring the warning voice in my head, I let him lead me away.

CHAPTER
SIXTY-ONE

His palm was warm and calloused and the act of holding his hand felt intimate. I liked how it connected us.

I didn't have long to enjoy the feeling, though, because we didn't go far. He led me just across the alley to a door in a small building.

"What is this place?" I asked.

"I'm not sure. Let's find out," he said. He released my hand and I curled my fingers in so that I wouldn't reach for him again.

He began lifting nearby vases, and under one he found a key. I shook my head. If only things had been that easy for me with finding the treasury key. He put it into the lock and I heard the click. He pushed the door open.

Despite it being bright outside, the main room was darkened. It was a small home that had curtains drawn over the windows. "How did you know this would be empty?" I asked as he walked inside.

"An educated guess. They close this neighborhood down for the festival and the residents leave."

I knew that, but it didn't mean everyone followed the rules and vacated. "Isn't this trespassing?"

"I won't tell if you don't," he said.

"We're still breaking into someone's home."

"You've never had a problem breaking into places you're not supposed to before," he said, cajoling me to step inside.

He was impossible to resist. I entered and looked around. It didn't have a second floor, and so everything was in this main room. A table and two chairs, a fireplace for cooking, pots and pans hung up on the wall.

And one massive bed in the corner that seemed to draw my eye no matter where else I tried to look.

My heart thudded quickly. It got worse when Jason shut the door and I heard the lock click into place.

We were completely, utterly alone. We wouldn't be disturbed. I could stay here for the rest of the night and no one would know. My body ached with that knowledge.

He'd never had a problem with kissing me passionately in public places. What would it be like in private?

Where no one could accidentally interrupt us?

"Were you planning this?" I asked him, feeling a little apprehensive.

"How could I?" he said with a small smile, putting the key on the table. "I didn't know that you would find me tonight. I make things up as I go along."

His reassurance eased the knot that had been forming in my chest. "I'm the same way."

"I know." He seemed to fill all of the space, his broad shoulders and muscled arms blocking everything else out. Even if he had planned to bring me here, I didn't think I would have minded.

"Have I mentioned how much I like your green tunic?" he asked. "You look beautiful in it."

"I don't," I responded, immediately rejecting his words. I'd compared myself against Chryseis and found myself utterly lacking. I wasn't beautiful. Not like she was.

"You do," he insisted. "So much so that I'm having a hard time restraining myself."

"From what?"

Instead of answering my question, he asked his own: "If I asked you to stay with me tonight, would you even consider it? Allow me to have one night with you?"

The desire in his voice, the questions he'd asked, seared a path down my spine, exploding at the base and then spreading out to my limbs. I couldn't respond.

Because I was afraid I would say yes.

He gave me a sheepish grin and rubbed the back of his neck. "I shouldn't have said that. I'm sorry. I would not ask you to break your vow."

Jason might not have asked, but there was a distinct possibility that I would offer.

"I'm not sure you're worth getting buried alive for," I said, hoping a joke might break the tension building between us.

"Probably not," he agreed. "Better to refuse."

I had a sudden flash from my last dream with him. *When the time comes, say yes.*

Was this what that dream had meant? Had I somehow known that this moment was coming and prepared myself to accept him? To accept this?

Then, as if our souls were connected and he could hear my thoughts like I'd spoken them out loud, he said, "I dream of you. Almost every night."

His voice was so soft that at first I thought I'd misunderstood him. "You do?"

"Yes. And you always turn me away. It is the most frustrating thing I've ever experienced."

At that I had to smile. "I'm guessing that most women don't tell you no."

He grinned back but the look in his eyes sent a shiver across my skin. "Not usually."

A bit of my lust receded at the reminder that I was just one of many. "Maybe it's good for you to be denied."

He came closer and my breath caught at his nearness. "It is not good for me. Do you know that I wake up every night with your name on my lips, sweating, gasping, reaching for you, wanting you so badly that even my teeth ache?"

My knees threatened to buckle underneath me, that image searing itself into my brain.

The muscles in his throat were working and he put his hands gently on my bare shoulders. I gasped at the contact and then I noticed that his hands were shaking, unsteady.

That had never happened before. He always seemed so sure of himself, so confident.

Was he afraid? Or was it an indication that his declaration was true, that he wanted me so badly that he shook just by being close to me?

"Why can't I stay away from you?" I whispered the words.

He repeated my question back to me. "Why can't I stay away from you?"

"I asked you first."

Jason leaned in to nuzzle my hair with his nose. "I don't know the answer."

And for the first time in my life, I was fine with not having a response. It was enough to be here with him.

His lips took over where his nose had been and he began to kiss the side of my head, moving his way toward my face. Everywhere he touched me, with his hands or his mouth, was hot and feverish. I wound my fingers into his tunic, gripping with all my might so that I could stay upright.

"I don't know if this is a dream or if it's real," I said breathlessly.

"It's very real," he murmured against my cheek. "In your dreams, what do I do?"

His hands had traveled down my arms and came to rest on my waist. He brought me closer to him, fitting us together.

It was difficult to speak. "You make me feel lighter than air."

"How do I do that?"

My cheeks preemptively colored at what I was about to say. "You touch me and kiss me and pleasure me."

I heard his sharp intake of breath and felt the shudder that passed through him.

"Would you like me to do that to you now?" His voice was hoarse, raspy, laden with desire.

My heart was going to burst out of my chest because it was beating too fast. "I can't."

Now it really was like my dreams.

His hands stilled and he pulled his head back. I saw the way his eyes had darkened, his pupils blown. "Where do I touch you that you like best?"

It would be impossible to choose.

This is not a dream, I told myself. There would be real-world consequences to answering that question. I was dangerously close to breaking my vow. He was so tempting and somehow always seemed to appear at my greatest moments of weakness.

Or maybe he was my weakness.

"Tell me what you want," he urged as he dug his fingers into my hips possessively, and I tried not to moan from the delicious pressure.

Still I didn't answer.

"Do you want me to kiss you?" he asked. "If you don't, I'll leave now."

I had to say no to kissing. I tried to shake my head but it refused to cooperate. As did my voice. I wanted his kiss so desperately I couldn't think of anything else. It all faded away.

I moved my hands from the front of his tunic up to his neck. I made myself talk. "Have you been sent to tempt me? To make me forget myself?"

He shook his head, smiling wryly. "I ask myself the same thing. It's like we're two flames, drawn to each other, meant to burn brightly together."

"That also means we can destroy one another."

"Yes, but it would not be a bad way to die," he said. "I would be lying if I said I haven't imagined the softness of your skin against mine, exploring your body with my fingers and mouth and tongue. To watch you coming undone beneath me."

I didn't even know what that meant precisely, but his words turned me liquid and hot. I badly wanted what he was describing. Our strangled breathing had become loud, thick with hunger and longing.

"You didn't answer my question," he reminded me.

There would be repercussions that I couldn't even begin to fathom. I didn't care.

"Kiss me," I invited.

He reached up to frame my face with his hands, and the way he gazed at me, with a reverence like I was something sacred to him, made my breathing hitch.

Then he kissed me so intently that it was bruising. He parted my lips and expertly stroked my tongue with his and this time I did moan. Lust, sharp as a sword, pierced me over and over again until I was weak.

What passed between us in dreams was insubstantial. Not quite real. Touching him and kissing him in that dreamscape did not feel like it did in real life. In person was exponentially better in every way imaginable.

"You don't kiss like someone who has only been kissed a few times before this," he told me in between kisses.

"As I've told you, I'm a quick study. And I had an excellent teacher."

He grinned, but that moment of lightheartedness was quickly gone as his hands ran up my back, his mouth relentless on mine.

His hands left my body and I protested against his lips, but then I heard the sound of metal hitting the floor. He was taking off his weapons. I lost count after five. I was impressed by all his hiding places and was about to ask where they were coming from, but then he was touching me again and I was lost.

He kissed me like he hadn't eaten in months and I was a table laden with all of his favorite foods. He devoured me. His lips were rhythmic, smooth, insistent while also being all consuming.

I was lost in kissing him, a flame blazing, radiating heat and pleasure but without being burned.

That wasn't accurate. Because I was burning for him—every part of me he touched, he scalded. I was afraid that no part of my body would feel like my own again. That it would always be a place that Jason had touched or caressed or kissed, because I could feel him all over me. Even when his hands and fingers moved to a new spot, that phantom imprint stayed behind.

Like he was touching me everywhere all at once.

"You feel like magic," I said into his mouth.

He stopped kissing me long enough to say, "So do you."

I shook my head. "I'm just an ordinary woman."

That reverent look was back in his eyes, and he said in a rough, fire-inducing voice, "Lia, there is absolutely nothing ordinary about you."

I pulled the back of his neck down toward me so that I could kiss him, show him what his words meant to me. As he'd predicted, our fires burned together, lighting up the room and my soul.

"Did you still want to see me?" he asked suddenly, surprising me.

"What?" I was confused, disoriented.

Up until the moment he reached up and undid his shoulder pin with one hand. His blue tunic fell to his waist, where his belt kept the rest of it in place.

Had I asked for this? I didn't remember doing so.

I had in my dreams. But how would he know that?

He kissed me again and I forgot my question, forgot my own name.

His skin was warm and I pushed my hands against him, backing up. I wanted to see him and touch him.

I let out a small sigh. His chest was so perfect that it should have been taken to the nearest statue maker so that they could create a mold from it. I planned on doing what he'd suggested earlier—I was going to explore him with my fingers and mouth and tongue.

I mapped out the topography of his torso, so very different from my own. Fascinated, I ran my fingertips along his muscles, rewarded with his sharp intakes of breath. Those muscles quivered and then hardened under my touch.

I always felt at a bit of a disadvantage in our encounters, his experience so evident and my lack of it just as glaring. But this was making me feel like I had the power. As if I could have him on his knees, begging for my touch and my kiss.

That he wanted me every bit as much as I wanted him.

It emboldened me. I ducked my head to kiss his stomach, letting my tongue flick out to taste him there. He made a sound so guttural that it was like it had been ripped from deep in his chest.

I felt his hand at the back of my head, massaging it and holding me against him at the same time. Just like in the dream I'd had of this moment. I kissed my way up, brushing my lips against his skin. There was so much strength under this warm softness.

His fingers curled into my hair and he pulled my mouth to his, his kiss raw with need and desire. He kissed me with a thoroughness, a ruthlessness, that made me want to collapse to the floor.

Were it not for the arm he had clamped around my waist, I probably would have.

He tore his lips away. "Do you want more?"

I only partially understood what he was asking but it didn't change my answer. "Yes."

He bent down, reaching an arm under my knees, and swept me off my feet. Surprised, I wrapped both of my arms around his neck. He carried me against his chest and I asked, "Where are we going?"

"I'm taking you to bed."

CHAPTER
SIXTY-TWO

In my dreams he had to beg me to change my mind, to give in, to yield, but that wasn't happening now.

I did not protest. I wanted this. All of him.

Demaratus had taught me that self-control was of the utmost importance. But Jason had obliterated mine.

He laid me gently on the bed, as if I were made of glass. He followed me down, caging me with his arms and body. "If you want to go, you should go now."

Because we might soon pass a point of no return.

Shaking my head I told him, "I don't want to leave. I want to be here with you." I wanted to lie with him, to be naked with him, to find out what happened where all my dreams left off.

When he kissed me again, it was more than just physical passion that I felt. There was an emotion there—a message he was conveying. He kissed me like he didn't want to ever let go of me.

Like he cared about me.

He reached down to outline my mouth, my cheeks, my jawline, with kisses. He kissed down to my throat, sliding his lips across my neck, and it made my nerves light up like a firefly. Then he was kissing the base of my throat, sucking at my skittering pulse, and fiery sensations glided along my skin, spiraling out from his mouth.

I dug my fingers into his shoulders while he kissed along my collarbone and over to my left shoulder. He pulled at my tunic, wanting access to more of my skin, and I hissed when he brushed against my wound. It was sensitive to touch.

"What's wrong?" he asked, sounding concerned.

I pulled the tunic away from my shoulder so that he could see. "I was stabbed."

His eyes darkened, full of fury. "Who do I have to kill?"

Again, his words shouldn't have excited me, but they did. "We were attacked at the temple. Another acolyte already took care of the man that did it."

"When was this?" he demanded.

"A few days ago."

His eyes widened in disbelief. "And you climbed over the wall in this condition?"

"It doesn't hurt." And it was the truth. I hadn't thought of it at all until he'd touched it. "Even if it did, it would be worth the pain to be close to you."

There was a long pause, an expression in his eyes that I didn't understand, and then he spoke. "I understand that all too well."

Before I could ask what he'd meant, he was kissing me again.

The kisses started out tiny, delicate, brushes of his lips against mine. But he built my pleasure the same way my sisters had built a fire. He began with the smaller things, the fleeting touch of his lips on mine, a whisper of his fingertips on my skin, a soft murmur of pleasure, piling them up. Then he ignited them, his touch firm, his lips demanding, until I was blazing and ready to consume everything within reach.

As that pleasure spread through me like warm honey, his kiss continued to smolder and burn. He incinerated whatever doubt I might have still had left. He reached over to knot his fingers in my hair, holding me in place while his tongue moved urgently against mine. His kisses were hot, tangling us together. They burned heavy, like the seal Io had pressed to my shoulder, and I did my best to burn him back.

This was everything—that way that all his attention was focused and intent on only me, how his fingers grasped my flesh, his chest grazing mine. He made me feel like a newly created sword being thrust into a fiery heat, and he would forge me into something new with his kiss and his touch.

Jason was magic, no matter what he'd said. He had created some kind of potion that emanated directly from his skin and lips and I was helpless against it. Like he was a shape-shifting terawolf with a special kind of venom that went into my bloodstream like a sickness, infecting every part of my being. The only solution was to keep kissing him, to touch more of him, to move against him.

As if he were both the cure and the disease.

He gently tugged at my tunic and attached his mouth to a spot of skin that was below my collarbone and just above my breast. He sucked and I felt his teeth as he tugged at the skin. I arched against him, my eyes blurring, fire lancing through me as he marked me.

When he finished he pulled back and surveyed his work. I glanced down and saw my skin had reddened.

"You're mine," he told me in a tone that brooked no argument.

"And you're mine." I needed to get closer to him. I tugged at him, wanting his body against me.

He shook his head. "I don't want to hurt you."

"You won't," I promised. "I'm tough."

"I noticed," he said with a grin.

"Please." I had thought only minutes ago that I could have him pleading with me for more and now I was the one doing it.

I wasn't even embarrassed.

He gave me what I wanted and shifted himself over me and then lowered down slowly. I let out a moan when his taut body finally molded itself against me. It was both a relief and a demand for something new.

When his mouth found mine, ravenous and consuming, I realized that he liked this just as much as I did. Maybe even more. We wound ourselves together, one of his legs settling between mine. It felt like we were trying to possess each other, each kiss hungrier and deeper than the one before it.

I had found the right key, the right door, and now I was going to be led to the treasure waiting for me.

Then he slowed the kiss, taming it deliberately. As if he meant to calm me down, but somehow his precision and technique only added more fuel to the fire he had built.

"You're always in such a rush," he told me, nuzzling his nose against mine. "We have all night. You don't know how many times I've imagined this. I want it to last."

I was so mindless with need that I didn't understand the words the way he was using them.

"But first, this has been digging into me," he said. He rolled away and it was like someone had torn my skin off.

Then he was pushing my tunic up and running his hand up my left leg. He leaned over to kiss me and I felt him grin against my lips when his hand came across my sword. He disarmed me and tossed it to the ground.

I trembled, my breath quickening, as his fingers brushed against the bare skin of my inner thigh, undoing the straps there so that he could tug the sheath away and let it fall as well. It felt incredible.

"Better," he said, but his fingers were still running along my thigh and I couldn't stop shaking.

He took his hand away and again I wanted to protest but then he was back on top of me and a buzz of pleasure started in my spine, traveling along all of my nerves. I needed something. Something more from him. I didn't know what it was, but these sensations were building inside me, desperate to get out.

It seemed he intended to kiss me slowly but it didn't happen according to his plan. I didn't allow it. I plundered his mouth and he immediately responded.

He broke it off and said, "We can wait—"

But I interrupted him. "I need you to make me forget."

He reached up to softly stroke my face. "Forget what?"

"Forget that tomorrow I will be parted from you."

Then he kissed me the way I wanted, the way I'd been aching for. His hands moved like liquid over my body, over my curves, leaving heat in his wake. I pulled him against me, searching for . . . something.

We burned so hotly and brightly together, bigger than even the bonfire in the temple courtyard.

He ground his hips against me, right where I needed him most, and it caused all my other senses to turn off. I couldn't see, hear, taste, or smell anything else—I was consumed by the white-hot spikes of desire he created inside me. I arched up into him. Fire lit up my bones while he continued to move against me.

Now I understood the urge to bite. To devour. To consume. I sank my teeth where his neck met his shoulder and he groaned with pleasure.

I soothed it with my tongue and lips, tasting the saltiness of his skin again. He was undeniably delicious.

"You're even better than the wine I had tonight, and that was exquisite." I murmured the words into his strong neck.

He immediately stilled. "You were drinking at the festival? Before you came over the wall?"

"Yes." What did that have to do with anything?

Jason let out a groan of disbelief and rolled onto his back, covering his eyes with his hands. "I know what's in that wine! Everyone knows what that wine does to the celebrants." He let his hands drop from his face so that he could look at me. "You are not yourself. Your judgment has been impaired."

"It has not!"

"Tomorrow you will wake up with the memory of this and you will hate yourself for what we almost did."

I opened my mouth to tell him that he was wrong, but the words wouldn't come out.

Why were we talking? I didn't want to talk. It didn't matter if I'd had some wine. It was unimportant. I was sure I could coax him into kissing me again.

I leaned toward him but he scrambled off the bed and went over to the far corner of the room. "You have to go back."

"I don't want to leave you."

His voice was raspy and tortured. "Go now, before I stop you and convince you to stay."

My heart was both breaking and beating with anticipation. I sat up on the bed, my bare feet making contact with the floor.

"Now, Lia." He said my name like it pained him, as if he knew exactly what I was thinking.

I got my sword and sheath and, not able to help myself, took a step toward him.

He shook his head. "If you kiss me again, I will take you back to that bed and not let you go. And you don't actually want that."

Jason was rejecting me. Because he thought I couldn't make my own decisions. That I wasn't able to think clearly. I marched over to the door and unlocked it, throwing it open as I went out into the alley.

Anger and humiliation filled every empty space inside me. Which was good because my body was urging me to turn around and take him up on his offer to be trapped in that bed with him. There was no need to climb back over the wall as the party had spread. Fortunately, no one seemed to notice me leaving the house and they were all intent on their celebrating. As I came out of the alley and onto the street, someone handed me a cup of wine, filled to the brim. I took it and drank the entire thing down. Warmth flooded through my veins.

I didn't care what kind of mystery ingredients were in it. Whatever they were, they must have been fast acting because they immediately ate away at my anger, giving the part of me that wanted to turn around and go back a much louder voice.

Only the tiny sliver of pride I had left kept me from doing so. The longer I thought about returning to that little house, the more it seemed like a good idea. To distract myself I looked for my sisters, but it was impossible to find them in this crowd. I knew I should just go back to my room and fall asleep.

It was embarrassing to admit it, but part of me hoped that when I drifted off, I would see my dream Jason, because I wasn't very happy with the real one.

As I pushed my way through the throng of women, I came across Io, who was swaying to the music, a cup of wine in her hand. Her eyes were glassy, her cheeks a bright pink.

"Lia! There you are!" she exclaimed, rushing over to hug me. "Where have you been? Did you enjoy your walk?"

I spotted Zalira a bit farther off and she grinned and mouthed the word "Jason?" I turned from her, not wanting to give anything away. I did not want to relive what had just happened.

"The walk didn't turn out the way I thought it would," I told Io.

"Your poor hands are so empty. You need a drink!" She grabbed one off the tray of a passing attendant and handed it to me.

When she did she asked me, "Do you think the goddess has a body that you can touch, or do you think she's made of aether, like the stars?"

"I can either discuss the transcendent nature of the goddess, or I can have more wine. I can't do both."

Her smile got bigger. "Drink!"

So I drank quickly again. Another spike of warmth.

She looped her arm through mine. "Come and sit with me!"

I wanted to sneak off to bed. To put my pillow over my head and let this day be over. But I had the distinct impression that drunk Io would follow me and ask me questions until she squeezed the entire story out of me. It was easier to play along.

As we walked toward a bench, I stumbled a bit. I realized that I was unsteady. Maybe I was drunk now, too. That had been a big cup I'd had back there. Not to mention what I'd drunk earlier and what I was currently carrying around with me.

I'd never been drunk before. It was a strange experience. Both Io and I sat down a bit too hard, misjudging the distance, splashing some of our wine on the ground. She broke out into peals of laughter and I couldn't help but smile back.

"Did you see the horses earlier? I love white horses!" she exclaimed.

"I didn't. I've decided I'm not interested in sacred animals." Which made me think of the terawolves and something began to nag at the back of my mind. It was a phrase Io had said the night we were attacked by those creatures, and I had overlooked it in the heat of the moment.

When I read about them.

Io could read.

"How do you know how to read?" I asked her.

"What?" She shrieked the word and then laughed. "Why do you think I can read?"

"Because you said you could. The night of the terawolves."

She glanced up and to the right, as if trying to recall what she'd said. "I did, didn't I? Shouldn't have done that."

"Why not?"

She put an unsteady finger to her lips and made a shushing sound. "Because it's a secret."

"What is?"

"I'll tell you. My secret," she added on unnecessarily.

"I think I know all of your secrets already," I told her.

"You don't!" she said insistently, shaking her head. "Not this. No one knows this. Not Zalira, not Ahyana. Not even Suri."

That was serious. "Tell me."

Io looked to our left, then to our right, before leaning in close to me and slurring her words. "I'm a princess."

CHAPTER SIXTY-THREE

For a moment I thought I had accidentally spoken and revealed my own background, but no, it was definitely Io who had said those words out loud.

"A princess?" I asked, making certain I'd heard correctly.

She nodded. "Yes."

"Of Ilion?" I clarified.

"The only one. And I ran away from the palace to join the temple." She sounded pleased with herself.

"Why would you do that?" I had done the same thing, but for very different reasons. It occurred to me that this was another way Io and I were connected. We were more alike than I'd even realized.

"I told you. My stepmother wanted to make an arranged marriage for me with an older man." She practically spat the words but somehow still managed to slur them.

Here I'd thought Io incapable of keeping a secret, but she'd been keeping a huge one from me. From all of us.

"You were almost my sister-in-law," I said with a laugh before I took another drink.

"Are you related to the old, gross man?" she asked, confused.

A part of my brain warned me to hold my tongue, but it only seemed logical that if she shared such a monumental secret with me, I was obligated to do the same. "You're not the only one who is a princess. I'm a princess, too. And I was betrothed to your brother."

Her mouth dropped open. "What? You're Princess Thalia of Locris? You were supposed to marry Xander?"

Xander? It must have been a nickname for Alexandros. Regardless, revealing my own secret identity almost seemed like more information than she could handle. Her eyes were so wide, her mouth still agape.

"I suppose I can't marry him now," I said before finishing up my wine.

"No. You took vows. To us, the temple, and the goddess."

"Yes, I did. You're stuck with me."

Her face broke back into the smile I was used to. "I'm so glad!" Her smile faded again. "You won't tell our sisters about who I really am, will you?"

"I won't tell them. I promise. Will you promise that you won't tell them about me, either?"

She held a hand over her heart. "I swear I won't tell our adelphia."

With a nod I thanked her and put my cup on the ground. I was very tired and needed to use the washroom and then head to bed. I leaned over and gave Io a loud kiss on the forehead. "Good night, almost-sister-in-law."

"Good night, my fellow princess turned priestess. Well, princess turned acolyte," she amended, giving me a cheery wave.

It took me longer than it should have to find my way back to our dormitory. After I had used the toilet, I went into our room. Kunguru was on the windowsill and he squawked at me but I ignored him. So, so tired.

I climbed into my bed and turned on my side to fall asleep.

My own thoughts from earlier returned to me. Like I'd missed something.

Io can read.

If she could read, that meant she could have taken the book. She would have been able to read it herself and personally gone over the content. She had been so upset when I'd told her what I'd discovered about priestess marriages and their dowries. What if she had wanted to hide the truth? And had destroyed the book to do so?

I couldn't believe that of her, though. She didn't seem the deceptive type.

Demaratus's voice filled my head.

Stupid girl! She cheated to become an acolyte and hid her true identity from everyone!

That was true. And if she was willing to cheat to get what she wanted and lie about her background, she might have been willing to steal to protect something she believed so strongly in.

I woke with a start, having heard a noise coming from the window. I sat up and saw that there was a man on the windowsill, about to jump into our room.

My sword was missing. I frantically fished around under my pillow but it wasn't there. What had I done with it?

Then the man was on the move and he ran over to my bed. I pulled in a deep breath, intending to scream so that I could draw the guard to help me, wake my sisters up.

"I told you I would sneak in." Jason's voice immediately calmed me and my shoulders dropped as I relaxed. He sat down next to me on my bed and it took every bit of strength I still had not to throw my arms around him.

I was angry at him for his rejection. I needed to remember that.

"Antiope will kill you," I said.

"Who?"

"My battle master. She's a Scythian who—" I shook my head. Why was I explaining this to him? "You have to go."

"Not yet. I think we have some unfinished business."

My traitorous heart leapt with excitement. "You're speaking too loud. You're going to wake everyone up."

He glanced over his shoulder. "Who?"

All my sisters' beds were empty. I reached up to my head and felt the long strands of my hair against my fingertips.

Oh. This was another dream. It wasn't real. It was only my fevered imagination bringing Jason here so that we could finish what he'd so skillfully started.

This was what I'd hoped for when I'd gone to bed, but instead of feeling excited, I just felt pathetic.

"Go away," I told him. "I need to sleep."

He reached for my hand and held it with his own and it had the desired effect. I didn't tell him to leave again. I let him breach my defenses once more.

I'd never considered myself weak but I was quickly learning that, when it came to him, that wasn't true.

"Why are you here?" I asked.

"Why are you fighting what exists between us?" he asked.

My gaze flew up to his. "You know why. Nothing can happen."

"Even if the goddess wills it to be so?"

"You have said that before. She doesn't. Her laws say that we can't be together."

He shrugged one shoulder. "It's her magic that connects us."

"What do you mean?"

"This is a dream," he said, looking around the room before his eyes returned to mine. "But I'm here."

"And obviously I'm here," I said. What did that have to do with anything?

That beautiful smile of his lit up his face. "Yes. You are in your bed and I am in mine but we exist in this space together."

Now I took my hand away from his. "What are you saying? That this is real? I'm not imagining you, you're actually here?"

He nodded.

"That can't be," I protested.

"It is."

"Are you saying that everything that's happened between us has been real? That we have both been here in our dreams the entire time?"

"Yes."

Images flooded my mind and I put my head in my hands. All the things we did, the words we had exchanged—all of it had actually happened? "Everything you've said to me . . ."

I trailed off, not able to complete the sentence.

He laid his hand out flat, offering it to me. Leaving it to be my choice whether I wanted to touch him again. Not able to help myself, I took it. I saw the way the tension left his body when I did so.

"I meant everything I've ever said to you," he told me and my heart froze in place, refusing to beat.

He had all but confessed to being in love with me.

"Why didn't you tell me about this earlier?" I demanded.

"I thought you knew!"

This was too bizarre to be a true possibility. "Or I'm dreaming that you're saying all this to me now. How do I know you're not a figment of my imagination?"

He smiled slightly. "I don't know. I've never had to prove my realness before."

His hand squeezed mine gently and I looked at where we were joined, still not quite able to comprehend what was happening.

"I have kissed you a thousand times," he said, "and would kiss you a thousand more if fate allowed it. When I made you that pledge? I meant every word. You know how I feel, Lia. I have shown you over and over again. I would gladly give up my life to save you."

My heart wanted so badly to believe him but I was still afraid that my desperate mind had conjured this up.

"Do you feel the connection between us?" he asked in that growly voice that made my insides flutter and shake.

I swallowed back what I was feeling. "What connection?"

"You know what I'm speaking of. I've never had this happen with anyone else before. Like we were fated to be together. Like the goddess herself ordained it. As if you were made for me. I feel so much that whenever I see you, I forget myself and all I want is to touch you and kiss you and let the world fall away."

I wanted the same thing, which was why we should stay away from each other. "It doesn't matter. None of this matters. I don't even know if I believe this tale you've told me."

He lifted my hand up near his face. "The next time I see you, I'll kiss your hand. Like this." He pressed his warm mouth against the back of my hand and my fingers tightened in response, wanting to reach for him.

"You've never done that before."

"Correct. That is how you'll know that this is real and has been the entire time." He kissed my hand again and then placed it back on the bed. "Because I will see you. There will be obstacles in our path, but we are fated. Destined. I know us and what we will be. I know you."

I shook my head. "No one really knows me."

"But I do." He paused and then asked, "How do you feel about me? Do you love me?"

"I don't know." It was the only answer I could give him. It was also the truth.

My non-answer didn't seem to bother him. "I think you do. You might need time before you realize it, but you'll see that we belong together."

I tried very hard not to let his words affect me. He was painting a picture that I wanted desperately to be a part of, even if my plans made it impossible. "If all of what you're saying is true, and you're actually here, then what did you mean when you told me to say yes? Were you talking about the festival?"

He opened his mouth to respond but he was suddenly gone and I was alone in my dark bedroom.

"Jason?"

The ground beneath my bed gave way and I was falling. I landed with a thud in a meadow of wildflowers. I spotted him in the far-off distance. I called his name but he didn't move or respond. I ran toward him but I didn't seem to be making any progress. He never got closer, no matter how hard or how long I ran. I couldn't reach him.

The landscape swirled around me and I was back in Locris. But not the Locris I knew. It looked like Ilion. Everything was green. Trees, flowers, plants of every kind, blooming and growing all around me.

I smelled the irises first and then I turned to see the goddess standing not far away from me. Again I was overwhelmed by her love for me, one that went beyond human understanding. She was so beautiful and radiant that for a moment I couldn't speak.

But I wasn't going to let this opportunity pass by.

"Is this what's possible?" I asked her. "Can Locris be restored this way? Will I be the one to save my nation?"

There will be a time when you have need of me. When you do, call on my name.

What did that mean? Call on her name? I would just say Damara and she would appear? And what, point me in the direction of the lost eye?

"I don't understand," I said, but she vanished by turning into a shimmering golden and green light.

When I awoke for real, I lay in my bed for several minutes, listening to my sisters sleeping around me, contemplating what I had just seen in my dreams.

Call on my name.

I had need of the goddess now. She could tell me precisely where the eye was located.

With my heart clanging in my chest like a bell, I breathed out the word.

"Damara."

CHAPTER
SIXTY-FOUR

Nothing happened.

Frustrated, I sat up and immediately regretted the decision. My head hurt so much it was like someone was banging on it with a hammer. I let out a small groan and put my hands against my skull, as if I could push the pain away.

The second thing I noticed after the headache was the flood of regret I was currently feeling.

Jason had correctly predicted my reaction last night.

Thinking of him only made my head hurt worse. When he'd told me in that house that my judgment was compromised, I had been angry with him. I hadn't thought that I was drunk. But considering what I'd confessed to Io last night, I clearly hadn't had my wits about me.

I glanced over at her bed but it was empty. She was already awake. I hoped she wouldn't remember what I'd told her.

Even if she did, would it matter? I knew her secret as well. She couldn't afford for it to get out, either. They would expel her from the temple for being a member of the royal family.

Mutually assured destruction.

All this time I'd pictured Prince Alexandros as being some kind of monster, but if Io was his sister, he couldn't have been all bad.

Or maybe that was the leftover wine in my body talking.

Thinking about drinking immediately turned my thoughts back to Jason and our last in-person encounter and I wondered if things would have gone differently if I'd been sober. I was fairly certain that I still would have made the same choice. I'd wanted him so badly—even now I ached for him.

It would have been the wrong decision. I understood that logically. I knew the promises I'd made. I could not do those kinds of things with him. Especially not if I wanted to find the eye and restore Locris to the way I'd seen it in my dream last night. I imagined that the goddess would not be interested in helping an acolyte who had blasphemed one of her basic laws.

But I now understood why those other priestesses had risked being buried alive. From what I had experienced, it might have even been a little bit worth it.

I let out a deep sigh as I realized how close I'd come to throwing everything away for Jason. For a man who made me no promises, a man who didn't want marriage or a relationship, a man who would happily move on to the next woman as soon as he tired of me.

I was such a fool. I'd never felt this kind of humiliation before. Without the spiked wine to alter my perceptions and thinking, I could see everything clearly. It would have been a huge mistake if I'd stayed.

And I had no idea how to interpret what had happened with him in my dreams. Him saying he was actually there and that everything was real?

How could that even be possible?

It had to have been my own psyche, trying to convince me that I hadn't come so close to wrecking everything for a worthless man who didn't actually care about me. To paint him as a devoted lover, willing to die for me.

That wasn't who he was.

Then why did he send you away? a little voice asked me. *If he didn't care about you, he could have taken advantage of you last night and you would have welcomed it.*

I didn't want to think of him as being an honorable man, just a self-ish one. It made things easier. Maybe he didn't really want me. Maybe he'd only felt sorry for me and let things go too far. Who was to say?

Disgusted with myself I went into the washroom and found Io there, happily scrubbing her face and whistling a tune to herself.

"Too loud," I muttered. "How are you not hungover?"

"When you're skilled with herbs and medicines, you have a hang-over cure. Here's one for you. Add it to some water and drink it," she said, putting a small vial in my hand.

"You are my favorite person," I told her, truly meaning it.

"You're not the first sister to say that to me," she said with a wink.

"Io, about last night . . ." I let my voice trail off, not sure how to broach the subject with her. I certainly didn't want to bring it up if she had been so drunk that she no longer remembered.

"What about it? It's all one giant blur," she said. "I think there was dancing, maybe music. I *know* there was wine."

I smiled. It sounded like my secret was safe. "Nothing. It just seemed like you were having a good time."

She nodded. "I was. And everything has been so hard lately that I really needed a night like that."

"I'm glad you had it." I waited a moment and then said, "What are you doing up so early?"

"Tryphosa, the new lead healer, the one who took over for Daphne?" I heard her voice catch on Daphne's name, but she pressed forward. "There is a farm nearby that has requested our help with their olive tree grove and we're going out to assist. It should only be for a few days."

She had mentioned this trip when she'd found out that Daphne had died. "Do you think that's safe?"

"The farm is not far from the city walls. There will be a few of us and I think we'll be all right. I might mention it to Tryphosa to see if she wants to ask Antiope for an additional guard or two."

I didn't like the idea of her leaving the temple grounds after all the recent attacks and losses we'd suffered, but it wasn't my choice to make. "Good luck and safe travels. We'll miss you."

"I'll be back before you know it," she promised.

She was gone when I came back from using the toilet, and I hurried over to complete my chores. The courtyard was in complete shambles and there was no way for me to finish everything up before my morning class. I focused on the temple itself and then did my best in the courtyard. I was going to need help.

During my tutorial Maia was telling me about the goddess's siblings and how they ruled over different parts of the world, far from here.

"Is the goddess's name Damara?" I asked, interrupting her while she was speaking about the sister of the goddess who presided over the seas.

She sucked in a sharp breath. "Where did you hear that word?"

"At the festival. I overheard some women speaking." Another lie, but I wasn't going to tell her anything about Jason.

"That is not the goddess's name. Damara is a title that means 'mother of life' that is sometimes used for her. We do not speak her true name. It is too sacred."

Or, as Jason had suggested, it would give me some kind of power if I knew it. Hadn't the goddess essentially told me the same thing in my dream?

No wonder they kept it hidden.

Another thing I would have to learn in order for my quest to be successful.

I was grateful that throughout the rest of the day none of my sisters brought up the festival. Not even Zalira, and I had fully expected her to tease me further about Jason. Last night she'd obviously intuited that he and I had been together but she said nothing about it.

It made me a little suspicious because it seemed out of character for all of them to not ask questions.

They were all helpful, though, when I begged them to assist me with mapping out potential points of interest, places I might want to investigate in my search for the eye. Some private residences with substantial libraries, booksellers near the docks who might have religious texts, the palace.

I wondered if Io knew of a secret way into her old home. I would have to ask her when she returned.

We were at dinner when there was some kind of commotion outside. I heard women calling to one another, saw Antiope get up and run out with her weapon in hand.

Were we under attack again?

Everyone in the dining hall emptied outside into the courtyard. There were soldiers lining the street for several blocks. Armed and armored.

All facing the temple.

As if they were about to lay siege.

Antiope had her sword out, facing the army gathered in front of her. The soldiers parted then, creating a pathway down the middle of the street.

Black stallions pulled a chariot as it slowly made its way toward us. I couldn't see who was coming and it suddenly seemed vitally urgent that I do so. I climbed up the steps to the temple patio to get a better view.

My sisters followed me.

"What's going on?" Ahyana asked. "Are we going to have to fight?"

They easily outnumbered us. If this was to be a battle, we would eventually lose.

The chariot moved agonizingly slowly, making certain to create a spectacle of itself before it reached the archway. It was meant to intimidate, to show the wealth and strength of the person driving it.

When it finally arrived I realized that I recognized the man holding the reins. He was tall, muscled, built like a warrior. Blue tattoos covered nearly every patch of his pale, exposed skin. He had a dark gray tunic and light eyes.

And bright red hair.

I knew him. Fury tinged my vision, while adrenaline spiked in my gut.

With a growl I spun on my heel, intending to return to the dormitory.

"Where are you going?" Zalira asked.

"That is the man who killed my sister," I said through clenched teeth. "I'm getting my sword because I'm going to run him through."

"You can't leave the temple," Ahyana said. "As soon as you step foot onto the street, he can harm you."

"He can try." Now that I had him within my sights, I wasn't going to let him escape with his life.

He owed it to me after what he'd taken.

"Don't get your weapon," Zalira told me. "Not before we know what's happening. You can't rush out there and murder the man in front of all those soldiers."

She was right but I didn't want her to be. I wanted to see the expression in his eyes as I plunged my xiphos straight into his chest so that he would know exactly what it felt like to have his heart destroyed.

Because he had obliterated mine.

The redheaded demon handed his reins to a soldier standing behind him on the chariot and then held up both of his hands, asking for the crowd to be quiet.

"I am Thrax, captain of Prince Alexandros's royal guard. I have come for the princess."

For Io? I knew she had cheated to get in here, that serving the goddess was the most important thing in her life, but had she joined without her family's knowledge or permission?

Had they finally tracked her down and decided to demand her back? Would they force her into that arranged marriage?

"There is no princess here," Antiope called back scornfully. "There are only servants of the goddess."

"You harbor a foreign princess in your midst," Thrax said and then he seemed to make eye contact with me.

My heart plummeted down to my feet.

No, no, no.

This was not happening.

My time had run out.

"As I told you," Antiope retorted, "there are only humble servants here."

"I have come for Princess Thalia to honor the betrothal contract she made with Prince Alexandros."

The temple crowd seemed confused, exchanging glances and whispering to one another.

It wouldn't take them long to figure out who he meant.

"There is no one here named Thalia," Antiope said.

His gaze still locked with mine, he said, "The Locrian maiden. I demand that you turn her over to me."

CHAPTER
SIXTY-FIVE

How did the royal family know that I was at the temple? My first thought was that the witness must have told them. That he had seen me at the Golden Lamb, realized who I was, and somehow told the palace.

My second thought was that Io must have told everyone. But she wasn't even here and I'd only just confided in her. How could she have shared my secret already? She had sworn she wouldn't.

Or maybe someone at the festival had overheard us and passed the information along to the prince. They were probably paid a good amount of coin for it.

It had been so foolish of me to tell Io. If I had just kept my mouth shut, this wouldn't be happening.

That wine had led me to so many bad decisions last night. All the eyes in the courtyard turned toward me. Some wore questioning expressions, others accusing.

Suri's eyebrows raised as Ahyana asked, "Is that true?"

Well, at least now I had proof that Io had kept silent. Our sisters would have been the first people she told.

"Yes, it's true."

Ahyana looked devastated. "Why didn't you tell us?"

"You know why," Zalira interjected. "They'll never let her stay here now that they know who she is."

"I didn't say anything because I was trying to prevent this from happening. The prince is going to demand that I marry him to solidify his claim to the throne. I had hoped I had another week at least. I'm sorry I kept this from you. But, as you can see, this secret coming out is going to jeopardize everything I've done."

Soon I wouldn't have a choice. I imagined that Theano would happily hand me over to this Thrax, and as soon as I got close to him, I was going to kill him. Which meant I was going to wind up in prison or executed for crimes against the soon-to-be king and his personal representative.

To my surprise, Antiope turned toward me and said, "Lia, do you want to go with this man?"

"No, I do not," I called back.

She returned her gaze to the captain. "There. You heard her. She doesn't want to go with you. She is under our protection and will not leave the temple grounds. No woman here will be taken by the likes of you. You're welcome to come and try to claim her but I wouldn't recommend it."

Everyone was going to wind up dead. I was about to be the reason for a war between the royal family and the temple.

He nodded, as if he had expected this response. "The temple is surrounded and will continue to be until Princess Thalia is handed over. No one will be allowed to leave and no supplies will be permitted in."

"Io," Ahyana breathed. "Will she and the others be able to return? Or will they take them captive?"

"They won't hurt Io," I said confidently. "She will be fine." These were her people, after all.

Although I couldn't predict what might happen to Tryphosa and the other acolytes.

Antiope scowled. I could see she didn't like this threat. She might even go out there and eliminate the king's army by herself.

The historical sieges I'd read about usually did not end well for the people being invaded. This Thrax had robbed me of Quynh and now he was going to starve us into submission.

To force us into a position where we would have no choice but to surrender.

I wasn't going to let him hurt any more of my sisters. But if I went with him, this would all be over. Locris would be doomed and I would never get the answers I'd been looking for.

"Back inside!" Antiope called to the crowd, and we all filed into the dining room. Again I was treated with names and curses and glares from women who obviously wished me dead.

It wasn't anything new but it was never easy to deal with.

My sisters lined up next to me, shoulder to shoulder. I knew they would fight to help me if necessary.

There was a lot of yelling and confusion until Antiope stood up on the dais and ordered, "Shut your mouths! Now! I will not have this kind of disorder!"

"Our supply of food is not limitless!" an older priestess said. "We will be fine for a time but eventually we will run out."

"We can ration," Antiope said.

"What if they cut off our water supply again?"

Were the prince's men responsible for that? But if they had been, wouldn't Io have said something? Wouldn't she have recognized the red dirt?

Or maybe she had kept quiet to not risk giving away her own identity.

Did that mean Prince Alexandros was responsible for the pirate attack on the *Nikos*? Why would he have done it?

Had he wanted to eliminate me before I ever came to Ilion so that he would be free to marry his precious Chryseis?

That didn't make sense. He could have just canceled the contract. There would have been a fine to pay, but he certainly could have afforded it. He didn't have to end my life to have his way. And why would he want me to turn myself over now?

Whoever had stopped up the spring wasn't working for the prince.

"We will go out now and fill up as many vases as we can from the fountain," Antiope said. "An attack on one of our acolytes is an attack on all of us. The prince does not get to dictate our actions or our choices. We are not subject to him. We are one sisterhood."

"I should turn myself in," I said, shaking my head. Despite Antiope's rallying speech I could see that not everyone felt the same way she did. "I'm not going to put everyone in danger."

One for many. I knew that it was the right thing to do.

"Didn't you hear Antiope?" Zalira said, coming to stand in front of me. "We stand together. We are sisters."

My heart clenched at her words, wanting to believe them but knowing how this would eventually turn out.

I couldn't hold out forever. Neither could the women of the temple.

Eventually I would have to do what the prince wanted to save everyone here.

And I would do so willingly.

I would find a way to still save Locris. That wouldn't change.

What would change was getting to see my adelphia every day. I knew that at some point that would have happened regardless, but if I was being honest with myself, I'd dreamed about convincing all of them to return to Locris with me, with Jason captaining our ship.

It was a ridiculous fantasy and I shouldn't have even entertained it.

"Everyone go back to your responsibilities!" Antiope yelled over the fray. "If our decision changes, we will let you know!"

Zalira took me by the arm and led our sisters back to our room. When the door was shut she said, "We have to smuggle you out."

Ahyana nodded enthusiastically. "Yes! We'll get you out of the temple and then you'll be safe. You can hide in Troas until you find whatever it is you're looking for and then you can go home. You can have all of my coins." She went over to her heavy box. "I don't have a need for them."

I bit the inside of my cheek so that I wouldn't cry. I knew how long she'd been collecting her drachmas. "I won't take your money."

"It's actually Kunguru's money since he was the one who stole it, but he would want you to have it, too."

Suri went over to the window and looked out, as if she expected to see a mob with torches calling for my head.

"There won't be a way to leave," I said. "Did you see how many soldiers were out there? That Thrax said they've surrounded the entire temple. I'll never be able to sneak past them. Even with distractions and cloud cover."

"I don't accept that," Zalira said with a shake of her head. "There has to be a way. I won't let them march in here and grab you and force you into a marriage you don't want."

"We may be left with little choice." Demaratus had impelled me to be realistic. If I knew what the outcome would most likely be, then I could prepare for it and maybe even find a way to circumvent it.

"There's always a choice! We just have to find it," Zalira countered. "But in the meantime, one of us should always be with you. I don't think things are going to be safe for you going forward."

I thought she'd meant from outside the temple but I soon discovered that the greater threat came from within.

The army did not leave. True to their word, they laid a serious siege outside the temple walls. They never entered the grounds, but they stayed put. They didn't allow any messengers or supplies in or out. Our pantries were well stocked and every available vase had been filled with water. It seemed unnecessary because the water continued to flow.

Every evening at dinnertime Thrax came to the archway in his chariot and made the same announcement. His name, that he was captain of the prince's royal guard, and a demand that I be turned over to him to honor the contract.

I always came out to see him when he arrived, planning all the ways I was going to make him bleed as soon as I got the chance.

When there wasn't a literal army between us.

Zalira, Ahyana, and Suri kept trying to come up with a plan for me to sneak out but nothing they thought of was viable. The vise had been applied too tightly. There was no way to escape.

On the morning of the fourth day, I headed out to do my morning chores. My sisters had stayed up late last night plotting and I hadn't wanted to wake any of them this morning. They deserved their rest.

I was filling a vase with water when something hit me hard in the back of my head. My knees gave way and I turned onto my shoulder to cushion my fall. I quickly rolled over, my head throbbing, and pulled out my xiphos and got back on my feet.

Artemisia stood with a staff, along with the remaining members of her adelphia behind her. "Once again you bring nothing but trouble to the temple. You're going to get us all killed. I'm going to hand you over before that happens."

Several of these girls were part of the Chosen. This was not going to be an easy fight. Not only was I outnumbered but I was outclassed. They were more skilled at combat than I was.

"I'm not going anywhere," I said. I'd had the same thoughts. That I should turn myself over to Thrax, if for no other reason than to get close enough to take my revenge, regardless of what the consequences would be after.

But I wasn't going to let Artemisia force me out. I would go on my own terms, in a way that I chose.

I bent down to retrieve my broom and I broke the shaft away from the brush. They were all wielding staves, which would give them a distance advantage over my sword. I expected them to rush me but they didn't.

"Do you know how much I'm going to enjoy watching you bleed?" Artemisia asked. "You come in here and betray everything we stand for. You defile this temple and all the people who serve. Your nation is responsible for so much death and so much chaos. You have taken a sister from me. You have cursed us, and the only way to make things right is a blood sacrifice. There is more than one way for you to leave this temple."

No more vague threats, no more pretending to get along.

She intended to kill me.

CHAPTER SIXTY-SIX

I had always suspected that this was the kind of person she was—bloodthirsty, evil, preying on those weaker than herself—but now she had proven me right. I tightened my grip on my weapons.

"You won't take me without a fight."

She gave me a malicious grin. "Oh, I'm absolutely counting on it."

Her sisters spread out, intending to attack from different sides at the same time. I wouldn't be able to use the surprise tactics Antiope had taught us. They knew them as well and would be expecting them.

I kept backing up but eventually I would hit an actual wall. Which was probably what they were trying to do. Forcing me to corner myself.

Crossing one foot over the other, I headed away from the stone fence and back toward the temple.

One of the women leapt forward, arcing her staff down at me. I shoved the butt of the broom handle into her gut, causing her to double over, and then immediately whirled to meet the next attacker with my sword.

While I was engaged, someone jabbed their staff into my still-healing left shoulder and I swore in pain and backed up, breaking off the standstill I'd been stuck in.

"So, so fragile," Artemisia said, watching while her sisters attacked me. "Have you ever asked yourself why so many people want you dead?"

She meant to distract me but I wouldn't allow her to do so. I kept all her sisters in my line of vision, and when one of them tried to get behind me to attack, I was there, ready to block her blow.

But I wasn't quite fast enough to stop the woman coming from the opposite direction and she hit me hard across my shoulder blades, knocking the air from my lungs.

I hit her staff away and tried to back up again so that I could stay at the fringe of their group, but they were no longer allowing me to do so. They made their circle tighter, moving in to finish me.

Another swing that I blocked but it meant that I missed the one aimed at my head. That blow drove me down, blurring my vision.

I lifted my eyes to see one of them being jerked to the ground and another being hit with something, knocking her sideways.

My sisters.

Suri was grappling with one of Artemisia's adelphia while Zalira punched another in the face. Ahyana swung her own staff high and then brought it down hard on an attacker trying to reach her.

I saw Io.

Io was here. She was safe.

She also had Antiope with her.

"What is going on?" Antiope demanded. She had obviously been pulled from her bed and didn't look pleased.

"They attacked Lia while she was doing her chores," Io said. "I saw the whole thing when we arrived a few minutes ago."

"She's lying," Artemisia said.

"I'm the only one who has a reason to be out here," I said, reaching up to touch the blood trickling out of my nose. "You ambushed me."

"You told me to meet you out here and then you tried to attack me," she countered. I couldn't tell if Antiope believed her.

"We are sisters," Antiope fumed. "And it is against the rules of the temple to attack one another."

"She is no sister of mine," Artemisia said and then spat on me.

"That isn't your choice!" Antiope roared. "Return to your rooms immediately. I will consult with Nysa as to what your punishment will be. Pray that it isn't banishment."

The rest of Artemisia's adelphia picked up their staves and headed for their dormitory. When she got close to me, Artemisia leaned in and said, "This isn't over."

"Anywhere, anytime," I told her. "I'm not afraid of you."

"Then you're an even greater fool than I thought."

She left and my sisters came over to help me stand. I was so tired of being beaten up. They took me to the infirmary.

"How did you get inside the temple?" I asked Io.

"I don't know. They just let us pass. A soldier told me that they won't let anyone here leave and that they won't allow any supplies to come in, but that it was fine to let priestesses return," she said.

I wondered if there was more to her story that she wasn't sharing. Had it been her royal blood that had made it possible for them to get through?

Regardless, I was glad she was back. We had all worried about her. Ahyana convinced Io to go back to the dormitory and get cleaned up. Zalira stayed with me while Tryphosa looked me over and declared me fine. "It looks like you have a bruise here."

My tunic had slipped slightly and the spot she was pointing at was where Jason had sucked my skin into his mouth. I felt my cheeks turning pink. "I've had that for a few days."

She nodded. "Drink water, get rest. I find that tends to heal most things over time."

As I walked with Zalira to the dining hall, she said, "What were you thinking? Didn't I tell you not to go anywhere alone?"

"I know. I'm sorry. It honestly didn't occur to me that Artemisia might take this as her golden opportunity to kill me."

"It did to me," she said. "Not everyone here honors their vows the way that they should."

Including me.

A Tribute of Fire

I swallowed down my guilt.

"Promise me that you'll always have someone with you," she said.

"I promise."

"Good. Now that Io's back, maybe she can help us come up with a means of sneaking you out. She might have a potion that makes you appear dead and we can get you out that way."

I wasn't sure I wanted to risk my life on a potion that would make me seem dead. Knowing Io, it might work a little too well.

"Thank you for coming to my rescue today," I said.

"That's what we're here for. You can always count on us. We can get through anything together. Don't forget that."

"I won't."

I was so glad I had them. My sisters made me feel like nothing bad could ever happen to me so long as they were willing to stand shoulder to shoulder with me.

◆ ◆ ◆

The fifth day of the siege destroyed that notion entirely.

Theano woke up, back to her old terrible self. Being prayed to at every meal, staring at all of us from behind her veil, watching our every move during training. She had Maia fetch me. We went into Theano's office and I was struck by my last vivid and horrible memories of being in this room.

"Sit."

I did as the high priestess requested. Maia stayed in the doorway. Not sitting with me but not leaving me alone, either. I wondered if there was a reason for that.

When Antiope arrived a few seconds later, I got my answer. This wasn't just an interrogation. They were going to make a decision about me and my place in the temple.

I'd been so worried that they'd remove me when they found out my background, and now the time was up on that, as well.

"I should have guessed that you were royal when you said you were Aianteioi. But Ajax had many illegitimate children, didn't he?" Theano shifted slightly and then said, "So, Princess Thalia, why should we keep you at the temple? We have a rule against allowing daughters of noble or royal households to join us."

I didn't have an answer for her.

Thankfully, Maia stepped in. "That policy only applies to Ilionian daughters."

Theano's head snapped up. "What?"

"I can recite it from memory," Maia said. "And it clearly states 'Ilionian.' Lia is not Ilionian. Therefore, she cannot be subject to that rule as she is Locrian."

Maia was the best mentor in the whole world. I wished that I could hug her.

It took a few moments for Theano to collect herself. "Be that as it may, the princess has a marriage offer on the table from the Ilionian prince. We cannot afford to make him our enemy."

"He hasn't declared war on us," Antiope offered. "Only that we cannot leave the temple grounds. Which we generally try not to do anyways."

The level of logic being directed at the high priestess seemed to infuriate her, if her balled-up hands were any indication. But her voice was even when she answered. "My messenger is not being permitted to approach. We are not receiving gifts and sacrificial offerings from the citizens of Troas, which means that we will not be able to send supplies to the women's shelters under our jurisdiction."

Theano said this like it was my fault. I was not the one who had directed an army to encamp outside.

"What do you want me to do about it?" I asked.

"Make them leave."

It was very difficult not to scoff. "Every day the captain says they won't unless I agree to go with him."

She leaned back in her chair. "This stalemate will have to end. It cannot be tolerated. Today you will have to speak with this captain and convince him to vacate the street."

"I don't know how to do that!"

Another few beats passed by. "Maia claims that you are a capable girl. I'm sure you'll come up with something."

She waved her hand toward the door, indicating that I could go. How was I supposed to make Thrax and his soldiers leave?

Maybe Zalira had the right idea and the best thing to do was to find a way out of the temple so that they would have to decamp.

"Are we still voting on whether Lia will be allowed to stay?" Maia asked.

"As you so clearly pointed out, Princess Thalia is not subject to that particular law. I see no reason to vote. You may all go," Theano said.

Antiope clasped my shoulder briefly before leaving. As I walked back to my dormitory with Maia, I said, "What am I supposed to do? I don't know how to make them leave."

Especially since every plan I'd come up with so far all centered around slitting Thrax's throat. I didn't think that would be very good from a negotiating standpoint.

"I will talk to some of the priestesses and see if we can come up with something," she said apologetically. "I have heard such terrible stories about the prince. I don't want you to end up in that palace. You won't be safe."

That just made everything a thousand times worse. As soon as I could find Io, I was going to force her to tell me what her older brother had done that would make even the tranquil Maia worried.

But as it turned out, I didn't need to ask Io.

Because the prince decided to grace us with his presence.

CHAPTER SIXTY-SEVEN

The brass horns blowing were our first clue that today would be different. I was struck with the memory of them being used to begin the race through Troas, and I had to push that thought aside.

Then we heard the criers calling out, "Make way for Prince Alexandros! Make way!"

Instead of their words clearing people off the street, they had the opposite effect. Members of the neighborhood hung out of their windows and crowded the sidewalks to catch sight of the prince.

"No one has seen him in over a year," Ahyana told me. "He won't attend state functions and doesn't leave the palace. They say he's hideous."

Io was far enough away that she probably didn't hear what Ahyana was telling me. I wanted to shush her but couldn't risk her asking why. I didn't want Io's feelings to be hurt.

I walked over to Io and put an arm around her shoulders. "Are you doing all right?"

She nodded, her eyes bright. "I haven't seen him in so long. I'm sorry, I know this is hard for you, but I've missed him."

"Then I'm glad that you'll be able to see him again." I was personally hoping that he would be a reasonable, rational man and that I could do what Theano had ordered me to do—find a way to end this siege so that life could return to normal.

His chariot was being pulled by white horses draped in purple, the color of the royal family. People cheered for him as he went by, the horns getting louder as they came closer. There was a long processional behind him.

Prince Alexandros was certainly putting on a show.

Was this for my benefit? I almost smiled. It was a waste. He wasn't going to intimidate me into leaving the temple. Or impress me with his wealth. I wasn't that shallow.

The chariot reached the archway and the horns came to a sudden halt. I couldn't see him because of all the women crowding the courtyard.

"Princess Thalia, come forth!" That was Thrax's voice. I'd heard it enough over the last few days to recognize it, that accent of his that made him roll his *Rs*.

"Do you want to come with me?" I asked Io. I wanted her to have the chance to reunite with her brother.

"I can't. If I do, everyone will know who I am."

I hadn't considered that. I was the only one who knew Io's true identity. "I understand."

"I'm going to our room." She took a few steps backward and then said, "Lia, I'm so, so sorry."

I frowned at her strange response and then began to push my way through the crowd. They didn't part easily and I had to ask people to move more than once.

But then I broke through the final line, only to see . . .

Jason.

Jason was standing there with Thrax.

What was he doing?

I actually pinched myself to make sure I wasn't dreaming, that this was really happening.

It was then that I noticed the cut of his dark purple tunic. The quality, the expensive and detailed embroidery along the edges. The confident way that he stood.

The anger on his face.

But not surprise at seeing me. There was only fury.

I was misinterpreting this scene. I had to be. Maybe he was a messenger for the prince. "What are you—"

"You will kneel before Prince Alexandros," Thrax said to me.

My heart beat so hard that it was cutting off my air supply and I felt sweat breaking out on my back.

Not a dream. Not a messenger.

Jason was Prince Alexandros.

By the goddess.

"I will not kneel," I said, my throat tight. "He is not my prince."

My mind was reeling. What was happening? Jason was Alexandros? It felt like I couldn't put coherent thoughts together to figure this situation out.

Thrax drew his sword at my disrespect and I did the same. I would welcome the fight.

"Put your sword away," Jason said. No, not Jason. Alexandros. Alexandros told Thrax to put his weapon down.

He did as his prince commanded him and sheathed his sword.

I, however, did not.

Instead I gripped my sword so fiercely I worried I was going to leave permanent marks in my hand.

Alexandros was not surprised that I was Princess Thalia.

He knew it. I saw on his face that he knew exactly who I was. He'd been expecting me.

My brain was flooded with unanswerable questions.

How long had he known?

From the beginning?

Why had he pretended to be someone else?

To what end? What was the purpose of all of this?

Did Io know that Jason and Alexandros were the same person? Was that why she had just apologized to me?

Was this all one giant trap that I had happily walked into, completely unaware that I was being manipulated the entire time?

When the time comes, say yes.

That bastard. He had known exactly what was going on the whole time. He knew we were headed for this moment and he had expected me to roll over and offer myself up to him.

Everything that had passed between us had been a lie. He had worn me down, tricked me, manipulated me at every single interaction that had occurred between us. He had taken advantage of my inexperience and naivete when it came to relationships between men and women in order to seduce me into agreeing to this marriage.

And I had been fool enough to fall for it. To even fancy myself in love with him.

Now he was forcing my hand, threatening people that I loved, to make me comply.

And all of this after he had destroyed my nation with his excessive tariffs, slowly choking us to death by devaluing the few goods we had left to trade with.

He was the reason my brother was dead.

I couldn't even confront him about all of that. Hundreds of witnesses surrounded us—his army, the women of the temple, the locals who had come out to watch this scene unfold. I was not going to let my personal business be the gossip of Troas.

Gritting my teeth, I put my sword away. I wouldn't draw his blood. I wouldn't give him the satisfaction of behaving that way.

Not yet.

"What do you want, Alexandros?" I said, emphasizing his name.

He didn't even flinch.

Thrax, however, put his hand on his hilt again. "That is Prince Alexandros to you."

Ignoring his guard dog, I directed my attention to the royal liar, waiting for him to answer.

He moved as close as he could to the archway without stepping over and technically entering the courtyard. "You know what I want. We have a signed betrothal contract. Come out and keep your word."

I wanted to rage and shout and make him admit to what he'd done. How he had used me, tried to coerce me. I would have had more respect for him if he'd just been honest with me from the beginning and admitted who he was and what he wanted.

I had no respect for this kind of targeted, constant deception.

So I stepped up to the line as well so that we could speak without every single person being able to hear what we were saying.

"I am not going anywhere with you," I said. "You can set that contract on fire. Ball it up and throw it in the ocean. Eat it, for all I care."

His honey eyes flashed with anger. "You will marry me. There is no other choice for you here."

"I will stay in the temple, where I have made vows to serve," I snapped back.

Alexandros leaned in closer so that he could breathe the next words against my skin. "Perhaps I should go tell your high priestess what you were doing with me the night of the festival."

I gasped. I had never wanted to hit someone so badly in my entire life. "You bastard."

"I assure you, my parents were married and I'm entirely legitimate."

Fury wrapped itself around me like a water dragon, all sinews and teeth, urging me to strike out at him. "It would be your word against mine."

"My word is royal," he countered.

"So's mine. Which they all know now, thanks to you."

He shook his head and clasped his arms behind his back. "Don't stand here and pretend to be pious when we both know you have no problem skirting dangerously close to breaking the vows you've made."

Again I was so angry that I was afraid I was going to physically attack him.

He pushed his suit. "You will leave and you will marry me."

"No, I won't." As I'd told Thrax, Alexandros wasn't my prince. He couldn't order me around. I was not subject to him.

There was only an invisible line separating us. I realized that he could reach out and yank me to him, force me into his chariot.

The laws he was so easily dismissing were the only things keeping me safe at the moment. He couldn't enter the temple and he couldn't force me into marriage. I had to agree.

Which was why he had stooped to so much subterfuge to get me to do so.

He also had to know that Antiope was itching for an excuse to come out here and slaughter some soldiers.

His gaze was hot, intense, and despite how incandescently angry I was with him, despite all the things I blamed him for, I could feel my body responding. It urged me to step forward, to go with him if it meant he would kiss me again.

I let out a small sound of disgust. All I could think about was that while we stood here, being watched by so many, I still had the mark he'd made on my chest. I was glad he couldn't see it. That no one could.

But I knew it was there.

"You are being unreasonable," he said. "Honor the contract that you and your father made."

He wanted to speak to me of honor?

"I am giving you one last chance," he said. "Or you will not like the consequences."

"Do your worst," I hissed at him.

He pressed his lips into a thin line. "Remember this tomorrow when I show you my worst—you told me to do it."

Then he reached out and grabbed my hand so quickly that I didn't have time to react. For a second I was worried that he might do what I'd imagined and attempt to pull me over the dividing line.

But he wouldn't dare risk that.

"Let go of me!" I told him.

He stared intently at me and, keeping his gaze on mine, brought my hand up to his mouth and kissed it.

My throat closed in on itself.

Then Alexandros whirled about and climbed into his chariot, turning his white stallions back into the street and driving away much quicker than he had when he'd arrived.

I put a hand over my stomach and walked back into the courtyard, in complete shock.

He had let me know just how deep the deception had gone. How was it even possible? I had a very limited understanding of the power of life mages. Could they connect dreams?

Had he used their power to set out to seduce me even when I was sleeping?

There weren't any answers to be had from Alexandros or his entourage, but there was someone at the temple who could give them to me.

CHAPTER SIXTY-EIGHT

When I got into my room, I slammed the door shut and locked it. This wasn't a moment for my other sisters and I knew they would follow.

This was going to be between Io and me.

She was sitting on her bed crying. She looked at me, her eyes full of guilt. "I'm so, so sorry," she said. "He came because I told him about you."

It was like she had punched me in the gut. I had considered the possibility that Io had told him who I was and immediately dismissed it as impossible. But she had betrayed me. "You promised me you wouldn't tell anyone."

"I promised not to tell our adelphia and I didn't. I had to tell Xander."

This family and their obsession with technicalities! This was not the time to be splitting hairs. "Why? Why would you do that?"

"There are so many reasons," she said, trying to dry her tears and steady her voice so that she could speak to me. "I'm so sorry. I know you must be furious with me. But I cannot let my nation fall into my stepmother's hands. She is making a play for the throne for my younger half brother. There is so much more here at stake than you realize. A much bigger picture."

"So to make your brother king, you sacrificed me?"

"No, Lia, that's not what this is." She let out a sigh. "I'm explaining it all wrong."

"Did you know that Alexandros is Jason?" I demanded.

Io made a confused face. "What?"

"When I met him, he told me his name was Jason. I have been seeing him. Kissing him. And . . ." I let my voice trail off. I wouldn't tell her how far I'd been willing to let things go.

For one brief moment she looked shocked but then she quickly recovered. "That's good, isn't it?" she asked hopefully. "You like each other. It will make things easier."

"No, it's not good! He has been tricking me this entire time to get me to agree to marry him."

She shook her head. "That doesn't sound like Xander."

I wasn't going to stand here and let her defend her evil brother. "How long has he known who I am?"

How long had he been teasing and kissing and manipulating me into submission?

"I saw him at the festival, before I went to bed. He comes to the temple and checks on me regularly to make certain that I am all right. It was after I'd talked to you. He told me about some of the moves our stepmother has been making and I told him who you were. He needs you to marry him to keep the throne out of her hands."

Io talked to Alexandros? I realized that this had happened more than once. "The day I snuck out into the city. You were worried about me going alone. You told him. That's how he found me."

"Yes." She sounded miserable. "But I didn't know he was telling you that he was someone else."

I had thought these were coincidences. Happy accidents. But there had been a more sinister design behind it all the entire time.

Had he known from the moment he'd stepped foot into Locris? He could have bribed someone in the palace to point me out. And then I went into the tree courtyard and kissed him, like a complete fool. I hadn't even made him try to catch me. Like a fish deliberately swimming into a net, voluntarily catching itself.

I collapsed onto my bed, hard.

From her body language it was obvious that Io wanted to comfort me. I knew she hated hurting me, but it didn't make the pain of her betrayal sting any less. I didn't think she was the reason he knew who I was. I believed that he had known for a while now, but it still hurt that she was so willing to break my trust. She hadn't told him anything that he didn't already know, but her confession might have forced him into acting sooner than he'd planned.

"I left the palace to avoid being forced into a marriage," she said. "I know what that's like. I don't want that for you but I also need you to know that I love my brother and he is a good man."

Jason, or Alexandros, was a lying, deceiving, philandering, self-centered, vile . . . I couldn't even think of a bad enough word to call him. I should have paid closer attention when Demaratus was cursing at us for not performing up to his standards.

But I wouldn't say any of that to Io. I would never be able to convince her of the kind of person her brother really was. "If you say so."

Several quiet moments passed between us before she said, "Do you know how my brother got his scar?"

"He said something about a woman with a jealous lover."

She frowned, as if she didn't like my answer. "My stepmother was worried that I would marry a foreign prince, obtain a powerful marriage, and then throw my support to Xander for the crown. She decided to eliminate me and thought no one would care if a daughter was killed. Xander fought off her assassins but was left with a permanent reminder of her treachery on his face."

That didn't change anything. I could see that Io wanted it to, but it didn't erase either one of their betrayals.

"When the attempt failed, that's when she tried to marry me off to one of her cronies and I came here instead."

I put my head into my hands. There was too much pain, too much confusion, too much emotion.

"There's something else," she added.

"What else can there be?" I asked, throwing my hands into the air. I couldn't begin to imagine what she had to say that she thought I would want to hear.

She looked down at her hands, folded on her lap. As if she were considering where to begin. "When I was young, I had an illness that threatened my life. No life mage could fix me. No medicines or potions healed me. The physicians told my father that I was going to die. As a last resort my father brought me to the temple. Daphne was the one who took me. She brought me into the flower garden and laid me on the ground and left. The goddess appeared to me there."

As angry as I was at her, I couldn't help but be caught up in her story.

"What I remember most was how beautiful she was, how loving. The way that she glowed, her golden hair and green eyes. She knelt down on the ground next to me and asked me what I wanted. I said I wanted to live. I told her that if she saved my life, I would devote myself to her. She reached over and touched my head. I was immediately healed and have not suffered from that sickness ever since."

"I don't understand what that has to do with me."

She gave me a small smile. "I'm getting to that. After she healed me, she kissed me on my brow and said that she had a special quest for me to fulfill. She told me that I was to protect her savior. The one who would save all of Ilion. I vowed to her that I would."

Now I was growing impatient. "And?"

"And you're the promised savior, Lia. You aren't safe here at the temple. I think you'll be safer at the palace. Xander won't let anything happen to you."

I sucked in a big breath. She wasn't making any sense. "I am not Ilion's savior." I would still be happy to see the entire place burned to the ground.

Especially now that I knew who Alexandros was and what he had done.

"You are," she insisted. "I suspected it from the first moment I met you."

Now I was on my feet, walking over to the farthest wall so that I could get as far away from her as possible. "You can't be serious."

"I am. You are flame-kissed in more than one way. Your red hair, your skin when I burned you. And you bear the mark of the goddess on your left shoulder. The seal. It's her symbol."

"No, it's Theano's seal, nothing more."

"You are marked."

"By you!"

She just shook her head like I was being the ridiculous one. "The prophecy never said the person was born with the mark—only that they would bear it. Which you do. You are fated to restore magic and save Ilion. I will keep my promise to the goddess and do what I must to see to your safety. And I can't think of anyone better to watch over you than my brother."

Io couldn't mean what she was saying right now. It was all nonsense. I was the last person who could be expected to protect her nation. I would not sacrifice anything for these people who had done nothing but try to kill me since I'd left Locris.

Except your sisters, a voice reminded me, and I immediately silenced it.

"I need you to leave," I told her. It was all too much, especially with her sitting there, watching me.

She stood up. "I'm here if you need me." She walked over to the door and unlocked it. Then she paused in the doorway. "I did what had to be done. I am sorry for hurting you. I didn't want to do that."

The problem was that she had.

She shut the door, leaving me in silence.

I couldn't even think about Io's "promised savior" nonsense. It was a problem for another day.

My immediate issues were with her brother.

Jason was Alexandros.

No matter how many times I said it, I couldn't bring myself to accept it. The Jason I had come to know was nothing like the man I'd met today.

I didn't understand why he had been so angry with me. Shouldn't he have been attempting to charm me? Cajole me into accepting his marriage proposal?

Maybe deep down he was angry with himself for tricking me. No, that couldn't have been it. Alexandros struck me as the kind of man who would do whatever he had to in order to achieve his desired outcome.

Was he mad because he knew what my answer would be?

No one really knows me.

But I do.

Out of sheer frustration I picked up my pillow and tossed it across the room.

I remembered what else he'd told me. That he would be returning in twenty-four hours and he was going to do his worst.

His worst, I scoffed. He could try. I would be ready for it.

And I felt that way until I reminded myself that he was the prince of one of the wealthiest nations in the world. He had a great deal of resources available to him.

Alexandros's worst might destroy me.

I refused to come out of my room. I wouldn't do my chores, wouldn't go to training or my classes. My sisters all tried talking to me but I wouldn't speak. Io didn't come back to our room that night or the next day. I wasn't sure where she had slept and I didn't care.

Just so long as she stayed away from me.

I wouldn't eat, either. Kunguru kept coming into the room and dropping off berries and pieces of bread for me.

While I knew both Demaratus and Antiope would be telling me to prepare myself, to eat and sleep so that I was ready to face my enemy, I couldn't do it. Especially sleep. Alexandros might enter my dreams and I didn't want to deal with him in the dreamscape anymore. I was done with him. I stayed up and pet Kunguru, who insisted on cuddling close to me.

My answer was going to be no. There was nothing that Alexandros could say or do to me that would convince me otherwise.

It might have seemed selfish to refuse, potentially putting the priestesses and acolytes in danger, but now I knew for a fact that he would never attack the temple. His little sister was here. The one he would sneak out of the palace to talk to and watch over. Given the story she had told me about how he had risked his life to protect her, there was no way he would launch an assault and possibly put her in danger.

If he thought I would so easily cave because he had threatened to tell Theano that I had kissed him a couple of times, then he really didn't know me at all, no matter what he said.

I thought of all his pretty words, of the pledges and promises. He'd never meant a single one of them. Just more manipulation that I had eaten up like honey.

Like pasteli.

I groaned, upset that my own thoughts continued to betray me. I didn't want to remember how he had tricked me and how pieces of cheap food had won me over.

Or how he had tried so hard to get me to say that I loved him. I wouldn't have been able to refuse to marry him if I had said it. It would have bound me to him. It was why he'd never said the actual words to me. The goddess would have known they were false, and he would have been punished.

But he'd wanted me to say it. To trap me.

Everything between us had been a lie.

I knew my adelphia were worried about me. One of them stayed with me at all times. Even when I went to use the washroom.

And I didn't know if that was to keep me safe from other people, or to keep me safe from myself.

I kept running everything through my head, trying to find a way out of this situation. I decided that I would see what his worst was when he returned and then I would go from there. Perhaps Zalira was right and I should sneak out. I still didn't think it could be done, but it was better than sitting here and waiting for someone to come assassinate me or for Alexandros to figure out a way to punish me or the people I cared about.

I should have been relying on my sisters, letting them support me the way they clearly wanted to.

But this was now my fight, and my fight alone. I was going to have to figure out how to deal with all of this on my own because I was the only person that his demand affected.

When the horns announced the prince's return, I got my sword and strapped it on.

"What are you going to do with that?" Ahyana asked, the concern evident.

I didn't answer.

Instead I went out to the courtyard and shoved my way through the gathered crowd with three of my sisters following me.

Io still stayed away.

But everyone else was here for a show.

Prince Alexandros pulled up on his chariot and jumped down. He came back to the same spot he'd stood in yesterday and I did the same.

"Has your answer changed?" he asked.

"No greeting? You don't want to inquire after my health? Whether or not I've had a good day? You don't want to tell me about your sea voyages? Tell me how well you know me?"

He flinched, but it was only for a split second. "Are you done?"

"I am done. My answer has not changed."

Alexandros waited for a few beats and then took several steps back. "You will change your mind when you see what I've brought you. Bring out the prisoner!"

Prisoner? My panicked mind ran through a list of people he might have captured to hurt me. My parents? Kallisto? Demaratus?

My breathing became ragged and I struggled to pull air into my lungs. How long had he kept someone I loved locked up in his prison?

I narrowed my eyes at him. After I killed his friend Thrax, he was next. *I swear it.*

Thrax was the one who brought the prisoner forward, his hand under their left arm. The prisoner had a coarse, beige hood on their head and I couldn't see who it was. Their wrists were in chains, as were their ankles.

My heart beat louder with each step that they took.

I took out my sword.

Closer and closer.

"That's far enough!" Alexandros told them, his gaze never leaving mine. "Take it off."

My throat was burning and everything seemed to be happening so slowly. My pulse thundered in my ears as Thrax reached over and pulled the hood away from the prisoner.

Revealing their face.

I let out a sound of strangled anguish and dropped to my knees. It was as if I'd been stabbed in the gut, hit so hard that it caused my soul to leave my body.

Quynh.

Quynh was alive.

I couldn't speak, couldn't breathe, couldn't do anything but stare. My limbs trembled as a strange cold sensation filled my entire body. Was this actually happening?

Alexandros crouched down to my eye level. Fury radiated from him in waves but his voice was cold, precise. "You will leave the temple and you will marry me. Now. Or else . . ." His gaze drifted to Quynh and my heart stopped beating out of sheer dread.

Or else what?

Or else he'd kill her?

I didn't know this man or what he was capable of. What he would do to make certain he gained his throne. Alexandros doing his worst was beyond what I could have imagined. He had left me with no choice.

Because he knew my weaknesses.

I'd allowed him to get close to me and he had used that information to corner me, leaving me with no way out. Demaratus had warned me repeatedly about letting myself get trapped, and my naivete, my misplaced trust, had allowed this to happen.

I had lost this battle. And if I didn't agree to his terms, I might lose my sister.

Frenzied terror gripped my throat with sharp, icy fingers. I shook my head. No, I couldn't let fear take over. I wouldn't be able to think, to act. I had to master my emotions. I funneled that scared, sickly feeling into fury. Anger I knew. Anger I could control.

My blood pulsed quickly inside my veins, chasing away the coldness until all I felt was molten rage. I narrowed my gaze at the prince. I was not going to lose this war. He had forgotten that I knew his weaknesses, too. He wouldn't win. I wouldn't let him. I was still going to find the eye and go back to Locris.

After I had my revenge.

Prince Alexandros would pay for locking up my sister. For trying to trick me. I would make him regret forcing me into this marriage.

Then I would kill him for threatening to hurt Quynh.

As strength and resolve infused my spine, I recalled that I had once declared I wouldn't marry an Ilionian even if my life depended on it, but it turned out I would do so if my sister's life was on the line.

"Yes." The word burst bitterly out of my mouth, my chest heaving. "Yes, I will marry you."

AUTHOR'S NOTE

Thank you for reading my story (sorry not sorry about the cliff-hanger)! I grew up with two parents who loved to read—one loved romance and the other fantasy. Those were the books that filled our home. And I've been privileged to write fun, light romantic comedies, which I absolutely adore. But every time I've been asked in an interview, "What other genre would you like to write in?" my answer is always the same—fantasy. Being able to combine those two literary loves of mine into one story has been a dream come true, so I hope you've enjoyed reading it as much as I've adored writing it.

The idea for this book came from a Wikipedia entry. A few years ago I was writing my book *The Seat Filler* and was going to include a line about the Greek mythological character Cassandra. She was the Trojan princess who rejected Apollo's advances, and he cursed her to always see the future but to never be believed. (She tried to tell the Trojans there were Greeks inside that big wooden horse, but no one would listen.) I wasn't sure if I had used the reference correctly, so I quickly looked her up. As I read what happened to her, there was a note about Ajax the Lesser assaulting her in Athena's temple and how his nation, Locris, then had to provide two maidens to recompense for his vile actions. (Athena wanted the Greeks to punish him then and there, but they wouldn't. Which was why she had their ships blown off course and destroyed after the Trojan War ended. You might like to know that Ajax did receive a terrible end—Athena borrowed Zeus's lightning bolt and hurled it at Ajax's ship, killing almost everyone on board. Clinging to a rock while the seas raged, Ajax boasted that not even the gods could best him. Poseidon, particularly affronted by this claim, split the rock in half and then pulled Ajax into the ocean and drowned him.) The Locrian maidens crossed that same sea repeatedly and were supposed to try and reach the temple of Athena to serve, "but only if they made it there alive." That one line in the Wikipedia entry struck me hard, and the idea for this story immediately started to form in my head.

Just like the Trojan War, the Locrian maidens were real. Scholars have debated for a long time whether they were hunted and killed in the streets of Troy, or if it was merely a symbolic gesture and the maidens served their time and then returned home. The maiden ritual was mentioned in poems like *Alexandra* by Lykophron, and in histories by Apollodorus, Plutarch, Strabo, and Timaios. King Antigonos was asked to arbitrate when there was a disagreement about fulfilling the ritual; his ruling/direction about the maiden selection and how the Aianteioi (descendants of Ajax) were to be treated was inscribed onto stone that was discovered in modern times in Oiantheia. The Locrian maidens were sent to Troy for a thousand years because of Ajax the Lesser's crimes. There hasn't been a great deal of scholarship on these young women and what they might have endured for generation upon generation. I feel honored to have been given the opportunity to try and tell a tiny bit of their story.

If you'd like to be notified when the next book in this series comes out, make sure you sign up for my newsletter at www.sariahwilson.com.

And if you feel so inclined, I'd love for you to leave a review on Amazon, on Goodreads, or any other place you'd like. Thank you!

ACKNOWLEDGMENTS

This book has been like an answer to a prayer for me. My family and I have struggled through some really dark and difficult times over the last couple of years, and selling this book saved us financially. So thank you for picking up a copy, because this story means everything to me.

There are so many people to thank. I don't usually start with my agent, but this time I'm going to. When I was trying to come up with a way to pay off some massive medical debt, I told my agent that I had this idea for a book that I absolutely adored and hoped that maybe we could sell it and pay everything off in one fell swoop. It was a ridiculous pipe dream, and she would have been well within her rights to tell me as much. Instead she said, "Let's do it." She believed in me every step of the way and never once doubted that we could reach my goal. And she was right. Sarah Younger, you went above and beyond, and I am very, very grateful to you. Thank you for wielding your literary xiphos and shield to fight for me.

And thank you to Alison Dasho—my beloved editor who bought this book. I had posted online in my private readers' group that I was going to start writing a romantasy. When she and I had a phone call about another book we were working on together, she asked if I would tell her about the series I had planned. She gasped throughout my entire summation, and it made me believe that other people would actually want to read it. When she offered to buy the series in a preempt, something that has been my dream for a very long time, I was completely overwhelmed and so grateful. Thank you for believing in me and this series, and for being such a wonderful editor to me for the last five years. I will miss you.

Thank you to Lauren Plude, my new editor, who inherited this project. Authors hear horror stories all the time about "orphaned" manuscripts, and I was very worried about what would happen with this book. But you hit the ground running, every bit as excited about it as Alison had been, and I knew I was in good hands. I'm so appreciative of all your hard work and suggestions, and I'm so thrilled to be working with you. You have such good ideas about where this series should go!

Sending mountains of gratitude to Charlotte Herscher, my developmental editor, who has worked with me on countless books. It was so much fun seeing how little editorial input you had on this one, the way you just left me a bunch of notes that said how much you loved it and how you kept getting caught up in the story. It makes me very happy when that happens! Your recommendations were so appreciated, as always. (And she's the reason you didn't have an even bigger cliffhanger. I was going to end the book with the reveal about Quynh.)

A special thank-you to the team at Montlake—Kris Beecroft, Karah Nichols, Anh Schluep, and Stef Sloma—without whom none of this would have been possible. Thanks to the copy editors and proofreaders who hunt down my plethora of mistakes and continuity errors and help me correct them (and for leaving your notes on the things you enjoyed). Thank you to Elizabeth Turner Stokes for this amazing cover! It is absolutely stunning and I love it.

I am deeply indebted to many historical scholars, but I'd particularly like to mention James M. Redfield (*The Locrian Maidens: Love and Death in Greek Italy*), Dennis D. Hughes (*Human Sacrifice in Ancient Greece*), and Simon Hornblower (*Lykophron: Alexandra: Greek Text, Translation, Commentary, and Introduction*). I am also thankful to associate professor Seth Jeppesen for his insight and for coming up with the word "adelphia" for Lia's temple sisterhood. Thank you to Stephanie Rosera for naming the terawolves. Thank you to Brandon Sanderson for your class on fantasy writing and for inviting me to speak to your students. Thank you to my private readers' group for your support and enthusiasm and encouragement. They mean the world to me!

Sending thanks to those authors who paved the way for romantasy—I am so thrilled that my two great loves get to be combined in one genre!

As always, remember that #BenSoloDeservedBetter and #SoDoesRey.

For my kids—everything I do is for you. I'm so grateful I get to be your mom.

And for Kevin—you epitomize "one for many" every day. You are the best thing that ever happened to me.

ABOUT THE AUTHOR

Photo © 2020 Jordan Batt

Sariah Wilson is the *USA Today* bestselling author of *Hypnotized by Love, Almost Like Being in Love, The Hollywood Jinx, The Chemistry of Love, The Paid Bridesmaid, The Seat Filler, Roommaid, Just a Boyfriend,* the Royals of Monterra series, and the #Lovestruck novels. She happens to be madly, passionately in love with her soulmate and is a fervent believer in happily ever afters—which is why she writes romance. She currently lives with her family and various pets in Utah, and harbors a lifelong devotion to ice cream. For more information, visit her website at www.sariahwilson.com.